THE
MUMMY
OR
RAMSES
THE
DAMNED

Anne Rice

BALLANTINE BOOKS · NEW YORK

Library of Congress Catalog Card Number: 88-92225

ISBN 0-345-36917-3

Manufactured in the United States of America

First Trade Edition: June 1989
First International Edition: March 1990

This novel is dedicated with love

to

Stan Rice
and
Christopher Rice

And

to
Gita Mehta
an instant inspiration

And

to
Sir Arthur Conan Doyle
for his great mummy stories
"Lot No. 249" and "The Ring of Thoth"

And

to
H. Rider Haggard
who created the immortal *She*

And

to
All who have brought
"the mummy" to life
in stories, novels and film.

And lastly

to
My father
Howard O'Brien
who came more than once
to get me from the neighborhood show,
when "the mummy" had scared me
so badly that I couldn't even stay
in the lobby with the creepy music
coming through the doors.

A Very Special Thanks

to

Frank Konigsberg

and

Larry Sanitsky

for their enthusiastic encouragement
in connection with *The Mummy*
and for their contribution
to the development of the story.

THE MUMMY

PART · 1

1

THE CAMERA flashes blinded him for a moment. If only he could get the photographers away.

But they had been at his side for months now—ever since the first artifacts had been found in these barren hills, south of Cairo. It was as if they too had known. Something about to happen. After all these years, Lawrence Stratford was onto a major find.

And so they were there with the cameras, and the smoking flashes. They almost knocked him off balance as he made his way into the narrow rough-hewn passage towards the letters visible on the half-uncovered marble door.

The twilight seemed to darken suddenly. He could see the letters, but he couldn't make them out.

"Samir," he cried. "I need light."

"Yes, Lawrence." At once the torch exploded behind him, and in a flood of yellow illumination, the slab of stone was wonderfully visible. Yes, hieroglyphs, deeply etched and beautifully gilded, and in Italian marble. He had never seen such a sight.

He felt the hot silky touch of Samir's hand on his as he began to read aloud:

" 'Robbers of the Dead, Look away from this tomb lest you wake its occupant, whose wrath cannot be contained. Ramses the Damned is my name.' "

He glanced at Samir. What could it mean?

3

"Go on, Lawrence, translate, you are far quicker than I am," Samir said.

" 'Ramses the Damned is my name. Once Ramses the Great of Upper and Lower Egypt; Slayer of the Hittites, Builder of Temples; Beloved of the People; and immortal guardian of the kings and queens of Egypt throughout time. In the year of the death of the Great Queen Cleopatra, as Egypt becomes a Roman province, I commit myself to eternal darkness; beware, all those who would let the rays of the sun pass through this door.' "

"But it makes no sense," Samir whispered. "Ramses the Great ruled one thousand years before Cleopatra."

"Yet these are nineteenth-dynasty hieroglyphs without question," Lawrence countered. Impatiently, he scratched away at the loose rubble. "And look, the inscription's repeated—in Latin and in Greek." He paused, then quickly read the last few Latin lines.

" 'Be Warned: I sleep as the earth sleeps beneath the night sky or the winter's snow; and once awakened, I am servant to no man.' "

For a moment Lawrence was speechless, staring at the words he'd read. Only vaguely did he hear Samir:

"I don't like it. Whatever it means, it's a curse."

Reluctantly Lawrence turned and saw that Samir's suspicion had turned to fear.

"The body of Ramses the Great is in the Cairo Museum," Samir said impatiently.

"No," Lawrence answered. He was aware of a chill moving slowly up his neck. "There's *a* body in the Cairo Museum, but it's not Ramses! Look at the cartouches, the seal! There was no one in the time of Cleopatra who could even write the ancient hieroglyphs. And these are perfect—and done like the Latin and the Greek with infinite care."

Oh, if only Julie were here, Lawrence thought bitterly. His daughter, Julie, was afraid of nothing. She would understand this moment as no one else could.

He almost stumbled as he backed out of the passage, waving the photographers out of his path. Again, the flashes went off around him. Reporters rushed towards the marble door.

"Get the diggers back to work," Lawrence shouted. "I want the passage cleared down to the threshold. I'm going into that tomb tonight."

"Lawrence, take your time with this," Samir cautioned. "There is something here which must not be dismissed."

"Samir, you astonish me," Lawrence answered. "For ten years we've been searching these hills for just such a discovery. And no one's touched that door since it was sealed two thousand years ago."

Almost angrily, he pushed past the reporters who caught up with him now, and tried to block the way. He needed the quiet of his tent until the door was uncovered; he needed his diary, the only proper confidant for the excitement he felt. He was dizzy suddenly from the long day's heat.

"No questions now, ladies and gentlemen," Samir said politely. As he always did, Samir came between Lawrence and the real world.

Lawrence hurried down the uneven path, twisting his ankle a little painfully, yet continuing, his eyes narrow as he looked beyond the flickering torches at the sombre beauty of the lighted tents under the violet evening sky.

Only one thing distracted him before he reached the safety zone of his camp chair and desk: a glimpse of his nephew, Henry, watching idly from a short distance away. Henry, so uncomfortable and out of place in Egypt; looking miserable in his fussy white linen suit. Henry, with the inevitable glass of Scotch in his hand, and the inevitable cheroot on his lip.

Undoubtedly the belly dancer was with him—the woman, Malenka, from Cairo, who gave her British gentleman all the money she made.

Lawrence could never entirely forget about Henry, but having Henry underfoot now was more than he could bear.

In a life well lived, Lawrence counted Henry as his only true disappointment—the nephew who cared for no one and nothing but gaming tables and the bottle; the sole male heir to the Stratford millions who properly couldn't be trusted with a one-pound note.

Sharp pain again as he missed Julie—his beloved daughter, who should have been here with him, and would have been if her young fiancé hadn't persuaded her to stay at home.

Henry had come to Egypt for money. Henry had company papers for Lawrence to sign. And Henry's father, Randolph, had sent him on this grim mission, desperate as always to cover his son's debts.

A fine pair they are, Lawrence thought grimly—the ne'er-do-well and the chairman of the board of Stratford Shipping who clumsily funneled the company's profits into his son's bottomless purse.

But in a very real way Lawrence could forgive his brother, Randolph, anything. Lawrence hadn't merely given the family business to Randolph. He had dumped it on Randolph, along with all its immense pressures and responsibilities, so that he, Lawrence, could spend his remaining years digging among the Egyptian ruins he so loved.

And to be perfectly fair, Randolph had done a tolerable job of running Stratford Shipping. That is, until his son had turned him into an embezzler and a thief. Even now, Randolph would admit everything if confronted. But Lawrence was too purely selfish for that confrontation. He never wanted to leave Egypt again for the stuffy London offices of Stratford Shipping. Not even Julie could persuade him to come home.

And now Henry stood there waiting for his moment. And Lawrence denied him that moment, entering the tent and eagerly pulling his chair up to the desk. He took out a leather-bound diary which he had been saving, perhaps for this discovery. Hastily he wrote what he remembered of the door's inscription and the questions it posed.

"Ramses the Damned." He sat back, looking at the name. And for the first time he felt just a little of the foreboding which had shaken Samir.

What on earth could all this mean?

Half-past midnight. Was he dreaming? The marble door of the tomb had been carefully removed, photographed, and placed on trestles in his tent. And now they were ready to blast their way in. The tomb! His at last.

He nodded to Samir. He felt the ripple of excitement move through the crowd. Flashes went off as he raised his hands to his ears, and then the blast caught them all off guard. He felt it in the pit of his stomach.

No time for that. He had the torch in hand and was going in, though Samir tried once again to stop him.

"Lawrence, there could be booby traps, there could be—"

"Get out of my way."

The dust was making him cough. His eyes were watering.

He thrust the torch through the gaping hole. Walls decorated with hieroglyphs—again, the magnificent nineteenth-dynasty style without question.

At once he stepped inside. How extraordinarily cool it felt; and the smell, what was it, a curious perfume after all these long centuries!

His heart beat too fast. The blood rushed to his face, and he had to cough again, as the press of reporters raised the dust in the passage.

"Keep back!" he shouted crossly. The flashes were going off all around him again. He could barely see the painted ceiling overhead with its tiny stars.

And there, a long table laden with alabaster jars and boxes. Heaps of rolled papyri. Dear God, all this alone confirmed a momentous discovery.

"But this is no tomb!" he whispered.

There was a writing table, covered with a thin film of dust, looking for all the world as if the scholar had only just left it. An open papyrus lay there, with sharpened pens, an ink bottle. And a goblet.

But the bust, the marble bust—it was unmistakably Graeco-Roman. A woman with her tight wavy hair drawn back beneath a metal band, her drowsy half-lidded eyes seemingly blind, and the name cut into the base:

CLEOPATRA

"Not possible," he heard Samir say. "But look, Lawrence, the mummy case!"

Lawrence had already seen it. He was staring speechless at the thing which lay serenely in the very middle of this puzzling room, this study, this library, with its stacks of scrolls and its dust-covered writing table.

Once again, Samir ordered the photographers back. The smoking flashes were maddening Lawrence.

"Get out, all of you, get out!" Lawrence said. Grumbling, they retreated out of sight of the door, leaving the two men standing there in stunned silence.

It was Samir who spoke first:

"This is Roman furniture. This is Cleopatra. Look at the coins, Lawrence, on the desk. With her image, and newly minted. Those alone are worth—"

"I know. But there lies an ancient Pharaoh, my friend. Every detail of the case—it's as fine as any ever found in the Valley of the Kings.''

"But without a sarcophagus," Samir said. "Why?"

"This is no tomb," Lawrence answered.

"And so the King chose to be buried here!" Samir approached the mummy case, lifting the torch high above the beautifully painted face, with its darkly lined eyes and exquisitely modeled lips.

"I could swear this is the Roman period," he said.

"But the style . . .''

"Lawrence, it's too lifelike. It's a Roman artist who has imitated the nineteenth-dynastic style to perfection."

"And how could such a thing happen, my friend?"

"Curses," Samir whispered, as if he had not heard the question. He was staring at the rows of hieroglyphs that circled the painted figure. The Greek lettering appeared lower down, and finally came the Latin.

" 'Touch not the remains of Ramses the Great,' " Samir read. "It's the same in all three tongues. Enough to give a sensible man pause."

"Not this sensible man," Lawrence replied. "Get those workers in here to lift this lid at once."

The dust had settled somewhat. The torches, in the old iron sconces on the wall, were sending far too much smoke onto the ceiling, but that he would worry about later.

The thing now was to cut open the bundled human shape, which had been propped against the wall, the thin wooden lid of the mummy case carefully laid upright beside it.

He no longer saw the men and women packed at the entrance, who peered at him and his find in silence.

Slowly, he raised the knife and sliced through the brittle husk of dried linen, which fell open immediately to reveal the tightly wrapped figure beneath.

There was a collective gasp from the reporters. Again and again the flashes popped. Lawrence could feel Samir's silence. Both men stared at the gaunt face beneath its yellowed linen bandages, at the withered arms so serenely laid across the breast.

It seemed one of the photographers was begging to be allowed into the chamber. Samir angrily demanded silence. But of these distractions, Lawrence was only dimly aware.

He gazed calmly at the emaciated form before him, its wrappings the color of darkened desert sand. It seemed he could detect an expression in the shrouded features; he could detect something eloquent of tranquillity in the set of the thin lips.

Every mummy was a mystery. Every desiccated yet preserved form a ghastly image of life in death. It never failed to chill him, to look upon these ancient Egyptian dead. But he felt a strange longing as he looked at this one—this mysterious being who called himself Ramses the Damned, Ramses the Great.

Something warm touched him inside. He drew closer, slashing again at the outer wrapping. Behind him, Samir ordered the photographers out of the passage. There was danger of contamination. *Yes, go, all of you, please.*

He reached out and touched the mummy suddenly; he touched it reverently with the very tips of his fingers. So curiously resilient! Surely the thick layer of bandages had become soft with time.

Again, he gazed at the narrow face before him, at the rounded lids, and the sombre mouth.

"Julie," he whispered. "Oh, my darling, if only you could see . . ."

The Embassy Ball. Same old faces; same old orchestra, same old sweet yet droning waltz. The lights were a glare to Elliott Savarell: the champagne left a sour taste in his mouth. Nevertheless he drained the glass rather gracelessly and caught the eye of a passing waiter. Yes, another. And another. Would that it were good brandy or whisky.

But they wanted him here, didn't they? Wouldn't be the same without the Earl of Rutherford. The Earl of Rutherford was an essential ingredient, as were the lavish flower arrangements, the thousands upon thousands of candles; the caviar, and the silver; and the old musicians sawing wearily at their violins while the younger generation danced.

Everyone had a greeting for the Earl of Rutherford. Everyone wanted the Earl of Rutherford to attend a daughter's wedding, or an afternoon tea, or another ball such as this. Never mind that Elliott and his wife rarely entertained anymore in either their London town house or the country estate in Yorkshire—that Edith spent much of her time in Paris now with a widowed sister. The seventeenth Earl of Rutherford was the genuine article. The titles in his family went back—one way or another—to Henry VIII.

Why hadn't he ruined everything long ago? Elliott wondered. How had he ever managed to charm so many people in whom he had no more than a passing interest, at best?

But no, that wasn't the entire truth. He loved some of these people, whether he cared to admit it or not. He loved his old friend Randolph Stratford, just as he loved Randolph's brother, Lawrence. And surely he loved Julie Stratford, and he loved watching her dance with his son. Elliott was here on account of his son. Of course Julie wasn't really going to marry Alex. At least not any time soon. But it was the only clear hope on the horizon that Alex might acquire the money he needed to maintain the landed estates he would inherit, the wealth that was supposed to go along with an old title, and seldom did anymore.

The sad part was that Alex loved Julie. The money meant nothing to either of them, really. It was the older generation that did the scheming, and the planning, as they have always done.

Elliott leaned against the gilded railing, gazing down at the soft drift of young couples turning beneath him, and for a moment, he tried to shut out the din of voices, and hear only the sweet strains of the waltz.

But Randolph Stratford was talking again. Randolph was assuring Elliott that Julie needed only a little prodding. If only Lawrence would say the word, his daughter would give in.

"Give Henry a chance," Randolph said again. "He's only been in Egypt a week. If Lawrence will take the initiative . . ."

"But why," Elliott asked, "should Lawrence do that?"

Silence.

Elliott knew Lawrence better than Randolph knew him. Elliott and Lawrence. No one really knew the whole story, except the two men themselves. At Oxford years ago, in a carefree world, they had been lovers, and the year after they'd finished, they had spent a winter together south of Cairo in a houseboat on the Nile. Inevitably the world had separated them. Elliott had married Edith Christian, an American heiress. Lawrence had built Stratford Shipping into an empire.

But their friendship had never faltered. They had spent countless holidays in Egypt together. They could still argue all night long about history, ruins, archaeological discoveries, poetry, what have you. Elliott had been the only one who really understood when Lawrence retired and went to Egypt. Elliott had envied Lawrence. And there had been the first bitterness between them. In the small hours, when the wine flowed, Lawrence had called Elliott a coward, for spending his remaining years in London in a world he did not value; a world which gave him no joy. Elliott had criticized Lawrence for being blind and stupid. After all, Lawrence was rich beyond Elliott's wildest dreams; and Lawrence was a widower with a clever and independent daughter. Elliott had a wife and son who needed him day in and day out to regulate the successes of their wholly respectable and conventional lives.

"All I mean to say," Randolph pressed, "is that if Lawrence would express his wish about this marriage . . ."

"And the small matter of the twenty thousand pounds?" Elliott asked suddenly. The tone was soft, polite, but the question was unforgivably rude. Nevertheless he persisted. "Edith will be back from France in a week and she's certain to notice that the necklace is missing. You know, she always does."

Randolph didn't answer.

Elliott laughed softly, but not at Randolph, not even at himself. And certainly not at Edith, who had only a little more money now than Elliott did and most of it in plate and jewels.

Perhaps Elliott laughed because the music made him giddy; or something about the vision of Julie Stratford, dancing down there with Alex, touched his heart. Or perhaps because of late he had lost the ability to speak any longer in euphemisms and half-truths. It was gone along with his physical stamina, and the sense of well-being he had enjoyed throughout his youth.

Now his joints hurt more and more with every passing winter; and he could not walk half a mile any longer in the country without suffering a severe pain in his chest. He did not mind having white hair at fifty-five, perhaps because he knew he looked rather good with it. But it bruised him secretly and deeply to have to use a cane wherever he went. These were all mere shadows, however, of what was yet to come.

Old age, weakness, dependence. Pray that Alex was happily married to the Stratford millions, and not before too long!

He felt restless, suddenly; dissatisfied. The soft swooshing music annoyed him; sick to death of Strauss, actually. But it was something keener.

He wanted to explain it suddenly to Randolph, that he, Elliott, had made some crucial mistake a long time ago. Something to do with those long nights in Egypt, when he and Lawrence would walk through the black streets of Cairo together, or rail at each other drunkenly in the little saloon of the boat. Lawrence had somehow managed to live his life along heroic proportions; he had accomplished things of which others were simply incapable. Elliott had moved with the current. Lawrence had escaped to Egypt, back to the desert, the temples, to those clear star-filled nights.

God, how he missed Lawrence. In the last three years they had exchanged only a handful of letters, but the old understanding would never grow dim.

"Henry took some papers with him," Randolph said, "small matter of family stock." He glanced about warily, too warily.

Elliott was going to laugh again.

"If it goes as I hope," Randolph continued, "I'll pay you everything I owe you, and the marriage will take place within six months, I give you my word."

Elliott smiled.

"Randolph, the marriage may or may not happen; it may or may not solve things for both of us—"

"Don't say that, old boy."

"But I must have that twenty thousand pounds before Edith comes home."

"Precisely, Elliott, precisely."

"You know, you might say no to your son once in a while."

A deep sigh came from Randolph. Elliott didn't press it. He knew as well as anyone did that Henry's deterioration was no joke any longer; it had nothing to do with sowing wild oats, or going through a rough period. There was something thoroughly rotten in Henry Stratford and there always had been. There was very little that was rotten in Randolph. And so it was a tragedy; and Elliott, who loved his own son, Alex, excessively, had only sympathy for Randolph on that score.

More assurances; a positive din of assurance. You'll get your twenty thousand pounds. But Elliott wasn't listening. He was watching the dancers again—his good and gentle son whispering passionately to Julie, whose face wore that look of determination that flattered her for reasons that Elliott could never fully understand.

Some women must smile to be beautiful. Some women must weep. But with Julie, the real radiance shone only when she was serious—perhaps because her eyes were too softly brown otherwise, her mouth too guileless, her porcelain cheeks too smooth.

Fired with determination, she was a vision. And Alex, for all his breeding, and all his proffered passion, seemed no more than "a partner" for her; one of a thousand elegant young men who might have guided her across the marble floor.

It was the "Morning Papers Waltz" and Julie loved it; she had always loved it. There came back to her now a faint memory of dancing once to the "Morning Papers Waltz" with her father. Was it when they had first brought home the gramophone, and they had danced all through the Egyptian room and the library and the drawing rooms—she and Father—until the light came through the shutters, and he had said:

"Oh, my dear, no more. No more."

Now the music made her drowsy and almost sad. And Alex kept talking to her, telling her in one way or another that he loved her, and there was that panic inside her, that fear of speaking harsh or cold words.

"And if you want to live in Egypt," Alex said breathlessly, "and dig for mummies with your father, well then, we'll go to Egypt. We'll go straight after the wedding. And if you want to march for the vote, well then, I shall march at your side."

"Oh, yes," Julie answered, "that's what you say now, and I know you mean it with all your heart, but Alex, I'm just not ready. I cannot."

She couldn't bear to see him so deadly earnest. She couldn't bear to see him hurt. If only there were a little wickedness in Alex; just a little bit of meanness as there was in everyone else. His good looks would have been improved by a little meanness. Tall, lean and brown-haired, he was too angelic. His quick dark eyes revealed his entire soul too easily. At twenty-five, he was an eager and innocent boy.

"What do you want with a suffragette for a wife?" she asked. "With an explorer? You know I could very well be an explorer, or an archaeologist. I wish I was in Egypt with Father right now."

"Dearest, we'll go there. Only marry me before we go."

He leaned forward as if he meant to kiss her. And she moved back a step, the waltz carrying them almost recklessly fast, so that for a moment she felt light-headed and almost as if she were truly in love.

"What can I do to win you, Julie?" he whispered in her ear. "I'll bring the Great Pyramids to London."

"Alex, you won me a long time ago," she said, smiling. But

that was a lie, wasn't it? There was something truly terrible about this moment—about the music with its lovely compelling rhythm, and the desperate look on Alex's face.

"The simple truth is . . . I don't want to be married. Not yet." *And perhaps not at all?*

He didn't answer her. She'd been too blunt, too much to the point. She knew that sudden shrinking. It wasn't unmanly; on the contrary, it was gentlemanly. She had hurt him, and when he smiled again now, there was a sweetness and a courage in it that touched her and made her feel all the more sad.

"Father will be back in a few months, Alex. We'll all talk then. Marriage, the future, the rights of women, married and unmarried, and the possibility that you deserve far better than a modern woman like me who's very likely to turn your hair grey within the first year and send you running into the arms of an old-fashioned mistress."

"Oh, how you love to be shocking," he said. "And I love to be shocked."

"But do you, dearest, really love to be shocked?"

Suddenly he did kiss her. They had stopped in the middle of the dance floor, other couples swirling around them as the music swept on. He kissed her and she allowed it, yielding to him completely as if she must somehow love him; must somehow meet him halfway.

It didn't matter that others must be looking at them. It didn't matter that his hands were trembling as he held her.

What mattered was that, though she loved him terribly, it was not enough.

It was cool now. There was noise out there; cars arriving. The braying of a donkey; and the sharp high-pitched sound of a woman laughing, an American woman, who had driven all the way from Cairo as soon as she had heard.

Lawrence and Samir sat together in their camp chairs at the ancient writing table, with the papyri spread out before them.

Careful not to put his full weight on the fragile piece of furniture, Lawrence hastily scribbled his translations in his leather-bound book.

Now and then he glanced over his shoulder at the mummy, the great King who for all the world looked as if he merely slept. Ramses the Immortal! The very idea inflamed Lawrence. He knew that he would be in this strange chamber until well after dawn.

"But it must be a hoax," Samir said. "Ramses the Great guarding the royal families of Egypt for a thousand years. The lover of Cleopatra?"

"Ah, but it makes sublime sense!" Lawrence replied. He set down the pen for a moment, staring at the papyri. How his eyes ached. "If any woman could have driven an immortal man to entomb himself, Cleopatra would be that woman."

He looked at the marble bust before him. Lovingly he stroked Cleopatra's smooth white cheek. Yes, Lawrence could believe it. Cleopatra, beloved of Julius Caesar and beloved of Mark Antony; Cleopatra, who had held out against the Roman conquest of Egypt far longer than anyone dreamed possible; Cleopatra, the last ruler of Egypt in the ancient world. But the story—he must resume his translation. . . .

Samir rose and stretched uneasily. Lawrence watched him move towards the mummy. What was he doing? Examining the wrappings over the fingers, examining the brilliant scarab ring so clearly visible on the right hand? Now that was a nineteenth-dynasty treasure, no one could deny it, Lawrence thought.

Lawrence closed his eyes and massaged his eyelids gently. Then he opened them, focusing on the papyrus before him again.

"Samir, I tell you, the fellow is convincing me. Such a command of languages would dazzle anyone. And his philosophical perspective is quite as modern as my own." He reached for the older document, which he had examined earlier. "And this, Samir, I want you to examine it. This is none other than a letter from Cleopatra to Ramses."

"A hoax, Lawrence. Some sort of little Roman joke."

"No, my friend, nothing of the kind. She wrote this letter from Rome when Caesar was assassinated! She told Ramses she was coming home to him, and to Egypt."

He laid the letter aside. When Samir had time he would see for himself what these documents contained. All the world would see. He turned back to the original papyrus.

"But listen to this, Samir—Ramses' last thoughts: 'The Romans can not be condemned for the conquest of Egypt; we were conquered by time itself in the end. And all the wonders of this brave new century should draw me from my grief and yet I can not heal my heart; and so the mind suffers; the mind closes as if it were a flower without sun.' "

Samir was still looking at the mummy, looking at the ring. "Another reference to the sun. Again and again the sun." He turned to Lawrence. "But surely you don't believe it—!"

"Samir, if you can believe in the curse, why can't you believe in an immortal man?"

"Lawrence, you play with me. I have seen the workings of many a curse, my friend. But an immortal man who lived in Athens under Pericles and Rome under the Republic and Carthage under Hannibal? A man who taught Cleopatra the history of Egypt? Of this I know nothing at all."

"Listen again, Samir: 'Her beauty shall forever haunt me; as well as her courage and her frivolity; her passion for life, which seemed inhuman in its intensity while being only human after all.' "

Samir made no answer. His eyes were fixed on the mummy again, as if he could not stop looking at it. Lawrence understood perfectly, which is why he sat with his back to the thing in order to read the papyrus, so that he would get the crucial work done.

"Lawrence, this mummy is as dead as any I have ever seen in the Cairo Museum. A storyteller, that is what the man was. Yet these rings."

"Yes, my friend, I observed it very carefully earlier; it is the cartouche of Ramses the Great, and so we have not merely a storyteller but a collector of antiquities. Is that what you want me to believe?"

But what did Lawrence believe? He sat back against the sagging canvas of the camp chair and let his eyes drift over the contents of this strange room. Then again he translated from the scroll.

" 'And so I retreat to this isolated chamber; and now my library shall become my tomb. My servants shall anoint my body and wrap it in fine funerary linen as was the custom of my time now so long forgotten. But no knife shall touch me. No embalmer shall extract the heart and brain from my immortal form."

A euphoria overcame Lawrence suddenly; or was it a state of waking dream? This voice—it seemed so real to him; he felt the personality, as one never did with the ancient Egyptians. Ah, but of course, this was an immortal man. . . .

Elliott was getting drunk, but no one knew it. Except Elliott, who leaned on the gilded rail of the half-landing again in a rather casual manner that he almost never assumed. There was a style to even his smallest gestures, and now he carelessly violated it, keenly aware that no one would notice; no one would take offense.

Ah, such a world, made up almost wholly of subtleties. What a horror. And he must think of this marriage; he must talk of this marriage; he must do something about the sad spectacle of his son, quite obviously defeated, who, after watching Julie dance with another, came now up the marble stairs.

"I'm asking you to trust in me," Randolph was saying. "I guarantee this marriage. All it takes is a little time."

"Surely you don't think I enjoy pressing you," Elliott answered. Thick-tongued. Drunk all right. "I'm much more comfortable in a dream world, Randolph, where money simply doesn't exist. But the fact is, we cannot afford such reverie, either of us. This marriage is essential for us both."

"Then I shall go to see Lawrence myself."

Elliott turned to see his son only a few steps away, waiting like a schoolboy for the adults to acknowledge him.

"Father, I badly need consolation," Alex said.

"What you need is courage, young man," Randolph said crossly. "Don't tell me you've taken no for an answer again."

Alex took a glass of champagne from the passing waiter.

"She loves me. She loves me not," he said softly. "The simple fact is I cannot live without her. She's driving me mad."

"Of course you cannot." Elliott laughed gently. "Now, look. That clumsy young man down there is stepping on her feet. I'm sure she'd be very grateful if you came to her rescue at once."

Alex nodded, scarcely noticing as his father took the half-full glass from him and drank down the champagne. He straightened his shoulders and headed back to the dance floor. Such a perfect picture.

"The puzzling part is this," Randolph said under his breath. "She loves him. She always has."

"Yes, but she's like her father. She loves her freedom. And frankly I don't blame her. In a way she's too much for Alex. But he'd make her happy, I know that he would."

"Of course."

"And she would make him supremely happy; and perhaps no one else ever will."

"Nonsense," Randolph said. "Any young woman in London

would give her eyeteeth for the chance to make Alex happy. The eighteenth Earl of Rutherford?''

"Is that really so important? Our titles, our money, the endless maintenance of our decorative and tiresome little world?'' Elliott glanced around the ballroom. This was that lucid and dangerous state with drinking, when everything began to shimmer; when there was meaning in the grain of the marble; when one could make the most offensive speeches. "I wonder sometimes if I should be in Egypt with Lawrence. And if Alex shouldn't peddle his beloved title to someone else."

He could see the panic in Randolph's eyes. Dear God, what did the title mean to these merchant princes, these businessmen who had all but the title? It wasn't only that Alex might eventually control Julie, and thereby control the Stratford millions, and that Alex himself would be far easier than Julie to control. It was the prospect of true nobility, of nieces and nephews roaming the park of the old Rutherford estate in Yorkshire, of that miserable Henry Stratford trading on the alliance in every despicable way that he could.

"We're not defeated yet, Elliott," Randolph said. "And I rather like your decorative and tiresome little world. What else is there when you get right down to it?''

Elliott smiled. One more mouthful of champagne and he must tell Randolph what else there was. He just might. . . .

"I love you, fine English," Malenka said to him. She kissed him, then helped him with his tie, the soft touch of her fingers against his chin making the hairs rise on his neck.

What lovely fools women were, Henry Stratford thought. But this Egyptian woman he had enjoyed more than most. She was dark-skinned, a dancer by profession—a quiet and luscious beauty with whom he could do exactly what he wanted. You never knew that kind of freedom with an English whore.

He could see himself settling someday in an Eastern country with such a woman—free of all British respectability. That is, after he had made his fortune at the tables—that one great win he needed to put him quite beyond the world's reach.

For the moment, there was work to be done. The crowd around the tomb had doubled in size since last evening. And the trick was to reach his uncle Lawrence before the man was swept up utterly by the museum people and the authorities—to reach him now when he just might agree to anything in return for being left alone.

"Go on, dearest." He kissed Malenka again and watched her wrap the dark cloak about herself and hurry to the waiting car. How grateful she was for these small Western luxuries. Yes, that kind of woman. Rather than Daisy, his London mistress, a spoilt and demanding creature who nevertheless excited him, perhaps because she was so difficult to please.

He took one last swallow of Scotch, picked up his leather briefcase, and left the tent.

The crowds were ghastly. All night long he'd been awakened by the grind and huff of automobiles, and frenzied voices. And now the heat was rising; and he could already feel sand inside his shoes.

How he loathed Egypt. How he loathed these desert camps and the filthy camel-riding Arabs, and the lazy dirty servants. How he loathed his uncle's entire world.

And there was Samir, that insolent, irritating assistant who fancied himself Lawrence's social equal, trying to quiet the foolish reporters. Could this really be the tomb of Ramses II? Would Lawrence grant an interview?

Henry didn't give a damn. He pushed past the men who were guarding the entrance to the tomb.

"Mr. Stratford, please," Samir called after him. A lady reporter was on his heels. "Let your uncle alone now," Samir said as he drew closer. "Let him savor his find."

"The hell I will."

He glared at the guard who blocked his path. The man moved. Samir turned back to hold off the reporters. Who was going into the tomb? they wanted to know.

"This is a family matter," he said quickly and coldly to the woman reporter trying to follow him. The guard stepped in her path.

So little time left. Lawrence stopped writing, wiped his brow carefully, folded his handkerchief and made one more brief note:

"Brilliant to hide the elixir in a wilderness of poisons. What safer place for a potion that confers immortality than among potions that bring death. And to think they were her poisons—those which Cleopatra tested before deciding to use the venom of the asp to take her life."

He stopped, wiped his brow again. Already so hot in here.

And within a few short hours, they'd be upon him, demanding that he leave the tomb for the museum officials. Oh, if only he had made this discovery without the museum. God knows, he hadn't needed them. And they would take it all out of his hands.

The sun came in fine shafts through the rough-cut doorway. It struck the alabaster jars in front of him, and it seemed he heard something—faint, like a whispered breath.

He turned and looked at the mummy, at the features clearly molded beneath the tight wrappings. The man who claimed to be Ramses had been tall, and perhaps robust.

Not an old man, like the creature lying in the Cairo Museum. But then this Ramses claimed that he had never grown old. He was immortal, and merely slept within these bandages. Nothing could kill him, not even the poisons in this room, which he had tried in quantity, when grief for Cleopatra had left him half-mad. On his orders, his servants had wrapped his unconscious body; they had buried him alive, in the coffin he had had prepared for himself, supervising every detail; then they had sealed the tomb with the door that he himself had inscribed.

But what had rendered him unconscious? That was the mystery. Ah, what a delicious story. And what if—?

He found himself staring at the grim creature in its bindings of yellow linen. Did he really believe that something was alive there? Something that could move and speak?

It made Lawrence smile.

He turned back to the jars on the desk. The sun was making the little room an inferno. Taking his handkerchief, he carefully lifted the lid of the first jar before him. Smell of bitter almonds. Something as deadly as cyanide.

And the immortal Ramses claimed to have ingested half the contents of the jar in seeking to end his cursed life.

What if there were *an immortal being under those wrappings?*

There came that sound again. What was it? Not a rustling; no, nothing so distinct. Rather like an intake of breath.

Once again he looked at the mummy. The sun was shining full on it in long, beautiful dusty rays—the sun that shone through church windows, or through the branches of old oaks in dim forest glens.

It seemed he could see the dust rising from the ancient figure: a pale gold mist of moving particles. Ah, he was too tired!

And the thing, it did not seem so withered any longer; rather it had taken on the contour of a man.

"But what were you really, my ancient friend?" Lawrence asked softly. "Mad? Deluded? Or just what you claim to be— Ramses the Great?"

It gave him a chill to say it—what the French call a frisson. He rose and drew closer to the mummy.

The rays of the sun were positively bathing the thing. For the first time he noticed the contours of its eyebrows beneath the wrappings; there seemed more expression—hard, determined— to its face.

Lawrence smiled. He spoke to it in Latin, piecing together his sentences carefully. "Do you know how long you've slumbered, immortal Pharaoh? You who claimed to have lived one thousand years?"

Was he murdering the ancient language? He had spent so many years translating hieroglyphs that he was rusty with Caesar's tongue. "It's been twice that long, Ramses, since you sealed yourself in this chamber; since Cleopatra put the poisonous snake to her breast."

He stared at the figure, silent for a moment. Was there a mummy that did not arouse in one some deep, cold fear of death? You could believe life lingered there somehow; that the soul was trapped in the wrappings and could only be freed if the thing were destroyed.

Without thinking he spoke now in English.

"Oh, if only you were immortal. If only you could open your eyes on this modern world. And if only I didn't have to wait for permission to remove those miserable bandages, to look on . . . your face!"

The face. Had something changed in the face? No; it was only the full sunlight, wasn't it? But the face did seem fuller. Reverently, Lawrence reached out to touch it but then didn't, his hand poised there motionless.

He spoke in Latin again. "It's the year 1914, my great King. And the name Ramses the Great is still known to all the world; and so is the name of your last Queen."

Suddenly there was a noise behind him. Henry:

"Speaking to Ramses the Great in Latin, Uncle? Maybe the curse is already working on your brain."

"Oh, he understands Latin," Lawrence answered, still staring at the mummy. "Don't you, Ramses? And Greek also. And Persian and Etruscan, and tongues the world has forgotten. Who knows? Perhaps you knew the tongues of the ancient northern barbarians which became our own English centuries ago.'' Once again, he lapsed into Latin. ''But oh, there are so many wonders in the world now, great Pharaoh. There are so many things I could show you. . . .''

''I don't think he can hear you, Uncle,'' Henry said coldly. There was a soft chink of glass touching glass. ''Let's hope not, in any case.''

Lawrence turned around sharply. Henry, a briefcase tucked under his left arm, held the lid of one of the jars in his right hand.

''Don't touch that!'' Lawrence said crossly. ''It's poison, you imbecile. They're all full of poisons. One pinch and you'll be as dead as he is. That is, if he's truly dead.'' Even the sight of his nephew made him angry. And at a time such as this. . . .

Lawrence turned back to the mummy. Why, even the hands seemed fuller. And one of the rings had almost broken through the wrapping. Only hours ago. . . .

''Poisons?'' Henry asked behind him.

''It's a veritable laboratory of poisons,'' Lawrence answered. ''The very poisons Cleopatra tried, before her suicide, upon her helpless slaves!'' But why waste this precious information on Henry?

''How incredibly quaint,'' his nephew answered. Cynical, sarcastic. ''I thought she was bitten by an asp.''

''You're an idiot, Henry. You know less history than an Egyptian camel driver. Cleopatra tried a hundred poisons before she settled on the snake.''

He turned and watched coldly as his nephew touched the marble bust of Cleopatra, his fingers passing roughly over the nose, the eyes.

''Well, I fancy this is worth a small fortune, anyway. And these coins. You aren't going to *give* these things to the British Museum, are you?''

Lawrence sat down in the camp chair. He dipped the pen. Where had he stopped in his translation? Impossible to concentrate with these distractions.

''Is money all you think about?'' he asked coldly. ''And what have you ever done with it but gamble it away?'' He looked up at his nephew. When had the youthful fire died in that handsome face? When had arrogance hardened it, and aged it; and made it so deadly dull? ''The more I give you, the more you lose at the tables. Go back to London, for the love of heaven. Go back to your mistress and your music hall cronies. But get out.''

There was sharp noise from outside—another motor car back-firing as it ground its way up the sandy road. A dark-faced servant in soiled clothes entered suddenly, with a full breakfast tray in his hands. Samir came behind him.

''I cannot hold them back much longer, Lawrence,'' Samir said. With a small graceful gesture, he bid the servant set down the breakfast on the edge of the portable desk. ''The men from the British embassy are here also, Lawrence. So is every re-porter from Alexandria to Cairo. It is quite a circus out there, I fear.''

Lawrence stared at the silver dishes, the china cups. He wanted nothing now but to be alone with his treasures.

''Oh, just keep them out as long as you can, Samir. Give me a few more hours alone with these scrolls. Samir, the story is so sad, so poignant.''

''I'll do my best,'' Samir answered. ''But do take breakfast, Lawrence. You're exhausted. You need nourishment and rest.''

''Samir, I've never been better. Keep them out of here till noon. Oh, and take Henry with you. Henry, go with Samir. He'll see that you have something to eat.''

''Yes, do come with me, sir, please,'' Samir said quickly.

''I have to speak to my uncle alone.''

Lawrence looked back at his notebook. And the scroll opened above it. Yes, the King had been talking of his grief after, that he had retreated here to a secret study far away from Cleopatra's mausoleum in Alexandria, far away from the Valley of the Kings.

''Uncle,'' Henry said frostily, ''I'd be more than happy to go back to London if you would only take a moment to sign . . .''

Lawrence refused to look up from the papyrus. Maybe there would be some clue as to where Cleopatra's mausoleum had once stood.

''How many times must I say it?'' he murmured indifferently. ''No. I will sign no papers. Now take your briefcase with you and get out of my sight.''

''Uncle, the Earl wants an answer regarding Julie and Alex. He won't wait forever. And as for these papers, it's only a matter of a few shares.''

The Earl . . . Alex and Julie. It was monstrous. ''Good God, at a time like this!''

''Uncle, the world hasn't stopped turning on account of your discovery." Such acid in the tone. "And the stock has to be liquidated."

Lawrence laid down the pen. "No, it doesn't," he said, eyeing Henry coldly. "And as for the marriage, it can wait forever. Or until Julie decides for herself. Go home and tell that to my good friend the Earl of Rutherford! And tell your father I will liquidate no further family stock. Now leave me alone."

Henry didn't move. He shifted the briefcase uneasily, his face tightening as he stared down at his uncle.

"Uncle, you don't realize—"

"Allow me to tell you what I *do* realize," Lawrence said, "that you have gambled away a king's ransom and that your father will go to any lengths to cover your debts. Even Cleopatra and her drunken lover Mark Antony could not have squandered the fortune that has slipped through your hands. And what does Julie need with the Rutherford title anyway? Alex needs the Stratford millions, that's the truth of it. Alex is a beggar with a title the same as Elliott. God forgive me. It's the truth."

"Uncle, Alex could buy any heiress in London with that title."

"Then why doesn't he?"

"One word from you and Julie would make up her mind—"

"And Elliott would show his gratitude to you for arranging things, is that it? And with my daughter's money he'd be very generous indeed."

Henry was white with anger.

"What the hell do you care about this marriage?" Lawrence asked bitterly. "You humiliate yourself because you need the money. . . ."

He thought he saw his nephew's lips move in a curse.

He turned back to the mummy, trying to shut it all out—the tentacles of the London life he'd left behind trying to reach him here.

Why, the whole figure looked fuller! And the ring, it was plainly visible now as if the finger, fleshing out, had burst the wrappings altogether. Lawrence fancied he could see the faint color of healthy flesh.

"You're losing your mind," he whispered to himself. And that sound, there it was again. He tried to listen for it; but his concentration only made him all the more conscious of the noise outside. He drew closer to the body in the coffin. Good Lord, was that hair he saw beneath the wrappings about the head?

"I feel so sorry for you, Henry," he whispered suddenly. "That you can't savour such a discovery. This ancient King, this mystery." Who said that he couldn't touch the remains? Just move perhaps an inch of the rotted linen?

He drew out his penknife and held it uncertainly. Twenty years ago he might have cut the thing open. There wouldn't have been any busybody officials to deal with. He might have seen for himself if under all that dust—

"I wouldn't do that if I were you, Uncle," Henry interrupted. "The museum people in London will raise the roof."

"I told you to get out."

He heard Henry pour a cup of coffee as if he had all the time in the world. The aroma filled the close little chamber.

Lawrence backed into the camp chair, and again pressed his folded handkerchief to his brow. Twenty-four hours now without sleep. Maybe he should rest.

"Drink your coffee, Uncle Lawrence," Henry said to him. "I poured it for you." And there it was, the full cup. "They're waiting for you out there. You're exhausted."

"You bloody fool," Lawrence whispered. "I wish you'd go away."

Henry set the cup before him, right by the notebook.

"Careful, that papyrus is priceless."

The coffee did look inviting, even if Henry was pushing it at him. He lifted the cup, took a deep swallow, and closed his eyes.

What had he just seen as he put down the cup? The mummy stirring in the sunlight? Impossible. Suddenly a burning sensation in his throat blotted out everything else. It was as if his throat were closing! He couldn't breathe or speak.

He tried to rise; he was staring at Henry; and suddenly he caught the smell coming from the cup still in his trembling hand. Bitter almonds. It was the poison. The cup was falling; dimly he heard it shatter as it hit the stone floor.

"For the love of God! You bastard!" He was falling; his hands out towards his nephew, who stood white-faced and grim, staring coldly at him as if this catastrophe were not happening, as if he were not dying.

His body convulsed. Violently, he turned away. The last thing he saw as he fell was the mummy in the dazzling sunlight; the last thing he felt was the sandy floor beneath his burning face.

* * *

For a long moment Henry Stratford did not move. He stared down at the body of his uncle as if he did not quite believe what he saw. Someone else had done this. Someone else had broken through the thick membrane of frustration and put this horrid plot into motion. Someone else had put the silver coffee spoon into the jar of ancient poison and slipped that poison into Lawrence's cup.

Nothing moved in the dusty sunlight. The tiniest particles seemed suspended in the hot air. Only a faint sound originated within the chamber; something like the beat of a heart.

Imaginings. It was imperative to follow through. It was imperative to stop his hand from shaking; to prevent the scream from ever leaving his lips. Because it was there all right—a scream which once released would never stop.

I killed him. I poisoned him.

And now that great hideous and immovable obstacle to my plan is no more.

Bend down; feel the vein. Yes, he's dead. Quite dead.

Henry straightened, fighting a sudden wave of nausea, and quickly took several papers from his briefcase. He dipped his uncle's pen and wrote the name Lawrence Stratford neatly and quickly, as he had done several times on less important papers in the past.

His hand shook badly, but so much the better. For his uncle had had just such a tremor. And the scribble looked all the better when it was done.

He put the pen back and stood with his eyes closed, trying to calm himself again, trying to think only, It is done.

The most curious thoughts were flooding him suddenly, that he could undo this! That it had been no more than an impulse; that he could roll back the minutes and his uncle would be alive again. This positively could not have happened! Poison . . . coffee . . . Lawrence dead.

And then a memory came to him, pure and quiet and certainly welcome, of the day twenty-one years ago when his cousin Julie had been born. His uncle and he sitting in the drawing room together. His uncle Lawrence, whom he loved more than his father.

"But I want you to know that you will always be my nephew, my beloved nephew . . ."

Dear God, was he losing his mind? For a moment he did not

even know where he was. He could have sworn someone else was in this room with him. Who was it?

That thing in the mummy case. Don't look at it. Like a witness. Get back to the business at hand.

The papers are signed; the stock can be sold; and now there is all the more reason for Julie to marry that stupid twit Alex Savarell. And all the more reason for Henry's father to take Stratford Shipping completely in hand.

Yes. Yes. But what to do at the moment? He looked at the desk again. Everything as it was. And those six glittering gold Cleopatra coins. Ah, yes, take one. Quickly, he slipped it into his pocket. A little flush warmed his face. Yes, the coin must be worth a fortune. And he could fit it into a cigarette case; simple to smuggle. All right.

Now get out of here immediately. No, he wasn't thinking. He couldn't still his heart. Shout for Samir, that was the appropriate action. Something horrible has happened to Lawrence. Stroke, heart attack, impossible to tell! And this cell is like a furnace. A doctor must come at once.

"Samir!" he cried out, staring forward like a matinee actor at the moment of shock. His gaze fell directly again on that grim, loathsome thing in the linen wrappings. Was it staring back at him? Were its eyes open beneath the bandages? Preposterous! Yet the illusion struck a deep shrill note of panic in him, which gave just the right edge to his next shout for help.

2

FURTIVELY THE clerk read the latest edition of the *London Herald,* the pages folded and held carefully out of sight behind his darkly lacquered desk. The office was quiet now because of the board meeting, the only sound the distant clack of a typewriting machine from an adjoining room.

MUMMY'S CURSE KILLS
STRATFORD SHIPPING MAGNATE
"RAMSES THE DAMNED" STRIKES DOWN
THOSE WHO DISTURB HIS REST

How the tragedy had caught the public imagination. Impossible to walk a step without seeing a front-page story. And how the popular newspapers elaborated upon it, indulging in hastily drawn illustrations of pyramids and camels, of the mummy in his wooden coffin and poor Mr. Stratford lying dead at his feet.

Poor Mr. Stratford, who had been such a fine man to work for; remembered now for this lurid and sensational death.

Just when the furore had died down, it had been given another infusion of vitality:

HEIRESS DEFIES MUMMY'S CURSE
"RAMSES THE DAMNED" TO VISIT LONDON.

The clerk turned the page now quietly, folding the paper into a narrow thick column width again. Hard to believe Miss Stratford was bringing home all the treasure to be placed on exhibit in her own home in Mayfair. But that is what her father had always done.

The clerk hoped that he'd be invited to the reception, but there was no chance of it, even though he had been with Stratford Shipping for some thirty years.

To think, a bust of Cleopatra, the only authenticated portrait in existence. And freshly minted coins with her image and name. Ah, he would have liked to see those things in Mr. Stratford's library. But he would have to wait until the British Museum claimed the collection and put it on display for lord and commoner alike.

And there were things he might have told Miss Stratford, if ever there had been an opportunity, things perhaps old Mr. Lawrence would have wanted her to know.

For instance, that Henry Stratford hadn't sat behind his desk for a year now, yet he still collected a full salary and bonuses; and that Mr. Randolph wrote him cheques on the company funds at random and then doctored the books.

But perhaps the young woman would find out all this for herself. The will had left her full control of her father's company. And that's why she was in the boardroom, with her handsome fiancé, Alex Savarell, Viscount Summerfield, right now.

Randolph could not bear to see her crying like this. Dreadful to be pressing her with papers to sign. She looked all the more fragile in her black mourning; her face drawn and shimmering as if she were feverish; her eyes full of that odd light that he had first seen when she told him that her father was dead.

The other board members sat in sullen silence, eyes downcast. Alex held her arm gently. He looked faintly baffled, as if he really didn't understand death; it was just that he didn't want her to suffer. Simple soul. Out of place among these merchants and men of business; the porcelain aristocrat with his heiress.

Why must we go through with this? Why are we not alone with our grief?

Yet Randolph did it because he had to do it, though never had the whole thing seemed so meaningless. Never had his love for his only son been so painfully tried.

"I simply cannot make decisions yet, Uncle Randolph," she said to him politely.

"Of course not, my dear," he answered. "No one expects you to. If you'll only sign this draft for emergency funds and leave the rest to us."

"I want to go over everything, to take a hand in things," she said. "That's clearly what Father intended. This whole situation with the warehouses in India, I don't understand how it could have come to such a crisis." She paused, unwilling to be caught up in things, perhaps utterly incapable of it, and the tears flowed silently again.

"Leave it to me, Julie," he said wearily. "I've been handling crises in India for years."

He pushed the documents towards her. Sign, please, sign. Do not ask for explanations now. Do not add humiliation to this pain.

For that is what was so surprising, that he missed his brother so much. We don't know what we feel for those we love until they're taken. All night he'd lain awake remembering things . . . the Oxford days, their first trips to Egypt—Randolph, Lawrence and Elliott Savarell. Those nights in Cairo. He had awakened early and gone through old photographs, and papers. Such marvelously vivid memories.

And now, without spirit or will, he tried to cheat Lawrence's daughter. He tried to cover for ten years of lies and deceit. Lawrence had built Stratford Shipping because he really didn't care about money. Oh, the risks that Lawrence used to take. And what had Randolph done since he took over? Hold the reins and steal.

To his utter amazement Julie lifted the pen and signed her name quickly on all the various papers, without so much as reading them. Well, he was safe from her inevitable questions for a little while.

I'm sorry, Lawrence. It was like a silent prayer. Perhaps if you knew the whole story.

"In a few days, Uncle Randolph, I want to sit down and go over everything with you. I think that's what Father wanted. But I'm so tired. It's really time to go home."

"Yes, let me take you home now," Alex said immediately. He helped her to her feet.

Dear good Alex. Why couldn't my son have had a mere particle of that gentleness? The whole world could have been his.

Quickly Randolph went to open the double doors. To his

amazement he found the men from the British Museum waiting. An annoyance. He would have spirited her out another way, if he had known. He did not like the unctuous Mr. Hancock, who behaved as if everything Lawrence had discovered belonged to the museum and the world.

"Miss Stratford," the man said now as he approached Julie. "Everything has been approved. The first showing of the mummy will take place in your home, just as your father would have wished. We will of course catalogue everything, and remove the collection to the museum as soon as you wish it. I thought you would want to have my personal assurance. . . ."

"Of course," Julie answered wearily. This interested her no more than the board meeting, obviously. "I'm grateful to you, Mr. Hancock. You know what this discovery meant to my father." There was a pause again as if she would begin crying. And why not? "I only wish I'd been with him in Egypt."

"Darling, he died where he'd been most happy," Alex offered lamely. "And among the things he loved."

Pretty words. Lawrence had been cheated. He'd had his momentous find for only a few short hours. Even Randolph understood as much.

Hancock took Julie's arm. They moved towards the door together.

"Of course it's impossible to authenticate the remains until we make a thorough examination. The coins, the bust, these are quite unprecedented discoveries. . . ."

"We'll make no extravagant claims, Mr. Hancock. I only want a small reception for Father's oldest friends."

She offered her hand now, in effect dismissing him. She managed such things so decisively, so like her father. So like the Earl of Rutherford when you thought about it. Hers had always been an aristocratic manner. And if only the marriage were to take place. . . .

"Good-bye, Uncle Randolph."

He bent to kiss her check.

"I love you, darling," he whispered. It surprised him. And so did the smile that spread across her face. Did she hear what he had meant to tell her? I am so sorry, sorry for everything, my dear.

Alone at last on the marble staircase. All of them gone but Alex, and in her heart of hearts, she wished that he were gone too.

She wanted nothing so much now as the quiet interior of her Rolls-Royce limousine with the glass shutting out the noise of the world around her.

"Now, I'm going to say this only once, Julie," Alex said as he helped her down the stairs. "But it comes from my soul. Don't let this tragedy postpone the marriage. I know your feelings, but you're alone in that house now. And I want to be with you, to take care of you. I want us to be husband and wife."

"Alex, I'd be lying to you," she said, "if I told you I could make a decision now. More than ever I need time to think."

She couldn't bear to look at him suddenly; he seemed so young always. Had she ever been young? The question would have made Uncle Randolph smile perhaps. She was twenty-one. But Alex at twenty-five seemed a boy to her. And it hurt her so much not to love him as he deserved to be loved.

The sunlight hurt her eyes as he opened the door to the street. She brought the veil down from the brim of her hat. No reporters, thank God no reporters, and the big black motor car there waiting with the door open.

"I won't be alone, Alex," she said gently. "I have Rita and Oscar there. And Henry's moving back into his old room. Uncle Randolph insisted upon it. I'll have more company than I need."

Henry. The last person in the world she wanted to see was Henry. What an irony that he had indeed been the last person her father saw before his eyes closed in death.

The reporters mobbed Henry Stratford as he came ashore. Had the mummy's curse frightened him? Had he glimpsed anything supernatural at work in the little rock chamber where the death of Lawrence Stratford had taken place? Henry fought his way through customs in silence, ignoring the noisy, smoky flashes of the cameras. With icy impatience he glared at the officials, who checked his few suitcases and then waved him past.

His heart thudded in his ears. He wanted a drink. He wanted the quiet of his own home in Mayfair. He wanted his mistress, Daisy Banker. He wanted anything but the dreary ride with his father. He avoided Randolph's eyes altogether as he climbed into the back of the Rolls.

As the long cumbersome saloon forced its way out of the thick traffic, he caught a glimpse of Samir Ibrahaim greeting a group of black-dressed men—undoubtedly busybodies from the museum. What a fortunate thing that this corpse of Ramses the Great concerned everyone far more than the corpse of Lawrence Stratford, which had been buried without ceremony in Egypt, just as Lawrence had wished.

Good Lord, his father looked dreadful, as if he'd aged overnight some ten years. He was even a little disheveled.

"Do you have a cigarette?" Henry asked sharply.

Without looking at him his father produced a small thin cigar and a light.

"The marriage is still the essential thing," Randolph murmured almost as if he were speaking to himself. "A new bride simply doesn't have time to think about business. And for the time being, I've arranged for you to stay with her. She cannot remain alone."

"Good Lord, Father, this is the twentieth century! Why the hell can't she remain alone!"

Stay in that house, and with that disgusting mummy on display in the library? It sickened him. He closed his eyes, savored the cigar silently, and thought of his mistress. A series of sharp, erotic images passed quickly through his mind.

"Damn it, you do what I tell you," his father said. But the voice lacked conviction. Randolph gazed out the window. "You'll stay there and keep an eye on her and do what you can to see she consents to the marriage as quickly as possible. Do your best to see that she doesn't move away from Alex. I think Alex has begun to irritate her slightly."

"Small wonder. If Alex had any gumption . . ."

"The marriage is good for her. It's good for everyone."

"All right, all right, let's drop it!"

Silence as the car moved on. There was time for dinner with Daisy, and a long rest at the flat before he hit the gambling tables at Flint's, that is, if he could force a little immediate cash out of his father. . . .

"He didn't suffer, did he?"

Henry gave a little start.

"What? What are you talking about?"

"Your uncle?" his father asked, turning to him for the first time. "The late Lawrence Stratford, who has just died in Egypt? Did he suffer, for the love of God, or did he go quietly?"

"One minute he was fine, the next he was lying on the floor. He was gone within seconds. Why do you ask about something like that?"

"You're such a sentimental young bastard, aren't you?"

"I couldn't prevent it!"

For one moment, the atmosphere of that close little cell came back to him, the acrid smell of the poison. And that thing, that thing in the mummy case, and the grim illusion that it had been watching.

"He was a pigheaded old fool," Randolph said almost in a whisper. "But I loved him."

"Did you really?" Henry turned sharply and peered into his father's face. "He's left everything to her, and you loved him!"

"He settled plenty on both of us a long time ago. It ought to have been enough, more than enough—"

"It's a pittance compared to what she's inherited!"

"I won't discuss this."

Patience, Henry thought. Patience. He sat back against the soft grey upholstery. I need a hundred pounds at least and I won't get it like this.

Daisy Banker watched through the lace curtains as Henry stepped out of the cab below. She lived in a long flat above the music hall, where she sang every night from ten P.M. until two in the morning; a soft ripe peach of a woman with big drowsy blue eyes and silver blond hair. Her voice was nothing much and she knew it; but they liked her, they did. They liked her very much.

And she liked Henry Stratford, or so she told herself. He was certainly the best thing that had ever happened to her. He'd got her the job below, though how she could never quite work out; and he paid for the flat, or at least he was supposed to. She knew there was quite a bit owing, but then he was just back from Egypt. He'd make it right or shut up anyone who questioned him about it. He was very good at doing that.

She ran to the mirror as she heard his tread on the stairs. She pulled down the feathered collar of her peignoir and straightened the pearls at her throat. She pinched her cheeks to work up the blush just as his key turned in the lock.

"Well, I'd just about given up on you, I had!" she bawled as he came into the room. But oh, the sight of him. It never failed to work on her. He was so very handsome with his dark brown hair and eyes; and the way he conducted himself; so truly the gentleman. She loved the way he removed his cloak now and threw it carelessly over the chair, and beckoned for her to come into his arms. So lazy he was; and so full of himself! But why shouldn't he be?

"And my motor car? You promised me a motor car of my own before you left. Where is it! That wasn't it downstairs. That was a cab."

There was something so cold in his smile. When he kissed her, his lips hurt her a little; and his fingers bit into the soft flesh of her upper arm. She felt a vague chill move up her spine; her mouth tingled. She kissed him again and when he led her into the bedroom she didn't say a word.

"I'll get you your motor car," he whispered into her ear as he tore off the peignoir and pressed her against him so that her nipples touched the scratchy surface of his starched shirt. She kissed his cheek, then his chin, licking the faint stubble of his beard. Lovely to feel him breathe this way, to feel his hands on her shoulders.

"Not too rough, sir," she whispered.

"Why not?"

The telephone rang. She could have ripped it from the wall. She unbuttoned his shirt for him as he answered.

"I told you not to call again, Sharples."

Oh, that bloody son of a bitch, she thought miserably. She wished he was dead. She'd worked for Sharples before Henry Stratford had rescued her. And Sharples was a mean one, plain and simple. He had left his scar on her, a tiny half-moon on the back of her neck.

"I told you I'd pay you when I got back, didn't I? Suppose you give me time to unpack my trunk!" He jammed down the little cone of a receiver into the hook. She pushed the phone back out of the way on the marble-top table.

"Come here to me, sweetheart," she said as she sat on the bed.

But her eyes dulled slightly as she watched him staring at the telephone. He was broke still, wasn't he? Stone broke.

Strange. There had been no wake in this house for her father. And now the painted coffin of Ramses the Great was being carried carefully through the double drawing rooms as if by pallbearers, and into the library, which he had always called the Egyptian room. A wake for the mummy; and the chief mourner was not here.

Julie watched as Samir directed the men from the museum to

place the coffin carefully upright in the southeast corner, to the left of the open conservatory doors. A perfect position. Anyone entering the house could see it immediately. All those in the drawing rooms would have a good view of it; and the mummy himself would appear to have a view of all assembled to pay him homage when the lid was lifted and the body itself was revealed.

The scrolls and alabaster jars would be arranged on the long marble table beneath the mirror to the left of the upright coffin, along the east wall. The bust of Cleopatra was already being placed on a stand in the centre of the room. The gold coins would go in a special display case beside the marble table. And other miscellaneous treasures could now be arranged any way that Samir saw fit.

The soft afternoon sunlight poured in from the conservatory, throwing its intricate dancing patterns over the golden mask of the King's face and his folded arms.

Gorgeous it was, authentic obviously. Only a fool would question such a treasure. But what did the whole story mean?

Oh, if only they were all gone, Julie thought, and she could be alone now to study it. But the men would be here forever examining the exhibit. And Alex, what to do about Alex, who stood beside her, and gave her not a moment to herself?

Of course she'd been glad to see Samir, though it had stirred her own pain to see the pain in him.

And he looked stiff and uncomfortable in his black Western suit and starched white shirt. In the silks of his native dress, he was a dark-eyed prince, quite removed from the dreary routines of this noisy century and its bludgeoning drive to progress. Here he looked foreign, and almost servile in spite of the imperious manner in which he ordered the workmen about.

Alex stared at the workmen and their relics with the strangest expression. What was it? These things meant nothing to him; they had to do with some other world. But did he not find them beautiful? Ah, it was so difficult for her to understand.

"I wonder if there is a curse," he whispered softly.

"Oh, please, don't be ridiculous," Julie answered. "Now, they're going to be working for some time. Why don't we go on back into the conservatory and have tea?"

"Yes, we should do that," he said. It was dislike in his face, wasn't it? Not confusion. He felt nothing for these treasures. They were alien to him; they did not matter one way or the other. She might have felt the same way gazing at a modern machine she did not understand.

It saddened her. But everything saddened her now—and most of all the fact that her father had had so little time with these many treasures, that he had died on the very day of his greatest discovery. And that she was the one who must savour each and every article that he had uncovered in this mysterious and controversial grave.

Perhaps after tea, Alex would understand that she wanted to be alone. She led him down the hall now, past the double doors of the drawing rooms, past the doors of the library and out through the marble alcove into the glass room of ferns and flowers that ran across the entire back of the house.

This had been Father's favourite place when he was not in the library. No accident that his desk and his books were only a few feet away, through those glass doors.

They sat down at the wicker table together, the sun playing beautifully on the silver tea service before them.

"You pour, dearest," she said to Alex. She laid out the cakes on the plates. Now that gave him something to do which he understood.

Had she ever known a human being who could do all the little things so well? Alex could ride, dance, shoot, pour tea, mix delicious American cocktails, slip into the protocol of Buckingham Palace without batting an eyelash. He could read an occasional poem with such a simulation of feeling that it made her weep. He could kiss very well, too, and there was no doubt that marriage with him would have its deeply sensuous moments. No doubt whatsoever. But what else would it have?

She felt selfish suddenly. Wasn't all that enough? It hadn't been for her father, a merchant prince whose manners were indistinguishable from those of aristocratic friends. It had meant nothing at all.

"Drink it, darling, you need it," Alex said to her, offering her the cup the way she liked it. No milk, no sugar. Only a thin slice of lemon.

Imagine anyone really needing tea.

It seemed the light changed around her; a shadow. She looked up to see that Samir had come silently into the room.

"Samir. Sit down. Join us."

He motioned for her to remain where she was. He was holding a leather-bound book in his hands.

"Julie," he said with a slow and deliberate glance in the direction of the Egyptian room, "I brought your father's notebook to you. I didn't want to give it to the people at the museum."

"Oh, I'm so glad. Do join us, please."

"No, I must return to work immediately. I want to make sure things are done as they should be. And you must read this notebook, Julie. The newspapers, they published only the bare bones of this story. There is more here. . . ."

"Come, sit down," she pressed again. "We'll take care of that together, later."

After a moment's hesitation, he gave in. He took the chair beside her, giving a little polite nod to Alex, to whom he'd been introduced before.

"Julie, your father had only begun his translations. You know his command of the ancient tongues. . . ."

"Yes, I'm eager to read it. But what is really troubling you?" she said earnestly. "What is wrong?"

Samir pondered, then: "Julie, I am uneasy about this discovery. I am uneasy about the mummy and the poisons contained in the tomb."

"Were they really Cleopatra's poisons?" Alex said quickly. "Or is that something the reporters dreamed up?"

"No one can say," Samir answered politely.

"Samir, everything is carefully labelled," Julie said. "The servants had been told."

"You don't believe in the curse now, do you?" Alex asked.

Samir made a little polite smile. "No. Nevertheless," he said, turning back to Julie. "Promise me that if you see anything strange, even if you suffer a presentiment, you will call me at the museum at once."

"But, Samir, I never expected you to believe—"

"Julie, curses are rare in Egypt," he said quickly. "And the admonitions written on this mummy case are most severe. The story of the creature's immortality, there are more details in this little book."

"But you don't think Father really succumbed to a curse, Samir."

"No. But the things found in the tomb defy explanation. Except if one believes . . . But then that is absurd. I ask only that you take nothing for granted. That you call me if you need me at once."

He took his leave of her abruptly, and went back into the library. She could hear him speaking Arabic to one of the workmen. She watched them uneasily through the open doors.

Grief, she thought. It's a strange and a misunderstood emotion. He grieves for Father as I do, and so the whole discovery is ruined for him. How difficult all this must be.

And he would have so enjoyed all of it if only . . . Well, she understood. It was not so with her. She wanted nothing so much as to be alone with Ramses the Great and his Cleopatra. But she understood. And the pain of Father's loss would be there forever. She didn't really want it to go away. She looked at Alex, poor lost boy staring at her with such concern.

"I love you," he whispered suddenly.

"Why, what on earth has come over you!" She laughed softly.

He looked baffled, childlike. Her handsome fiancé was really suffering suddenly. She couldn't bear it.

"I don't know," he said. "Maybe I'm having a presentiment. Is that what he called it? I only know I want to remind you—I love you."

"Oh, Alex, dear Alex." She bent forward and kissed him, and felt his sudden desperate clasp of her hand.

The gaudy little clock on Daisy's dressing table rang six.

Henry sat back, stretched, then reached for the champagne again, filling his glass, then hers.

She looked drowsy still, the thin satin strap of her nightgown fallen down over one rounded arm.

"Drink, darling," he said.

"Not me, lovey. Singing tonight," she said with an arrogant lift of her chin. "I can't drink all day like some I know." She tore off a bit of meat from the roasted fowl on her plate, and put it in her mouth crudely. Beautiful mouth. "But this cousin of yours! She's not afraid of the bloody mummy! Putting it right there in her own house!"

Big stupid blue eyes fixed on him; just the kind he liked. Though he missed Malenka, his Egyptian beauty; he really did. The thing about an Eastern woman was she didn't have to be stupid; she could be clever, and just as easy to manage. With a girl like Daisy, the stupidity was essential; and then you had to talk to her—and talk to her and talk to her.

"Why the hell should she be afraid of the damned mummy!" he said irritably. "The daft part is giving the whole treasure to a museum. She doesn't know what money is, my cousin. She has too much of it to know. He increased my trust fund by a pittance and he leaves her a shipping empire. He's the one who was . . ."

He stopped. The little chamber; the sunlight falling in shafts on that thing. He saw it again. Saw *what he had done!* No. Not right. Died of a heart attack or a stroke, he did—the man lying sprawled on the sandy floor. I didn't do it. And that thing, it hadn't been staring through the wrappings, that was absurd!

He drank the champagne too quickly. Ah, but it was good. He filled his glass again.

"But a bleeding mummy in the very house with her," Daisy said.

And suddenly, violently, he saw those eyes again, beneath rotted bandages, staring at him. Yes, staring. Stop it, you fool, you did what you had to do! Stop it or you will go mad.

He rose from the table a bit clumsily and put on his jacket, and straightened his silk tie.

"But where are you going?" Daisy asked. "You're a bit too drunk to be going out now, if you ask me."

"But I didn't," he answered. She knew where he was going. He had the hundred pounds he'd managed to squeeze out of Randolph, and the casino was open. It had opened at dark.

He wanted to be there alone now, so that he could truly concentrate. Merely thinking of it, of the green baize under the lamps and the sound of the dice and roulette wheel, engendered a deep excitement in him. One good win, and he'd quit, he promised himself. And with a hundred pounds to start. No, he couldn't wait. . . .

Of course he'd run into Sharples, and he owed Sharples too much money, but how the hell was he supposed to pay it back if he didn't get to the tables, and though he didn't feel lucky—no, not lucky at all tonight—well, he had to give it a try.

"Just wait now, sir. Sit down, sir," Daisy said, coming after him. "Have another glass with me and then a little nap. It's barely six o'clock."

"Let me alone," he said. He put on his greatcoat and pulled on his leather gloves. Sharples. A stupid man, Sharples. He felt in his coat pocket for the knife he'd carried for years. Yes, still there. He drew it out now, and examined the thin steel blade.

"Oh no, sir," Daisy gasped.

"Don't be a fool," he said offhandedly, and closing the knife and putting it back into his pocket he went out the door.

No sound now but the low gurgling of the fountain in the conservatory, the ashen twilight long gone, the Egyptian room lighted only by the green shaded lamp on Lawrence's desk.

Julie sat in her father's leather chair, back to the wall, her silk peignoir soft and comfortable, and surprisingly warm, her hand on the diary which she had not yet read.

The glittering mask of Ramses the Great was ever so slightly frightening, the large almond-shaped eyes peering into the soft shadows; the marble Cleopatra appeared to glow. And so beautiful the coins mounted on black velvet against the far wall.

She had inspected them carefully earlier. Same profile as the bust, same rippling hair beneath its gold tiara. A Greek Cleopatra, not the silly Egyptian image so popular in programmes for Shakespeare's tragedy, or in the engravings which illustrated Plutarch's *Lives* and popular histories galore.

Profile of a beautiful woman; strong, not tragic. Strong as Romans loved their heroes and heroines to be strong.

The thick scrolls of parchment and papyrus looked all too fragile as they lay heaped on the marble table. The other items could also be easily destroyed by prying hands. Quill pens, ink pots, a little silver burner meant for oil, it seemed, with a ring in which to position a glass vial. The vials themselves lay beside it—exquisite specimens of early glasswork, each with a tiny silver cap. Of course all these little relics, and the string of alabaster jars behind them, were protected by small, neatly inscribed signs which read: "Please do not touch."

Nevertheless, it worried her, so many coming here to view these things.

"Remember, it's poison, most definitely," Julie had told Rita and Oscar, her indispensable maid and butler. And that had been enough to keep them out of the room!

"It's a body, miss," Rita had said. "A dead body! Never mind it's an Egyptian King. I say leave the dead alone, miss."

Julie had laughed softly to herself. "The British Museum is full of dead bodies, Rita."

If only the dead *could* come back. If only the ghost of her father would come to her. Imagine such a miracle. Having him again, speaking to him, hearing his voice. *What happened, Fa-*

ther? Did you suffer? Was there even one second when you were afraid?

Yes, she wouldn't have minded such a visitation at all. But no such thing would ever happen. That was the horror. We went from the cradle to the grave beset by mundane tragedies. The splendour of the supernatural was a thing for stories and poems, and Shakespeare's plays.

But why dwell on it? Now had come the moment to be alone with her father's treasures, and to read the last words he wrote.

She turned the pages now to the date of the discovery. And the first words she saw made her eyes fill with tears.

Must write to Julie, describe everything. Hieroglyphs on the door virtually free of error; must have been written by one who knew what he was writing. Yet the Greek is entirely of the Ptolemaic period. And the Latin is sophisticated. Impossible. Yet there it is. Samir uncommonly fearful and superstitious. Must sleep for a few hours. Am going in tonight!

There was a hasty ink sketch of the door of the tomb and its three broad paragraphs of writing. Hastily she turned to the next page.

Nine P.M. by my watch. Inside the chamber at last. Appears to be a library rather than a tomb. The man has been laid to rest in a King's coffin beside a desk on which he has left some thirteen scrolls. He writes entirely in Latin, with obvious haste but no carelessness. There are droplets of ink all over, but the text is completely coherent.

"Call me Ramses the Damned. For that is the name I have given myself. But I was once Ramses the Great of Upper and Lower Egypt, slayer of the Hittites, Father of many sons and daughters, who ruled Egypt for sixty-four years. My monuments are still standing; the stele recount my victories, though a thousand years have passed since I was pulled, a mortal child, from the womb.

"Ah, fatal moment now buried by time, when from a Hittite priestess I took the cursed elixir. Her warnings I would not heed. Immortality I craved. And so I drank the potion in the brimming cup. And now, long centuries gone by—amid the poisons of my lost Queen, I hide the potion which she would not accept from me—my doomed Cleopatra.''

Julie stopped. The elixir, hidden amongst these poisons? She realized what Samir had meant. The papers had not told that part of the little mystery. Tantalizing. These poisons hide a formula that can grant eternal life.

''But who would create such a fiction!'' she whispered.

She found herself staring at the marble bust of Cleopatra. Immortality. Why would Cleopatra not drink the potion? Oh, but really, she was beginning to believe it! She smiled.

She turned the page of the diary. The translation was interrupted. Her father had written only:

> Goes on to describe how Cleopatra awakened him from his dream-filled sleep, how he tutored her, loved her, watched her seduce the Roman leaders one by one. . . .

''Yes,'' Julie whispered. ''Julius Caesar first and then Mark Antony. But why would she not take the elixir?''

There was another paragraph of translation:

> ''How can I bear this burden any longer? How can I endure the loneliness anymore? Yet I can not die. Her poisons can not harm me. They keep my elixir safe so that I may dream of still other Queens, both fair and wise, to share the centurion with me. But is it not her face I see? Her voice I hear? Cleopatra. Yesterday. Tomorrow, Cleopatra.''

Latin followed. Several scribbled paragraphs in Latin which Julie could not read. Even with the aid of a dictionary she could not have translated it. Then there were a few lines of demotic Egyptian, even more nearly impenetrable than that Latin. Nothing more.

She laid down the book. She fought the inevitable tears. It was almost as if she could feel the presence of her father in this room. How excited he must have been, what a lovely scribble his handwriting had become.

And how lovely the whole mystery was.

Somewhere among all those poisons, an elixir that conveyed immortality? One need not take it literally to find it beautiful.

And behold that tiny silver burner and the delicate vial. Ramses the Damned had believed it. Perhaps her father had believed it. And for the moment, well, maybe she did too.

She rose slowly and approached the long marble table against the opposite wall. The scrolls were too fragile. There were tiny bits and pieces of papyrus scattered everywhere. She had seen this damage done as the men lifted them ever so carefully from their crates. She dared not touch them. Besides, she couldn't read them.

As for the jars, she mustn't touch them either. What if some of that poison were spilled, or somehow released into the air?

She found herself suddenly looking at her own reflection in the mirror on the wall. She went back to the desk, and opened the folded newspaper that lay there.

Shakespeare's *Antony and Cleopatra* was enjoying a long run in London. She and Alex had meant to go and see it, but then Alex fell asleep during serious plays. Only Gilbert and Sullivan entertained Alex, and even then he was usually nodding off by the end of the third act.

She studied the little announcement for the performance. She stood up and reached for Plutarch on the bookshelf above the desk.

Where was the story of Cleopatra? Plutarch had not devoted a full biography to her. No, her story was contained in that of Mark Antony, of course.

She paged quickly to the passages she only dimly remembered. Cleopatra had been a great Queen, and what we call now a great politician. She had not only seduced Caesar and Antony, she kept Egypt free of Roman conquest for decades, finally taking her own life when Antony was dead by his own hand, and Octavius Caesar had stormed her gates. The loss of Egypt to Rome had been inevitable, but she had almost turned the tide. Had Julius Caesar not been assassinated, he might have made Cleopatra his Empress. Had Mark Antony been a little stronger, Octavian might have been overthrown.

Even in her final days, however, Cleopatra had been victorious in her own way. Octavian wanted to take her to Rome as a royal prisoner. She had cheated him. She had tried out dozens of poisons on condemned prisoners, and then chosen the bite of a snake to end her life. The Roman guards had not prevented her suicide. And so Octavian took possession of Egypt. But Cleopatra he could not have.

Julie closed the book almost reverently. She looked at the long row of alabaster jars. Could these really be those very poisons?

She fell into a strange reverie as she gazed at the magnificent coffin. A hundred like it she had seen here and in Cairo. A hundred like it she had examined ever since she could remember. Only this one contained a man who claimed to be immortal. Who claimed to be entering not death when he was buried, but "a dream-filled sleep."

What was the secret of that slumber? Of being awakened from it? And the elixir!

"Ramses the Damned," she whispered. "Would you wake for me as you did for Cleopatra? Would you wake for a new century of indescribable marvels even though your Queen is dead?"

No answer but silence; and the large soft eyes of the golden King staring at her, graven hands folded over his chest.

"That's robbery!" Henry said, barely able to contain his anger. "The thing's priceless." He glared at the little man behind the desk in the back office of the coin shop. Miserable little thief in his stuffy world of dirty glass cases and bits and pieces of money displayed as if they were jewels.

"If it's genuine, yes," the man answered slowly. "And if it's genuine, where did it come from? A coin like this with a perfect image of Cleopatra? That's what they will want to know, you see, where did it come from? And you have not told me your name."

"No, I haven't." Exasperated, he snatched the coin back from the dealer, slipped it into his pocket and turned to go. He stopped long enough to put on his gloves. What did he have left? Fifty pounds? He was in a fury. He let the door slam behind him as he walked into the biting wind.

The dealer sat quite still for a long moment. He could still feel the coin that he had let slip literally from his hand. Never in all these long years had he seen anything quite like it. He knew it was genuine, and suddenly he felt the fool as never before in his life.

He should have bought it! He should have taken the risk. But he knew it was stolen, and not even for the Queen of the Nile could he become a thief.

He rose from the desk, and passed through the dusty serge curtains that separated his shop from a tiny drawing room where he spent much of his time, even during business hours, quite alone. His newspaper lay beside the wing chair where he'd left it. He opened now to the headline:

STRATFORD MUMMY AND HIS CURSE
COME TO LONDON

The ink drawing beneath showed a slender young man disembarking from the P&O H.M.S. *Melpomine* along with the mummy of the famed Ramses the Damned. Henry Stratford, nephew of the dead archaeologist, said the caption. Yes, that was the man who had just left his shop. Had he stolen the coin from the tomb where his uncle died so suddenly? And how many more like it had he taken? The dealer was confused; relieved on the one hand, and full of regret on the other. He stared at the telephone.

Noon. The club dining room was quiet, the few scattered members eating their lunch alone on white-draped tables in silence. Just the way Randolph liked it, a true retreat from the noisy streets outside, and the endless pressure and confusion of his office.

He was not happy when he saw his son standing in the door some fifty feet away. Hasn't slept all night, more than likely. Yet Henry was shaven, neatly dressed, Randolph gave him that much. The little things were never out of Henry's control. It was the great disaster with which he couldn't cope—that he had no real life any longer. That he was a gambler and a drinker with no soul.

Randolph went back to his soup.

He didn't look up as his son took the chair opposite, and called to the waiter for a Scotch and water "at once."

"I told you to stay at your cousin's last night," Randolph said gloomily. There was no point to this conversation. "I left the key for you."

"I picked up the key, thank you. And my cousin is no doubt doing quite well without me. She has her mummy to keep her company."

The waiter set down the glass and Henry drained it at once.

Randolph took another slow spoon of the hot soup.

"Why the hell do you dine in a place like this? It's been out of fashion for a decade. It's positively funereal."

"Keep your voice down."

"Why should I? All the members are deaf."

Randolph sat back in the chair. He gave a small nod to the waiter, who moved in to take the soup plate. "It's my club and I like it," he said dully. Meaningless. All conversation with his son was meaningless. He would weep if he thought of it. He would weep if he lingered too long on the fact that Henry's hands trembled, that his face was pale and drawn, and that his eyes fixed on nothing—eyes of an addict, a drunk.

"Bring the bottle," Henry said to the waiter, without looking up. And to his father. "I'm down to twenty pounds."

"I can't advance you anything!" Randolph said wearily. "As long as she's in control, the situation is very simply desperate. You don't understand."

"You're lying to me. I know she signed papers yesterday. . . ."

"You've drawn a year's salary in advance."

"Father, I must have another hundred. . . ."

"If she examines the books herself, I may have to confess everything; and ask for another chance."

It filled him with surprising relief merely to say it. Perhaps it was what he wanted. He gazed at his son from a great remove suddenly. Yes, he should tell his niece everything, and ask for her . . . what? Her help.

Henry was sneering.

"Throwing ourselves on her mercy. Oh, that's lovely."

Randolph looked away, across the long vista of white-draped tables. Only one stooped grey-haired figure remained now, dining alone, in a far corner. The elderly Viscount Stephenson—one of the old landed gentry who still had the bank account to support his vast estates. Well, dine in peace, my friend, Randolph thought wearily.

"What else can we do!" he said softly now to his son. "You might come to work tomorrow. At least make an appearance. . . ."

Was his son listening, his son who had been miserable for as long as Randolph could remember, his son who had no future, no ambitions, no plans, no dreams?

It broke his heart suddenly, the thought of it—the long years since his son had been anything but desperate, and furtive, and bitter as well. It broke his heart to see his son's eyes darting anxiously over the simple objects of the table—the heavy silver, the napkin which he had not yet unfolded. The glass and the bottle of Scotch.

"All right, I'll give you some on account," he said. What would another hundred pounds matter? And this was his only son. His only son.

A sombre yet undeniably exciting occasion. When Elliott arrived, the Stratford house was crowded to overflowing. He had always loved this house, with its uncommonly large rooms, and its dramatic central stairway.

So much dark wood, so many towering bookshelves; and yet it had a cheerful atmosphere with the wicked abundance of electric light and the never-ending stretches of gilded wallpaper. But he missed Lawrence sharply as he stood in the front hall. He felt Lawrence here; and all the wasted moments of their friendship came back to torment him. And the long-ago love affair that haunted him still.

Well, he had known it would happen. But there was nowhere else on earth that he wanted to be tonight, except in Lawrence's house for the first official showing of Ramses the Damned, Lawrence's discovery. He made a light dismissive gesture to fend off those who immediately came towards him, and bowing his head he pushed his way gently through strangers and old friends until he reached the Egyptian room. The pain in his legs was bad tonight, because of the damp, as he always said. But luckily he wouldn't have to stand long. And he had a new walking stick that he rather liked, a fancy affair with a silver handle.

"Thank you, Oscar," he said with the usual smile as he took his first glass of white wine.

"Not a moment too soon, old boy," Randolph said to him wearily. "They're going to unveil the ghastly thing now. Might as well come along."

Elliott nodded. Randolph looked dreadful, no doubt about it. He'd had the wind knocked out of him by Lawrence's death. But he was doing his best here, it was obvious.

They moved together into the front ranks—and for the first time, Elliott laid eyes upon the startlingly beautiful coffin of the mummy.

The innocent, childlike expression of the golden mask charmed him. Then his eyes moved to the bands of writing that girded the lower portion of the figure. Latin and Greek words written as if they were Egyptian hieroglyphs!

But he was distracted as Hancock of the British Museum called for quiet, tapping a spoon loudly on a crystal glass. Beside Hancock stood Alex, with his arm around Julie, who looked exquisite in her black mourning, her hair drawn severely back from her pale face, revealing to all the world that her features had never needed fancy coifs or other adornments.

As their eyes met, Elliott gave Julie a little melancholy smile, and saw the immediate brightening in her that always greeted him. In a way, he thought, she is more fond of me than of my son. What an irony. But then his son was staring at these proceedings as if he were utterly lost. And perhaps he was, and that was the problem.

Samir Ibrahaim appeared suddenly at Hancock's left. Another old friend. But he did not see Elliott. A bit anxiously, he directed two young men to take hold of the lid of the mummy case and wait for his instructions. They stood with eyes downcast as if faintly embarrassed by the act they were about to perform. And the room went dead silent.

"Ladies and gentlemen," Samir said. The two young fellows at once hoisted the lid and moved it gracefully to one side. "I give you Ramses the Great."

The mummy lay exposed for all to see; the tall figure of a man with arms crossed on his breast, seemingly bald and naked under its thick discoloured wrappings.

A collective gasp rose from the crowd. In the golden light of the electric chandeliers and the few scattered candelabra, the form was faintly horrible as they always are. Death preserved and mounted.

There was an uneasy sprinkling of applause. Shudders, even uneasy laughter; and then the thick bank of spectators broke up, some drawing in for a closer look, then backing off as if from the heat of a fire, others turning their backs on the thing altogether.

Randolph sighed and shook his head.

"Died for this, did he? I wish I understood why."

"Don't be morbid," said the man next to him, someone Elliott ought to remember, but didn't. "Lawrence was happy—"

"Doing what he wanted to do," Elliott whispered. If he heard it said even one more time, he would weep.

Lawrence would have been happy examining his treasure.

Lawrence would have been happy translating those scrolls. Lawrence's death was a tragedy. Anyone who tried to make anything else out of it was a perfect fool.

Elliott gave Randolph's arm a gentle squeeze and left him, moving slowly towards the venerable corpse of Ramses.

It seemed the younger generation had decided en masse to block his progress as they surrounded Alex and Julie. Elliott could hear her voice in snatches as conversation regained its spirited volume all around.

". . . a remarkable story in the papyri," Julie explained. "But Father had only begun his translation. I should like to know what you think, Elliott."

"What was that, my dear?" He had just reached the mummy itself and he was staring at the face, marvelling at how easily one could discern an expression under so many layers of decomposing cloth. He took her hand now as she moved close to him. Others pressed in, trying to get a good look, but Elliott stood his ground rather selfishly.

"Your opinion, Elliott, of the whole mystery," Julie said. "Is this a nineteenth-dynasty coffin? How did it come to be fashioned in Roman times? You know, Father told me once, you knew more about Egyptology than all the men at the museum."

He laughed softly to himself. She glanced about nervously to make sure Hancock was nowhere near. Thank God, he was in the thick of his own little crowd, explaining something about those scrolls, no doubt, and the row of exquisite jars along the wall beneath the mirror.

"What do you think?" Julie prodded again. Had seriousness ever been so seductive?

"Can't possibly be Ramses the Great, my dear," he said. "But then you know that." He studied the painted lid of the coffin again, and once more the body nestled in its dusty swathing. "An excellent job, I must say that. Not many chemicals were used; no smell of bitumen whatsoever."

"There is no bitumen," Samir said suddenly. He had been standing on Elliott's left and Elliott had not even seen him.

"And what do you make of that?" Elliott asked.

"The King has given us his own explanation," Samir said. "Or so Lawrence told me. Ramses had himself wrapped with all due ceremony and prayers; but he was not embalmed. He was never taken from the cell where he wrote his story."

"What an amazing idea!" Elliott said. "And have you read

these inscriptions yourself?'' He pointed to the Latin as he translated: " 'Let not the sun shine on my remains; for in darkness
I sleep; beyond all suffering; beyond all knowledge. . . .' Now
that is hardly an Egyptian sentiment. I think you'll agree.''

Samir's face darkened as he looked at the tiny letters. "There
are curses and warnings everywhere. I was a curious man until
we opened this strange tomb.''

"And now you're frightened?'' Not a good thing for one man
to say to another. But it was true. And Julie was merely en-
thralled.

"Elliott, I want you to read Father's notes,'' she said, "before the museum gathers up everything and locks it in a vault.
The man doesn't merely claim to be Ramses. There's a good
deal more.''

"You're not referring to the nonsense in the papers,'' he asked
her. "About his being immortal, and loving Cleopatra.''

Strange the way she looked at him. "Father translated some
of it,'' she repeated. She glanced to the side. "I have the notebook. It's on his desk. Samir will agree with me, I think. You'll
find it interesting.''

But Samir was being dragged away by Hancock and some
other fellow with a brittle smile. And Lady Treadwell had accosted Julie before she could go on. Wasn't Julie afraid of the
curse? Elliott felt her hand slip away from his. Old Winslow
Baker wanted to talk to Elliott right now. No, go away. A tall
woman with withered cheeks and long white hands stood before
the coffin and demanded to know if the whole thing might be a
practical joke.

"Certainly not!'' said Baker. "Lawrence always dug up the
real thing, I'd stake my life on it.''

Elliott smiled. "Once the museum has these wrappings off,''
he said, "they'll be able to date the remains successfully. There
will be internal evidence of age, of course.''

"Lord Rutherford, I didn't recognize you,'' said the woman.

Good Lord, was he supposed to recognize her? Someone had
stepped in front of her; everyone wanted to see this thing. And
he ought to move, but he didn't want to.

"I can't bear to think of their cutting him open,'' Julie said
half in a whisper. "This is the first time I've seen him,'' she
said. "I didn't dare to open the case on my own.''

"Come along, darling, there's an old friend I want you to

meet," Alex said suddenly. "Father, there you are! Do get off your feet! Do you want me to help you to a chair?"

"I can manage, Alex, go on," Elliott replied. The fact was, he was used to the pain. It was like tiny knives in his joints; and tonight he could feel it even in his fingers. But he could forget about it, entirely, now and then.

And now he was alone with Ramses the Damned, with a lot of backs and shoulders turned to him. How splendid.

He narrowed his eyes as he drew very close to the mummy's face. Amazingly well formed; not desiccated at all. And certainly not the face of an old man, such as Ramses would have been at the end of a sixty-year reign.

The mouth was a young man's mouth, or at least that of a man in his prime. And the nose was slender, but not emaciated—what Englishmen call aristocratic. The ridges of the brows were prominent and the eyes themselves could not have been small. Probably a handsome man. In fact, there seemed little doubt of it.

Someone said crossly that the thing ought to be in the museum. Another that it was perfectly gruesome. And to think, these had been Lawrence's friends? Hancock was examining the gold coins on display in their velvet-lined case. Samir was beside him.

In fact, Hancock was making a fuss about something, wasn't he? Elliott knew that officious tone.

"There were five, only five? You're sure of it?" And he was speaking so loudly one would have thought Samir was deaf, not merely Egyptian.

"Quite sure. I told you," Samir said with a touch of irritation. "I cataloged the entire contents of the chamber myself."

Quite unmistakably, Hancock shifted his gaze to someone across the room. Elliott saw it was Henry Stratford, looking quite splendid in his dove-grey wool, with a black silk tie at his throat. Laughing and talking nervously, too, it seemed, with Alex and Julie and that crowd of young people whom Henry secretly loathed and resented.

Handsome as ever, Elliott thought. Handsome as when he was a boy of twenty, and that narrow elegant face could flash from a beguiling vulnerability to a chilling viciousness.

But why was Hancock staring at him? And what was he whispering now in Samir's ear? Samir looked at Hancock for a long moment, then gave a languid little shrug, his eyes moving slowly over Henry also.

How Samir must loathe all this, Elliott thought. How he must loathe that uncomfortable Western suit; he wants his *gellebiyya* of watered silk, and his slippers, and he should have them. What barbarians we must seem.

Elliott moved to the far corner and slipped into Lawrence's leather chair, easing it back against the wall. The crowd opened and closed at random, revealing Henry again moving away from the others, and glancing uncomfortably to right and left. Very subtle, not like a stage villain, but he's up to something, isn't he?

Henry slowly passed the marble table, his hand hovering as if he meant to touch the ancient scrolls. The crowd closed again, but Elliott merely waited. The little knot of persons in front of him shifted finally, and there was Henry, yards away, peering at a necklace on a little glass shelf, one of those many relics which Lawrence had brought home years ago.

Did anyone see Henry pick up the necklace and look at it lovingly as if he were an antiquarian? Did anyone see him slip it into his pocket and walk away, face blank, mouth rigid?

Bastard.

Elliott only smiled. He took a sip of the chilled white wine, and wished it were sherry. He wished he had not seen the little theft. He wished he had not seen Henry.

His own secret memories of Henry had never lost their painful edge, perhaps because he had never confessed what had happened to anyone. Not even to Edith, though he had told her many other sordid things about himself when wine and philosophy had made it seem imperative that he do so; and not to the Roman Catholic priests to whom he occasionally went to speak of heaven and hell in passionate ways no one else would tolerate.

He always told himself that if he did not relive those dark times, then he would forget them. But they were horridly vivid even now, some ten years after.

He had loved Henry Stratford once. And Henry Stratford was the only lover Elliott had ever had who tried to blackmail him.

Of course it had been an utter failure. Elliott had laughed in Henry's face. He'd called his bluff. "Shall I tell your father all about it? Or shall I tell your uncle Lawrence first? He's going to be furious with me . . . for perhaps five minutes. But you, his favourite nephew, he will despise till the day you die because I shall tell him all of it, you see, down to the sum of money you're demanding. What was it? Five hundred pounds? You've made yourself a wretch for that, imagine.''

How sullen and hurt Henry had been; how utterly confounded.

It should have been a triumph; but nothing took the sting from the overall humiliation. Henry at twenty-two—a viper with an angel's face, turning on Elliott in their Paris hotel as if he were a common boy out of the gutter.

And then there had been the little thefts. An hour after Henry had left, Elliott had discovered that his cigarette case, his money clip and all his cash were missing. His dressing gown was gone; his cuff links. Other items he could no longer remember.

He could never bring himself to mention the whole disaster. But he would have liked to needle Henry now, to slip up beside him and ask about the necklace that had just found its way into his pocket. Would Henry put it with the gold cigarette case, and the fine engraved money clip, and the diamond cuff links? Or lay it off on the same pawnbroker?

It was all too sad really. Henry had been a gifted young man; and it had all gone wrong, despite education and blood and countless opportunities. He'd started to gamble when he was no more than a boy; his drinking had become a disease by the time he was twenty-five; and now at thirty-two he had a perpetually sinister air that deepened his good looks and made him curiously repulsive in spite of them. And who suffered for it? Randolph, of course, who believed against all evidence that Henry's descent was his father's failure.

Let him go to hell, Elliott thought. Maybe he'd sought some glimmer with Henry of the flame he'd known with Lawrence, and it was all his own fault—seeing the uncle in the nephew. But no, it had started as an honest thing in its own right. And Henry Stratford had pursued him, after all. Yes, to hell with Henry.

It was the mummy Elliott had come to see. And the crowd had backed off a little again. He caught a fresh glass of wine from a passing tray, climbed to his feet, ignoring the outrageous stab of pain in his left hip, and made his way back to the solemn figure in the coffin.

He looked at the face again, the grim set of the mouth with its firm chin. A man in his prime all right. And there was hair cleaving to the well-shaped skull beneath the swollen bandages.

He lifted his glass in salute.

"Ramses," he whispered, drawing closer. And then speaking in Latin, he said, "Welcome to London. Do you know where London is?" He laughed softly at himself speaking Latin to this thing. Then he quoted a few sentences from Caesar's account of his conquest of Britain. "That's where you are, great King," he said. He made a feeble attempt to switch to Greek, but it was simply too hard for him. In Latin, he said: "I hope you like the damn place better than I do."

There was a faint rustling sound suddenly. Where had it come from? How odd to hear it so distinctly when the roar of conversation all around him was such a persistent nuisance. But it sounded as if it had come from the coffin itself, right in front of him.

He scanned the face again. Then the arms and hands, which appeared to be snagged in the rotted linen, as if they might fall loose at any moment. In fact, there was a distinct tear in the dark, dirty cloth, exposing a bit of the undergarment of the body right where the wrists were crossed. Not good. The thing was deteriorating right here before his eyes. Or there were tiny parasites at work. Must be stopped immediately.

He looked down at the mummy's feet. This was alarming. A tiny pile of dust accumulating even as he watched, falling, it seemed, from the twisted right hand, on which the wrappings had been badly broken.

"Good Lord, Julie must send this over to the museum immediately," he whispered. And then he heard that sound again. Rustling? No, it was fainter. Yes, the thing must be properly taken care of. God only knew what the London damp was doing to it. But surely Samir knew this. And so did Hancock.

In Latin, he spoke to the mummy again. "I don't like the damp either, great King. It gives me pain. And that's why I'm going home now, to leave you to your worshippers."

He turned away, leaning heavily on his cane, to ease the ache in his hip. He glanced back only once. And the thing looked so robust. It was as if the Egyptian heat had not dried it out whatsoever.

Daisy looked at the tiny necklace as Henry clasped it at the back of her neck. Her dressing room was packed with flowers, bottles of red wine, champagne cooling in ice, and other offerings, but none from a man as handsome as Henry Stratford.

"Looks funny to me," she said, cocking her head to one side. Thin gold chain and a little trinket with paint on it, or that's what it looked like. "Wherever did you get it?"

"It's worth more than that trash you took off," Henry said, smiling. His speech was thick. He was drunk again. And that meant he would be mean, or very, very sweet. "Now come on, ducky, we're going to Flint's. I feel uncommonly lucky, and there's a hundred pounds burning a hole in my pocket. Get a move on."

"And you mean to say that loony cousin of yours is all alone in that house now with that bloomin' mummy case wide open right there in the parlour?"

"Who the hell cares?" He snatched up the white fox wrap he'd bought for her and put it over her shoulders, and pulled her out of the dressing room and towards the stage door.

Flint's was packed when they got there. She hated the smoke, and the sour smell of drink; but it was always fun to be with him here when he had money and he was excited; and he kissed her now on the cheek as he led her towards the roulette wheel.

"You know the rules. You stand on my left, and only on my left. That's always been lucky."

She nodded. Look at all the fine gentlemen in this room; and the women just loaded with jewels. And she with this silly thing around her neck. It made her anxious.

Julie jumped; what was that sound? She found herself vaguely embarrassed as she stood alone in the shadowy library.

There was no one else here, but she could have sworn she heard another person. Not a step, no. Just all the tiny little sounds of another in the room very near to her.

She looked at the mummy slumbering in its case. In the semi-darkness, it looked as if it were coated with a thin layer of ashes. And what a sombre, brooding expression it had. She really hadn't noticed before. It looked for all the world as if it were struggling with a bad dream. She could almost see a crease in the forehead.

Was she glad now that they had not replaced the lid? She wasn't certain. But it was too late. She had sworn not to touch these things herself; and she must get to bed; she was more weary than she'd ever been. Her father's old friends had stayed forever. And then the newspaper people had barged in. What brazen effrontery! The guards had finally forced them out, but not before they had taken a whole series of pictures of the mummy.

And now the clock was striking one. And there was no one here. So why was she trembling? She went quickly to the front door, and was about to throw the bolt when she remembered Henry. He was supposed to be her chaperon and her protector. Strange that he hadn't spoken a civil word to her since he'd come home. And he certainly had not been in his room upstairs. But nevertheless. . . . She left the door unbolted.

It was bitter cold as he stepped out into the deserted street. He slipped on his gloves quickly.

Shouldn't have slapped her, he thought. But she shouldn't have butted in, damn her. He knew what he was doing. He had doubled his money ten times! If only on that last throw! And then as he argued to sign a note, she'd butted in! "But you mustn't!"

Infuriating, the way they'd looked at him. He knew what he owed. He knew what he was doing. And Sharples there, that scum. As if he were afraid of Sharples.

It was Sharples who stepped out of the alleyway now in front of him. For a moment he wasn't entirely certain. It was so dark, with the fog rolling just above the ground, but then in the seam of light from the window above, he saw the man's pockmarked face.

"Get out of my way," he said.

"Another streak of bad luck, sir?" Sharples fell into step beside him. "And the little lady costing you money. She was always expensive, sir, even when she worked for me. And I'm a generous man, you know."

"Let me alone, you bloody fool." He stepped up the pace. The street lamp was out up ahead. And there wouldn't be a cab at this hour.

"Not without a little interest on account, sir."

Henry stopped. The Cleopatra coin. Would the imbecile realize what it was worth? Suddenly he felt the man's fingers digging into his arm.

"You dare!" He pulled away. Then slowly he removed the coin from his inside coat pocket, held it out in the dim light and raised his eyebrow as he looked at the man, who gathered it out of his palm immediately.

"Ah, now that's a beauty, sir. A real ar . . . kay . . . o . . .

logical beauty!'' He turned the coin over, as if the inscriptions actually meant something to him. ''You pinched it, didn't you, sir? From your uncle's treasure, am I right?''

''Take it or leave it!''

Sharples made his hand a fist around the coin, like a man doing a magic trick for a child.

''Butter wouldn't melt in your mouth, would it, sir?'' He slipped the coin into his pocket. ''Was he still lying there, gasping, sir, when you pinched it? Or did you wait till he'd breathed his last?''

''Go to hell.''

''This won't cover it, sir. No, sir, not by a long shot, sir. Not what you owe me and the gentlemen at Flint's, sir.''

Henry turned on his heel; he made a small adjustment of his top hat against the driving wind; he began to walk fast towards the corner. He could hear the scrape of Sharples's heels on the pavement behind him. And no one ahead in the misty dark; no one behind, that little seam of light from the door of Flint's no longer visible.

He could hear Sharples drawing close to him. Into the pocket of his coat he reached. His knife. Slowly he drew it out, opened the blade, and gripped the handle tight.

Suddenly he felt the pressure of Sharples against his back.

''Seems to me you need a little lesson in paying your debts, sir,'' the bastard said to him.

Sharples's hand came down on his shoulder; but Henry turned swiftly, forcing his knee against Sharples and knocking him off balance a step. For the brilliant silk of his vest Henry aimed, where the knife might go in between the ribs, with no impediment. And to his astonishment he felt it sink into the man's chest, and saw the white of Sharples's teeth as he opened his mouth in a dry scream.

''Bloody fool! I told you to leave me alone!'' He drew out the knife and stabbed the man again. He heard the silk rip this time, and he stepped back, trembling violently all over.

The man took a few faltering steps. Then he fell down on his knees. Gently he pitched forward, shoulders hunched, and then softly heaved to one side, his body going limp and loose on the pavement.

Henry couldn't see his face in the dark. He saw only the lifeless form sprawled there. The bitter cold of the night paralyzed him. His heart thudded in his ears as it had in the chamber in Egypt when he had gazed down at Lawrence lying dead on the floor.

Well, damn him! He shouldn't have tried that with me! The rage choked him. He could not move his right hand, so cold it was, in spite of the glove, the knife clutched in it. Carefully, he lifted his left hand, and closed the knife and put it away.

He glanced from right to left. Darkness, silence. Only the faraway rumble of a motor car on a distant street. Water dripping somewhere, as if from a broken gutter. And the sky above lightening ever so faintly—the color of slate.

He knelt down in the thinning darkness. He reached out for that gleaming silk again, and careful not to touch the great dark wet spot spreading there, he reached under the lapel of the coat. The man's wallet. Fat, full of money!

He did not even examine the contents. Instead he slipped it in the same pocket with the knife. And then he turned on his heel, lifted his chin and walked off with crisp loud steps. He even began to whistle.

Later, when he was comfortably settled in the back of a cab, he drew the wallet out. Three hundred pounds. Well, that was not bad. But as he stared down at the wad of dirty bills, a panic seized him. It seemed he couldn't speak or move, and when he looked out the little window of the hansom, he saw only the soiled grey sky over the roofs of the dreary tenements, and there seemed nothing he wanted, or could want, or could ever have that would alleviate the hopelessness he felt.

Three hundred pounds. But he had not killed the man for that. Why, who could say he had killed anyone! His uncle Lawrence had died of a stroke in Cairo. And as for Sharples, a despicable moneylender he had made the acquaintance of in Flint's one evening, well, one of Sharples's confederates had killed him. Sneaked up on him in a dark street and sunk a knife in his ribs.

Of course that's what had happened. Who would connect him to these sordid affairs?

He was Henry Stratford, vice chairman of Stratford Shipping, a member of a distinguished family soon to be connected by marriage to the Earl of Rutherford. No one would dare. . . .

And he would call now on his cousin. Explain that he was a little down on his luck. And she would surely come up with a comfortable sum, three times perhaps what he held in his hand, because she would understand it was only temporary, these losses. And it would be a great relief to make them right.

His cousin, his only sister. Once they had loved each other, Julie and he. Loved each other as only a sister and a brother can. He would remind her. She wouldn't give him any trouble, and then he could rest for a little while.

That was the worst part of it of late. He couldn't rest.

3

JULIE PADDED softly down the stairs in her slippers, the full folds of her lace peignoir gathered in one hand so that she did not trip, her brown hair in loose waves over her shoulders and down her back.

She saw the sun before she saw anything else, as she entered the library—the great blessed flood of yellow light filling the glass conservatory beyond the open doors, a dazzle amid the ferns, and in the dancing water of the fountain and in the great mesh of green leaves curling beneath the glass ceiling.

Long slanting rays fell on the mask of Ramses the Damned in its shadowy corner, on the dark colours of the Oriental carpet, and on the mummy himself as he stood upright in his open case, the tightly wrapped face and limbs becoming golden in the haze, golden as desert sand at midday.

The room lightened before Julie's eyes. The sun exploded suddenly on the gold Cleopatra coins on their bed of velvet. It shimmered on the smooth marble bust of Cleopatra with its demure, half-lidded gaze. It caught the translucent alabaster of the long row of jars. It gleamed on tiny bits and pieces of old gold throughout the room, and on the gilded titles of the many leather-bound books. It struck the deep-graven name "Lawrence Stratford" written on his velvet-covered diary that lay on the desk.

Julie stood still, feeling the warmth surround her. The dark musty smell was fading. And the mummy, it seemed to move in the brightening light, as if responding to the heat. To sigh almost like a flower opening. What a tantalizing illusion. Of course it had not moved at all; yet it did seem fuller, somehow, its powerful shoulders and arms more rounded, its fingers poised as if alive.

"Ramses . . ." she whispered.

There came that sound again, the sound that had startled her the night before. But no, it wasn't a sound, not really. Just the breath of this great house. Of timbers and plaster in the warmth of the morning. She closed her eyes for a moment. And then Rita's step sounded in the hall. Of course, it had been Rita all along . . . the sound of another very near—heartbeat, breath, the subtle shift of garments in motion.

"Well, miss, I tell you I don't like that thing in the house," Rita said. Was that her feather duster softly brushing the living room furniture?

Julie didn't turn around to look. She looked at the mummy. She approached it now and looked up into its face. Good Lord, she had not really seen it last night. Not as she was seeing it now in this great warm glare. It had been a living breathing man, this thing, locked forever in its cerements.

"I do declare, miss, it gives me the shivers."

"Don't be absurd, Rita. Bring me some coffee, like a good girl." She drew even closer to the thing. After all, there was no one here to stop her. She could touch it if she wished. She listened for Rita's retreat. Heard the kitchen door open and close. Then she did reach out and touch the linen bandages that covered the right arm. Too soft, too fragile. And hot from the sun!

"No, this is not good for you, is it?" she asked, glancing up at the thing's eyes as if it were rude to do otherwise. "But I don't want them to take you away. I'll miss you when you're no longer here. But I won't let them cut you open. That much, I promise you."

Was that dark brown hair she saw beneath the bandages that surrounded the skull? It seemed there was a great thickness of it there, bound painfully tight to the bones, giving a horrid effect of baldness. But it was the overall spectacle that really caught her and carried her away now from the details. The thing had a distinct personality, rather like a fine sculpture would have. Tall, broad-shouldered Ramses with his head bowed, and his hands in that attitude of resignation.

The words in the diary came back to her with painful clarity.

"You *are* immortal, my love," she said. "My father's seen to it. You may curse us for opening your tomb, but thousands will come to see you; thousands will eventually speak your name. You will live forever. . . ."

So strange that she was on the verge of tears. Father dead. And this which had meant so much to him. Father in an unmarked grave in Cairo as he had wanted it to be; and Ramses the Damned the toast of London.

Suddenly she was startled by Henry's voice.

"You're talking to that damned thing, just the way your father did."

"Good Lord, I didn't know you were here! Where did you come from?"

He stood in the archway between the two drawing rooms, his long serge cape hanging loosely from one shoulder. Unshaven, very likely drunk. And that smile of his. It was chilling.

"I'm supposed to be looking out for you," he said, "remember?"

"Yes, of course. I'm sure you are absolutely delighted."

"Where's the key to the drinks cupboard? It's locked, you know. Why the devil does Oscar do that?"

"Oscar's gone till tomorrow. Perhaps you should have coffee, besides. That would do you the most good."

"Would it now, my dear?" He removed the cape as he walked arrogantly towards her, his eyes sweeping the Egyptian room as if he did not entirely approve of it. "You never let me down, do you?" he asked, and flashed that bitter smile again. "My childhood playmate, my cousin, my little sister! I loathe coffee. I want some port or sherry."

"Well, I have none," she said. "Go on upstairs and sleep it off, why don't you?"

Rita had come to the door, was waiting as if for instructions.

"Coffee for Mr. Stratford, too, please, Rita," Julie said, because he hadn't moved. It was perfectly clear he wasn't going anywhere. He was staring at the mummy, in fact, as if it had startled him. "Did Father really speak to him like that?" she asked. "The way I was doing?"

He didn't immediately answer. He turned away, and moved to inspect the alabaster jars, even his posture slouching and arrogant.

"Yes, talked to it as if it could talk back. And Latin of all things. If you ask me, your father had been sick for some time.

Too many years in the desert heat squandering money on corpses and statues and trinkets and trash.''

How his words stung her. So careless, yet so hateful. He paused before one of the jars, with his back to her. In the mirror she saw him scowling down at it.

"It was *his* money, wasn't it?" she asked. "He made enough for all of us, or so he thought."

He turned around sharply.

"What's that supposed to mean?"

"Well, you haven't managed yours very well, have you?"

"I've done the best I can. Who are you to judge me?" he asked. Suddenly, with the sunlight harshly illuminating his face, he looked frighteningly vicious.

"And what about the shareholders of Stratford Shipping? Have you done your best for them? Or is that quite beyond my judgment also?''

"Be careful, my girl," he said. He drew close to her. He gave one arrogant glance to the mummy on his left almost as if it were another presence, another full person, and then he turned his shoulder to it a little, and narrowed his eyes as he looked at her. "Father and I are the only family you have left now. You need us more than you think, perhaps. After all, what do you really know about trade or shipping?''

How curious. He had made a good point and then ruined it. She needed them both, but it had nothing to do with trade and shipping. She needed them because they were her blood, and to hell with trade and shipping.

She didn't want him to see the hurt in her. She turned away and looked down the length of the double drawing rooms, towards the pale northern windows on the front of the house, where the morning seemed scarcely to be happening.

"I know how to add two and two, my dear cousin," she said. "And that has put me in a very awkward and painful position."

With relief, she watched Rita enter from the hall, her back bent uncomfortably as she carried the heavy silver coffee service. On the center table of the rear drawing room she set it down, only a few feet from where Julie stood.

"Thank you, dear. That's all for now."

With a pointed glance at the thing in the coffin, Rita was gone. And once again Julie was alone with this exquisitely painful moment. Slowly she turned and saw that her cousin was standing directly in front of Ramses.

"Then I should come right to the point," he said, and he turned around to face her. He reached up and loosened his silk tie, and then pulled it off and stuffed it in his pocket. His gait was almost shambling as he approached her.

"I know what you want," she said. "I know what you and Uncle Randolph both want. And more important, I know what you both need. What Father left you won't begin to cover your debts. Lord, but you've made a mess of things."

"So sanctimonious," Henry said. He stood only a foot from her now, his back to the brightening sun and the mummy. "The suffragette, the little archaeologist. And now you'll try your hand at business, will you?"

"I'll try," she said coldly. His anger was igniting hers. "What else can I do?" she asked. "Let it all slip through your father's hands! Lord, but I pity you!"

"What are you trying to tell me?" he asked. His breath stank of liquor, and his face was shadowed with coarse unshaven hair. "That you'll ask for our resignations? Is that it?"

"I don't know yet." She turned her back on him. She walked into the front drawing room and opened the small *secrétaire*. She sat down before it, and removed her book of bank drafts. And uncapped the inkwell.

She could hear him pacing behind her as she wrote the cheque.

"Tell me, cousin, does it feel good to have more than you can ever spend, more than you can ever count? And to have done nothing to get it?"

She turned, her eyes down, and she gave him the cheque. She rose and went to the front window. She lifted the lace curtain and looked out at the street. Please go away, Henry, she thought dully, disconsolately. She didn't want to hurt her uncle. She didn't want to hurt anyone. But what could she do? She'd known for years about Randolph's embezzling. She and her father had discussed it last time she was in Cairo. Of course he had meant to take the situation in hand, always meant. And now it fell to her.

She turned suddenly. The silence made her uneasy. She saw her cousin standing in the Egyptian room. He was staring at her, his eyes cold and seemingly lifeless.

"And when you marry Alex, will you disinherit us as well?"

"For the love of heaven, Henry. Go away and leave me alone."

There was something stunning about his expression, about

the sheer hardness of his face. He wasn't young anymore, was he? He looked ancient in his habits and in his guilt and in his self-deception. Have pity, she thought. What can you do to help him? Give him a fortune and it will be gone within a fortnight. She turned round again and looked out into the wintry London street.

Early passersby. The nurse from across the way with the twins in their wicker carriage. An old man hurrying along with a newspaper under his arm. And the guard, the guard from the British Museum, slouching idly on the front steps just beneath her. And down the street, in front of her uncle Randolph's, Sally the parlour maid shaking a rug out the front door because she was sure that no one was awake to see.

Why was there no sound behind her in the double rooms? Why didn't Henry storm out, slamming the front door? Perhaps he had left, but no, she heard a tiny furtive noise suddenly, a spoon touching china. The damned coffee.

"I don't know how it could have come to this," she said, still gazing at the street before her. "Trust funds, salaries, bonuses, you had everything, both of you."

"No, not everything, my dear," he said. "You have everything."

Sound of coffee being poured. For the love of heaven!

"Look, old girl," he said, his voice low and strained. "I don't want this quarrel any more than you do. Come. Sit down. Let's have a cup of coffee together like civilized people."

She couldn't move. The gesture seemed more sinister than his anger.

"Come and have a cup of coffee with me, Julie."

Was there any way out of it? She turned, her eyes downcast, and moved towards the table, only looking up when it seemed unavoidable, to see Henry facing her, the steaming cup in his outstretched hand.

There was something unaccountably odd about this, about the way he was offering it to her, about the peculiarly blank expression on his face.

But this had no more than a second to register. For what she saw behind him caused her to freeze in her tracks. Reason ruled against it, but the evidence of her senses was undeniable.

The mummy was moving. The mummy's right arm was outstretched, the torn wrappings hanging from it, as the being stepped out of its gilded box! The scream froze in her throat.

The thing was coming towards her—towards Henry, who stood with his back to it—moving with a weak, shuffling gait, that arm outstretched before it, the dust rising from the rotting linen that covered it, a great smell of dust and decay filling the room.

"What the devil's the matter with you!" Henry demanded. But the thing was now directly behind him. The outstretched hand closed on Henry's throat.

Her scream would not break loose. Petrified, she heard only a dry shriek inside her, like the impotent cries of her worst dreams.

Henry turned, hands rising reflexively to protect himself, the coffee cup falling with a clatter to the silver tray. A low roar escaped his lips as he fought the thing strangling him. His fingers clasped at the filthy wrappings; the dust rose in gusts as the creature tore its left arm loose from the bindings, and sought to pinion its victim with both hands.

With an ignominious scream, Henry threw the creature off him, and pitched forward on all fours. In an instant he was on his feet and scrambling across the carpet. He ran through the front room and over the marble tile of the front hall to the door.

Speechless, terrified, Julie stared at the ghastly figure who knelt beside the center table. The thing was panting, struggling for breath. She scarcely heard the front door open or slam shut.

Never in her whole life had there been a moment so devoid of reason. Shivering violently, she backed away in horror from this ragged being, this dead thing that had come to life, and seemed now unable to rise to its feet

Was it looking at her? Were those eyes glinting through the ragged bandages? Blue eyes? It reached out for her. Her body was caught in a cold involuntary shudder. A wave of dizziness passed over her. *Don't faint. Whatever happens, don't faint.*

Suddenly it turned away. Quite deliberately it looked towards its coffin, or was it the conservatory with the light pouring through its roof? It lay as if exhausted on the Oriental carpet, and then it reached out as if towards the great flood of morning sun.

She could hear its breathing again. Alive! Dear God, alive! It struggled to move forward, lifting its powerful torso only a little off the carpet and propelling itself with a sluggish movement of its knees.

Out of the shadowy drawing room it crawled inch by inch away from her until suddenly it reached the farthest rays of the sun penetrating the library. There it stopped, and seemed to breathe deeply as if actually breathing not air but light. It lifted itself a little higher on its elbows, and began to crawl towards the conservatory again with greater speed. The linen bandages trailed from its legs. A path of dust was left on the rug. The bandages on its arms were falling to pieces. Fragments of linen broke loose and appeared to disintegrate in the light.

Without a conscious decision, she moved behind it, keeping a safe distance, yet quite unable to stop herself from following it, from staring as if spellbound at its grim progress through the conservatory doors.

Into the hottest glare of the sun it moved, and suddenly it stopped beside the fountain and rolled over on its back. One hand reached up towards the glass ceiling; the other fell limp on its chest.

Silently, Julie moved into the conservatory. Still trembling uncontrollably, she went closer and closer until she was staring directly down at this thing.

The body was filling out in the sunlight! It was growing ever more robust as she watched! She could hear the sound of the wrappings releasing it. She could see the chest rising and falling with regular breath.

And the face, my God, the face. There were eyes there, great shining blue eyes under the thin wrappings. It reached up suddenly and tore loose the bandages. Yes, large and beautiful blue eyes. With another rip, it tore the bandages from its skull and released a soft mop of brown hair.

Then it rose on its knees with quiet grace and reached down into the fountain with its bandaged hands, scooping up the sparkling water to its lips. It drank and drank the water, with deep sighing gulps. Then it stopped and turned towards her, wiping away more of the thick ashen layer of linen from its face.

A man looking at her! A blue-eyed man with intelligence looking at her!

That scream rose again, but was not released. Only a soft sigh came out of her. Or was it a gasp? She realized she had taken a step backwards. The thing climbed to its feet.

It rose now to its full height and gazed calmly at her, its fingers working almost absently to clear the rest of the rotted bandages from its head as if they were cobwebs. Yes, a full head of dark wavy brown hair. It fell to just below the ears, and came now softly over the forehead. And the eyes evinced fascination as it looked at her. Good Lord, imagine! Fascination as *it* looked at *her*!

She was going to faint. She had read about it. She knew what it was, though it had never happened to her. But her legs were literally going out from under her and things were going dim. No. Stop! She couldn't faint with this thing staring at her.

This was the mummy come to life!

She backed into the Egyptian room, legs trembling; her body moist all over, her hands clawing at her lace peignoir.

It watched her as if genuinely curious as to what she meant to do. Then it wiped more of the bandages away from its neck and its shoulders and its chest. Its broad naked chest. She closed her eyes, and then opened them slowly. Still there, with those powerful arms, and the dust falling from its lustrous brown hair.

It took a step towards her. She backed away. It took another step. She backed up farther. In fact, she was backing up all the way across the library, and very suddenly she felt the centre table of the second drawing room behind her. She felt her hands touch the edge of the silver coffee tray.

With silent, even steps it came towards her—this thing, this beautiful man with the splendid body and the large gentle blue eyes.

Good Lord, are you losing your reason! Never mind that it's handsome! It just tried to strangle Henry! Quickly she darted around the table, groping behind her with outstretched hands as she moved towards the front drawing room doors.

It stopped as it reached the table. It looked down at the silver coffeepot and the overturned cup. It picked up something off the tray. What was it? A wadded handkerchief. Had Henry left it there? Quite unmistakably it pointed to the spilt coffee, and then in a soft, resonant and distinctly masculine voice it spoke:

"Come and have a cup of coffee with me, Julie!" it said.

Perfect British accent! Familiar words! Julie felt a shock course through her. This was no invitation from the thing. Why, it was imitating Henry. Same precise intonation. That's what Henry had said!

It held out the handkerchief, which it had opened. White powder, sparkling as if full of tiny crystals. It pointed to the distant row of alabaster jars. The top was missing from one of the jars! And again it spoke with the same flawless, crisp English accent:

"Drink your coffee, Uncle Lawrence."

A groan escaped her lips. The meaning was unmistakable. She stood there staring, the words echoing in her head. Henry had poisoned her father and this creature had witnessed it. Henry had tried to poison her. With all her spirit she tried to deny it. She tried to find some reason that it could not be so. But she knew it was so. Just as surely as she knew this thing was alive and breathing and occupying space before her, and that it was the immortal Ramses come to life out of those decayed wrappings, standing before her in the drawing room with the sun at its back.

Her legs were going out from under her. No way to prevent it, and the darkness was rising. And as she felt herself slip downwards, she saw the tall figure dart forward, and she felt the strong arms catch her and lift her and hold her quite firmly, so that she felt almost safe.

She opened her eyes, and looked up into its face. No, *his* face. His beautiful face. She heard Rita scream from the hallway. And the darkness rose again.

"What the hell are you saying!" Randolph was not really fully awake. He struggled out of the tangle of covers, reaching for his crumpled silk robe at the foot of the bed. "You're telling me you left your cousin there alone in that house with this thing!"

"I'm telling you it tried to kill me!" Henry roared like a madman. "That's what I'm telling you! The damned thing got out of the coffin and tried to strangle me with its right hand!"

"Damn it, where are my slippers! She's alone in that house, you fool!"

Barefoot he ran into the hall and down the stairway, his robe ballooning behind him.

"Hurry, you imbecile!" he shouted to his son, who hesitated at the top of the steps.

She opened her eyes. She was sitting on the sofa, and Rita was clinging to her. Rita was hurting her. Rita was making little whimpering sounds.

And there was the mummy, standing right there. Nothing about it imagined. Not the dark lock of hair fallen down on his smooth broad forehead. Or his deep shadowy blue eyes. He had torn loose more of the rotted stuff that covered him. He was bare to the waist, a god, it seemed at the moment. Especially with that smile. That warm and embracing smile.

His hair seemed to be moving as she looked at it, as if it were growing before her eyes. It was fuller and more lustrous than it had been before she fainted. But what in God's name was she doing, staring at this creature's hair!

He drew a little closer. His bare feet were free of the cumbersome wrappings.

"Julie," he said softly.

"Ramses," she whispered back.

The creature nodded, the smile lengthening. "Ramses!" he said emphatically, and he made her a very subtle bow with his head.

Dear God, she thought, this is not merely a man gifted with beauty; this is the most beautiful man I've ever seen.

In a daze, she forced herself to climb to her feet. Rita clung to her, but she struggled free of Rita, and then the mummy—the man—reached out and took her hand and helped her to stand.

The fingers were warm, dusty. She found herself staring right into his face. Skin like the skin of any other human being, only smoother, perhaps softer, and full of more high colour—like that of a man who had been running, the cheeks faintly flushed.

He turned his head sharply. She heard it too. Voices outside; argument. A motor car had pulled up in front of the house.

Rita made an awkward dash to the window as if the mummy were going to stop her.

"It's Scotland Yard, miss, thank God for that."

"No, but this is a disaster! Bolt the door at once."

"But miss!"

"Bolt it. Now."

Rita ran to obey. Julie took Ramses' hand.

"Come with me, upstairs, immediately," she said to him. "Rita, put the lid on that coffin. It weighs almost nothing. Close it up fast and come."

No sooner had Rita slid the bolt than they were knocking and pulling the bell. The shrill clanging from the back of the house startled Ramses. His eyes moved quickly over the ceiling and to the back of the house as though he had heard the sound traveling the wire to the kitchen wall.

Julie tugged him gently but urgently, and to her amazement he followed easily as they made their way up the stairs.

She could hear little cries of distress coming from Rita. But Rita was doing as she had been told. Julie heard the thump as the lid of the coffin slid into place.

And Ramses, he was staring at the wallpaper, at the framed portraits, at the knickknack shelf nestled in the corner at the top of the stairs. He was looking at the stained-glass window. He looked down at the wool carpet with its pattern of feathers and twisted leaves.

The pounding was becoming quite impossible. Julie could hear her uncle Randolph calling her name.

"What shall I do, miss?" Rita called out.

"Come up at once." She looked at Ramses, who was watching her with a strange mixture of patience and amusement. "You look normal," she whispered. "Perfectly normal. Beautiful, but normal." She pulled him on down the hallway. "The bath, Rita!" she shouted as Rita appeared, quivering and tentative, behind him. "Quick. Run the bath."

She brought him on towards the front of the house as Rita hurried past. They had stopped their pounding for a minute. She could hear the grind of a key in the lock. But the bolt, thank God for that! The pounding started again.

Ramses was truly smiling at her now, as if he were about to laugh. He peered into the bedrooms as he passed them. Suddenly he saw the electric chandelier hanging on its dusty chain from the ceiling rose above. The tiny light bulbs looked dull and opaque in the daylight, but they were burning, and he narrowed his eyes to study this, gently resisting her for the first time.

"Later you can see it!" she said in panic. The water was roaring into the tub. The steam was pouring out of the door.

He gave her another decorous little nod with a slight lift of his eyebrows, and followed her into the bath. The shining tile seemed to please him. He turned slowly to the window and stared at the sunlight sparkling in the frosted glass. Gently he examined the latch and then he opened the window, pushing out on the two sides until he could see the rooftops spread out before him and the brilliant morning sky above.

"Rita, Father's clothes," Julie said breathlessly. They were going to break down that door any minute. "Hurry, get his robe, slippers, a shirt, whatever you can lay hands on at once."

Ramses lifted his chin and closed his eyes. He was drinking in the sunlight. Julie could see his hair moving ever so slightly; tiny tendrils at his forehead curling. The hair seemed to grow thicker. It *was* growing thicker.

Of course. This is what woke him from the dream-filled sleep, she realized. The sun! And he had been too weak to do more than struggle with Henry. He had had to crawl into the sunlight before he could gain his full strength.

There were shouts of "Police" from below. Rita came running with a pair of slippers in her hand, and a pile of clothing over her arm.

"There's reporters out there, miss; a whole crowd of them, and Scotland Yard and your uncle Randolph . . ."

"Yes, I know. Go down now and tell them we'll be right there, but don't draw back the bolt!"

Julie took the silk bathrobe and white shirt and put them on the hook. She touched Ramses' shoulder.

He turned and looked at her and the immediate warmth of his smile astonished her.

"Britannia," he said softly, his eyes moving from right to left as though to encompass the spot on which they stood.

"Yes, Britannia!" she said. A sudden lovely giddiness took hold of her. She pointed to the bath. *"Lavare!"* she said. Didn't that mean wash?

He nodded, his eyes taking in everything around him—the brass taps, the steam billowing up from the deep tub. He looked at the clothing.

"For you!" she said, pointing at the robe and then at Ramses. Oh, if only she could remember the Latin. "Vestments," she said desperately.

And then he did laugh. Softly, gently, indulgently. And she found herself petrified again, staring at him, at the smooth shimmering beauty of his face. Lovely even white teeth he had, flawless skin and such an oddly commanding manner as he gazed at her. But then he was Ramses the Great, wasn't he? She was going to faint again if she didn't stop this.

She backed out the door.

"Reste!" she said. *"Lavare."* She made pleading gestures with both her hands. Then she went to leave, and quite suddenly his powerful right hand closed on her wrist.

Her heart stopped altogether.

"Henry!" he said softly. His face took on an air of menace, but not towards her.

Slowly she caught her breath. She could hear Rita screaming at the men to stop their banging. Someone was shouting back from the street.

"No, don't worry about Henry. Not now. I'll take care of

Henry, you can be sure.'' Oh, but he wouldn't understand this. Again she gestured for his patience, his forbearance, and then she gently removed his hand from her wrist. He nodded, let her go. She backed away again, and then shut the door and ran down the hallway and down the stairs.

"Let me in, Rita!" Randolph was shouting.

Julie almost stumbled on the bottom step. She rushed into the drawing room. The lid was in place on the coffin! Would they see that faint trail of dust on the floor? But no one would believe it! She wouldn't have believed it!

She stopped, closed her eyes, breathed deeply, and then told Rita to go ahead and open the door.

She turned, a rather prim expression fixed on her face, and watched as her uncle Randolph, dishevelled and barefoot, wearing only his dressing gown, came into the room. The museum guard was right behind him, and two gentlemen who appeared to be police in plain clothes, though she did not know precisely why.

"What in the world is the matter?" she asked. "You woke me from a sound sleep on the sofa. What time is it?" She looked about in confusion. "Rita, what is going on?"

"I'm sure I don't know, miss!" Rita almost screamed. Julie gestured for her to be quiet.

"Oh, my dear, I was terrified," Randolph answered. "Henry said . . ."

"Yes? Henry said what?"

The two gentlemen in greatcoats were looking at the spilled coffee. One of them was staring at the open handkerchief with its white powder spilled out on the floor. How very like sugar it looked in the sunlight. And there was Henry, suddenly, hovering at the hallway door.

She stared at him for a sullen moment. *Killed my father!* But she could not allow herself to feel it just now. She could not allow herself to believe it or she would go mad. She saw him again in her mind's eye, holding out that coffee cup for her; she saw his wooden expression, his pale face.

"Whatever is the matter with you, Henry?" she asked coldly, suppressing the quaver in her voice. "You ran out of here half an hour ago as if you'd seen a ghost."

"You know damned well what happened," he whispered. He was blanched and sweating. He had taken out his handkerchief and he wiped his upper lip, his hand trembling so badly that she could see it.

"Get a grip on yourself," Randolph said, turning to his son. "Now what the devil did you see?"

"The question is, miss," said the shorter of the two Scotland Yard men, "has there been some sort of intruder in this house?"

A gentleman's voice and manner. The fear was leaving her. She could feel her conviction returning as she spoke. "Indeed not, sir. My cousin saw an intruder? Henry, you must have a guilty conscience. You're having hallucinations. I saw no one here."

Randolph eyed Henry furiously. The Scotland Yard men appeared confused.

Henry himself was in a silent rage. He glared at her as if he meant to strangle her with his bare hands. And she glared right back at him, thinking coldly, You killed my father. You would have killed me.

We do not know how we shall feel at such moments. We cannot know, she thought. I only know that I hate you, and I have never hated another human being in my life.

"That mummy case!" Henry blurted out suddenly. He clung to the door as if he didn't dare to come into the room. "I want that mummy case opened now."

"You are really past all patience. No one shall touch that mummy case. It contains a priceless relic, which belongs to the British Museum and must not be exposed to the air."

"What the hell do you mean saying these things!" he shouted. He was becoming hysterical.

"Be quiet," Randolph said to him. "I've heard quite enough!"

There was noise from outside, voices. Someone had come all the way up the steps and was peering through the front door.

"Henry, I won't have this confusion in my house," Julie said shortly.

The Scotland Yard man studied Henry coldly.

"Sir, if the lady does not want the premises searched . . ."

"Indeed, I do not," Julie responded. "I think quite enough of your time has been wasted. As you can see, nothing here has been disturbed."

Of course the coffee cup was lying on its side on the plate and the handkerchief was on the floor, but she stood her ground coldly, eyes moving from Henry to the officer. And then to the other officer, who was scrutinizing her just a little too carefully, though he did not offer a word.

None of them saw what she saw—the figure of Ramses coming slowly down the stairs. They did not see him come across the front hallway and silently enter the room. That is, until Julie could not tear her eyes off him, and the others realized it and turned to see the source of her fascination—the tall brown-haired man in the dark burgundy silk bathrobe standing in the door.

She was breathless looking at him. Majestic. It was what all Kings should be. Yet he looked otherworldly as though his court had been a place of superhumans. Men of uncommon strength and grand bearing, with vivid and piercing eyes.

Even the robe with its satin lapels looked exotic on him. The slippers were like those from an ancient tomb. The white shirt he wore was unbuttoned, yet that looked curiously "normal," perhaps because his skin had that robust glow to it, and because he thrust his chest slightly forward and stood with feet firmly planted on the floor at parade rest as no modern man would do. This was the posture for commanding subservience, but there was nothing arrogant in his expression. He merely looked at her and at Henry, who had flushed red to the roots of his dark hair.

Henry stared at the open shirt. He stared at the scarab ring that Ramses wore on his right hand. Both the inspectors were staring at him. And Randolph seemed absolutely baffled. Did he recognize the robe he'd given his brother? Rita had backed up against the wall and covered her mouth with her hands.

"Uncle Randolph," Julie said as she stepped forward. "This is a good friend of Father's, just arrived here from Egypt. An Egyptologist whom Father knew quite well. Ah . . . Mr. Ramsey, Reginald Ramsey. I want you to meet my uncle, Randolph Stratford, and this is his son, Henry . . ."

Ramses studied Randolph, then locked his eyes on Henry again. Henry was staring stupidly back at Ramses. Julie made a little gesture to Ramses for patience.

"I think this is not the time for a social gathering," she said awkwardly. "Really, I am quite tired, and caught off guard by all this. . . ."

"Well, Miss Stratford, perhaps it was this gentleman your cousin saw," said the genial policeman.

"Oh, it very well might have been," she answered. "But I must take care of my guest now. He's had no breakfast. I must . . ."

Henry knew! She could see it. She struggled to say something civil and appropriately meaningless. That it was past eight o'clock. That she was hungry. Henry was shrinking into the corner. And Ramses was staring at Henry as Ramses moved behind the two Scotland Yard men, towards that handkerchief, and now with a very graceful and quick gesture, he gathered it up from the floor. No one saw this but Julie and Henry. Glaring at Henry, Ramses shoved the handkerchief into the pocket of his robe.

Randolph was staring at her in utter perplexity; one of the Scotland Yard men was plainly bored.

"You're all right, my dear!" said Randolph. "You're certain."

"Oh, yes, I am indeed." She went to him at once, and taking his arm, guided him to the door. The Scotland Yard men followed.

"My name is Inspector Trent, madam," said the vocal one. "And this is my partner, Sergeant Galton. You must call us if you need us."

"Yes, of course," she said. Henry appeared on the verge of an outburst. Suddenly he bolted, almost knocking her over, and rushed out the open door and through the crowd gathered on the steps.

"Was it the mummy, sir!" someone shouted. "Did you see the mummy walk!"

"Was it the curse!"

"Miss Stratford, are you unharmed!"

The Scotland Yard men exited immediately, Inspector Trent ordering the crowd to disperse at once.

"Well, what the devil is the matter with him!" Randolph muttered. "I don't understand all this."

Julie held his arm all the tighter. No, he couldn't possibly know what Henry had done. He would never have done anything to hurt Father, not really. But how could she be sure? On impulse she kissed him. She slipped her hand onto the back of her uncle's neck, and kissed his cheek.

"Don't worry, Uncle Randolph," she said suddenly. And she felt herself on the verge of tears.

Randolph shook his head. He was humiliated, even a little afraid, and she felt tragically sorry for him as she watched him go. Sorrier than she had ever felt for anyone in her life. She did not realize he was barefoot until he was halfway down the street.

The reporters were following him. As the Scotland Yard men drove away, a pair of the reporters doubled back, and she retreated quickly, slamming the door. She peered out through the glass at the distant figure of her uncle rushing up his own front steps.

Then slowly she turned and came back into the front room.

Silence. The faint singing of the fountain in the conservatory. A horse passing at a brisk trot in the street outside. Rita shivering in the corner, with her apron a little knot in her feverishly working hands.

And Ramses, motionless, in the middle of the room. He stood with his arms folded, looking at her, feet slightly apart as before. The sun was a warm golden haze behind him, leaving his face in shadow. And the deep radiance of his eyes was almost as distracting as the high sheen of his full hair.

For the first time she understood the simple meaning of the word *regal*. And another word came to her, quite unfamiliar yet perfectly appropriate. It was comely. And it struck her that no small part of his beauty was his expression. He appeared wonderfully clever, and wonderfully curious, though quite collected, all at the same time. Otherworldly, yet perfectly normal. Grander than human; but human nonetheless.

He merely looked at her. The deep folds of the long heavy satin robe moved ever so faintly in the soft current of warm air from the conservatory doors.

"Rita, leave us," she whispered.

"But miss . . ."

"Go."

Silence again. Then he came towards her. No trace of a smile; only a gentle seriousness, eyes widening a little as he appeared to study her face, her hair, her dress.

How must this flimsy lace peignoir look to him? she thought suddenly. Good Lord, does he think the women of these times wear such things about the house and on the street? But he was not looking at the lace. He was staring at the shape of her breasts beneath the loose silk, at the contour of her hips. He looked at her face again and there was no mistaking his expression. It was passionate suddenly. He drew closer and reached out for her shoulders and she felt his warm fingers tighten.

"No," she said.

She shook her head emphatically and she stepped back. She straightened her shoulders, trying not to admit her fear, or the sudden delicious chill that ran up her back and down her arms. "No," she said again with a faint touch of disapproval.

And as she watched, on the edge of fear, the warmth in her breasts astonishing her, he nodded, backed away and smiled. He made a little open gesture with his hands. He spoke in a soft riff of Latin. She caught her name, the word *regina*, and the word she knew meant house. *Julie is Queen in her house.*

She nodded.

Her sigh of relief was impossible to disguise. She was shaking again, all over. Could he see it? Of course.

He made a gesture of asking:

"Panis, Julie," he whispered. *"Vinum. Panis."* He narrowed his eyes, as if searching for a proper word. *"Edere,"* he whispered, and gestured gracefully to his lips.

"Oh! I know what you're saying. Food, you want food. You want wine and bread." She hurried to the doorway. "Rita," she called out. "He's hungry. Rita, we must get him something to eat at once."

She turned around to see him smiling at her again, with that great warmth of affection she had seen upstairs. He found her pleasing to look at, did he? If only he knew that she found him almost irresistible, that a moment before she had almost locked her arms around him and— Best not to think of that. No, mustn't think of that at all.

4

ELLIOTT SAT back in the wing chair, staring forward at the coal fire. He was as close as possible to the grate, his slippered feet on the fender. The heat soothed the pain in his legs and in his hands. He was listening to Henry, veering between impatience and an unexpected fascination. God's vengeance upon Henry had been almost complete for his sins. Henry was a scandal.

"You must have imagined it!" Alex said.

"But I am telling you that damned thing got out of that mummy case and came at me. It strangled me. I felt its hand on me; I looked up into its filthy bandaged face."

"Definitely imagined it," Alex said.

"Imagined it, hell!"

Elliott glanced up at the two young men at the end of the mantel shelf to his right. Henry, unshaven, trembling, the glass of Scotch in his hand. And Alex, immaculate, his hands as clean as a nun's.

"And this Egyptologist fellow, you're saying that he and the mummy are one and the same? Henry, you've been out all night, haven't you? You've been drinking with that girl from the Music Hall. You've been—"

"Well, where the hell did the bastard come from if he's not the mummy!"

Elliott laughed softly. He gave the coals a poke with the tip of his silver cane.

Henry went on undaunted.

"He wasn't there last night! He came down the stairs in Uncle Lawrence's bathrobe! And you haven't seen this man! He's no ordinary man. Anybody who looks at him can tell he's not ordinary."

"He's alone there now? With Julie?"

It took so long for Alex to put things together, trusting soul.

"That's what I've been trying to tell you. My God! Isn't there anyone in London who will listen to me?" Henry gulped the Scotch, went to the sideboard and filled his glass again. "And Julie's protecting him. Julie knows what happened. She saw the thing come at me!"

"You're doing yourself a disservice with this story," Alex said gently. "No one's going to believe—"

"You realize those papyri, those scrolls," Henry sputtered. "They talk about some kind of immortal something. Lawrence was talking about it to that Samir fellow, something about Ramses the Second wandering for a thousand years—"

"I thought it was Ramses the Great," Alex interrupted.

"They are one and the same, you numbskull. Ramses the Second, Ramses the Great, Ramses the Damned. It was all in those scrolls, I tell you—about Cleopatra and this Ramses. Didn't you read it in the papers? I thought Uncle Lawrence was going soft from the heat."

"I think you need a rest, possibly in hospital. All this talk of a curse—"

"Damn it, don't you understand me! It's worse than a curse. The thing tried to kill me. It moved, I tell you. It's alive."

Alex stared at Henry with a thinly veiled look of revulsion. Same look he reserves for newspapers, Elliott thought glumly.

"I'm going to see Julie. Father, if you'll excuse . . ."

"Of course, that's exactly what you should do." Elliott looked into the fire again. "See about this Egyptologist person. Where he came from. She shouldn't be alone in that house with a stranger. It's absurd."

"She's alone in that house with the damned mummy!" Henry growled.

"Henry, why don't you go home and get some sleep?" Alex asked. "I shall see you later, Father."

"You bloody twit!"

Alex ignored the insult. It seemed an amazingly easy insult

to ignore. Henry emptied the glass again and went back to the sideboard.

Elliott listened to the chink of the bottle against the glass. "And this man, this mysterious Egyptologist, did you catch his name?" he asked.

"Reginald Ramsey, try that one on for size. And I could swear she made it up on the spot." He came back to the mantel shelf, resting his elbow on it, with a full tumbler of Scotch, which he sipped slowly, his eyes darting anxiously away as Elliott looked up. "I didn't hear him speak a word of English; and you should have seen the look in his eye. I'm telling you—you've got to *do* something!"

"Yes, but precisely what?"

"How the hell should I know? Catch the damned thing, that's what!"

Elliott gave a short laugh. "If this thing or person or whatever it is tried to strangle you, why is Julie protecting it? Why hasn't it strangled her?"

Henry stared forward blankly for a moment. Then he took another deep gulp from the glass. Elliott eyed him coldly. Not mad. No. Hysterical, but not mad.

"What I am asking," Elliott said softly, "is why would it try to harm you?"

"For the love of hell, it's a mummy, isn't it? I was the one traipsing about over there in its bloody tomb! Not Julie. I found Lawrence dead in the damned tomb—"

Henry stopped, as if he had just realized something. He was no longer merely blank-faced; he was in a visible state of shock.

Their eyes locked, but only for an instant. Elliott looked down at the fire. This is the young man I once cared for, he thought, once caressed with tenderness and hunger; once loved. And now he is reaching the end of something, the very end. And revenge ought to be sweet, but it isn't.

"Look," Henry said. He was almost stammering. "There's some sort of twist to this, some sort of explanation. But the thing, whatever it is, has to be stopped. It could have Julie in some sort of spell."

"I see."

"No, you don't see. You think I'm mad. And you despise me. You always have."

"No, not always."

Again they looked at each other. Henry's face was wet now

with perspiration. His lip trembled slightly, and then he looked away.

Utterly desperate, Elliott thought. He has nowhere to hide anymore from himself, that's the crux of it.

"Well, whatever you think," Henry said, "I'm not spending another night in that house. I'm having my things sent to the club."

"You can't leave her alone there. It isn't proper. And in the absence of a formal engagement between Julie and Alex, I cannot properly interfere."

"The hell you can't. And the hell I won't go where I wish. I tell you I won't stay there."

He heard Henry turn to go. He heard the glass slammed down on the marble-top sideboard. He heard the heavy steps retreating, leaving him alone.

Elliott leaned back against the damask. There was a dull resonating sound that meant the front door had been slammed shut.

He tried to see the entire incident in perspective, Henry coming here because Randolph did not believe him. What a strange story for a young man to have invented, even one as crazed and desperate as Henry. It did not make sense at all.

"Lover of Cleopatra," he whispered, "guardian of the royal house of Egypt. Ramses the Immortal. Ramses the Damned."

Suddenly he wanted to see Samir again. Talk to him. Of course the story was ridiculous, but . . . No. The whole point was that Henry was deteriorating more rapidly than anyone could have predicted. Nevertheless he wanted Samir to know about this.

He removed his pocket watch. Why, it was still very early. He had plenty of time before his afternoon appointments. If only he could manage to get himself out of this chair.

He had planted the cane firmly on the hearthstones in front of him when he heard his wife's soft tread on the carpet near the door. He sank back again, relieved that he wouldn't feel that excruciating pain for a few more moments, and then he looked up into her eyes.

He had always liked his wife; and now in the middle of his life, he had discovered that he loved her. A woman of impeccable grooming and subtle charm, she looked ageless to him, perhaps because he was not erotically attracted to her. But he knew that she was twelve years his senior, and therefore old, and this disturbed him only because he feared age himself, and he feared losing her.

He had always admired her, enjoyed her company; and he needed her money desperately. She had never minded that. She appreciated his charm, his social connections, and forgave him his secret eccentricities.

She had always known something was wrong with him philosophically, that he was "the tainted wether of the flock," wholly out of sympathy with his peers and his friends and enemies. But she never made an issue of it. Her happiness did not depend upon his happiness, it seemed; and she was eternally grateful that he went through the motions of social life, and had not run off like Lawrence Stratford to live in Egypt.

He was too crippled now with arthritis to be unfaithful to her any longer, and he wondered sometimes whether this was a relief to her, or whether it saddened her. He could not make up his mind. They still shared the marriage bed, and probably always would, though there was never any urgency or real need, except that of late, he'd been keenly aware that he depended upon her and loved her deeply.

He was glad she was home. It lessened the pain of Lawrence's death. But of course he'd have to recover her diamond necklace very soon, and that Randolph had promised to pay him tomorrow morning for the money he had borrowed against the thing was a great relief to him.

Edith looked especially pretty to him now, in her new Paris suit of green wool. She had a tailored look about her, except for her bouffant silver hair, which looked all the more lovely because of the severity of her clothes and the absence of any jewelry. She never wore the diamonds he had borrowed against, except to attend balls. He took pride in the fact that she was a handsome woman in her old age, and invariably impressive. People liked her, more even than they liked him, which was as it should be.

"I'm going out for a while," he said to her. "Little errand. You shan't miss me. I'll be back in good time for lunch."

She didn't answer. She sat down on the tufted ottoman beside him, and slipped her hand over his. How light it felt. Her hands were the only part of her which revealed age without question.

"Elliott, you've borrowed again against my necklace," she said.

He was ashamed. He said nothing.

"I know you did it for Randolph. Henry's debts again. Always the same story."

He looked at the coals in front of him. He didn't answer. After all, what was there to say? She knew it was safe in the hands of a jeweller trusted by both of them, that the advance had been relatively small—easy for her to manage, even if Randolph did not come through.

"Why didn't you come to me and tell me you needed money?" she asked him.

"It's never been easy to do that, my dear. Besides, Henry has made things so difficult for Randolph."

"I know. And I know you meant well, as usual."

"As vulgar as it may sound, a loan against a diamond necklace is a small price to pay for the Stratford millions. And that's where we are, my dear, trying to make a good marriage, as they say, for our son."

"Randolph cannot persuade his niece to marry Alex. He has no influence with her at all. You lent the money because you felt sorry for Randolph. Because he's your old friend."

"Perhaps that's true."

He sighed. He wouldn't look at her. "Perhaps, in some way, I feel responsible," he said.

"How could you be responsible? What have you to do with Henry, and what's become of him?" she asked.

He didn't answer. He thought of the hotel room in Paris, and the look of dull misery in Henry's eyes when his attempt at extortion had failed. Strange how clear it all was to him, the furnishings of that room. Later, when he had discovered the theft of the cigarette case and the money, he had sat thinking: I must remember this; I must remember all of it. This mustn't happen to me again.

"I'm sorry about the necklace, Edith," he whispered, suddenly stung to think that he had stolen from his wife as Henry had stolen from him. He found himself smiling at her, even winking, flirting a little as he always did. He gave her a little shrug.

She acknowledged all this with a wicked little smile of her own. Years ago she would have said, Don't play the bad boy with me. The fact that she didn't say it anymore didn't mean she didn't find him charming.

"Randolph has the money now to cover the loan," he assured her, more seriously.

"Not necessary," she whispered. "Leave it to me." And now she rose slowly and waited. She knew that he could use her help to get up and on his feet. And much as it humiliated him, he knew it too.

"Where are you going?" she asked as she held out her hands.

"Samir Ibrahaim at the museum."

"This mummy again."

"Henry's come up with the strangest story. . . ."

5

"A LEX, MY darling," she said, taking both his hands in hers. "Mr. Ramsey was a good friend of Father's. It's quite all right his being here."

"But you're alone. . . ." He looked disapprovingly at her white peignoir, as well he might.

"Alex, I'm a modern girl. Don't question me! Now off you go and let me take care of my guest. In a few days, we'll have lunch, and I'll explain the entire thing—"

"Julie, a few days!"

She kissed him quickly on the lips. She pressed him towards the front door. He gave another one of those determined glances back down the hall towards the conservatory.

"Alex, go now. The man's from Egypt; I'm to show him London. And I'm rushed. Please, darling dear, do as I ask you."

She all but shoved him out the door. He was too much of a gentleman to protest further. He gave her that innocent, baffled look, and then said softly that he would call her this evening on the telephone if that was all right.

"Of course," she said. "You're a sweetheart." Blowing him a little kiss off the tips of her fingers, she shut the door immediately.

She turned and leaned against the wall for a moment, staring back down the hall herself at the glass doors. She saw Rita dash by. She heard the sound of the kettle in the kitchen. The house was full of warm pungent fragrances of cooking food.

Her heart was pounding again; thoughts did drift through her brain, but they had no immediate emotional impact. What mattered for this moment, this absolutely extraordinary moment, was that Ramses was there. The immortal man was there. He was in the conservatory.

She made her way back down the hall and stood in the doorway looking at him. He wore Father's robe still, though he had removed the shirt with a faint look of distaste for the stiff starched fabric. And his hair had reached its fullness now, a great glossy mane of soft waves that hung down just below the lobes of his ears, with a deep full lock falling again and again on his forehead.

The white wicker table was covered with plates of steaming food. As he read the copy of *Punch* propped before his plate, he ate delicately with his right hand from the meat here, and the fruit there, and the bread to his left, and the bits of roasted fowl in front of him. It was quite a miracle, in fact, the fastidiousness with which he ate, not touching the knives and forks, though he had loved the ornate designs in the old silver.

He had been reading and eating steadily for the last two hours. He had devoured quantities of food beyond her wild imaginings. It was like fuel to him, it seemed. He had drunk four bottles of wine, two bottles of seltzer, all the milk in the house, and now he was taking occasional gulps of brandy.

He was not drunk; on the contrary, he seemed extraordinarily sober. He had gone through her English/Egyptian dictionary so rapidly that his scanning and turning the pages had made her almost dizzy. The English/Latin dictionary had taken him no more time. The system of Arabic numbers side by side with Roman numerals he apparently absorbed within minutes. The full concept of zero she could not explain, but she had certainly been able to demonstrate it. Then he'd gone through the *Oxford English Dictionary* with the same haste, turning back and forth, running his finger down column after column.

Of course he was not reading every word. He was getting the gist, the roots, the fundamental scheme of the language; that she understood as he made her name every object in sight and repeated the words rapidly with perfect inflection. He had memorized the names of every plant in the room—ferns, banana trees, orchids, begonias, daisies, bougainvillea. It had thrilled her to hear his rapid inventories repeated moments later without a mistake: fountain, table, plates, china plates, silver, floor tiles, Rita!

Now he was working his way through purely English texts, finishing off the *Punch* as he had already finished two issues of the *Strand* magazine, the *Harper's Weekly* from America, and every issue of *The Times* in the house.

He scanned the pages with great care, fingers touching words, pictures, even designs as if he were a blind man somehow miraculously able to see through touch. With the same loving attention, he fingered the Wedgwood plates and the Waterford crystal.

He looked up excitedly now as Rita brought him a glass of beer.

"I've got nothing else, miss," she said with a little shrug, standing well back of him as she held out the glass.

He snatched it from her and drained it immediately. He gave her a nod and smile.

"Egyptians love beer, Rita. Get some more, hurry."

Keeping Rita on the go was keeping Rita from losing her mind.

Julie made her way through the ferns and potted trees and took her place at the table opposite Ramses. He glanced up, then pointed to a picture of "the Gibson girl" before him. Julie nodded.

"American," she said.

"United States," he responded.

She was stunned. "Yes," she said.

He quickly devoured a sausage whole, and folded another thin slice of bread and ate it in two bites, as he turned the pages with his left hand, scanning a picture of a man on a bicycle. This made him laugh out loud.

"Bicycle," she said.

"Yes!" he said, precisely as she had said it a moment ago. Then he said something softly in Latin.

Oh, she had to take him out, show him everything.

The telephone sounded suddenly, a shrill ring from Father's desk in the Egyptian room. He was immediately on his feet. He followed her into the Egyptian room and stood quite close, looking down at her as she answered it.

"Hello? Yes, this is Julie Stratford." She covered the mouthpiece. "Telephone," she whispered. "Talking machine." She held the receiver so that he might hear the voice on the other end. Henry's club calling; they would come round for Henry's trunk. Could she have it ready?

"It's ready now. You'll need two men, I should think. Please do hurry."

She clasped the wire and held it up to Ramses' attention. "The voice goes through the wire," she whispered. She hung up the telephone, looked about. Taking his hand, she led him back into the conservatory, and pointed to the wires outside, which ran from the house to the telegraph pole at the far end of the garden.

He studied all this with keen concentration. Then she took an empty glass from the table and approached the wall that divided the far end of the conservatory from the kitchen. She placed the mouth of the glass against the wall and pressed her ear to the bottom of the glass, and listened. It amplified the sound of Rita moving about. Then she invited him to do it. He heard the amplification just as she had heard it.

He stared at her, thoughtful, dazzled, excited.

"The wire of the telephone conducts sound," she said. "It's a mechanical invention." That's what she must do, show him what machines were! Explain the great leap forward which machines had accomplished; the complete transformation of thinking about how to do things.

"Conducts sound," he repeatedly thoughtfully. He moved to the table and lifted the magazine he'd been reading. He made a gesture as if to say Read aloud. Quickly, she read a paragraph of commentary on home affairs. Too dense with abstractions, but he was merely listening to the syllables, wasn't he? Impatiently he took the magazine from her, and then answered:

"Thank you."

"Very good," she said. "You're learning with amazing speed."

Then he made a curious little series of gestures. He touched his temple, his forehead, as though making some reference to his brain. And then he touched his hair, and his skin. What was he trying to tell her? That the organ of thought responded as quickly as his hair and body had responded to the sunlight?

He turned to the table. "Sausages," he said. "Beef. Roast chicken. Beer. Milk. Wine. Fork. Knife. Napkin. Beer. More beer."

"Yes," she said. "Rita, bring him some more beer. He likes

beer." She lifted a fold of her peignoir. "Lace," she said. "Silk."

He made a little buzzing noise.

"Bees!" she said. "Exactly. Oh, you are so wonderfully clever."

He laughed. "Say again," he said.

"Wonderfully clever." Now she pointed to her head, tap, tap, tap. The brain, thought.

He nodded. He glanced down at the silver-handled paring knife on the table. He picked it up, as if asking her permission, and slipped it into his pocket. Then beckoning for her to follow, he went into the Egyptian room. He approached an old dim map of the world behind a dusty glass in a heavy frame and he pointed carefully to England.

"Yes, England. Britannia," she said. She pointed to America. "The United States," she said. Then she identified continents, oceans. Finally she identified Egypt, and the Nile River, a tiny line on this small map. "Ramses, King of Egypt," she said. She pointed to him.

He nodded. But he wanted to know something else. Very carefully he articulated the question:

"Twentieth century? What means anno Domini?"

She was speechless, looking at him. He had slept through the birth of Christ! Of course he had no way to grasp how long that sleep had lasted. That he was a pure pagan did not disturb her so much as it fascinated her. But she feared the shock she would give him now when she answered his question.

Roman numerals, where was that book? She took down Plutarch's *Lives* from her father's shelves and found the date of publication in Roman numerals, only three years before, perfect.

Taking a sheet of notepaper from her father's desk, and dipping his pen, she hastily wrote out the correct date. But how to make it known to him the beginning of the system?

Cleopatra was close enough, but she feared to use Cleopatra's name, for all the obvious reasons. Then the clearest example came to her.

She wrote out in hard printed letters the name Octavius Caesar. He nodded. She made a Roman numeral one beneath it. Then she drew a long horizontal line, moving to the very right edge of the page, and she wrote her own name Julie, and the full date in Roman numerals. And after that the Latin word: *annum*.

He blanched. He looked at the paper for a long time, and then the colour appeared to dance in his cheeks. There was no doubt he understood her. His expression became grave, then curiously philosophical. He seemed to be pondering rather than absorbing a shock. She wrote the word *century*, and then the Roman numeral for one hundred, and the word *annus*. He nodded a little impatiently, yes, yes, he understood.

Then he folded his arms and walked slowly around the room. She could not guess what he was thinking.

"A long time," she whispered. "Tempus . . . tempus fugit!" She was embarrassed suddenly. Time flies? But it was all the Latin she could think of. He was smiling at her. Was it a cliché two thousand years ago?

He approached the desk, and leaning over her gently, he took the pen and carefully drew the Egyptian cartouche which spelled his name in hieroglyphs, Ramses the Great. Then he too drew a horizontal line stretching across the page almost to the edge, where he wrote Cleopatra. In the very middle of that line he wrote the Roman numeral M meaning one thousand years; and then the arabic numbers for it which she had only taught him an hour ago.

He gave her a moment to read this. And then he wrote beneath his cartouche the arabic numerals 3000.

"Ramses is three thousand years old," she said, pointing to him, "and Ramses knows it."

He nodded again, and smiled. What was his expression? Sad, resigned, merely thoughtful? There was a great dark flicker of pain in his eyes. The smile did not break, but she saw it, and she saw a subtle puckering of the lids beneath his eyes as he pondered this himself, and apparently moved back from it emotionally. He looked about the room now as if he were seeing it for the first time. He looked at the ceiling, and then at the floor, and then directly at the bust of Cleopatra. His eyes were as wide as before, his smile as soft and agreeable, but the something was gone from his face. The vigour. It had completely vanished.

When he looked at her again, there was a thin glaze of tears in his eyes. She couldn't bear it. She reached out and clasped his left hand. His fingers curled around hers, squeezing them tenderly.

"Very many years, Julie," he said. "Very many years. The world unseen by me. Do I speak clearly?"

"Oh, yes, indeed you do," she said.

He studied her, whispering slowly, and almost reverently, "Very many many years, Julie." And then he smiled. And his smile became broader. And then his shoulders began to shake. And she realized he was laughing. "Two thousand years, Julie." He laughed outright. And the look of wild excitement returned, the look of heightened vitality. Only slowly did his eyes turn to the bust of Cleopatra. He stared at it for a long moment, and then he looked at Julie again, and the curiosity and optimism had returned. For that was it, a great vigorous optimism.

She wanted to kiss him. In fact, the urge was so strong it amazed her. It wasn't merely the beauty of his face, it was the deep resonant quality of his voice, and the look of pain in his eyes, and the way he smiled at her now, and reached up and touched her hair ever so respectfully. Chills ran down her back.

"Ramses is immortal," she said. "Ramses has *vitam eternam.*"

A small polite laugh of acknowledgment came from him. A nod. "Yes," he said. *"Vitam eternam."*

Was she feeling love for this man? Or merely an infatuation so overpowering it swept every other consideration out of her mind? Even Henry and what he had done, that he had killed her father?

Henry must wait. Justice had to wait. Unless she was to kill Henry herself, and that was quite unthinkable. But this, this was everything now, this man sitting before her. Her hatred for Henry would have its day. Henry was heading towards God's justice more surely than any human being she had ever known.

And she stood gazing into these magnificent blue eyes, feeling the warmth of the hand that held hers, swept into this man's future by a miracle.

There was a violent noise from the street. It could only have been a motor car. He heard it, there was no doubt of that; but only very slowly did he respond, looking away from her and towards the front windows. Then placing his arm very lightly on her shoulder, he guided her with him to the front of the house.

What a gentleman he was; what a strange courtly being. He peered out through the lace at what must surely have been a shocking spectacle—an Italian roadster idling, with two young men in the front seat, both of them waving at a young lady who was walking on the pavement opposite. The driver sounded the horn, a nasty loud thing, and it gave Ramses a bad start. But he continued to look at the rumbling, backfiring open car, not with fear, but with curiosity. As the thing began to move, and then lurched down the street, his curiosity gave way to utter astonishment.

"Motor car," she said. "It runs on gasoline. It is a machine. An invention."

"Motor car!" He moved immediately to the front door, and opened it.

"No, you must come, get properly dressed," she said. "Vestments, proper vestments."

"Shirt, tie, trousers, shoes," he said.

She laughed. He made a gesture for her to wait. She watched as he went into the Egyptian room, and studied the long line of alabaster jars. He selected one, and turned it to reveal a small hidden compartment at the base, which was now opened. Out of this he took several gold coins. He brought these to her.

"Vestments," he said.

She studied them only a second or two in the light from the windows. More of the flawless Cleopatra coins.

"Oh, no," she said, "these are worth far too much for us to spend them. Put them away. You are my guest here. I shall take care of everything."

She took him by the hand and led him up the stairs. Once again, he studied everything about him. Only this time he paused to examine the porcelain whatnots on the shelf. He stopped beneath her father's portrait in the upstairs hall.

"Lawrence," he said. Then, looking intently at her: "Henry? Where is Henry?"

"I shall take care of Henry," she said. "Time and the courts of law . . . *judicium* . . . justice shall take care of Henry."

He indicated he was not satisfied with this answer. He drew the paring knife out of his pocket and ran his thumb along the blade. "I, Ramses, shall kill Henry."

"No!" Her hands flew to her lips. "No. Justice. Law!" she said. "We are a people of courts and laws. When the time comes . . ." But she broke down. She could say no more. The tears welled in her eyes. It was hitting her again. Henry robbed Father of this triumph, this mystery, this very moment. "No," she said as he tried to steady her.

He put his hand on his chest. "I, Ramses, am justice," he said. "King, court, justice."

She sniffled, trying to stop her tears. She wiped at her lips with the back of her hand.

"You're a very fast learner of words," she said, "but you cannot kill Henry. I cannot live if you kill Henry."

Suddenly he took her face in his hands, and forcing her to him, he kissed her. It was brief, yet absolutely devastating. She reeled, and turned her back on him.

Quickly, she walked to the end of the hall and opened her father's door. She did not turn around and look at him again as she took the clothing out of the wardrobe. She laid out the shirt, the trousers, the belt. Socks, shoes. She pointed to the pictures on the wall, all the old photographs her father had treasured of himself and Elliott and Randolph and other cronies, from Oxford days to the present. The coat, she'd forgotten the coat. She dragged that out too and laid it down on the bed.

Then and only then did she look up. He stood in the door, watching her. The robe was open now to his waist; surely there was something profoundly primitive in the way he stood there, arms folded, feet apart, yet it seemed at the moment the very height of decorous sophistication.

He moved into the room now, surveying it with the same curiosity with which he approached everything else. He saw the photographs of her father, along with Randolph and Elliott at Oxford. He turned to look at the clothing laid out on the bed. Clearly he was comparing the clothes with that of the men in the pictures.

"Yes," she said, "you should dress like that."

His eyes darted to the *Archaeology Journal* on the dressing table. He picked it up and leafed through it, stopping at a full engraving of the great pyramid at Giza which contained also the Mena Hotel. What in the world was he thinking? He closed it.

"RRRRR . . . kay . . . ology," he said. With the utter guilelessness of a child, he smiled.

His eyes positively glittered as he looked at her. There was a scant bit of hair on his massive chest. She must get out of here now.

"You dress, Ramses. Like the pictures. I'll help you later if you make any mistakes."

"Very well, Julie Stratford," he said in that paralyzingly perfect British accent. "I dress alone. I have done this before."

Of course. Slaves. He had always had them, hadn't he? Probably by the dozens. Well, there was nothing to be done about it. She could not start removing that robe with her own hands. Her cheeks were burning. She could feel it. She hurried out, and quietly shut the door.

6

HENRY WAS now as drunk as he had ever been in his life. He had finished the bottle of Scotch which he had taken without permission from Elliott, and the brandy was going down like water. But it did not help.

He was smoking one Egyptian cheroot after another, filling Daisy's flat with the pungent fragrance he had grown accustomed to in Cairo. And all it did was make him think of Malenka, and how he wished he was with Malenka, though he also wished he had never set foot in Egypt, that he had never entered that chamber in the side of the mountain where his uncle Lawrence had been poring over a stack of ancient scrolls.

That thing had been alive! That thing had seen him slip the poison into Lawrence's cup. No mistaking now the memory of those eyes open under the bandages; no mistaking that the thing had come out of its coffin in Julie's house and clamped its filthy hand on his neck.

No one understood the danger he was in. No one understood because no one knew the thing's motive! Never mind the reason for its filthy existence! The thing knew what he had done. And that Reginald Ramsey—though he could not entirely associate the man with the filthy creature that had tried to strangle him— he knew intellectually they were one and the same. Would the man disappear into the rotted linen bandages again when it came to get him?

God! He shuddered all over. He heard Daisy say something,

and when he looked up he saw her standing by the mantel shelf, posing, as it were, in her corset and silk stockings, her breasts pouring over the lace cups of the corset, her blond ringlets tumbling onto her shoulders. Ought to be quite something to look at, to touch. It meant nothing.

"And you're telling me a bloomin' mummy came right out of the mummy case and put its bloomin' hands around your throat! And you're telling me it's got on a bloomin' robe and slippers and is walking around the bloomin' house!"

Go away, Daisy. In his mind's eye, he saw himself taking the knife out of his pocket, the knife with which he'd killed Sharples, and he saw himself stabbing Daisy with it, in the throat.

The bell sounded. She wasn't going to the door in that getup, was she? Perfect idiot. What the devil did he care! The door. He shrank back in the chair, fumbling in his pocket for the knife.

Flowers. She came back with a big bouquet of flowers, babbling about an admirer. He slumped back in the chair. What was she doing? Staring at him like that?

"I need a pistol," he said without looking at her. "Surely one of your guttersnipe friends can get me a pistol?"

"I'll have nothing to do with it!"

"You'll do as I tell you!" he said. If only she knew; he had killed two men. He had almost killed a woman. Almost. And the thing was, he would have liked to hurt Daisy, he would have liked to see the expression on her face when the knife went into her throat. "Now get on the telephone," he said to her. "Call that worthless brother of yours. I need a pistol small enough to keep under my coat."

Was she going to cry?

"Do as I tell you," he said. "Now, I'm going to my club to get some of my clothing. If anyone calls here for me, you're to say I'm staying there, do you hear?"

"You're in no condition to go anywhere!"

He struggled out of the chair, and towards the door. The floor was tilting. He steadied himself at the frame. For a long moment he rested his forehead against it. He could not remember a time when he wasn't tired, desperate, angry. He looked back at her.

"If I come back here and you haven't done what I said . . ."

"I'll do it," she whimpered. She threw the flowers down and folded her arms and turned her back to him and bowed her head.

Some instinct, upon which he had always relied without question, told him to temper it now. This was the moment to appear gentle, almost affectionate, though the very sight of her bent back infuriated him, though her sobs made him grit his teeth.

"You like this flat well enough, don't you, darling?" he said. "And you like the champagne you're drinking and the furs you're wearing. And you'll like the motor car well enough as soon as I get it. But what I need right now is a little loyalty and time."

He saw her nod. She was turning around to come to him. He went down the hall and out the door.

Henry's trunk had just been taken away.

Julie stood at the window watching the awkward, noisy German motorcar move out of sight down the street. In her heart of hearts, she did not know what to do about Henry.

To call the authorities at this point was unthinkable. Not only was there no explainable witness to what Henry had done; but the thought of wounding Randolph was more than Julie could bear.

Randolph was innocent. She knew it instinctively. And she knew as well that knowledge of Henry's guilt would be the final blow for Randolph. She would lose her uncle as she had lost her father. And though her uncle had never been the man her father was, he was her flesh and blood, and she loved him very much.

Dimly, she remembered Henry's words to her this morning. "We are all you have." She found herself paralysed with hurt, on the verge of tears again.

A footstep on the stairs interrupted her. She turned. And she saw the one person in the world who could sweep away this burden, even for a little while.

She had dressed very carefully for this moment. Telling herself that everything she did was an education for her honoured guest, she had chosen the most exquisite suit she owned; her best black-brimmed hat with silk flowers; and gloves of course; all this to acquaint him with the fashions of the time.

But she had also wanted to look beautiful for him. And she knew that the burgundy wool flattered her. Her heart was knocking again as she saw him come down the stairs.

In fact, her breath left her altogether as he stepped into the front hall and looked down at her, coming perilously close to her as if he meant to kiss her.

She did not step back.

He had done well with her father's wardrobe. Dark socks and

shoes perfect. Shirt buttoned properly. Silk tie knotted rather eccentrically but quite beautiful. Even the cuff links were properly done. In fact, he was disturbingly handsome in the silk waistcoat, sleek black frock coat and gray wool flannel trousers he wore. Only the cashmere scarf was all wrong. He had tied it as a sash about his waist as an old-fashioned soldier might have done.

"May I?" she asked as she removed it, and then slipped it over his head and around his neck, inside the coat. She smoothed it carefully, trying not to be overpowered by him, by his blue eyes looking down at her intently, and that strange philosophical smile.

Now came the big adventure. They were going out together. She was going to show Ramses the Great the twentieth century. This was the most exciting moment she had ever known.

He caught her hand as she opened the door. He drew her to him swiftly. Again, it was as if he were going to kiss her, and her excitement turned suddenly to fear.

He felt it; he stopped, holding her hand a little more loosely, a little more gently. And then he bent and kissed it reverently. And gave her a very mischievous little smile.

How in God's name was she going to resist him!

"Come, let's go. The world waits!" she said. There was a hansom coming along right now. She waved quickly, and then gave him a little tug.

He had stopped. He was looking up and down the broad expanse of street at all the many houses with their iron railings and massive doors, and lace curtains; and the chimney pots smoking above.

How vital, how passionate, how full of sheer lust for it all he appeared. With a spring in his step he came after her, and climbed into the back of the little cab.

It occurred to her that never in her life had she seen even a smattering of that passion in her beloved Alex. It made her sad for an instant, not because she was really thinking about Alex, but because she had the first inkling of how her old world was fading, of how things were never, never going to be the same.

Samir's office at the British Museum was small, packed with books, and overcrowded perhaps by the large desk and the two leather chairs. But Elliott found it comfortable enough. And thank God the little coal fire kept it very warm.

"Well, I'm not sure that I can tell you that much," Samir said. "Lawrence had only translated a fragment: the Pharaoh claimed to be immortal. He had roamed the world, it seems, since the end of his official reign. He'd lived among peoples the ancient Egyptians didn't know existed. He claimed to have been in Athens for two centuries, to have lived in Rome. Finally he retreated to a tomb from which only the royal families of Egypt could call him. Certain priests knew the secret. It had become a legend by Cleopatra's time. But apparently the young Queen believed."

"And she did whatever was necessary to awaken him."

"So he wrote. And he fell deeply in love with her, approving her liaison with Caesar in the name of necessity and experience, but not with Mark Antony. This embittered him, Lawrence said. There was nothing there to contradict our history. He condemned Antony and Cleopatra for their excesses and their bad judgment just as we have done."

"Did Lawrence believe the story? Did he have any theory—"

"Lawrence was deliriously happy with the mystery. Such an incomprehensible combination of artifacts. Lawrence would have spent the rest of his life trying to solve it. I'm not sure what he really believed."

Elliott reflected. "The mummy, Samir. You examined it. You were with Lawrence when he first opened the case."

"Yes."

"Did you detect anything out of the ordinary?"

"My Lord, you've seen a thousand such mummies. The baffling part was the writing, the command of languages, and, of course, the mummy case."

"Well, I have a little story to tell you," Elliott said. "According to our mutual friend and acquaintance Henry Stratford, the mummy is quite alive. This very morning he stepped out of his coffin, crossed Lawrence's library and tried to strangle Henry in the drawing room. Henry was lucky to escape with his life."

For a moment Samir didn't respond at all. It was as if he hadn't heard. Then softly, "You are joking with me, Lord Rutherford?"

Elliott laughed. "No. I am not joking, Mr. Ibrahaim. And I am willing to wager that Henry Stratford wasn't joking when he told me the story this very morning. In fact, I'm certain he wasn't joking. He was badly shaken; damn near hysterical. But joking, no.''

Silence. This is what it means to be speechless, Elliott thought as he looked at Samir.

"You don't have a cigarette, do you, Samir?" he asked.

Without taking his eyes off Elliott, Samir opened a small delicately carved ivory box. Egyptian cigarettes. Perfectly delicious. Samir lifted the gold lighter and handed it to Elliott.

"Thank you. I might add . . . for I suppose you are wondering . . . this mummy did not hurt Julie at all. And has become in fact her honoured guest."

"Lord Rutherford . . ."

"I'm perfectly serious. My son, Alex, went there immediately. As a matter of fact, there were police on the scene even before that. It seems an Egyptologist is staying at the Stratford house, a Mr. Reginald Ramsey, and that Julie is being quite emphatic that she must take her guest about London. She has no time to discuss Henry's inane hallucinations. And Henry, who had seen this Egyptologist, maintains that he is in fact the mummy, walking about in Lawrence's clothes."

Elliott lit the cigarette and inhaled deeply.

"You're going to hear about all this soon enough from others," he said casually. "The reporters were there in force. 'Mummy Walks in Mayfair.' " He shrugged.

Samir was clearly more stunned than amused. He appeared positively distressed.

"You'll forgive me," he said, "but I don't have a very high opinion of Lawrence's nephew, Henry."

"Of course not, how could you?"

"This Egyptologist. You said that his name was Reginald Ramsey. I have never heard of an Egyptologist by that name."

"Of course you haven't. And you know them all, don't you? From Cairo to London or Manchester, or Berlin or New York."

"I think I do."

"So none of this makes sense."

"Not a particle of sense."

"Unless, of course, we entertain for a moment the notion that this mummy is immortal. Then everything falls into place."

"But you don't believe—" Samir stopped. The distress was plain again. In fact, it had worsened.

"Yes?"

"This is preposterous," Samir murmured. "Lawrence died

of a heart attack in that tomb. This thing did not kill him! This is madness."

"Was there the slightest evidence of violence?"

"Evidence? No. But there was a feeling about that tomb, and the curses written all over the mummy case. The thing wanted to be left in peace. The sun. It did not want the sun. But it was asking to be left in peace. That is what the dead always want."

"Do they?" Elliott asked. "If I were dead, I'm not sure I would want to be at peace. If it meant being purely dead, that is."

"We're allowing our imaginations to run away with us, Lord Rutherford. Besides . . . Henry Stratford was in the tomb when Lawrence died!"

"Hmmmmm. That's true. And Henry didn't see our ragged, rotted friend moving about until this morning."

"I do not like this story. I do not like it at all. I do not like that Miss Stratford is alone in the house with these relics."

"Perhaps the museum should look into it further," Elliott said. "Check up on the mummy. After all, the thing is extremely valuable."

Samir didn't answer. He had sunk into that speechless state again, staring at the desk before him.

Elliott took hold of his cane firmly and rose to his feet. He was getting quite good at hiding the inevitable discomfort of that simple operation. But he had to stand quite still for a few moments to allow the pain to stop. He crushed out his cigarette slowly.

"Thank you, Samir. It's been a most interesting conversation."

Samir looked up as if waking from a dream.

"What the hell do you think is happening, Lord Rutherford!" Slowly he rose to his feet.

"You want my frank opinion of the moment?"

"Well, yes, I do."

"Ramses the Second is an immortal man. He found some secret in ancient times, some compound which rendered him immortal. And he is walking about London with Julie right now."

"You're not serious."

"Yes, I am," said Elliott. "But then I also believe in ghosts, and spirits, and bad luck; I throw salt over my shoulder and touch wood all the time. I should be surprised—no, flabbergasted—if any of this turned out to be true, you understand. But I believe it. At the moment, I believe it. And I'll tell you why. It's the only explanation for what's happened that makes any sense.''

Speechless again.

Elliott smiled. He slipped on his gloves, took hold of his walking stick and left the office as if every step were not causing him pain.

7

THIS WAS the great adventure of her life. Nothing after could ever equal it, of that she was sure. And how utterly surprising that it should be in London, at midday, rushing to and fro amid the noisy, crowded streets she'd known all her life.

Never before had the vast, grimy city seemed magical to her. But it did now. And how did *he* perceive it—this overgrown metropolis, with its towering brick buildings, its rumbling trams and belching motor cars, and hordes of dark horse-drawn carriages and cabs choking every street. What was he to make of the never-ending advertising, signs of all sizes and descriptions offering goods, services, directions and advice? Were the dim department stores with their stacks of ready-made clothing ugly to him? What did he make of the little shops where the electric lights burned all day long because the streets themselves were too smoky and dark to admit the natural light of the daytime sky?

He loved it. He embraced it. Nothing frightened him or repelled him. He rushed off the kerb to lay hands on the motor cars as they idled. He scampered up the winding steps of the omnibuses to see from the top deck. Into the telegraph office, he sped to study the young secretary at her typewriter. And she, at once charmed by this blue-eyed giant of a man bending over her, sat back to let him strike the keys with his own deft fingers,

105

which he did, at once pounding out Latin sentences which sent him into peals of laughter until he could not go on.

To the offices of *The Times*, Julie spirited him. He must see the giant printing presses, smell the black ink, hear the deafening noise that filled those immense rooms. He must make the connection among all these inventions. He must see how simple it all was.

She watched as he charmed people everywhere that they went. Men and women deferred to him, as if they knew instinctively that he was royalty. His bearing, his great strides, his radiant smile, subdued those at whom he stared fixedly, those whose hands he hastily clasped, those whose conversation or casual words he listened to, as if receiving a secret message which must not be misunderstood.

There were philosophical words to describe his state of being, surely, but Julie could not think what they were. She only knew that he took joy in things, that the steam shovel and the steam roller failed to terrify him because he anticipated shocks and surprises and wanted only to comprehend.

So many questions to ask him. So many concepts she struggled to express. That was the hardest part. Concepts.

But talk of abstractions became easier by the hour. He was learning English with dizzying speed.

''Name!'' he would say to her if she ceased for so much as a minute her endless commentary. ''Language is names, Julie. Names for people, objects, what we feel.'' He hammered on his breast as he said the last words. The Latin *quare, quid, quo, qui* had dropped completely from his speech by midafternoon.

''English is old, Julie. Tongue of barbarians from my time, and now filled with Latin. You hear the Latin? What is that, Julie! Explain this to me!''

''But there is no order to what I am teaching you,'' she said. She wanted to explain about printing, relate it to the stamping of coins.

''I make the order later,'' he assured her. He was too busy now ducking into the back of bakers and soup kitchens, into the shoemaker's and the milliner's, and studying the refuse thrown in the alleyways, and eyeing the paper parcels which people carried, and staring at women's clothes.

And staring at the women, too.

If that isn't lust, I am no judge of character, Julie thought. He would have frightened the women had he not been so expensively dressed, and oddly self-possessed. In fact, his whole manner of standing, gesturing, speaking, had a great compelling force to it. This is a King, she thought, out of time and place, yet nevertheless a King.

She steered him into the bookseller's. She pointed out the old names, Aristotle, Plato, Euripedes, Cicero. He stared at the Aubrey Beardsley prints on the wall.

Photographs positively delighted him. Into a little studio, Julie took him to have his own portrait taken. His pleasure was almost childlike. Even more wonderful, he exclaimed, was that even the poor of this great city could have such pictures made.

But when he beheld moving pictures, he was positively stunned. In the crowded little cinema, he gasped, clinging tight to Julie's hand, as the giant luminescent figures scurried about on the screen before them. Tracing the projectionists' beams with his eye, he made at once for the little room in back, tearing open the door without hesitation. But the old projectionist fell prey to his charm as did everyone else, and was soon explaining the entire mechanism in detail.

At last as they entered the giant dark cavern of Victoria Station, the mighty chugging locomotives brought him to a dead halt. But even these he approached fearlessly. He touched the cold black iron, and stood dangerously close to the giant wheels. Behind the departing train, he put his foot on the track to feel the vibration. Dazed, he stared at the crowds.

"Thousands of people, transported from one end of Europe to the other," she cried out over the noise around them. "Journeys which once took months now take but a few days."

"Europe," he whispered. "Italia to Britannia."

"The trains are carried on ships across the water. The poor of the open country can come into the cities. All men know the cities, do you see?"

He nodded gravely. He squeezed her hand. "No haste, Julie. All will be understood in time." Flash of his brilliant smile again, that great sudden warmth of affection for her which made her blush and look away.

"Temples, Julie. The houses of the *deus . . . di.*"

"Gods. But there is only one now. One God."

Disbelief. One God?

Westminster Abbey. They walked together under the high arches. Such splendor. She showed him the cenotaph of Shakespeare.

"Not the house of God," she said. "But the place where we gather to talk to him." How explain Christianity? "Brotherly love," she said. "That is the basis."

He looked at her in confusion. "Brotherly love?" Keenly, he watched the people around him.

"Do they believe this religion?" he asked. "Or is it habit alone?"

By late afternoon he was speaking coherently in whole paragraphs. He told her that he liked English. It was a good language for thinking. Greek and Latin had been excellent for thinking. Egyptian, no. With each new language he had learned in his earlier existence his capacity for understanding had improved. Language made possible whole kinds of thinking. Ah, that the common people of this era read newspapers, crowded with words! What must the thinking of the common man be?

"Are you not the least bit tired?" Julie asked, finally.

"No, never tired," he said, "except in the heart and the soul. Hungry. Food, Julie. I desire much food."

They entered the quiet of Hyde Park together, and despite his disclaimers he did seem relieved by the sudden timeless trees around him, by the vision of the sky through branches as it might have been seen at any moment or from any vantage point on earth.

They found a little bench on the path. He fell into silence watching the strollers. And how they stared at him—this man of powerful build with his fiercely exuberant expression. Did he know he was handsome? she wondered. Did he know that the mere touch of his hand sent a frisson through her which she tried to ignore?

Oh, so much to show him. She took him to the offices of Stratford Shipping, praying that no one would recognize her, and led him into the wrought-iron lift, and pressed the button for the roof.

"Wires and pulleys," she explained.

"Britannia," he whispered as they looked out on the rooftops of London; as they listened to the scream of the factory whistles, to the jangling of the tram bells far below. "America, Julie." He turned to her excitedly, clasping her shoulders, his fingers surprisingly gentle. "How many days by mechanical ship to America?"

"Ten days, I believe. One could be in Egypt in less time than that. A passage to Alexandria is six days."

Why had she said those words? His face darkened ever so slightly. "Alexandria," he whispered, pronouncing it as she had. "Alexandria still stands?"

She led him to the lift. So much more to see. She explained there was still an Athens, still a Damascus, still an Antioch. And Rome, of course there was Rome.

A wild idea had come to her. Hailing a hansom, she told the driver: "Madame Tussaud's."

All those costumed figures in the wax museum. Hastily she explained what it was, a panorama of history. She would show him American Indians, she would show him Genghis Khan or Attila the Hun—creatures who had brought terror to Europe after Rome fell.

She could not envision the mosaic of facts being created for him. His equanimity amazed her more and more.

But they had been in Madame Tussaud's only a few moments when she realized her error. His composure crumbled at the first sight of Roman soldiers. He recognized the figure of Julius Caesar instantly. And then in disbelief he stared at the Egyptian Cleopatra, a wax doll which bore no resemblance to the bust he had cherished or the coins he still possessed. But her identity was unmistakable as she reclined on her gilded couch, the snake coiled in her hands, its fangs just beneath her breast. The stiff figure of Mark Antony stood behind her, a characterless man in Roman military dress.

Ramses' face coloured. There was something savage in his eyes as he turned to Julie, then looked back at the printed labels beneath this display.

Why hadn't she realized these figures would be here? Why hadn't she remembered? She caught his hand as he backed away from the glass. He turned around, almost stumbling into a couple who blocked his path. The man said something threatening, but Ramses didn't seem to hear it. He was hurrying towards the exit. She ran after him.

He appeared calmer when she reached the street. He was scanning the traffic. He reached out for her hand without looking at her, and together they proceeded slowly until he stopped to watch the workmen on a construction sight. The great cement mixer was churning. The sound of hammering echoed against distant walls.

A faint bitter smile passed over Ramses' lips. Julie hailed a passing hansom.

"Where shall we go now?" she asked. "Tell me what you want to see."

He was staring at a beggar woman, a ragged figure in broken-down shoes who extended her hand now as she passed.

"The poor," he said, glancing at the woman. "Why are the poor still here?"

They rode silently through cobblestone streets. Strings of laundry closed out the damp gray sky. The smoke of cooking fires rose in the alleys. Barefoot children with soiled faces turned to watch them pass.

"But cannot all this wealth help these people? They are as poor as the peasants of my land."

"Some things don't change with time," Julie said.

"And your father? He was a rich man?"

She nodded. "He built a great shipping company—ships that carry merchandise from India and Egypt to England and America. Ships that circle the world."

"For this wealth, Henry tried to kill you, as he killed your father in the tomb."

Julie stared straight forward. It seemed the words would strip away every vestige of control she had. This day, this adventure, it had carried her to the heights, and now she felt herself descending. *Henry killed Father.* It was near impossible for her to speak.

Ramses took her hand in his.

"There should have been enough wealth for all of us," she said, her voice strained. "Enough for me, for Henry, for Henry's father."

"Yet your father dug in Egypt for treasure."

"No, not for treasure!" She looked at him sharply. "He dug to find evidence of the past. Your writings meant more to him than the rings on your fingers. The story you told, that was his treasure. That and the painted coffin because it was a pure thing, from your time."

"Archaeology," Ramses said.

"Yes." She smiled in spite of herself. "My father was not a robber of tombs."

"I understand you. Don't become angry."

"He was a scholar," she said, a little more gently. "He had all the money he needed. If he made a mistake, it was that he left his company to his brother, and to his nephew, but then he paid them so very well."

She stopped. She felt weary suddenly. Beneath the euphoria, she had been ever mindful of what happened; and the pain had only begun.

"Something went wrong," she whispered.

"Greed is what went wrong. Greed is what always goes wrong."

He was looking out the window at the dull, broken windows above. Foul smells rose from the puddles and from the doorway. The stench of urine, and decay.

She herself had never been in this part of London. It saddened her; it exacerbated her own pain.

"This Henry should be stopped," Ramses said firmly. "Before he tries again to hurt you. And your father's death, surely you want it avenged."

"It will kill my uncle Randolph when he finds out what happened. That is, if he doesn't already know."

"The uncle, the one who came this morning with such fear for you—he's innocent and is afraid for his son. But cousin Henry is evil. And the evil is unchecked."

She was trembling. The tears had risen to her eyes.

"I can't do anything now. He's my cousin. They're my only family. And when something is done, it will have to be in a court of law."

"You are in danger, Julie Stratford," he said to her.

"Ramses, I am not a Queen here. I cannot act on my own."

"But I am a King. I always will be. My conscience can bear this burden. Let me act when I see fit."

"No!" she whispered. She looked up at him imploringly. He pressed his arm against her, gently, then reached as if to embrace her. She held steady. "Promise me you will do nothing. If something happens, it will be on my conscience too."

"He killed your father."

"Kill him and you kill my father's daughter," she said.

There was a silent moment in which he merely looked at her, marvelling perhaps, she couldn't tell. She felt his right arm on her left arm. Then he drew her close to him, her breasts against his chest, and he kissed her, his mouth opening over hers. The heat was immediate and utterly consuming. She reached up to push him away, and found her fingers slipping up through his hair. She cradled his head gently. And then drew back, thoughtlessly, astonished.

For a moment she couldn't speak. Her face was flushed, and

she felt soft all over, and utterly exposed. She closed her eyes. She knew that if he touched her again, the game was up. She would end up making love to him in this cab, if she didn't do something. . . .

"What did you think I was, Julie?" he asked. "A spirit? I'm an immortal *man*."

He moved to kiss her again; she moved away, her hand up.

"Shall we speak again of Henry?" he asked. He took her hand and clasped it and kissed her fingers. "Henry knows what I am. He saw, because I moved to save your life, Julie. He saw. And there is no reason to let him live with this knowledge, since he is evil and deserves to die."

He knew she could hardly concentrate on the words he was speaking. It made her angry suddenly, his lips grazing her fingers, his blue eyes flashing like lights in the dim cab.

"Henry made a fool of himself with that story," she said. "And he won't try to hurt me again." She withdrew her hand and looked out the window. They were leaving this sad, miserable slum. Thank God.

He gave a little thoughtful shrug.

"Henry's a coward," she said. Her body was under control again. "A terrible coward. The way he did it to Father, such a coward."

"Cowards can be more dangerous than brave men, Julie," he said.

"Don't hurt him!" she whispered. She turned again to face Ramses. "For my sake, leave it to God. I can't be his judge and jury!"

"So like a Queen," he said. "And wiser than most Queens."

He bent slowly to kiss her again. She knew she ought to turn away, but she didn't. And the heat flooded her again, weakening her completely. When she pulled away, he tried to hold her; but her immediate resistance won out.

When she looked at him again, he was smiling.

"A guest in your court," he said with a little gesture of acceptance, "my Queen."

Elliott had not the slightest difficulty overwhelming Rita. Even as she begged him to understand that her mistress was not at home, and surely he must come back another time, he moved past her, directly into the Egyptian room.

"Ah, these lovely treasures. Not enough time in the world to examine them. Do get me a glass of sherry, Rita. I find I'm tired. I'll rest for a moment before going home.''

"Yes, sir, but—"

"Sherry, Rita."

"Yes, sir."

How anxious and pale she looked, poor girl. And what a mess this library was. There were books scattered everywhere. He looked at the table in the conservatory. He could see from where he stood that there were dictionaries stacked on the wicker table; papers and magazines in neat little piles all about the chairs.

But Lawrence's diary was here on the desk, just as he hoped. He opened it, confirmed that there was no mistake, then slipped it under his coat.

He was staring at the mummy case when Rita came to him, with the glass of sherry on a small silver tray.

Leaning heavily on his cane, he lifted the glass and took only a taste of it. "You wouldn't let me have a look at the mummy, now would you?" he asked.

"Good Lord, no, sir! Please don't touch it!" Rita said. Pure panic as she stared at the mummy case. "It's very heavy, sir! We mustn't try to lift it."

"There, there. You know as well as I do that it's a thin wooden shell, and not very heavy at all."

The girl was terrified.

He smiled. He took out a sovereign and gave it to her. She was astonished. She shook her head.

"No, take it, dearest. Buy yourself something pretty."

And before she could think what to say, he moved past her and towards the front door. She hurried to open it for him.

He paused only when he had reached the bottom of the steps. Now, why hadn't he forced the issue? Why hadn't he looked in that case?

His man Walter came forward to assist him. Good old Walter, who had been with him since he was a boy. He let Walter help him up into the idling car now, and he sat back, the pain in his hip biting deeply as he stretched out his legs.

Would he have been surprised to find that case empty, to discover that this was not a little game? On the contrary. He realized that he fully believed the case was empty. And he had been afraid to see that for himself.

* * *

Mr. Hancock of the British Museum was not a patient man. All his life he had used his devotion to Egyptian antiquities to bully people, to justify rudeness and downright meanness to others. This was part of his nature, as much as his genuine love for the relics and papyri which he had been studying all his life.

He read aloud the headline before him to the three other gentlemen in the room.

" 'Mummy Walks in Mayfair.' " He folded the papers. "This is perfectly disgusting. Is young Stratford out of his mind?"

The older gentleman who sat directly opposite on the other side of the desk merely smiled.

"Henry Stratford's a drunkard, and a gambler. The mummy climbed out of its case, indeed!"

"But the point is," said Hancock, "we have entrusted a priceless collection of antiquities to a private household, and now we have this little scandal! With Scotland Yard coming and going and reporters from the gutter press on the steps."

"If you will forgive me," the elder gentleman countered. "The matter of the stolen coin is much more disturbing."

"Yes," said Samir Ibrahaim quietly from the outer edge of the circle where he sat. "But I tell you there were only five when I cataloged the collection, and none of us has seen this so-called stolen coin."

"Nevertheless," said Hancock, "Mr. Taylor is a reputable coin dealer. He was certain the coin was authentic. And that it was Henry Stratford who offered it for sale."

"Stratford could have stolen it in Egypt," said the elder gentleman. There were a couple of nods from the circle.

"The collection should be in the museum," said Hancock. "We should be making our examinations of the Ramses mummy now. The Cairo Museum is angry about this controversy. And now, this coin—"

"But, gentlemen," Samir interrupted. "Surely we can make no decision about the safety of the collection until we've talked to Miss Stratford."

"Miss Stratford is very young," Hancock said snappishly. "And she is in a state of grief which clouds her judgment."

"Yes," said the elder gentleman. "But surely everyone present realizes that Lawrence Stratford contributed millions to this museum. No, I think Samir is right. We cannot move the collection until Miss Stratford gives her permission."

Hancock glanced again at the newspapers. " 'Ramses Rises from the Grave,' " he read. "I tell you I don't like it."

"Perhaps another guard should be posted," said Samir. "Perhaps two."

The elder gentleman nodded. "Good suggestion. But again, Miss Stratford's feelings are to be considered."

"Perhaps you should call on her!" Hancock said, glaring at Samir. "You were her father's friend."

"Very well, sir," Samir answered in a low voice. "I shall certainly do that."

Early evening: the Hotel Victoria. Ramses had been dining since four o'clock, when the sun was still slanting through the leaded glass, onto the white-draped tables. Now it was dark; candles blazed everywhere; the ceiling fans turned very slowly, barely stirring the fronds of the tall, elegant dark-green palms in their brass pots.

Liveried waiters brought plate after plate of food without comment, eyebrows arched as they opened the fourth bottle of Italian red wine.

Julie had finished her scant meal hours ago. They were deep in conversation now, the English flowing as easily as the wine flowed.

She had taught Ramses how to use the heavy silver, but he ignored it. In his time only a barbarian would have shoveled food into the mouth.

In fact, he had remarked after a little consideration, no one had shoveled food into the mouth. There was time for Julie to explain how silverware had come about. For now, she must agree that he was most, most . . . fastidious, she volunteered. Elegant, civilized, deft at the breaking of bread and meat into small portions, and the placing of them on the tongue without the fingers touching the lips.

She was now deep into her discussion of revolution. "The first machines were simple—for weaving, tilling the fields. It was the idea of the machine that caught the mind."

"Yes."

"If you make a machine to do one thing, then you can perfect a machine to do another. . . ."

"I understand you."

"And then came the steam engine, the motor car, the telephone, the aeroplane."

"I want to do it, fly in the sky."

"Of course, and we shall do it. But do you understand the concept, the revolution in thinking?"

"Of course. I don't come to you, as you say, from the nineteenth dynasty of Egypt's history, I come to you from the first days of the Roman Empire. My mind is, how do you say it, flexible, adaptable. I am constantly in, how do you say it, revolution?"

Something startled him; at first she didn't realize what it was. The orchestra had begun, very softly, so that she scarcely heard it over the hum of conversation. He rose, dropping his napkin. He pointed across the crowded room.

The soft strains of the "Merry Widow Waltz" rose strongly over the hum of conversation. Julie turned to see the little string orchestra assembled on the other side of the small polished dance floor.

Ramses rose and went towards them.

"Ramses, wait," Julie said. But he didn't listen to her. She hurried after him. Surely everyone was looking at the tall man who marched across the dance floor and came to a quick stop right in front of the musicians as if he were the conductor himself.

He positively glared at the violins, at the cello; and then as he studied the huge golden harp, the smile came back, so clearly ecstatic that the female violinist smiled at him and the old grey-haired male cellist seemed vaguely amused.

They must have thought him a deaf mute as he stepped up and laid his fingers right on the cello, drawing back at the power of the vibration, then touching it again.

"Oooh, Julie," he whispered aloud.

Everyone was looking. Even the waiters were glancing at them in obvious alarm. But nobody dared question the handsome gentleman in Lawrence's best suit and silk waistcoat, even when he shuddered all over and clamped his hands to the sides of his head.

She tugged on him. He wouldn't budge. "Julie, such sounds!" he whispered.

"Then dance with me, Ramses," she said.

No one else was dancing, but what did that matter? There was the dance floor, and she felt like dancing. She felt like dancing more than anything in the world.

Baffled, he looked at her, then allowed himself to be turned, and his hand to be taken properly as she slipped her arm about his waist.

"Now, this is the way the man leads the woman," she said, beginning the waltz step and moving him easily. "My hand should really be on your shoulder. I shall move, and you . . . that's it. But allow me to lead."

They turned faster and faster, Ramses following her lead beautifully, only glancing down now and then at his feet. Another couple had joined them; then came another. But Julie didn't see them; she saw only Ramses' rapt face, and the way his eyes moved over the commonplace treasures of the room. It was a haze suddenly, the candles, the gilded fan blades turning above, the drowsing flowers on the tables, and the shimmer of silver everywhere, and the music surrounding them, the music carrying them along ever faster.

He laughed out loud suddenly. "Julie, like music poured from a goblet. Like music that has become wine."

She turned him rapidly in small circles.

"Revolution!" he cried out.

She threw back her head and laughed.

Quite suddenly it was over. There must have been a finale. All she knew was that it was finished, and that he was about to kiss her, and she didn't want him to stop. But he hesitated. He noted the other couples leaving. He took her hand.

"Yes, time to go," she said.

The night outside was cold and foggy. She gave the doorman a few coins. She wanted a hansom.

Ramses paced back and forth, staring at the crowds of commercial travellers coming and going from motor cars and carriages, at the newsboy dashing up to him with the latest edition.

"Mummy's Curse in Mayfair!" the boy cried shrilly. "Mummy Rises from the Grave!"

Before she could reach him, Ramses had snatched the paper from the boy. Flustered, she gave the child a coin.

There it was all right, the whole silly scandal. An ink sketch of Henry running away from her front stairs.

"Your cousin," Ramses said gloomily. " 'Mummy's Curse Strikes Again . . .' " he read slowly.

"No one believes it! It's a joke."

He continued to read: "Gentlemen of the British Museum say that the Ramses collection is entirely safe and will be returned to the museum soon.'' He paused. "Museum,'' he said. "Explain this word *museum*. What is the museum, a tomb?''

The poor girl was miserable, Samir could see it. He ought to go. But he had to see Julie. And so he waited in the drawing room, sitting stiffly on the edge of the sofa, refusing Rita's third offer of coffee, tea, or wine.

Now and then he glanced down the length of the house to see the gleaming Egyptian coffin. If only Rita did not stand there, but clearly she was not going to leave him alone.

The museum had been closed for hours. But she wanted him to see it. She let the cab go and followed him to the iron fence. He gripped the pickets as he looked up at the door and the high windows. The street was dark, deserted. And a light rain had begun to fall.

"There are many mummies inside,'' she said. "Your mummy, it would have gone here eventually. Father worked for the British Museum, though he paid his own costs.''

"Mummies of Kings and Queens of Egypt?''

"There are more in Egypt, actually. A mummy of Ramses the Second has been there for years in a glass case.''

He gave a short bitter laugh as he looked at her. "Have you seen this?'' He looked back at the museum. "Poor fool. He never knew that he was buried in Ramses' tomb.''

"But who was he?'' Her heart quickened. Too many questions on the tip of her tongue.

"I never knew,'' he said quietly, eyes still moving slowly over the building as though he were memorizing. "I sent my soldiers to find a dying man, someone unloved and uncared for. They brought him back to the palace by night. And so I . . . how do you say? Made my own death. And then my son, Meneptah, had what he wanted, to be King.'' He considered for a moment. His voice changed slightly. It deepened. "And now you tell me this body is in a museum with other Kings and Queens?''

"In the Cairo Museum,'' she said softly. "Near Saqqara, and the pyramids. There's a great city there.''

She could see how this was affecting him. Very gently, she continued, though she could not tell whether or not he heard:

"In ancient times, the Valley of the Kings was looted. Grave robbers despoiled almost every tomb. The body of Ramses the

Great, it was found with dozens of others in a mass grave made for it by the priests.''

He turned and looked at her thoughtfully. Even in great distress, his face seemed open, his eyes searching.

"Tell me, Julie. Queen Cleopatra the Sixth, who ruled in the time of Julius Caesar. Her body lies in this Cairo Museum? Or here?'' He turned back to the dark building. She saw the subtle changes in him; the high colour again in his face.

"No, Ramses. No one knows what became of the remains of Cleopatra.''

"But you know this Queen, whose marble portrait was in my tomb.''

"Yes, Ramses, even schoolchildren know the name Cleopatra. All the world knows it. But her tomb was destroyed in ancient times. Ancient times were those times, Ramses.''

"I understand, better than I speak, Julie. Continue.''

"Nobody knows where her tomb stood. Nobody knows what happened to her body. The time of mummies had passed.''

"Not so!'' he whispered. "She was buried properly, in the old Egyptian fashion, without the magic, and the embalming, but she was wrapped in linen as was fitting, and then taken to her grave by the sea.''

He stopped. He put his hands to his temples. And then he rested his forehead against the iron fence. The rain came a little heavier. She felt chilled suddenly.

"But this mausoleum,'' he said, collecting himself, folding his arms and stepping back now as if he meant to say what he had to say. "It was a grand structure. It was large and beautiful and covered with marble.''

"So the ancient writers tell us. But it is gone. Alexandria contains no trace of it. No one knows where it stood.''

He looked at her in silence. "I know, of course,'' he said.

He walked away from her down the pavement. He stopped under the street lamp and gazed up into the dim yellow incandescent light. Tentatively, she followed. Finally he turned to her, and put out his hand for her and drew her close.

"You feel my pain,'' he said calmly. "Yet you know so little of me. What do I seem to you?''

She reflected. "A man,'' she said. "A beautiful and strong man. A man who suffers as we all suffer. And I know things . . . because you wrote them down yourself and you left the scrolls there.''

Impossible to tell if this pleased him.

"And your father read these things, too," he said.

"Yes. He made some translations."

"I watched him," he whispered.

"Was it true what you wrote?"

"Why should I lie?"

Suddenly he moved to kiss her, and again she backed off.

"Ah, but you choose the oddest moments for your little advances," she said breathlessly. "We were talking of . . . of tragedy, were we not?"

"Of loneliness, perhaps, and folly. And the things grief drives one to do."

His expression was softening. There was that playfulness again, that smile.

"Your temples are in Egypt. They still stand," she said. "The Ramasseum, at Luxor. Abu Simbel. Oh, these aren't the names by which you know them. Your colossal statues! Statues all the world has seen. English poets have written of them. Great generals have journeyed to see them. I've walked past them, laid my hands on them. I've stood in your ancient halls."

He continued to smile. "And now I walk these modern streets with you."

"And it fills you with joy to do it."

"Yes, that is very true. My temples were old before I ever closed my eyes. But the mausoleum of Cleopatra had only just been built." He broke off, letting go her hand. "Ah, it is like yesterday to me, you see. Yet it is dreamlike and distant. Somehow I felt the passage of the centuries as I slept. My spirit grew as I slept."

She thought of the words in her father's translation.

"What did you dream, Ramses?"

"Nothing, my darling dear, that can touch the wonders of this century!" He paused. "When we are weary, we speak lovingly of dreams as if they embodied our true desires—what we *would* have when that which we *do* have so sorely disappoints us. But for this wanderer, the concrete world has always been the true object of desire. And weariness came only when the world seemed dreamlike."

He stared off into the driving rain. She let his words sink in, trying in vain perhaps to grasp their full meaning. Her brief life had been marked with just enough pain to make her cherish what she had. The death of her mother years before had made her cleave all the more closely to her father. She had tried to love Alex Savarell because he wanted her to; and her father hadn't minded it. But what she really loved were ideas, and things, just as her father had. Was that what he meant? She wasn't certain.

"You don't want to go back to Egypt, you don't need to see the old world for yourself?" she asked.

"I am torn," he whispered.

A gust of damp wind swept the forlorn pavements; dry leaves scuttered and banked along the high iron fence. There came a dim zinging from the electric wires above, and Ramses turned to look at them.

"Ever more vivid than a dream," he whispered, staring again at the solitary yellow lamp above him. "I want this time, my darling dear," he said. "You forgive me if I call you this? My darling dear? As you called your friend, Alex."

"You may call me that," she said.

For I love you more than I ever loved him!

He gave her one of those warm, generous smiles. He came to her with his arms out and swept her up off her feet, suddenly.

"Light little Queen," he said.

"Put me down, great King," she whispered.

"And why should I do that?"

"Because I command you to do it."

He obeyed. He set her down gently and gave her a deep bow.

"And now where do we go, my Queen, home to the palace of Stratford, in the region of Mayfair, in the land of London, England, lately known as Britannia?"

"Yes, we do, because I am weary to the bone."

"Yes, and I must study in your father's library, if you permit. I must read the books now to 'put in order,' as you say, the things you've shown me."

Not a sound in the house. Where had the girl gone? The coffee Samir had finally accepted was now quite cold. He could not drink this watery brew. He had not wanted it in the first place.

He had stared fixedly at the mummy case for over an hour, it seemed, the clock chiming twice in the hallway, an occasional pair of headlights piercing the lace curtains and sweeping this high-ceilinged large room, and firing the mummy's gold face with life for an eerie instant.

Suddenly he rose. He could hear the creak of the floor beneath the carpet. He walked slowly towards the case. Lift it. And you will know. Lift it. Imagine. Could it be empty?

He reached out for the gilded wood, his hands poised, trembling.

"I wouldn't do that, sir!"

Ah, the girl. The girl again in the hallway with her hands clasped, the girl very afraid, but of what?

"Miss Julie would be so angry."

He could think of nothing to say. He gave an awkward little nod, and went back to the sofa.

"Perhaps tomorrow you should come," she said.

"No. I must see her tonight."

"But, sir, it's so very late."

The clop of a horse outside, the low creak of the hansom's wheels. He heard a sudden little laugh, very faint, but he knew it was Julie.

Rita hurried to the door and drew back the bolt. He stared speechless as the pair entered the room, Julie, radiant, her hair studded with sparkling droplets of rain; and a man, a tall, splendid-looking man, with dark brown hair and glittering blue eyes, beside her.

Julie spoke to him. She said his name. But it did not register.

He could not take his eyes off this man. The skin was pale, flawless. And the features exquisitely moulded. But the spirit inhabiting the man was the overwhelming characteristic. The man exuded strength and a sudden wariness that was almost chilling.

"I only wanted to . . . to look in on you," he said to Julie without so much as glancing at her. "To see that you were well. I worry on your account. . . ."

His voice trailed off.

"Ah, I know who you are!" said the man suddenly, in a faultless British accent. "You are Lawrence's friend, are you not? Your name is Samir."

"We have met?" Samir said. "I do not remember."

His eyes moved tentatively over the figure that approached him now, and suddenly he was staring fixedly at the outstretched hand, at the ruby ring, and the ring with the cartouche of Ramses the Great, and it seemed the room had become quite unreal; that the voices speaking to him were making no sense, and that there was no necessity to answer.

The ring he had seen through the mummy's wrappings! There

was no mistake. He could not make such a mistake. And what was Julie saying that could possibly matter now? Words so politely spoken, but all lies, and this being was staring back at him, knowing full well that he recognized the ring, knowing full well that words just didn't matter.

"I hope Henry didn't run to you with that nonsense of his. . . ." Yes, that was the meaning.

But it was not nonsense at all. And slowly he shifted his gaze and forced himself to see for himself that she was safe and sound and sane. Then he closed his eyes, and when he opened them again, he looked not at the ring but at the King's face, at the steady blue eyes which understood everything.

When he spoke to her again, it was a meaningless murmur: "Your father would not have wanted for you to be unprotected. Your father would have wanted me to come. . . ."

"Ah, but Samir, friend of Lawrence," the other said, "there is no danger now to Julie Stratford." And dropping suddenly into the ancient Egyptian with an accent Samir had never heard: "This woman is loved by me and shall be protected from all harm."

Stunning, that sound. He backed away. Julie was talking again. And again he wasn't listening. He had gone to the mantel shelf and held on to it now as if he might fall.

"Surely you know the ancient tongue of the Pharaohs, my friend," said the tall blue-eyed man. "You are Egyptian, are you not? All your life you have studied it. You can read it as well as you read Latin or Greek."

Such a carefully modulated voice; it was trying to dispel all fear; civilized, courteous. What more could Samir have wanted?

"Yes, sir, you are right," Samir said. "But I've never heard it spoken aloud, and the accent has always been a mystery. But you must tell me—" He forced himself to look at the man directly again. "You are an Egyptologist, I have been told. Do you believe it was the curse on the tomb that killed my beloved friend, Lawrence? Or did death take him naturally as we supposed?"

The man appeared to weigh the question; and in the shadows some feet away, Julie Stratford paled and lowered her eyes, and turned just a little away from both of them.

"Curses are words, my friend," the man said. "Warnings to drive away the ignorant and meddlesome. It requires poison or some other crude weapon to take a human life unnaturally."

"Poison!" Samir whispered.

"Samir, it's very late," Julie said. Her voice was raw, strained. "We mustn't speak of all this now, or I'll give way to tears again and feel foolish. We must speak of these things only when we really want to examine them." She came forward and took both his hands. "I want you to come another night, when we can all sit down together."

"Yes, Julie Stratford is very tired. Julie Stratford has been a great teacher. And I bid you good night, my friend. You are my friend, are you not? There are many things perhaps that we can say to each other. But for now, believe I shall protect Julie Stratford from anyone or anything that would hurt her."

Samir walked slowly to the door.

"If you need me," he said, turning back, "you must send for me." He reached into his coat. He took out his card and stared at it, quite baffled for a moment. Then he gave it to the man. He watched the ring glinting in the light as the man took it from him.

"I am in my office at the British Museum very late every night. I walk the corridors when everyone is gone. Come to the side door, and you will find me."

But why was he saying these things? What did he mean to convey? He wished suddenly the creature would speak the ancient tongue again; he could not understand the strange mixture of pain and joy that he felt; the strange darkening of the world, and the keen appreciation of light which had come with that darkening.

He turned and went out, hurrying down the granite steps and past the uniformed guards without so much as a glance in their direction. He walked fast through the cold damp streets. He ignored the cabs that slowed. He wanted only to be alone. He kept seeing that ring; hearing those old Egyptian words finally defined aloud as he had never heard them. He wanted to weep. A miracle had been revealed; yet somehow it threatened the miraculous all around him.

"Lawrence, give me guidance," he whispered.

Julie shut the door and slipped the bolt.

She turned to Ramses. She could hear Rita's tread on the floor above. They were alone, quite beyond Rita's hearing.

"You don't mean to trust him with your secret!" she asked.

"The harm is done," he said quietly. "He knows the truth.

And your cousin Henry will tell others. And others, too, will come to believe.''

"No, that's impossible. You saw yourself what happened with the police. Samir knows because he saw the ring; he recognized it. And because he came to see, and came to believe. Others will not do that. And somehow . . .''

"Somehow?''

"You wanted him to know. That's why you addressed him by name. You told him who you were.''

"Did I?''

"Yes, I think that you did.''

He pondered this. He didn't find the idea too agreeable. But it was true, she could have sworn so.

"Two who believe can make three,'' he said, as if she hadn't made the point at all.

"They cannot prove it. You're real, yes, and the ring is real. But what is there really to connect you with the past! You don't understand these times if you think it takes so little for men to believe that one has risen from the grave. This is the age of science, not religion.''

He was collecting his thoughts. He bowed his head and folded his arms and moved back and forth on the carpet. Then he stopped:

"Oh, my darling dear, if only you understood,'' he said. There was no urgency in his voice, but there was great feeling. And it seemed the cadence was English now, almost intimately so. "For a thousand years I guarded this truth,'' he said, "even from those I loved and served. They never knew whence I came, or how long I'd lived, or what had befallen me. And now I've blundered into your time, revealing this truth to more mortals in one full moon than ever knew it since Ramses ruled Egypt.''

"I understand,'' she said. But she was thinking something else quite different. *You wrote the whole story in the scrolls. You left them there. And that was because you could not bear this secret any longer.* "You don't understand these times,'' she said again. "Miracles aren't believed, even by those to whom they happen.''

"What a strange thing to say!''

"Were I to shout it from the rooftops no one would believe. Your elixir is safe, with or without these poisons.''

It seemed a shock of pain went through him. She saw it. She felt it. She regretted her words. What madness to think this creature is all powerful, that his ready smile doesn't conceal a vulnerability as vast as his strength. She was at a loss. She waited. And then his smile, once again, came to her rescue.

"What can we do but wait and see, Julie Stratford?"

He sighed. He removed his frock coat, and walked away from her into the Egyptian room. He stared at the coffin, his coffin, and then at the row of jars. He reached down and carefully switched on the electric lamp, as he had seen her do, and then looked up at the rows and rows of books rising over Lawrence's desk to the ceiling.

"Surely you need to sleep," she said. "Let me take you upstairs to Father's room."

"No, my darling dear, I do not sleep, except when I mean to take leave of life for the time being."

"You mean . . . day in and day out, you need no sleep whatsoever!"

"That is correct," he said, flashing her another little smile. "I shall tell you another wicked secret too. I do not need the food or the drink I take, I merely crave it. And my body enjoys it." He laughed softly at her shock. "But what I do need now is to read in your father's books, if you will allow me."

"Of course, you needn't ask me for such a thing," she said. "You must take what you need and what you want. Go to his room when you wish. Put on his robe. I want you to have every comfort." She laughed. "I'm beginning to speak the way you speak."

They looked at each other. Only a few feet separated them, and she was grateful for them.

"I'll leave you now," she said, but instantly he caught her hand, and closed the distance and locked her in his arms, and kissed her again. Then, almost roughly he let her go.

"Julie is Queen in her own domain," he said, a little apologetically.

"And your words to Samir, let us remember them. 'But for now, I shall protect Julie Stratford from anyone or anything that would hurt her.' "

"I did not lie. And I should like to lie at your side, the better to protect you."

She laughed softly. Better escape now while it was still morally and physically possible. "Oh, but there is one other thing," she said. She went to the far northeast corner of the room, and opened the cabinet gramophone. She cranked the thing, and looked at the RCA Victor records. Verdi's *Aïda*. "Ah, the very thing," she said. And no appalling picture on the front of the album to repel him. She put the heavy, brittle black disk on the velvet turntable. She set the arm in place. And then turned to watch his face as the triumphal march from the opera began, a low, faraway chorus of lovely voices.

"Oooh, but what is this magic! The machine is making music!"

"Just wind and play. And I shall sleep as mortal women do, dreaming, though real life has become all I ever dreamed it would be."

She glanced back once to see him rocking to the music, his arms folded, his head bowed. He was singing with it, very low, under his breath. And even the simple sight of the white shirt stretched taut over his broad back and powerful arms sent the shivers through her.

8

AS MIDNIGHT struck, Elliott closed the notebook. He had spent the evening reading Lawrence's translations through and through, and reexamining his dusty old biographies of the King called Ramses the Great, and the Queen known as Cleopatra. There was nothing in these historical tomes that could not accommodate the assertions of the mummy's preposterous story.

A man who ruled Egypt for sixty years might damn well have been immortal. And the reign of Cleopatra VI had been by any standards utterly remarkable.

But what intrigued him more than anything at the moment was a paragraph Lawrence had written in Latin and in Egyptian—the very last of his notes. Elliott had had no trouble reading this. He had kept his diary in Latin when he was in Oxford; and he had studied Egyptian for years along with Lawrence, and then on his own.

This was not a transcript of the material in Ramses' scrolls. Rather the paragraph contained Lawrence's private comments on what he'd read.

"Claims to have taken this elixir once and once only. No further infusion was required. Brewed the mix for Cleopatra, but felt it was unsafe to discard it. Reluctant to take it into his body for fear of adverse results. What if all chemicals in this tomb are properly tested? What if there is some chemical here which has a rejuvenating effect upon the human body, and can substantially prolong life?''

The two lines in Egyptian were incoherent. They said something about magic, secrets, natural ingredients combined to wholly new effect.

So that is what Lawrence had believed, more or less. And he had taken pains to conceal it in the ancient languages. Now what did Elliott really believe about this situation? Especially in light of Henry's story of the mummy coming to life?

It occurred to him again that he was playing a very dramatic little game; that belief is a word we seldom thoroughly examine. For example, he had all his life "believed" in the teaching of the Church of England. But he did not really for a moment expect to enter a Christian heaven when he died, and certainly not a Christian hell. He would not have gambled one farthing on the existence of either.

One thing was most certain. If he had actually seen the thing climb out of the coffin, as Henry claimed to have done, he would not be behaving like Henry. A man of no imagination, that was Henry. Perhaps the lack of imagination had always been the tragic flaw. It occurred to him that Henry was a man who did not grasp the *implications* of things.

Far from running from this mystery, as Henry had chosen to do, Elliott had become obsessed with it. If only he had stayed longer in the Stratford house, been a little more clever. He could have examined those alabaster jars; he could have taken one of the scrolls. That poor little Rita would have settled for just about any explanation.

He wished he had tried.

He also wished that his son, Alex, were not suffering. For that was the only unpleasant aspect of this entertaining mystery so far.

Alex had been calling Julie all day. He was in a great state of alarm over the guest in Julie's house, whom he had only glimpsed through the conservatory doors—"an enormous man, well, very tall, anyhow, with blue eyes. Quite a . . . a good-looking fellow, but certainly too old to be courting Julie!''

Then at eight this evening, there had come a call from one of those well-meaning friends who make a point of circulating rumours relentlessly. Julie had been seen dancing at the Victoria Hotel with a handsome and imposing stranger. Were not Alex and Julie engaged? Alex was now beside himself with worry.

Though he had called Julie every hour upon the hour all after-noon, there had been no response from her. Finally he had begged his father to intervene. Could not Elliott get to the bot-tom of this?

Yes. Elliott would get to the bottom of this. In fact, Elliott felt curiously enlivened by this entire development. Elliott felt almost young, daydreaming about Ramses the Great and his elixir hidden among poisons.

He rose now from his comfortable chair by the fire, ignoring the familiar pain in his legs, and went to his desk to write a letter.

Dearest Julie,

It has come to my attention that you are entertaining a guest, a friend of your father's, I believe. It would give me great pleasure to meet this gentleman. Perhaps I can be of some service to you during his stay, and certainly would not wish to miss such an opportunity.

May I ask you to join us here tomorrow night for family dinner. . . .

In a few moments he had finished this note. He put it in an envelope, sealed it, and took it into the front hall, where he laid it in a silver tray for his man, Walter, to deliver in the morning. Then he paused. Of course it was what Alex wanted him to do. But he knew that he was not doing it for Alex. And he knew that if any such dinner took place that Alex might be hurt even more than he had been already. On the other hand, the sooner Alex realized . . . He stopped. He did not really know what it was that Alex was supposed to realize. He knew only that he himself was inflamed with the mystery that was slowly unfolding before him.

He limped uneasily to the hook behind the stairs, removed his heavy serge cloak and then went out the side door of the house onto the street. There were four motor cars parked there.

But the Lancia Theta with the electric starter was the only one he ever drove. And a whole year had passed during which he had not enjoyed that extraordinary pleasure.

It delighted him now that he might take the thing out all alone, without having to consult a groom, a coachman, a valet or a chauffeur. What a lovely development, that such a complex in-vention took one back to simplicity.

The worst of it was easing himself onto the front seat, but he managed it. Then he pressed down on the starter pedal, gave it petrol and he was soon on horseback again, free, as he'd been when he was a young man, heading toward Mayfair at a gallop.

Leaving Ramses, Julie hurried up the stairs and into her room, closing the door behind her. For a long moment she leaned against the door, her eyes closed. She could hear Rita bustling about. She could smell the fragrant wax of the candles Rita always lighted by her bed. A romantic little touch that Julie retained from her childhood—before there had been electric lights—when the smell of the gaslights had always faintly sickened her.

She thought of nothing now except all that had happened: it filled her so completely there was no room for true reflection or evaluation. That pounding sense of an all-consuming adventure was the only attitude she could rationally identify within herself. Except of course for a physical attraction to Ramses that was acutely painful.

No, not merely physical. She was falling in love totally.

As she opened her eyes, she saw the portrait of Alex on her dressing table. And Rita in the shadows, who had just laid out her nightgown over the lace-covered counterpane. Then gradually she became aware of flowers everywhere. Bouquets of flowers in glass vases on the dressing table, on the night tables, on her desk in the corner.

"From the Viscount, miss," Rita said. "All these bouquets. I don't know what he's going to think, miss, about all this . . . these strange goings-on. I don't know what I think myself, miss. . . ."

"Of course you don't," Julie said, "but, Rita, you mustn't tell a soul, you know that."

"Who would believe me, miss!" Rita said. "But I don't understand it, miss. How did he hide in that box? Why does he eat all that food?"

For a moment Julie couldn't answer. What in the world was Rita thinking?

"Rita, there's nothing to worry about," she said firmly. She took Rita's hands in hers. "Will you believe me when I tell you that he is a good man, and there is a good explanation for everything!"

Rita stared blankly at Julie. Her small blue eyes grew very

wide suddenly. "But, Miss Julie!" she whispered. "If he's a good man, why did he have to sneak into London like that? And why didn't he smother under all that wrapping?"

Julie considered for a moment.

"Rita, my father knew of the plan," she said soberly. "He approved of it."

Can we really burn in hell for telling lies? Julie thought. Especially lies that calm other people immediately?

"I might even add," Julie said, "that the man had a very important purpose here. And only a few people in the government know about it."

"Ohhhh . . . ." Rita was dumbfounded.

"Of course a few very important people at Stratford Shipping know as well, but you mustn't breathe a word. Especially not to Henry, or Uncle Randolph, or Lord Rutherford or anyone else, you see. . . ."

Rita nodded. "Very well, miss. I didn't know it was like that."

After the door had closed, Julie started to laugh and put her hand to her mouth like a schoolgirl. But the truth was, it made perfect sense. For what Rita believed, mad as it seemed, was a great deal more plausible than what had really happened.

What had really happened. She sat down before her mirror. She began almost idly to take the pins from her hair, and her vision blurred as she looked at her own reflection. She saw the room as if through a veil; she saw the flowers; she saw the white lace curtains of her bed; she saw her world, remote, and no longer important.

She drifted slowly through the motions of brushing her hair, of rising, undressing, putting on her gown, and climbing under the covers. The candles still burned. The room had a soft lovely glow. The flowers gave a faint perfume.

Tomorrow she would take him to the museums, if he wanted. They would take a train perhaps out in the country. To the Tower of London they might go. Oh, so many things . . . so many, many things. . . .

And there came that great lovely cessation of all thought; she saw him; she saw herself and him together.

Samir had been sitting at his desk for the better part of an hour. He had drunk half a bottle of Pernod, a liqueur he had always loved, which he had discovered in a French café in Cairo. He wasn't drunk, however; he had merely blunted the palm-tingling agitation that had taken possession of him shortly after he left the Stratford house. But when he tried to really think about what was going on, the agitation would return again.

He was suddenly startled by a tap at his window. His office was at the back of the museum. And the only light shining in the entire building was his light, and perhaps another somewhere deep inside where the night guards took their cigarettes and coffee.

He could not see the figure outside. But he knew who it was. And he was on his feet before the tap came again. He went into the back corridor, and to a rear door and opened it on the back alleyway.

In a rain-spattered coat, his shirt open and unbuttoned halfway down the front, Ramses the Great stood waiting for him. Samir stepped out into the darkness. The rain had left a sheen on the stone walls, and on the pavement. But nothing seemed to shimmer quite like this tall, commanding figure before him.

"What can I do for you, sire?" Samir asked. "What service can I render?"

"I want to come in, honest one," Ramses said. "If you will permit, I would like to see the relics of my ancestors and of my children."

A lovely tremor passed through Samir at these words. He felt tears springing to his eyes. He could not have explained this bittersweet happiness to anyone.

"Gladly, sire," he said. "Let me be your guide. It is a great privilege."

Elliott saw the lights in Randolph's library. He parked his car at the kerb, right beside the old mews, climbed out and somehow managed to get up the steps and ring the bell. Randolph himself, in shirt-sleeves and with the stale smell of wine on his breath, came to answer.

"Good Lord, do you know what time it is?" he asked. He turned and allowed Elliott to follow him back into the library. What a grand affair it was, chock full of all the accoutrements money could buy for such a room, including prints of dogs and horses, and maps which no one ever looked at.

"I'll tell you the truth right off. I'm too tired for anything else," Randolph said. "You've come at a very good time to answer a very important question."

"And what is that?" Elliott said. He watched Randolph settle at his desk, a great monstrous thing of mahogany with heavy carving. There were papers and account books all over the top of it. There were bills in heaps. And a great huge ugly telephone, and leather containers for clips, pens, paper.

"The ancient Romans," Randolph said, sitting back and drinking his wine without a thought to offering Elliott any. "What did they do when they were dishonoured, Elliott? They slit their wrists, did they not? And bled to death gracefully."

Elliott eyed the man, his red eyes, the slight palsy of his hand. Then he put his walking stick to use as he climbed to his feet again. He went to the desk and poured himself a glass of wine from the decanter. He refilled Randolph's glass, and then retreated to his chair again.

Randolph watched all this but appeared to attach no significance to it whatsoever. He rested his elbows on the desk before him, and ran his heavy wrinkled fingers through his grey hair as he stared at the heap of papers.

"If memory serves me right," Elliott said, "Brutus fell on his sword. Mark Antony later tried the same trick, and made a mess of it. He then climbed a rope to Cleopatra's bedchamber. And there managed somehow to kill himself again, or to die finally. She chose the poison of a snake. But yes, to answer your question, Romans did from time to time slit their wrists, that's true. But will you allow me to observe that no amount of money is worth a man's life. And you must stop thinking of this."

Randolph smiled. Elliott tasted the wine. Very good. The Stratfords always drank good wine. Day in and day out, they drank vintages that others saved for momentous occasions.

"Is that so?" Randolph said. "No amount of money. And where am I going to get the amount of money I need to prevent my niece from understanding the full extent of my perfidy?"

The Earl shook his head. "If you take your life, she will undoubtedly find out everything."

"Yes, and I shall not be there to answer her questions."

"A small point, and not worth the price of your remaining years. You're talking nonsense."

"Am I? She isn't going to marry Alex. You know she isn't. And she wouldn't turn her back on Stratford Shipping even if she did. There's nothing standing between me and the final disaster."

"Oh, yes, there is."

"And what is that?"

"Give it a few days and see if I'm not right. Your niece has herself a new distraction. Her guest from Cairo, Mr. Reginald Ramsey. Alex is miserable about it, of course, but Alex will recover. And this Reginald Ramsey may very well sweep Julie away from Stratford Shipping as well as from my son. And your problems may find a very simple solution. She may forgive you everything."

"I saw that fellow!" Randolph said. "Saw him this morning when Henry made that asinine scene. You don't mean to tell me . . ."

"I have a hunch, as Americans say. Julie and this man . . ."

"Henry ought to be in that house!"

"Forget it. What you're saying doesn't matter."

"Well, you sound downright cheerful about this! I should have thought you'd be more upset than I am."

"It's unimportant."

"Since when?"

"Since I began to think, really think, about what our lives consist of. Old age and death await us all. And we cannot face that simple truth, so we look for endless distractions."

"Good God, Elliott! You're not talking to Lawrence, you're talking to Randolph. I wish I could share your grand perspective. At the moment I'd sell my soul for one hundred thousand pounds. And so would a lot of other men."

"I wouldn't," Elliott said. "And I don't have one hundred thousand pounds and I never will. If I had it, I'd give it to you."

"You would?"

"Yes, I believe so. But let me take this conversation in another direction. Julie may not wish to be questioned about her friend Mr. Ramsey. She may want some time alone, some real independence. And you might find everything in your hands again."

"You mean this?"

"Yes, and now I'm going home. I'm tired, Randolph. Don't slit your wrists. Drink all you want, but don't do anything so dreadful to all of us. Tomorrow night, come to my house for dinner. I've invited Julie and this mysterious man. Don't fail me. And when it's all over, perhaps we'll have a better idea as to where things stand. You may get everything you want. And I may have the solution to a mystery. Can I count on you for tomorrow night?"

"Dinner, tomorrow night?" Randolph said. "You came here at one in the morning to ask me this?"

Elliott laughed. He set down the glass and stood up.

"No," he said. "I came to save your life. Believe me, it's not worth it, one hundred thousand pounds. Just being alive . . . not being in pain . . . but then why try to explain?"

"Yes, don't put yourself out."

"Good night, my friend. Don't forget. Tomorrow night. I'll see myself to the door. Now go to bed like a good man, will you?"

With an electric torch, Samir had led Ramses rapidly through the entire collection. Whatever the King felt, the King did not confess. He studied each large object—mummy, sarcophagus, statue—in turn, barely observing the multitude of tiny relics that filled cases galore.

Their footsteps echoed carelessly on the stone floor. The lone guard, long used to Samir's nocturnal wanderings, left them alone.

"In Egypt are the real treasures," Samir said. "The bodies of the Kings. This is but a fraction of what has been saved from pillage and from time."

Ramses had paused. He was examining a Ptolemaic mummy case, one of those curious hybrid creations which consisted of an Egyptian coffin with a realistic Greek face painted upon it, rather than the stylized mask of earlier centuries. This was the coffin of a woman.

"Egypt," Ramses whispered. "Suddenly I cannot see the present for the past. I can't embrace this age until I have said my farewells to those years completely."

Samir found himself shivering in the dark. The sweet sadness gave way to fear again, a deep silent terror of this unnatural thing which he knew now to be true. There could be no error.

The King turned his back on the Egyptian rooms. "Lead me out, my friend," he said. "I am lost in this maze. I do not like the concept of a museum."

Samir walked quickly at his side, the beam shining on the floor directly before them.

"Sire, if you desire to go to Egypt, do it now. That is my advice to you, though I know you do not ask it. Take Julie Stratford if you will. But leave England."

"Why do you say this?"

"The authorities know that coins have been stolen from the collection! They want to reclaim the mummy of Ramses the Great. There is much talk and suspicion."

Samir could see the menace in Ramses' face. "The accursed Henry Stratford," he said under his breath, quickening his pace ever so slightly. "He poisoned his uncle, a man of learning and wisdom. His own flesh and blood. And stole from that man a golden coin as the body lay dying."

Samir stopped. The shock was more than he could bear. Instantly he knew it was true. He had known when he saw the body of his friend that something was terribly wrong. It had not been a natural death. But he had believed Henry Stratford a coward. Slowly he caught his breath. He looked at the tall shadowy figure standing beside him.

"You tried to tell me this earlier tonight," he whispered. "I didn't want to believe it."

"I saw it, my beloved servant," the King said. "With my own eyes. Just as I saw you come to the body of your friend Lawrence and begin to weep. These things were mixed with my waking dreams; but I remember them most clearly."

"Ah, but this cannot go unavenged." Samir was trembling.

Ramses placed a hand on his shoulder. They proceeded slowly.

"And this Henry Stratford knows my secret," Ramses said. "The tale he told was true. For when he tried by the same means to take the life of his cousin, I came out of the coffin to prevent it. Oh, if only I had had my full strength, I would have finished it, there and then. I should have embalmed him myself and wrapped him up and put him in the painted coffin for all the world to see as Ramses."

Samir smiled bitterly. "A just reward," he said under his breath. He felt the tears on his face, but there was none of the relief that tears should bring. "And what will you do now, sire?"

"Kill him, of course. For Julie's sake and for my sake. There is no other possibility."

"You wait for the opportunity?"

"I wait for permission. Julie Stratford has the delicate conscience of one unused to bloodshed. She loves her uncle; she shrinks from violence. And I understand her reasoning, but I grow impatient. And angry. I want this Henry to threaten us no more."

"And what of me? I too know your secret now, sire. Will you kill me to protect it?"

Ramses stopped in his tracks. "I don't ask kindnesses of those I mean to harm. But tell me. On your honour, who else knows the truth?"

"Lord Rutherford, the father of the young man who courts Julie. . . ."

"Ah, the one called Alex, with the gentle eyes."

"Yes, sire. The father is a man to be reckoned with. He suspects. More significantly, he may believe, more earnestly even than young Stratford."

"This knowledge is poison! As deadly as the poisons in my tomb. First there will be fascination, then greed, and finally desperation."

They had reached the side door. The rain was coming down. Samir could see it through the thick glass, though he could not hear it.

"Tell me why this knowledge isn't poison to you," Ramses asked.

"I don't wish to live forever, sire."

Silence.

"I know. I can see this. But in my heart of hearts, I don't understand it."

"Strange, sire, that I must give you explanations. You who must know things I shall never know."

"I shall be grateful for the explanation."

"I have found it hard enough to live this long as it is. I loved my friend. I fear for his daughter. I fear for you. I fear to acquire knowledge which I cannot use to any moral purpose."

Again there was a pause.

"You're a wise man," Ramses said. "But don't fear for Julie. I will protect Julie, even from myself."

"Take my advice and leave here. There are wild rumours. And the empty coffin, it will be discovered. But if you are gone, all this will die away. It has to die away. The rational mind cannot have it otherwise."

"Yes. I will go. I must see Egypt again. I must see the modern city of Alexandria covering the palaces and streets I knew. I must see Egypt again merely to be done with it, and go on to the modern world. But when, that is the question."

"You'll need papers to travel, sire. In this age, one cannot be a man without an identity. I can obtain those papers for you."

Ramses considered. Then: "Tell me where I can find Henry Stratford."

"I don't know that, sire. I might kill him myself now, if I did. He lodges with his father when he chooses. He keeps a mistress as well. I urge you to leave England now, and let this revenge wait for a proper moment. Let me get you the documents you need."

Ramses nodded, but this was not a nod of agreement. He was merely acknowledging the generosity of the advice, Samir knew that.

"How do I reward your loyalty, Samir?" he asked. "What do you want that I can give?"

"To be near you, sire. To know you. To hear now and then the smallest part of your wisdom. You have eclipsed the mysteries I loved. You are the mystery now. But I ask nothing, really, except that for your own safety you go. And that you protect Julie Stratford."

Ramses smiled approvingly.

"Get the travel documents for me," he said.

He reached into his pocket and produced a shining gold coin which Samir recognized immediately. He did not need to study the engraving.

"No, sire, I cannot. This is not a coin any longer. It is more. . . ."

"Use it, my friend. There are many, many more where it came from. In Egypt I have riches hidden which I myself can no longer measure."

Samir took the coin, though what he would do with it he was not certain.

"I can get what you want."

"And for yourself? Whatever is required that you might travel with us?"

Samir felt his pulse quicken. He stared at the King's face, only partially revealed by the grey light through the door.

"Yes, sire, if that's what you wish. I will gladly go with you."

Ramses made a small polite gesture; Samir at once opened the door; Ramses gave him a little bow and passed out into the rain silently.

For a long time, Samir stood there, feeling the cold spray from outside, yet not moving. Then he closed and locked the door. He walked through the dark corridors of the museum until he had reached the front foyer.

A great statue of Ramses the Great stood there as it had for many years, greeting all those who entered the museum.

It had brought only a passing smile from the King. But Samir stared at it, aware that his attitude was one of silent worship.

Inspector Trent sat at his desk at Scotland Yard pondering. It was past two. Sergeant Galton had long ago gone home. And he himself was tired. Yet he could not stop thinking of all the aspects of this strange case, which now encompassed a murder.

He had never become accustomed to examining corpses. Yet he'd gone to the morgue to see the body of Tommy Sharples for one very important reason. A rare Greek coin had been found in Sharples's pocket, a coin identical with the "Cleopatra coins" in the Stratford collection. And there had been a small address book on Sharples's person as well, which contained the name and addresses of Henry Stratford.

Henry Stratford, who had run out of his cousin's house in Mayfair this morning, crying that a mummy had climbed out of its coffin.

Yes, a puzzle.

That Henry Stratford possessed a rare Cleopatra coin would not have surprised anyone. He had tried to sell such a coin only two days ago, that was now almost certain. But why would he have tried to pay his debts with such a valuable piece of gold, and why did the thief who murdered Sharples not steal it?

Trent would call the British Museum about the coin first thing in the morning. That is, after he hauled Stratford out of bed and questioned him about the murder of Sharples.

But the whole thing didn't make sense. And then there was the question of the murder itself. Surely Henry Stratford hadn't done it. A gentleman like that could hold off his creditors for months. Beside, he just wasn't the sort to sink a knife into a man's chest, at least Trent didn't think so.

But he wasn't the sort to run screaming from his cousin's house that a mummy had tried to strangle him either.

And then there was another thing. A most disturbing thing. It was the manner in which Miss Stratford had responded when told of her cousin's mad story. She hadn't seemed shocked so much as coldly indignant. Why, the story itself didn't surprise her at all. And then there was that strange gentleman staying at her house and the way that Stratford had stared at him. The young woman had been hiding something, that was clear. Perhaps he should stop by and just have a look about the house, and talk with the guard for a little while.

After all, he wasn't going to get any sleep tonight anyway.

9

THE SMALL hours. Ramses stood in the hallway of Julie's palatial house, observing the intricately carved hands of the grandfather clock move into place. At last the big hand bisected the Roman numeral twelve, and the small hand bisected the Roman numeral four, and the clock began its deep, melodious chime.

Roman numerals. Everywhere he looked he saw them; on cornerstones, in the pages of books; on the facades of buildings. In fact, the art, the language, the spirit of Rome ran through this entire culture, hooking it firmly to the past. Even the concept of justice which so strongly influenced Julie Stratford had come down not from the barbarians who once ruled this place with their crude ideas of revealed law and tribal vengeance, but from the courts and judges of Rome where reason had reigned.

The great banks of the money changers were fashioned like Roman temples. Great marble statues of figures in Roman dress stood in public places. The curiously graceless houses that crowded this street had small Roman columns and even peristyles over the doors.

He turned around and went back into the library of Lawrence Stratford and sat down again in the man's comfortable leather chair. He had placed lighted candles all about this room for his own pleasure, and now it had the very pitch of light he so loved. Of course the little maidservant would faint dead away in the morning when she saw the dripping wax everywhere, but never mind. She would certainly clean it away.

He loved this room of Lawrence Stratford—Lawrence Stratford's books and his desk. Lawrence Stratford's gramophone playing "Beethoven," a medley of squeaky little horns that sounded oddly like a chorus of cats.

How curious that he had taken possession of so much that had belonged to this white-haired Englishman who had broken down the door of his tomb.

All day wearing Lawrence Stratford's stiff and heavy official garments. And now, at ease once again, in Lawrence Stratford's silk "pyjamas" and satin robe. The most puzzling part of modern dress had been the man's leather shoes. Surely human feet were not meant to wear this kind of covering. It was more than a soldier needed to protect him in the heat of battle. Yet even the poor wore these little torture chambers, though some were lucky enough to have worn holes through the leather, making a rough sandal of sorts so their feet could breathe.

He laughed at himself. After all he had seen today, he was thinking of shoes. His feet didn't hurt anymore. So why not forget it?

No pain ever stayed with him very long; or any pleasure. For example, he smoked Lawrence Stratford's delicious cigars now, drawing in the smoke slowly, so that it made him dizzy. But the dizziness went away at once. So it was with the brandy as it always had been. He experienced drunkenness only for an instant, when he first swallowed and the delicious heat of the drink was still in his chest.

His body simply threw off the effects of things. Yet he could taste and smell and feel. And the strange tinny music winding out of the gramophone gave him so much pleasure that he felt he might start weeping again.

So much to enjoy. So much to study! Since coming back from the museum, he had torn through five or six books in the library of Lawrence Stratford. He had read complex and exhilarating discussions of the "Industrial Revolution." He had dabbled a bit in the ideas of Karl Marx, which were sheer nonsense, as far as he could see. A rich man, it seemed, writing about poor men when he did not know how their minds worked. He had reexamined the world globe many times as he memorized the names of continents and countries. Russia, now that was an interesting country. And this America was the greatest mystery of all.

Then he had read Plutarch, the liar! How dare the bastard say that Cleopatra had tried to seduce Octavian, her last conqueror. What a monstrous idea! There was something about Plutarch which made him think of old men gossiping as they gathered on benches in public squares. No *gravitas* to the history.

But enough. Why think about that! There was a sudden confusion in him. What troubled him, made him a little afraid?

Not all the wonders he'd discovered in this twentieth-century world since morning; not the coarse abrasive English language, which he had mastered before afternoon; not the length of time that had passed since he'd closed his eyes. What troubled him was this entire question of the way his body constantly restored itself—wounds healing; cramped feet relaxing; brandy having little or no effect.

It was troubling him because for the first time in all his long existence he was beginning to wonder if his heart and mind were not subject to some similar system of uncontrollable renewal. Did mental pain leave him as easily as physical pain?

Not possible. Yet if that was not so, why hadn't his little trip to the British Museum made him cry out in agony? Numb and silent, he had walked among mummies and sarcophagi and manuscripts stolen from all the dynasties of Egypt even to the time in which he had retreated from Alexandria to his last tomb in the Egyptian hills. Yet Samir had been the one who suffered, beautiful golden-skinned Samir, whose eyes were black as Ramses' had once been. Great Egyptian eyes, those, the same after countless centuries. Samir, his child.

It was not that the memories weren't vivid. They were. Like yesterday, it seemed, that he had watched them carry the coffin of Cleopatra out of the mausoleum and down to the Roman cemetery by the sea. He could smell that sea again if he wanted to. He could hear the weeping all around him. He could feel the stones through the thin leather of his sandals as he'd felt it then.

Beside Mark Antony she had asked to be buried; and so it had been done. He'd stood in the crowds, a common man, with his coarse cloak wrapped around him, listening to the wailing of the mourners. "Our great Queen is dead."

His grief had been an agony. So why was he not weeping now? He sat in this room staring at her marble bust, and the pain was just beyond his reach.

"Cleopatra," he whispered. Playfully, he envisioned her not as the woman on her deathbed, but as the young girl who had awakened him: *Rise, Ramses the Great. A Queen of Egypt calls you. Come out of your deep sleep and be my counsel in this time of woe.*

No, he did not feel either the joy or the pain.

Did this mean the capacity to suffer had been affected by the powerful elixir that never ceased its work in his veins? Or was it something else, that he had long suspected; that when he slept, he somehow *knew* the passage of time? Somehow even in that unconscious state, he travelled away from the things that had hurt him; and his dreams were only one indication of the reasoning that went on in darkness and in stillness. Without panic, he had known before the sunlight ever touched his body that hundreds of years had passed.

Perhaps he was merely so shocked by all he'd seen about him in the twentieth century that the memories had not attained their full emotional force. The pain would return all at once and he would find himself weeping uncontrollably on the edge of madness—unable to embrace all the beauty that he saw.

There had been a moment in the wax museum, yes, when he had seen that vulgar effigy of Cleopatra, and the ludicrous, expressionless Antony beside her, when he had felt something akin to panic. It had soothed him to return to the noisy, bustling London streets outside. He had heard her crying in his memory: "Ramses, Antony is dying. Give him the elixir! Ramses!" It seemed a voice from somewhere outside of him, which he could not silence at will. It disturbed him that she had been so grossly represented. And his heart had been tripping like those steam hammers that broke the cement pavings of London. Tripping. But that was not pain.

And what did it matter that the wax statue had so cheapened her beauty? His statues bore no resemblance to him finally, and he had stood about in the hot sun chatting with the workmen who made them! Nobody expected public art to have anything much to do with the flesh-and-blood model, that is, not until the Romans started filling their gardens with portraits of themselves, down to the very warts.

Cleopatra had been no Roman. Cleopatra had been a Greek and an Egyptian. And the horror was, Cleopatra meant something to these modern people of the twentieth century which was altogether wrong. She had become a symbol of licentiousness, when in fact she had possessed a multitude of amazing talents. They had punished her for her one flaw by forgetting everything else.

Yes, that is what had shocked him in the wax museum. Remembered, but not for what she was. A painted whore lying on a silken couch.

Silence. His heart was thudding again. He listened. He heard the ticking of the clock.

A tray of savory pastries lay before him. There was the brandy; oranges and pears on a china plate. He should eat and drink, for that always calmed him, just as if he'd been starving when he was not starving at all.

And he did not want to feel the agony again, did he? Yet he was frightened. Because he did not want to lose his vast experience of human feeling. That would be like dying!

Once again he looked at her beautiful face, rendered there in marble, more truly Cleopatra than that wax horror. And something deep inside threatened the strange quiet of his mind. He saw images without meaning. He put his hands to his head and sighed.

Of course if he thought of Julie Stratford in her bed above him, his mind and heart would be instantly united. He laughed softly as he picked up one of the pastries—sticky and sweet. He devoured it. He wanted to devour Julie Stratford. Ah, this woman, this splendid woman; this delicate-boned modern Queen who needed no land to rule to make her regal. So wondrously clever and surprisingly strong. But then he had better not dwell on it, or he would go up and knock down her door.

Picture it: crashing into her bedchamber. The poor servant wakes in the attic and starts screaming. So what? And Julie Stratford rises in that lace bower of hers, which he glimpsed earlier from the hallway, and he covers her, ripping off her scant gown, caressing her hot little limbs and taking her before she can protest.

No. You cannot do that. Do that and you destroy the thing you desire. Julie Stratford was worth humility and patience, a great deal of it. He had known that when he had watched her from that strange numb half-awakened state, moving about this library, speaking to him in his coffin, never guessing that he could hear.

Julie Stratford had become a great mystery of body and soul and will.

He took another deep drink of the brandy. Delicious. Another long draw on the cigar. He sliced through the orange with the knife and picked it up and ate the sweet, wet meat of it.

The cigar filled the room with a perfume finer than any incense. Turkish tobacco, Julie had told him. He had not known what that meant then, but he knew now. Ripping through a little book called *History of the World*, he had read all about the Turks and their conquests. That was how he should start, really, with the little books full of generalities and summations: "Within a century and a half all of Europe had fallen to the barbarian hordes." The fine distinctions would come later, as he sought out the great wealth of printed material in all languages. Just thinking of it made him smile.

The gramophone stopped. He rose, went to the machine and found another black disk for it to play. This one had the curious title "Only a Bird in a Gilded Cage." For some reason that made him think of Julie again and wanting to crush her with kisses. He set the disk on the turntable and cranked the handle. A small fragile woman's voice began to warble. He laughed. He refilled his brandy and moved a little with the music, a slow dance without lifting his feet.

But it was time to do some work. The darkness was dissolving outside the windows. The first faint grey light of the dawn was coming. He could hear, even over the dull roar of the city around him, the faraway song of birds.

He went into the dark cold kitchen of the house, found "a glass," as they called them, these beautiful objects, and filled it with water from the miraculous little copper tap.

Then he went back into the library and studied the long row of alabaster jars under the mirror. All appeared unharmed. No cracks anywhere. Nothing missing. And there was his little burner, all ready for him, and the empty glass vials. All he needed was a little oil. Or one of these candles, burnt down now to a convenient stub.

Moving aside his scrolls rather carelessly, he set up the little burner properly. He slipped the candle into place, and blew out the flame.

Then he studied the jars again. His hand chose before his mind chose. And when he studied the crushed white powder he knew that his hand had been right.

Oh, if only Henry Stratford had dipped his spoon into this instead of the other! What a great shock he would have had. His uncle, a roaring lion, might have torn off his head.

It occurred to him suddenly that though the poisons might have frightened the people of his time, they would be no deterrent to the scientists of this age. A person with a spark of belief could easily have taken all these jars out of here, fed their contents slowly to animal victims, until he discovered the elixir. It would be simple enough.

As it stood now, of course, only Samir Ibrahaim and Julie Stratford knew of the elixir. And they would never divulge the secret to anyone. But Lawrence Stratford had partially translated the story. And his notebook was lying about somewhere—Ramses had been unable to find it—for anyone to read. Then of course there were the scrolls.

Whatever the case, this situation could not continue forever. He must carry the elixir on his person. And of course there was always the chance that the batch had lost its potency. Two thousand years almost, the powder had lain in the jar.

In that time, wine would have turned to vinegar, or some utterly undrinkable fluid. Flour would have turned into something no more edible than sand.

His hand trembled now as he poured all of the coarse granules into the metal dish of the burner. He tapped the jar to make sure that not so much as a speck remained. Then he mixed it in the dish gently with his finger, and added a liberal amount of water from the glass.

Now he relighted the candle. As it bubbled, he gathered the glass vials and laid them out—the ones that had been on display here on the table, and two others that had remained concealed or overlooked in an ebony box.

Four large vials with silver caps.

Within seconds the change had taken place. The raw ingredients, already quite potent in their own right, had been changed into a bubbling liquid, full of vague phosphorescent light. How ominous it looked, like something that might burn the skin off the mouth of anyone who tried to drink it! But it did not do that. It had not done it when eons ago, he had drunk down the full cup without hesitation, ready to suffer to be immortal! There had been no pain at all. He smiled. No pain at all.

Carefully he lifted the dish. He poured the steaming elixir into one vial after another until all four glass containers were full. Then he waited until the dish was cooled and he licked it clean, for that was the only safe thing to do. Then he capped the vials. And he took the candle and made the wax drip around these caps to seal them, all save one.

Three of the vials, he placed in the pocket of his robe. The fourth vial, the one which he had failed to seal, he carried with him into the conservatory. He stood there in the darkness, holding it, peering at the ferns and vines that crowded the room.

The glass walls were losing their dark opacity. He could still see his own reflection clearly, a tall figure in a wine-dark garment, with a warm room behind him—but the pale objects of the outside world were coming visible too.

He approached the potted fern nearest him; a thing of great airy dark-green fronds. He poured a bit of the elixir into the moist soil. Then he turned to the bougainvillea, whose fragile red blossoms were few and far between amid the dark foliage. He poured many droplets of the elixir into this pot as well.

There was a faint stirring; a crackling sound. To use any more would be madness. Yet he moved from pot to pot, pouring but a few drops in each. Finally half the vial remained. And he had done enough harm, had he not? If the magic no longer worked, he would know within a few moments. He looked to the glass ceiling. The first blush of the sun was there. The god Ra sending the first warm rays.

The leaves of the ferns rustled, lengthened; tender shoots unfurled. The bougainvillea swelled and trembled on its trellis, tiny tendrils shooting up along the wrought-iron grillwork, little blossoms opening suddenly, blood red as wounds. The entire glass room was alive with accelerated growth. He closed his eyes, listening to that sound. A dark deep shudder passed through him.

How could he have ever believed that the elixir had lost its effectiveness? It was as strong as ever it had been. One powerful draught had rendered him immortal forever. Why did he think the substance itself, once created, would be any less immortal than he?

He put the vial in his pocket. He unlatched the rear door of the house and went out into the murky wet dawn.

The pain in Henry's head was so bad he could not even see the two detectives clearly. He had been dreaming of that thing, that mummy, when they awakened him. In cold terror, he had taken his gun, cocked it, slipped it into his pocket and gone to the door. Now if they meant to search him . . .

"Everyone knew Tommy Sharples!" he said, fury masking his fear. "Everyone owed him money. For this you wake me at the crack of dawn?"

He squinted stupidly at the one called Galton, who now held up that damned Cleopatra coin! How the hell could he have been so stupid? To go off and leave that coin in Sharples's pocket. But for the love of hell, he had not planned to cut down Sharples! How could he be expected to think of things like this!

"Ever see this before, sir?"

Be calm. There is not a scintilla of evidence to connect you to anything. Let indignation serve you as well as it always has.

"Why, that's from my uncle's collection. The Ramses collection. How did you get it? It ought to be under lock and key."

"The question is," said the one called Trent, "how did Mr. Sharples get it? And what was he doing with it on his person when he was killed?"

Henry ran his hands back through his hair. If only the pain would stop. If only he could excuse himself for a minute, get a good stiff drink and have some time to think.

"Reginald Ramsey!" he said, looking Trent in the eye. "That's the fellow's name, wasn't it? That Egyptologist! The one staying with my cousin. Good God, what's going on in that house!"

"Mr. Ramsey?"

"You have questioned him, haven't you? Where did he come from, that man?" His face coloured as the two men stared at him in silence. "Do I have to do your job for you? Where the devil did the bastard come from? And what's he doing with all that treasure in my cousin's house?"

For an hour Ramses walked. The morning was cold and dreary. The great imposing houses of Mayfair gave way to the dingy tenements of the poor. He roamed narrow unpaved streets, like the alleyways of an ancient city—Jericho, or Rome. Tracks of the horse carts here, and the reek of damp manure.

Now and then some poor passerby would stare at him. Surely he should not be dressed in this long satin robe. But that did not matter. He was Ramses the Wanderer again. Ramses the Damned only passing through this time. The elixir still had its potency. And the science of this time was no more ready for it than the science of any other.

Look at this suffering, these beggars sleeping in the alleyway.

Smell the filth of that house, as if the door is a mouth that spews its fowl breath while gasping for clean air.

A beggar man approached him. "Spare a sixpence, sir, I haven't eaten in two days. Please, sir."

Ramses walked on by, his slippers damp and dirty from the puddles in which he had stepped.

And now comes a young woman, look at her; listen to the cough rattling deep from her chest.

"Want to have a good time, sir? I have a nice warm room, sir."

Oh, yes, he did want her services, so very much that he could feel himself hardening immediately. And the fever made her all the more fetching; she thrust out her small bosom gracefully as she forced a smile despite her pain.

"Not now, my fair one," he whispered.

It seemed the street, if it was in fact a street, had carried him into a great wilderness of ruins. Burnt-out buildings reeking of the smoke, with windows empty of drapery or glass.

Even here the poor camped in alcoves and shallow doorways. A baby cried desperately. The song of the hungry.

He walked on. He could hear the city coming alive around him; not the human voices; those he'd heard all along. It was the machines which awoke now as the dirty grey sky grew brighter and became almost silver overhead. From somewhere very far away, he heard a deep-throated train whistle. He stopped. He could feel the dull vibration of the great iron monster even here through the damp earth. What a beguiling rhythm it had, those wheels rolling on and on over the iron tracks.

Suddenly a spasm of shrill noise threw him into a panic. He turned in time to see an open motor car hurtling towards him, a young man bouncing on the high seat. He fell back against the stone wall behind him as the thing rattled and bumped over the ruts in the mud.

He was shaken, angry. A rare moment in which he felt helpless, exposed.

Dazed, he realized he was looking at a grey dove lying dead in the street. One of those fat dull grey birds which he saw everywhere in London, nesting on the windowsills and on the rooftops; this one had been struck by the motor car, and part of its wing had been crushed under the wheels.

The wind stirred it now, giving it a false semblance of life.

Suddenly a memory, one of the oldest and most vivid, caught

him off guard, ripping him from the present, cruelly, and planting him squarely in another time and place.

He stood in the cave of the Hittite priestess. In his battle garb, his hand on the hilt of his bronze sword, he stood looking up at the white doves circling in the sunlight under the high grate.

"They're immortal?" he asked her. He spoke in the crude, guttural Hittite tongue.

She had laughed madly. "They eat, but they do not need to eat. They drink, but they do not need to drink. It is the sun that keeps them strong. Take it away and they sleep, but they do not die, my King."

He had stared at her face, so old, shrunken with its deep wrinkles. The laughter had angered him.

"Where is the elixir!" he had demanded.

"You think it is a great thing?" How her eyes had gleamed as she approached him, taunting him. "And what if all the world were filled with those who could not die? And their children? And their children's children? This cave harbours a horrid secret, I tell you. *The secret of the end of the world itself, I tell you!*"

He had drawn his sword. "Give it to me!" he had roared.

She had not been frightened; she had only smiled.

"What if it kills you, my rash Egyptian? No human being has ever drunk it. No man, woman or child."

But he had already seen the altar, seen the cup of white liquid. He had seen the tablet behind it covered with tiny wedgelike letters.

He stepped up to the altar. He read the words. Could this possibly be the formula of the elixir of life? Common ingredients which he himself could have gathered from the fields and riverbanks of his native land? Half believing, he committed it to memory, never dreaming that he would never forget.

And the liquid, ye gods, look at it. With both hands he lifted the cup and drank it down. Somewhere far off he heard her laughing and laughing; it echoed through the endless chambers of the cave.

And then he'd turned, wiping his lip with the back of his hand, his eyes wide as the shock coursed through him, his face throbbing, his body hardening as if he were in his chariot before the battlefield, on the verge of raising his sword and giving the cry. The priestess had taken a step backwards. What had she seen? His hair stirring, writhing, as if lifted by a swift breeze; the grey hairs falling away as the strong brown hair replaced them; his black eyes fading, turning the colour of sapphires—the stunning transformation that he would verify later when he held up the mirror.

"Well, we shall see, shan't we?" he had cried, his heart pumping fiercely, his muscles tingling. Ah, how light and powerful he'd felt. He could have taken flight. "Do I live or die, priestess?"

Stunned, he stared at the London street before him. As if it were only hours ago! The moment whole and entire, and he could still hear the flapping of those wings against the grate. Seven hundred years had passed between that moment and the night he'd entered the tomb for his first long sleep. And two thousand since he'd been awakened, only to go to the grave within a few years again.

And now this is London; this is the twentieth century. Suddenly he was trembling violently. Again, the damp smoky wind stirred the feathers of the grey dove that lay dead in the street. He walked forward through the sludge and knelt down beside the bird and scooped it up in his hands. Ah, fragile thing. So full of life one moment, and now no more than refuse, though the white down fluttered on its warm, narrow little chest.

Oh, how the chill wind hurt him. How the sight of the dead thing pierced his heart.

Holding it in his right hand, he drew out the half-full vial of the elixir with his left. He pushed open the hinged cap with his thumb and poured the shimmering liquid over the dead creature, forcing one heavy drop after another into its open beak.

Not a second passed before the thing quickened. The tiny round eyes opened. The bird struggled to right itself, its wings flapping violently. He let it go, and up it went, circling as it soared beneath the heavy leaden sky.

He watched until it had disappeared from sight. Immortal now. To fly forever.

And another memory came, silent and swift as an assassin. The mausoleum; the marble halls, the pillars, and the gaunt figure of Cleopatra running beside him as he walked on, faster and faster, away from the dead body of Mark Antony lying on the gilded couch.

"You can bring him back!" she screamed. "You know you can. It's not too late. Ramses. Give it to us both, Mark Antony and me! Ramses, don't turn away from me.'' Her long nails had scratched at his arm.

In a rage he'd turned, slapped her, knocked her backwards. Astonished, she'd fallen, then crumpled into sobs. How frail she'd been, almost haggard, with the dark circles beneath her eyes.

The bird was gone over the London rooftops. The sun grew brighter, a shocking white light behind the rolling clouds.

His vision blurred; his heart was pounding thickly in his chest. He was weeping, weeping helplessly. Ye gods, what had made him think the pain would not come?

He'd wakened after centuries in a great luxurious numbness; and now that numbness was thawing, and the heat of his love and his grief would soon be wholly his once more. This was but the first taste of suffering, and what was the blessing, that he was alive, heart and soul, again?

He stared at the vial in his hand. He was tempted to crush it, and let its contents drip from his fingers into this foul and rutted street. Take the other vials out someplace far away from London where the grass grew high surely, and only the wild flowers would witness; and there pour all the liquid into the field.

But what were these vain fancies? *He knew how to make it.* He had memorized those words off that tablet. He could not destroy what was forever engraved on his own mind.

Samir left the cab and walked the remaining fifty yards to his destination, hands shoved in his pockets, collar turned up against the driving wind. Reaching the house on the corner, he went up the stone steps and knocked on the peeling door.

A woman draped all in black wool opened the door a crack, then admitted him. Quietly he entered a cluttered room where two Egyptians sat smoking and reading the morning papers, the shelves and tables around them covered with Egyptian goods. A papyrus and a magnifying glass lay to one side on the table.

Samir glanced at the papyrus. Nothing of importance. He glanced at a long, yellow mummy, its wrappings still quite well preserved, lying carelessly, it seemed, on a nearby shelf.

''Ah, Samir, don't trouble yourself,'' said the tallest of the two men, whose name was Abdel. ''Nothing but fakes on the market. Zaki's work, as you know. Except for that fellow. . . .'' The man pointed to the mummy. ''He's real enough, but not worth your time.''

Nevertheless Samir took a closer look at the mummy.

"The dregs of a private collection," Abdel said. "Not in your class."

Samir nodded, then turned back to Abdel.

"I did hear, however, that some rare Cleopatra coins have surfaced," Abdel said, a bit playfully. "Ah, if I could get my hands on one of those."

"I need a passport, Abdel," Samir said. "Citizenship papers. I need them fast."

Abdel did not immediately answer. He watched with interest as Samir reached into his pocket.

"And moncy. I need that too."

Samir held up the glittering Cleopatra coin.

Abdel reached for it before he was out of his chair. Samir watched him without expression as he examined it.

"Discretion, my friend," Samir said. "Speed and discretion. Let us discuss the details."

Oscar was back. Now that might be a problem, Julie thought, but only if Rita said something foolish, but then Oscar never listened to Rita. He thought Rita was a fool.

As Julie came down the stairs, she found her butler just closing the front door. He had a bouquet of roses in his arms. He gave her the letter that had come with them.

"Just arrived, miss," he said.

"Yes, I know."

With relief she saw it was from Elliott, not Alex, and hastily she read the letter as Oscar waited.

"Call the Earl of Rutherford, Oscar. Tell him I cannot possibly come tonight. And I shall call later myself to explain."

He was about to go when she took one of the roses out of the bouquet. "Put them in the dining room, Oscar," she said. She sampled the fragrance, then felt the soft petals with her finger. What was she going to do about Alex? Surely it was too soon to do anything, but every day only made matters worse.

Ramses. Where was he? That was really the first order of business. The door of her father's room had been open, the bed untouched.

She hurried back through the hall to the conservatory. Even before she reached the door, she saw the magnificent bougainvillea laden with red blossoms.

And to think that yesterday she hadn't noticed these beautiful blooms. And look at the ferns, magnificent. And the lilies that had opened early in their pots throughout the room.

"What a miracle," she said.

She saw Ramses seated in a wicker chair, watching her. And already dressed splendidly for the day's adventures. And this time he'd made no mistakes. How ruddy and beautiful he looked in the streaming sunlight; his hair fuller, richer, and his great blue eyes filled with a sombre melancholy as he looked at her, that is, before he brightened completely and gave her that irresistible smile.

For one moment a shock of fear passed through her. He seemed on the edge of tears. He rose from the chair and came towards her and lightly touched her face with his fingers.

"What a miracle *you* are!" he said.

A silence fell gently between them. She wanted to reach up and throw her arms about his neck. She merely looked at him, feeling his closeness, then she reached out and touched his face.

She should draw back, she knew it. But he surprised her. He drew back and then, kissing her almost reverently on the forehead, he said:

"I want to go to Egypt, Julie. Sooner or later, I shall have to go to Egypt. Let it happen now."

How weary and raw he sounded. All the gentleness that had been in him yesterday was mingled now with sadness. His eyes seemed darker and larger. And she'd been right—he was near to weeping, and it sent the fear again to her soul.

God, how great must be his capacity for suffering.

"Of course," she said. "We'll go to Egypt, you and I together. . . ."

"Ah, that was my hope," he said. "Julie, this age can never belong to me until I say farewell to Egypt, for Egypt is my past."

"I understand."

"I want the future!" he said, his voice dropping to a whisper. "I want . . ." He stopped, clearly unable to go on. Flustered, he turned away from her. He reached into his pocket and removed a handful of golden coins.

"Can we buy a ship with this, Julie, that will take us across the sea?"

"Leave everything to me," she said. "We are going. Now sit down, eat your breakfast. I know how hungry you are. You don't have to tell me."

He laughed in spite of himself.

"And I shall see to things at once."

She went into the kitchen. Oscar was just setting the breakfast tray for them. The room was full of the good smells of coffee, and cinnamon, and freshly baked muffins.

"Oscar, telephone Thomas Cook for me immediately. Book a passage for Mr. Ramsey and me to Alexandria. See if you can arrange for it straight away. We'll leave today if possible. Do hurry, and leave these things to me."

How amazed he was.

"But, Miss Julie, what about—"

"Do it, Oscar. Make the calls at once. Hurry. There's no time to lose."

Carrying the heavy tray, she came back out into the sunlight, and once more the great lovely flowers startled her. The purple orchids and the yellow daisies, equally beautiful.

"Why, look at it," she whispered. "And to think I scarcely noticed it before. Everything in bloom. Oh, so lovely. . . ."

He stood by the back door, watching her with that same sad and beautiful expression. "Yes, very lovely," he said.

10

HE HOUSE was in an uproar. Rita had all but lost her mind at the idea that she was going to Egypt. Oscar, remaining to keep the house, had been helping the cabbies get the trunks down the stairs.

Randolph and Alex were arguing furiously with Julie that she must not make this trip.

And the enigmatic Mr. Reginald Ramsey sat at the wicker table in the conservatory devouring an enormous meal, with glass after glass to wash it down. All the while he read the newspapers, two of them at a time, if Elliott was not mistaken. And now and then he lifted a book from the pile on the floor, and rushed through the pages as if searching for some dreadfully important item, and once finding it, dropped the book with a careless thud.

Elliott sat in Lawrence's chair in the Egyptian room watching all of this silently; glancing now and then to Julie in the drawing room; and then to Mr. Ramsey, who surely knew that he was being observed but did not seem to care.

The other silent and solitary watcher was Samir Ibrahaim, who stood to the very back of the conservatory, somewhat lost in the remarkable profusion of spring foliage, staring past the indifferent Mr. Ramsey into the shadowy front rooms.

Julie's call to Elliott had come over three hours ago. He had gone into action immediately. And he knew more or less what was going to happen now, as the little drama in the drawing room played itself out.

"But you simply cannot go off to Egypt with a man you know nothing about," Randolph said, trying to keep his voice down. "You can't take such a trip without a proper chaperon."

"Julie, I won't have it," Alex said, pale with exasperation. "I won't have you do this alone."

"Now, stop, both of you," Julie responded. "I'm a grown woman. I'm going. And I can take care of myself. Besides, I'll have Rita with me all the time. And Samir, Father's closest friend. I couldn't have a better protector than Samir."

"Julie, neither of them is a proper companion and you know this. This is nothing short of scandalous."

"Uncle Randolph, the boat leaves at four o'clock. We must be leaving here now. Let's get to the business at hand, shall we? I've had a power of attorney prepared, so that you can run Stratford Shipping with a free hand."

Silence. So at last we get to the heart of the matter, Elliott thought coolly. He could hear Randolph slowly clearing his throat.

"Well, I suppose that's necessary, my dear," he answered weakly.

Alex tried to interrupt, but Julie overrode him politely. Were there any other papers Randolph wanted her to sign? He could send them on to Alexandria immediately. She'd sign them and send them home from there.

Satisfied that Julie would be leaving on schedule, Elliott rose and walked casually out into the conservatory.

Ramsey went on eating superhuman amounts of food, quite undeterred. He now took one of three different lighted cigars and drew on it, then went back to his pudding, and his roast beef, and his buttered bread. It was a history of modern Egypt that lay open before him, the chapter entitled "The Mamluke Massacre." The man appeared to be scanning, so rapidly did his finger move down the page.

Suddenly Elliott realized he was surrounded by foliage. He was almost startled by the size of the fern beside him, and the immense heavy bougainvillea brushing his shoulder, as it partially blocked the door. Good Lord, what had happened here? Lilies everywhere he looked, and the daisies exploding out of their pots, and the ivy gone wild over the entire roof.

Concealing his shock, though from whom he wasn't certain,

since neither Ramsey nor Samir took official note of him, he tore off one of the blue-and-white morning glories blooming just over his head.

He stared at the perfect trumpet-shaped blossom. What sweetness. Then slowly he looked up to meet Ramsey's gaze.

Samir roused himself suddenly from his apparent state of meditation.

"Lord Rutherford, allow me . . ." Then he stopped as if at a complete loss for words.

Ramsey rose to his feet, wiping his fingers carefully on his linen napkin.

Absently the Earl slipped the morning glory in his pocket, and then extended his hand.

"Reginald Ramsey," he said, "a great pleasure. I'm an old friend of the Stratford family. Something of an Egyptologist myself. It is my son, Alex, who is engaged to be married to Julie. Perhaps you know."

The man hadn't known. Or he didn't understand. A faint flush came to his cheeks.

"Married to Julie?" he said in a half whisper. And then, with forced gaiety: "He is a fortunate man, your son."

The Earl eyed the table laden with food, because he couldn't stop himself, and the blossoms all but crowding out the sun above. He looked placidly at the man before him, who was certainly one of the handsomest creatures he'd ever seen. Downright beautiful, when you thought of it. The sort of large compassionate blue eyes that drive women mad. Add the ready smile and one has a near-fatal combination.

But the silence was becoming uncomfortable.

"Ah, the diary," Elliott said. He reached into his coat. Samir recognized it immediately, that was plain.

"This diary," Elliott said, "it belonged to Lawrence. It has valuable information on Ramses' tomb. Notes on a papyrus left by the man, it seems. I picked it up the other night. I must put it back."

There was a sudden coldness in Ramsey's face.

Elliott turned, leaning on his cane, and took a few painful steps toward Lawrence's desk.

Ramsey came along with him.

"The pain in your joints," Ramsey asked, "have you a modern . . . a medicine for it? There was an old Egyptian remedy. The willow bark. One had to boil it."

"Yes," Elliott answered, looking up again into those distracting blue eyes. "In this day and age we call it aspirin, don't we?" He smiled. This was going infinitely better than he had ever anticipated. He hoped the colour wasn't dancing in his face as it was in Ramsey's. "Where have you been all these years that you haven't heard of aspirin, my dear man? We produce it synthetically, and of course you are familiar with that word."

Ramsey's composure was unbroken, though he narrowed his eyes just a little as if he wanted the Earl to realize he was being appraised.

"I'm not a scientific man, Lord Rutherford," he answered. "I'm more an observer, a philosopher. So you call it aspirin. I am pleased to know it. Maybe I have spent too much of my time in distant lands." He raised his eyebrows almost playfully.

"Of course the ancient Egyptians had more potent medicines than willow bark, didn't they?" Elliott pushed it. He looked at the row of alabaster jars on the table across the room. "Potent medicines—elixirs, so to speak—which could cure more potent ailments than the pain I suffer in my bones."

"Potent medicines have their price," Ramses replied calmly. "Or shall I say, their dangers. But what an unusual man you are, Lord Rutherford. Surely you don't believe what you read in the notebook of your friend Lawrence."

"Oh, but I do believe it. Because, you see, I am not a scientific man either. Perhaps, we are both philosophers, you and I. And I fancy myself something of a poet, because so much of my wandering has been in my dreams alone."

The two men looked at each other in silence for a moment.

"A poet," Ramsey repeated, eyes moving over Elliott almost rudely to take his measure. "I understand you. But you do say most unusual things."

Elliott tried to hold steady. He could feel the sweat breaking out under his shirt. The man's face was so unexpectedly open, and almost inviting.

"I should like to know you," Elliott confessed suddenly. "I . . . I should like to . . . learn from you." He hesitated. The blue eyes fixed him in silence again. "Perhaps in Cairo or Alexandria we should have some time to talk to one another. Perhaps even on shipboard, we might become acquainted."

"You are going to Egypt?" Ramsey asked, cocking his head.

"Yes." Politely he moved past Ramsey, and into the drawing

room. He stood beside Julie, who had just signed another bank draft for her uncle, which she placed now in his hands.

"Yes," Elliott said, turning back to Ramsey and speaking loudly enough for the others to hear him. "Alex and I are both going. I booked passage on the same ship, as soon as Julie called. We wouldn't dream of letting her go alone, would we, Alex?"

"Elliott, I told you no," Julie said.

"Father, I didn't realize . . ."

"Yes, my dear," Elliott said to Julie, "but I couldn't take no for an answer. Besides, this may be the last time I see Egypt. And Alex has never been there. Surely you won't deny us the pleasure. Is there any reason why we should not all go?"

"Yes, I suppose I should see it," Alex said, by this time thoroughly confused.

"Well, your trunk's packed and on its way," Elliott said. "Come on, now, or we're all going to miss the boat, so to speak."

Julie was staring at him in a silent fury.

Ramsey gave a soft laugh behind him.

"So we all go to Egypt," he said. "I find this most interesting. We shall talk on board, Lord Rutherford, as you have said."

Randolph looked up after tucking the power of attorney into his coat.

"Well, that solves everything, doesn't it? Have a pleasant journey, my darling." He kissed his niece tenderly on the cheek.

The dream again, but he couldn't wake up. He turned over in Daisy's bed, into the scratchy lace pillow with its cloying perfume. "Just a dream," he murmured, "have to stop it." But he saw the mummy coming towards him, the long strips of darkened linen trailing from its shuffling feet. He felt the fingers lock on his throat.

He tried to scream, but he couldn't. He was suffocated, the smell of the filthy cerements choking him.

He turned over, thrashing at the bedcovers and suddenly striking out with his fist, only to feel fingers locked on it tightly.

When he opened his eyes, he saw his father's face.

"Oh, God," he whispered. He fell back on the pillow. The dream locked around him again for an instant, but he shuddered and stared again at his father standing over the bed.

"Father," he moaned. "What are you doing here?"

"I might ask you that question. Get out of that bed and get dressed. Your trunk's waiting downstairs, along with a cab to take you to the P and O docks. You're going to Egypt."

"The hell I am!" What was this, another stage of the nightmare?

His father removed his hat and took the bedside chair. When Henry reached for his cigar and matches, his father knocked them out of his hand.

"Damn you," Henry whispered.

"Now you listen to me. I have things in hand again and I intend to keep it that way. Your cousin Julie and her mysterious Egyptian friend are setting out for Alexandria this afternoon, and Elliott and Alex are going with them. Now you will be on that ship, too, do you understand? You are Julie's cousin, and therefore the only proper companion. And you will see that things remain seemly, that nothing intervenes to prevent Julie's eventual marriage to Alex Savarell. And you will see . . . you will see that this man, whoever he is, does not hurt my brother's only child."

"That man! You're mad if you think I'll—"

"And you are disinherited and penniless if you don't!" Randolph lowered his voice as he leaned forward. "I mean this, Henry. All your life I've given you everything you ever wanted. But if you don't toe the line now, and see this thing to the bloody end, I shall remove you from the board of Stratford Shipping. I shall terminate your salary and your personal income. Now you will be on that ship. And you will keep an eye on your cousin and see she doesn't elope with that revoltingly handsome Egyptian! And you will keep me posted as to everything that is going on."

Randolph removed a slim white envelope from his breast pocket. He laid it on the bedside table. There was a thick wad of money in the envelope. Henry could see that. His father rose to go.

"And don't wire me from Cairo that you're broke. Stay away from the gaming tables and the belly dancers. I shall expect a letter or a telegram within a week's time."

Hancock was beside himself.

"Left for Egypt!" he sputtered into the telephone. "But the whole collection is still there in that house! How could she do this!"

He motioned for silence to the clerk who meant to disturb him. Then he slammed down the black receiver in its hook.

"Sir, the newspapermen are here again, about the mummy."

"Oh, damn the mummy. That woman's gone off and left that treasure locked up in her living room, as if it were a collection of dolls!"

Elliott stood beside Julie and Ramsey watching from the high railing as Alex kissed his mother at the foot of the gangplank far below.

"But I'm not here to cluck over you like a mother hen," Elliott said to Julie. Alex embraced his mother again and then hurried to board. "I only want to be close at hand if you need me. Please don't be so distressed."

Lord, he meant it. It hurt him to see the look on her face.

"But Henry, why on earth has Henry come along? I don't want Henry with us."

Henry had boarded only moments before without a civil word to anyone, looking as pale and overwrought and generally miserable as he had looked the day before.

"Yes, I know." Elliott sighed. "But my dear, he's your next of kin and—"

"Give me space to breathe, Elliott. You know I love Alex, I always have. But a marriage to me may not be the best thing for him. And I've been perfectly honest about it all along."

"I know, Julie, believe me, I know. I always have. But your friend—" He gestured to the distant figure of Ramsey, who was watching all the goings-on of the harbour with obvious excitement. "How are we not to worry? What are we to do?"

She could not resist him. That had always been the case. One night several months back, when she'd had too much champagne and there'd been entirely too much dancing, she'd told Elliott she was more in love with him than she'd been with Alex. If he'd been free and asking for her hand, it would have been a fait accompli. Of course Alex had thought she was joking. But there had been a strange secret look in her eye that flattered Elliott immensely. And he saw a pale flicker of that same look now. And what a liar he was. What a liar he was being just now.

"All right, Elliott," she said. She kissed him on the cheek, and he loved it. "I don't want to hurt Alex," she whispered.

"Yes, darling," he said. "Of course."

There was a violent blast from the steam whistle. The last

call for boarding passengers. Parties had broken up in the state-rooms, and a steady stream of guests was going ashore.

Suddenly Ramsey came pounding towards them. He spun Julie around as if he didn't realize his own strength. She stared blankly.

"Feel it, Julie, the vibrations. I must see these engines."

Her face softened at once. It was as if his excitement were contagious.

"Of course you must. Elliott, excuse me. I have to take Ramse . . . I mean Mr. Ramsey . . . to the engine room, if it can possibly be arranged."

"Allow me," Elliott said agreeably, motioning for a young officer in a crisp white uniform who had just come out on deck.

Alex was unpacking already when Elliott entered the little drawing room between their staterooms. Two steamer trunks stood open. Walter moved to and fro with armfuls of clothes.

"Well, this is pleasant, isn't it?" Elliott said, surveying the little couch and chairs, the tiny portal. There had not been much time to arrange for proper accommodations, but Edith had stepped in finally and seen to everything herself.

"You look tired, Father. Let me order you some tea."

The Earl eased himself into the little gilded *fauteuil*. Tea did sound rather nice. What was that fragrance? Were there flowers in this room? He saw none. Only the champagne in its glistening ice bucket and the glasses ready on the silver tray.

Then he remembered. The morning glory he had crushed into his pocket. It was still giving off a latent perfume.

"Yes, tea would be fine, Alex, but there's no hurry," he murmured. Reaching into his pocket, he found the mangled little blossom and drew it out and lifted it to his nose.

A very pretty scent indeed. And then he thought of that conservatory, overgrown fantastically with leaves and blossoms. He looked at the morning glory. As he watched, it straightened, the creases in its waxy petals disappearing. It opened completely and within seconds had become again a perfect bloom.

Alex was talking, but Elliott did not hear him. He merely looked stupidly at the flower. Then he crushed it again, tightly in the palm of his hand.

Slowly he looked up to see that Alex was just putting down the telephone.

"Tea in fifteen minutes," Alex said. "What's the matter, Father? Father, you're white as a—"

"Nothing. No. It's nothing. I want to rest now. Call me when the tea comes."

He stood up, the flower clenched still in his fist.

When he had shut the door of his stateroom, he leaned against it, the sweat flooding down his back. He opened his hand. Again the blossom sprang back from a crushed and broken thing into a perfect flower, the blue-and-white petals lengthening before his eyes.

For an endless time, it seemed, he stared at it. The tiny bit of green leaf at its base curled as he watched. Then he realized he was looking at himself in the mirror. The grey-haired, partially crippled Earl of Rutherford, handsome still at fifty-five, though every step he took was an agony. He let go his walking stick, ignoring it as it fell, and with his left hand felt of his grey hair.

He could hear Alex calling him. The tea had already come. Carefully he took out his wallet. He crushed the flower again and slipped it into the leather folds. Then he bent over very slowly and picked up his cane.

In a daze, it seemed, he stared at his son, who poured the tea for him.

"You know, Father," Alex said, "I'm beginning to think it's going to work out after all. I've had a good look at Ramsey. He's quite a handsome fellow, but he's too old for her, don't you think?"

Oh, but this was too much fun, this great floating iron palace with little shops on board, and a great banquet room and a dance floor where musicians would later play!

And his quarters, why, never as a King had he had such splendid quarters aboard a seagoing vessel. He was laughing almost foolishly as the stewards finished unpacking the very last of Lawrence Stratford's clothes.

Samir closed the door after they'd gone, then turned and drew out a great deal of paper money from his coat.

"This will take care of your wants for a long time, sire, only you must not show it all at one time."

"Yes, my loyal one. That was the common wisdom when I'd slip out of the palace as a boy." He gave another exuberant laugh. He couldn't help himself. The ship even contained a library and a small cinema; and then all the marvels below deck. And the gentle, elegant members of the crew—all of whom had the manners of gentlemen—had told him he might move about as he wished.

"Your coin was worth a great deal more, sire, but I had little room to bargain."

"As they say in this day and age, Samir, don't give it another thought. And you are correct in your estimation of Lord Rutherford. He believes. In fact, I should say he knows."

"But it's Henry Stratford that presents the danger. Would a fall from the deck on the high seas be justice?"

"Not wise. It would destroy Julie's peace of mind. The more I learn of this age, the more I understand its complexities, its highly developed concepts of justice. They are Roman, but they are something more. We shall keep an eye on the progress of Mr. Henry Stratford. When his presence becomes more of a trial to his cousin, then perhaps his death will be the better of two evils, and you need not worry about that part of it. I shall do it alone."

"Yes, sire. But if for any reason you do not want this task, I shall be more than happy to kill this man myself."

Ramses laughed softly. How he liked this one; so shrewd, yet honest; patient, yet keenly clever as well.

"Maybe we should kill him together, Samir," he said. "But whatever the case I am ravenous. When do we take this great meal together on the pink tablecloths amid the great potted palms?"

"All too soon, sire, and please be . . . careful."

"Samir, do not worry," Ramses said. He took Samir's hand. "I have my instructions already from Queen Julie. I am to eat only one item of fish, one item of fowl, one item of meat, and not all at the same time."

It was Samir's turn to laugh softly.

"Are you unhappy still?" Ramses asked.

"No, sire. I am very happy. Don't ever be disappointed in my sombre expression. I have seen more in my life, as of this moment, than I ever dreamed I would see. When Henry Stratford is dead, I shall ask for nothing more."

Ramses nodded. His secret was safe forever with this one, he knew it, though he could not fully understand this quality of wisdom and resignation. He had never known it when he was mortal. He didn't know it now.

11

IT WAS a sumptuous first-class dining room, crowded already with gentlemen in white tie and tails and ladies in low-cut dresses. When Julie came in and took her chair, Alex rose to assist her. Henry and Elliott, already seated opposite, also rose, and though Julie nodded to Elliott, she found herself incapable of looking at her cousin.

She turned to Alex, and placed her hand on his. Unfortunately she could not help overhearing Henry continuing to talk angrily in Elliott's ear. Something about Alex being a fool that he could not have stopped Julie from taking this trip.

Alex, staring down at the plate before him, seemed somewhat at a loss. Was this the time or place for truth? She felt she must be honest from the beginning, or matters would only become worse for Alex, and she must see that they did not.

"Alex," she said in a low voice, "I may stay in Egypt. I don't know what my plans are. You know sometimes, my darling, I think you need someone as good as you are."

He wasn't surprised by her words. He thought for only a moment before answering. "But how could I want anyone better than you? I'll follow you into the jungles of the Sudan if that's where you want to go."

"You don't know what you're saying."

He bent forward, his voice dropping to the most intimate whisper. "I love you, Julie. Everything else in my life I take for granted. But not you. And you're more precious to me than all the rest put together. Julie, I mean to fight for you, if that's what must be done.''

What could she possibly say to him that would not wound him? He looked up suddenly. Ramses and Samir were here.

For a moment, she was speechless. Ramses was a vision in her father's white boiled shirt and beautifully cut tailcoat. As he took his seat, his every gesture seemed more graceful and more decorous than those of the Englishmen around him. He veritably glistened with vigour and well-being. The smile he flashed was like a light.

Then something happened. He stared at Julie's bare shoulders, at the plunging neck of her gown. He stared in particular at the tiny shadow between her half-naked breasts. And Alex stared at Ramses in polite outrage. And Samir, taking a seat to the left of the Earl, was obviously already alarmed.

She must do something. Still staring at her, as if he'd never laid eyes on a woman before, Ramses took the chair on her left.

Quickly, she opened his napkin for him, whispering:

"Here, in your lap. And stop staring at me. It's a ball gown, quite proper!'' She turned at once to Samir opposite. "Samir, I'm so glad you could make this journey with us.''

"Yes, and here we are,'' Elliott said immediately, filling the silence. "All having dinner together exactly as I'd planned. Isn't that marvellous! Seems I got my way after all.''

"So you did.'' Julie laughed. She was relieved suddenly that Elliott was there. He would smooth over one awkward moment after another; he did it instinctively. In fact, he probably couldn't stop himself. It was this buoyant charm among other things which kept him perpetually in demand.

She dared not look directly at Henry, but she could see he was hopelessly uneasy. He was already drinking. His glass was half full.

The waiters brought the sherry now, and the soup. Ramses had already reached for the bread. He had torn off a very large piece from the small loaf and eaten it whole.

"And tell me, Mr. Ramsey,'' Elliott continued, "how did you enjoy your stay in London? You weren't with us very long.''

Why the hell was Ramses smiling?

"I found it an overwhelming place,'' he said with immediate enthusiasm. "A curious blending of fierce wealth and inexplicable poverty. I do not understand how so many machines can produce so much for so few, and so little for so many. . . .''

"Sir, you're questioning the entire Industrial Revolution," Alex said, laughing nervously, which for him was most certainly a symptom of ill ease. "Don't tell me you're a Marxist. It's rather seldom that we encounter radicals in our . . . our circle."

"What is a Marxist! I am an Egyptian," Ramses said.

"Of course you are, Mr. Ramsey," said Elliott smoothly. "And you're no Marxist. How perfectly ridiculous. You knew our Lawrence in Cairo?"

"Our Lawrence. Briefly I knew him." Ramses was staring at Henry. Julie quickly lifted her soup spoon and, giving him a gentle nudge with her elbow, demonstrated how the soup was to be eaten. He didn't so much as glance at her. He picked up his bread, dipped it in the soup and began eating it, glaring at Henry again.

"Lawrence's death came as a shock to me, as I'm sure it did to everyone," he said, dipping another enormous piece of bread. "A Marxist is a type of philosopher? I do remember a Karl Marx. I discovered this person in Lawrence's library. A fool."

Henry had not touched his soup. He drank another deep gulp of his Scotch and motioned for the waiter.

"It's unimportant," Julie said quickly.

"Yes, Lawrence's death was a terrible shock," Elliott said soberly. "I was sure he had another good ten years. Maybe twenty."

Ramses was dipping yet another enormous piece of the bread into the soup. And Henry was now staring at him with veiled horror, careful to avoid his eyes. Everyone was more or less quietly watching Ramses, who wiped up the very last of the soup now with another chunk of bread, and then downed the sherry, and wiped his lips with the napkin and sat back.

"More food," he whispered. "It's coming?"

"Yes, it is, but slow down," Julie whispered.

"You were a true friend of Lawrence?" Ramses said to Elliott.

"Absolutely," said Elliott.

"Yes, well, if he were here, he'd be talking about his beloved mummy," said Alex with that same nervous laugh. "As a matter of fact, why are you taking this trip, Julie? Why go back to Egypt when the mummy lies there in London waiting for examination? You know, I don't really understand. . . ."

"The collection's opened several avenues of research," Julie said. ''We want to go to Alexandria and then perhaps Cairo. . . .''

''Yes, of course,'' Elliott said. He was clearly watching Ramses' reaction as the waiter set down the fish before him, a small portion in a delicate cream sauce. ''Cleopatra,'' he went on, ''your mysterious Ramses the Second claimed to have loved and lost her. And that happened in Alexandria, did it not?''

Julie had not seen this coming. Neither had Ramses, who had laid down his bread and was staring at the Earl with a blank expression on his face. There came those dancing points of colour beneath the smooth skin of his cheeks.

''Well, yes, there is that aspect of it,'' Julie struggled. ''And then we're going to Luxor, and to Abu Simbel. I hope you're all in fine form for an arduous journey. Of course if you don't want to continue . . .''

''Abu Simbel,'' Alex said. ''Isn't that where the colossal statues are of Ramses the Second?''

Ramses broke off half the fish with his fingers and ate it. Then he ate the second half. A curious smile had broken out on Elliott's face, but Ramses didn't see it. He was staring at Henry again. Julie was going to start screaming.

''Statues of Ramses the Great are everywhere, actually,'' Elliott said, watching Ramses mop up the sauce with the bread. ''Ramses left more monuments to himself than any other Pharaoh.''

''Ah, that's the one. I knew it,'' said Alex. ''The egomaniac of Egyptian history. I remember now, from school.''

''Egomaniac!'' Ramses said with a grimace. ''More bread!'' he said to the waiter. Then to Alex: ''What is an egomaniac? If you please?''

''Aspirin, Marxism, egomania,'' Elliott said. ''These are all new ideas to you, Mr. Ramsey?''

Henry was becoming positively agitated. He had drunk the second glass of Scotch and now sat plastered to the back of his chair, merely staring at Ramses' hands as he ate.

''Oh, you know,'' Alex said blithely. ''The fellow was a great braggart. He built monuments to himself all over the place. He bragged endlessly about his victories, his wives and his sons! So that's the mummy, and all this time I didn't realize.''

''What in the world are you talking about!'' Julie said suddenly.

''Is there any other Egyptian King in history who won so

many victories," Ramses said heatedly, "and pleasured so many wives, and fathered so many sons? And surely you understand that in erecting so many statues, the Pharaoh was giving to his people exactly what they wanted."

"Now, that's a novel view!" Alex said sarcastically, laying down his knife and fork. "You don't mean the slaves enjoyed being flogged to death in the burning sun to build all those temples and colossal statues?"

"Slaves, flogged to death in the hot sun?" Ramses asked. "What are you saying! This did not happen!" He turned to Julie.

"Alex, that's merely one theory of how the monuments were completed," she said. "No one really knows . . ."

"Well, I know," Ramses said.

"Everyone has his theory!" Julie said, raising her voice slightly and glaring at Ramses.

"Well, for heaven's sake," Alex said, "the man built enormous statues of himself from one end of Egypt to another. You can't tell me the people wouldn't have been a lot happier tending their flower beds. . . ."

"Young man, you are most strange!" said Ramses. "What do you know about the people of Egypt? Slaves, you speak of slaves when your slums are filled with starving children. The people wanted the monuments. They took pride in their temples. When the Nile overflowed its banks there could be no work in the fields; and the monuments became the passion of the nation. Labour wasn't forced. It didn't have to be. The Pharaoh was as a god, and he had to do what his people expected of him."

"Surely you're sentimentalizing it a bit," said Elliott, but he was plainly fascinated.

Henry had turned white. He was no longer moving at all. His fresh glass of Scotch stood untouched.

"Not in the least," Ramses argued. "The people of Egypt were proud of Ramses the Great. He drove back the enemies; he conquered the Hittites; he maintained the peace in Upper and Lower Egypt for sixty-four years of his reign! What other Pharaoh ever brought such tranquillity to the land of the great river! You know what happened afterwards, don't you?"

"Reginald," Julie said under her breath, "does this really matter so much!"

"Well, apparently it matters to your father's friend," said

Elliott. "I suspect the ancient Kings were perfect tyrants. I suspect they beat their subjects to death if they didn't work on those absurd monuments. The pyramids, how for example—"

"You are not so stupid, Lord Rutherford," said Ramses. "You are . . . how do you say . . . baiting me. Were Englishmen whipped in the streets when they built your St. Paul's or Westminster Abbey? The Tower of London, this is the work of slaves?"

"No one knows these answers," Samir said meekly. "Perhaps we should attempt to—"

"There's a great deal of truth in what you say," Elliott said, ignoring Samir. "But with regard to the great Ramses, you must admit, he was an exceptionally immodest ruler. The stele which brag of his accomplishments are laughable."

"Sir, really," Samir said.

"They are nothing of the sort," said Ramses. "This was the style of the times, the way the people wanted their ruler to represent himself. Don't you understand? The ruler was the people. For the people to be great, the ruler had to be great! The ruler was the slave of the people when it came to their wishes, their needs, their welfare."

"Oh, surely you don't mean the old fellow was a martyr!" Alex scoffed. Never had Julie seen him so aggressive.

"Perhaps it's not possible for a modern mind to comprehend an ancient mind so easily," Elliott conceded. "I wonder if the opposite is true. Whether a man of ancient times, brought to life again, in this era, could understand our values."

"You're not so difficult to understand," Ramses said. "You've learned to express yourselves too well for anything to remain veiled or mysterious. Your newspapers and books tell everything. Yet you are not so different from your ancient ancestors. You want love, you want comfort; you want justice. That is what the Egyptian farmer wanted when he went out to till his fields. That is what the labourers of London want. And as always the rich are jealous of what they possess. And greed leads to high crimes as it always has."

He turned his eyes mercilessly on Henry, who was now staring back at him directly. Julie looked in desperation to Samir.

"Why, you speak of this era as if you have nothing to do with it!" Alex said.

"So what you're saying," Elliott said, "is that we're no better and no worse than the ancient Egyptian."

Henry reached for his drink and suddenly knocked it over. Then he reached for the wine and drank it down. His white face was now moist all over. His lower lip was trembling. He looked for all the world like a man about to be seriously ill.

"No, that is not what I'm saying," Ramses said thoughtfully. "You are better. Better in a thousand ways. And yet you're still human. You haven't found all the answers yet. Electricity, telephones, these are lovely magic. But the poor go unfed. Men kill for what they cannot gain by their own labour. How to share the magic, the riches, the secrets, that is still the problem."

"Ah, there you have it. Marxism, I told you," Alex said. "Well, at Oxford they told us Ramses the Second was a bloody tyrant."

"Be quiet, Alex," said Elliott dismissively. He turned to Ramses. "Why does this concern you so, these questions of greed and power?"

"Oxford? What is Oxford?" Ramses asked, glancing at Alex. Then he stared again at Henry, and Henry moved his chair abruptly backwards. He appeared to be hanging on to the table as if to steady himself. The waiters, meantime, had taken the fish away and were setting down the roast chicken and potatoes. Someone poured another drink for Henry, which he emptied at once.

"You're going to be ill," Elliott said to him under his breath.

"Wait a minute," Alex said. "You've never *heard* of Oxford!"

"No, what is it?" Ramses asked.

"Oxford, egomania, aspirin, Marxism," Elliott said. "Your head is in the clouds, Mr. Ramsey."

"Yes, like that of a colossal statue!" Ramses smiled.

"But you're still a Marxist," Alex said.

"Alex, Mr. Ramsey is not a Marxist!" Julie said, unable any longer to contain her rage. "And as I recall, your favorite subject at Oxford was sports, wasn't it? Boat races and football? You've never studied Egyptian history or Marxism, am I right?"

"Yes, darling. I don't know a thing about ancient Egypt," he conceded, a bit crestfallen. "But there is that poem, Mr. Ramsey, that poem about Ramses the Great by Shelley. You have heard it, have you not? Let's see, some damnable old teacher made me memorize it."

"Perhaps we should return to the question of the journey,"

Samir said. "It shall be very hot in Luxor. Perhaps you will want to go only as far as—"

"Yes, and the reasons for the journey," Elliott said. "Are you investigating the claims made by 'the mummy'?"

"What claims?" Julie asked weakly. "I don't know what you mean specifically. . . ."

"You know. You told me yourself," Elliott answered. "And then there was your father's notebook, which I read, at your behest. The mummy's claim to be immortal, to have lived and loved Cleopatra."

Ramses looked down at his plate. Deftly he broke off a joint of the chicken and ate half of it in two quick, delicate bites.

"The museum will have to examine those texts," Samir said. "It's too early to draw conclusions."

"And is the museum content that you've left the collection locked up in Mayfair?" asked Elliott.

"Frankly," Alex said, "the whole thing sounded perfectly absurd to me. Romantic twaddle. An immortal being, living for a thousand years and then falling tragically in love with Cleopatra. Cleopatra!"

"I beg your pardon," Ramses said. He devoured the remaining chicken and wiped his fingers again. "At your famous Oxford, they said mean things about Cleopatra as well."

Alex laughed frankly and cheerfully.

"You don't have to go to Oxford to hear mean things about Cleopatra. Why, she was the trollop of the ancient world, a spendthrift, a temptress and an hysterical woman."

"Alex, I don't want to hear any more of this schoolboy history!" Julie said.

"You have many opinions, young man," Ramses said with a chilling smile. "What is your passion now? What interests you?"

There was a silence. Julie couldn't help but notice the curious expression on Elliott's face.

"Well," Alex said. "If you were an immortal—an immortal who'd once been a great King, would you have fallen in love with a woman like Cleopatra?"

"Answer the question, Alex," Julie said. "What is your passion? It's not history, not Egyptology, not government. What would you say it is that makes you want to wake up in the morning?" She could feel the blood rising in her face.

"Yes, I would have fallen in love with Cleopatra," said

Ramses. "She could have charmed a god. Read between the lines of your Plutarch. The truth is there."

"And what is the truth?" Elliott asked.

"That she was a brilliant mind; she had a gift for languages and for governing which defied reason. The greatest men of the time paid court to her. Hers was a royal soul in every sense of the word. Why do you think your Shakespeare wrote about her? Why do your schoolchildren know her name?"

"Oh, come now. Divine right?" said Alex. "You sound much better when you are talking Marxist theory."

"Which is what, precisely?"

"Alex," Julie said sharply. "You wouldn't know a Marxist if one punched you in the face."

"You must understand, my lord," Samir said to Alex. "We Egyptians take our history rather seriously. Cleopatra was by any standards a formidable Queen."

"Yes, well said," Ramses said. "And Egypt could use a Cleopatra now to rid it of British domination. She'd send your soldiers packing, you can be sure."

"Ah, there you see, a revolutionary. And what about the Suez Canal? I suppose she'd say 'No, thank you' for that? You do know what the Suez Canal is, don't you! Well, it was British financing that accomplished that little miracle, my friend, I hope you understand."

"Oh, yes, that little trench you dug between the Red Sea and the Mediterranean. Did you whip the slaves in the hot sun to dig that trench? Do tell me."

"Touché, old fellow, touché. Truth is, I haven't the foggiest notion." Alex put down his fork and sat back, smiling at Henry. "This has been the most exhausting dinner."

Henry stared at him with the same expressionless glassy eyes with which he regarded everything else.

"Tell me, Mr. Ramsey," said Elliott. "Your personal opinion, if you will. Is this mummy truly Ramses the Great? An immortal who lived until the time of Cleopatra?"

Alex laughed softly. He looked again at Henry, and this time apparently Henry's condition shocked him. He was about to say something when Ramses went on.

"And what do *you* think, Lord Rutherford?" Ramses asked. "You read the notes of your friend Lawrence. Is there an immortal man in that mummy case in Julie's house in Mayfair?"

Elliott smiled. "No, there isn't," he said.

Julie stared at her plate. Then slowly she looked up at Samir.

"Of course not!" Alex said. "And it's about time somebody said so. When they take him to the museum and cut him up, they'll discover he was a scribe with a lively imagination."

"Forgive me," Julie said. "But I am so weary of all this. We'll be in Egypt soon enough, among the mummies and the monuments. Must we go on?"

"I'm sorry, my dear," Elliott said, lifting his fork and taking a small morsel of chicken. "I've rather enjoyed our conversation, Mr. Ramsey. I find your perspective on ancient Egypt absolutely riveting."

"Oh? The present era is my fascination of late, Lord Rutherford. Englishmen such as yourself intrigue me. And as you were saying, you were a good friend of Lawrence, were you not?"

Julie saw the change in Henry before she realized that Ramses was once again glaring at him. Henry shifted, lifted the empty glass in his hand, then realized it was empty and stared at it as if he did not know what to do with it, and then stared just as stupidly at the waiter who took it from him and gave him another drink.

If Elliott noticed all this, he gave no sign.

"We had our differences, Lawrence and I," he answered, "but yes, we were very good friends. And we did agree upon one thing. We hoped that our children would soon be happily married."

Julie was stunned. "Elliott, please."

"But we needn't discuss this, you and I," Elliott said quickly. Obviously rudeness wasn't easy for him. "There are other things I should like to discuss with you. Where you came from, who you really are. All those same questions I ask myself when I look into the mirror."

Ramses laughed, but he was now angry. Julie could feel it.

"You'll probably find my answers brief and disappointing. As for the marriage of Julie to your son, Lawrence believed it was Julie's choice. Let me see. How did he put it?" He turned his eyes on Henry again. "English is rather new to me, but my memory is exceptional. Ah, yes. 'Julie's marriage can wait forever.' My dear Henry, were those not the words?"

Henry's lips worked silently, but only a faint moan came out of his lips. Alex was red-faced, hurt, looking at Ramses. Julie had to do something to stop this, but what?

"Well, you certainly do seem to have been a close friend of Julie's father," Alex said almost sadly. "Closer perhaps than we realized. Was there anything else that Lawrence made known to you before he died?"

Poor, poor Alex! But this was all aimed at Henry, and in another moment things were going to explode.

"Yes," Ramses said. Julie grabbed his hand and squeezed it, but he did not acknowledge this. "Yes, that he thought his nephew was a bastard." Again he glared at Henry. "Am I right? 'You bastard.' Weren't those his last words?"

Henry rose from the chair, upsetting it. He stumbled backwards as the chair went over with a thud on the carpeted floor. He stared at Ramses, his mouth open, a low sound coming from him, half gasp, half moan.

"Good God," said Alex. "Mr. Ramsey, you go too far."

"Do I?" asked Ramses, watching Henry.

"Henry, you're drunk, old man," Alex said. "I should help you to your room."

"Please do not do this," Julie whispered. Elliott was studying both of them. He had not so much as looked up at Henry, who turned now and half stumbled towards the far door.

Alex stared at his plate, his face reddening.

"Mr. Ramsey, I think there's something you must understand," Alex said.

"What is that, young man?"

"Julie's father was plainspoken with those he loved." Then something dawned on him. "But . . . you weren't there when he died, were you? I thought Henry was with him. Alone."

Elliott was silent.

"My, but this is going to be a very interesting trip," Alex said lamely. "I must confess—"

"It's going to be a disaster!" Julie said. She could take this no more. "Now, listen to me. All of you. I don't want any more talk of marriage; or of my father's death. I've had quite enough of both." She rose to her feet. "You must forgive me, but I'm leaving you now. I'll be in my cabin if you should need me." She looked down at Ramses. "But no more talk of these things, is that clear?"

She gathered up her small evening bag and walked slowly through the dining room, ignoring those who were staring.

"Oh, this is dreadful," she heard Alex say behind her. And

then he was at her side. "I am so sorry, darling, really! Things just got out of hand."

"I want to go to my room, I told you," she said, walking faster.

Nightmare. You are going to wake up, back in London, safe, and none of this will have happened. You did what you had to do. That creature is a monster and must be destroyed.

He stood at the bar waiting for the Scotch, which seemed to be taking forever, and then he looked up and saw him—that thing, that thing that wasn't human, standing in the door.

"Never mind," he growled under his breath. He turned and rushed through the little carpeted corridor to the deck. Slam of the door behind him, the thing was coming after him. He turned, his face stung by the wind, and almost fell on the narrow metal steps. The thing was only a few feet away from him, those big glassy blue eyes staring at him. He ran up the steps, the wind working against him as he ran along the deserted deck.

Where was he going? How would he get away from it? He pushed open another door into a little corridor. Numbers he didn't recognize on the polished doors of the staterooms. He looked back; the thing had entered the corridor; it was pounding after him.

"Damn you." His voice was a whimper. Out on the deck again and this time the wind was so damp it was like rain. He couldn't see where he was going. He clutched the railing for a moment, looking down at the boiling grey sea.

No! Get away from the railing. He rushed along until he saw another doorway, and ducked inside again. He felt the vibration right behind him, heard the thing breathing. His gun, where the hell was his gun?

Turning, he fumbled in his pocket. The thing had hold of him. Dear God! He felt a large warm hand close over his. The gun was wrenched out of his fingers. Groaning, he slumped against the wall, but the thing held him up by his lapel, peering into his face. An ugly light flashed through the porthole of the door, illuminating the thing in irregular bursts.

"A pistol, am I correct?" the thing said to him. "I read of it when perhaps I should have been reading of Oxford, egomania, aspirin and Marxism. It fires a small projectile of metal at high speed, as the result of intense combustion within the chamber behind the projectile. Very interesting, and useless when you are dealing with me. And were you to fire it, men would come and want to know why you did it.''

"I know what you are! I know where you came from.''

"Oh, you do! Then you realize that I know what you are. And what you have been up to! And I have not the slightest scruple about carrying you down to the coal furnaces which fuel this magnificent ship and feeding you to the fires which drive us now into the cold Atlantic.''

Henry's body convulsed. With every muscle he struggled, but he could not free himself from the hand that now locked on his shoulder, gently crushing the bones.

"Listen to me, foolish one.'' The thing drew in closer. He could feel its breath on his face. "Harm Julie and I shall do it. Make Julie cry and I shall do it! Make Julie *frown* and I shall do it! For the sake of Julie's peace of mind, you live. There is nothing more to it. Remember what I say.''

The hand released him. He slumped towards the floor, only catching himself before he actually fell. He gritted his teeth, his eyes closing as he felt the warm stickiness inside his pants, and smelled his own waste. His bowels had cut loose.

The thing stood there, its face veiled in shadow as it studied the gun which it held out to the grey light from the porthole in the door. Then it pocketed the gun and turned on its heel and left him.

A wave of sickness rose; he saw blackness.

When he awoke he was crouched in the corner of the passage. No one had passed, it seemed. Trembling, dizzy, he climbed to his feet and made his way to his stateroom. And once there he stood over the small toilet vomiting up the contents of his stomach. Only then did he strip off his soiled clothes.

She was crying when he came in. She had sent Rita off to supper with the other servants on board. He did not even knock. He opened the door and slipped inside. She wouldn't look at him. She pressed her handkerchief to her eyes, but her crying wouldn't stop.

"I'm sorry, my Queen. My gentle Queen. Believe me, I am.''

When she looked up she saw the sadness in his face. He stood helplessly before her, the lamp behind him filling the edges of his brown hair with an uneven golden light.

"Let it be for now, Ramses,'' she said desperately. "I can't bear it, the knowledge that he did it. Let it be, I beg you. I only want us to be in Egypt together.''

He sat down on the settee beside her, towering over her, and gently he turned her and this time when he kissed her she melted completely, letting him enfold her, letting him breathe into her that powerful heat. She kissed his face, his cheek where the flesh was so taut over the bones, and then his closed eyes. She felt his hands tighten on her naked shoulders and she realized he was pushing her gown down and away from her breasts.

She drew back, ashamed. She had led him on and she hadn't meant to.

"I don't want it to happen," she said, her tears coming again.

Not looking at him, she pushed the satin sleeves upwards. When finally their eyes met, she saw only patience, and that faint half smile, now tempered by the same sadness she'd seen before.

He reached out for her, and she stiffened. But he merely adjusted the sleeves of her dress for her. And straightened the pearls around her neck. Then he kissed her hand.

"Come out with me," he said in a low, soft voice, kissing her tenderly on her shoulder. "The wind is cool and fresh. And they are playing music in the public rooms. Can we dance together to the music? Ah, this floating palace. It is paradise. Come with me, my Queen."

"But Alex," she said. "If only Alex . . ."

He kissed her throat. He kissed her hand again. He turned her hand over and pressed his lips to her palm. The heat coursed through her again. To stay in this room would be folly, unless, of course. But no. She could not let it happen, until it was really what she wanted with her whole soul.

She might lose her soul utterly; that was the horror. There was a dim sense again of her world being destroyed.

"Let's go, then," she said drowsily.

He helped her to her feet. He took her handkerchief from her and wiped her eyes with it as if she were a child. Then he picked up her white fur from the arm of the chair and put it over her shoulders.

They walked together along the windy deck and into the corridor and towards the grand ballroom—a lovely confection of gilded wood and satin wall panels, of drowsing palms and stained glass.

He moaned as he looked at the distant orchestra. "Oooh, Julie, this music," he whispered. "It enslaves me."

It was a Strauss waltz again, only there were many musicians here, and the sound was louder and richer, flooding the great room.

No sign of Alex, thank God. She turned to him, and let him take her hand.

With a great sweeping turn, he began to waltz with her, beaming down at her, and it seemed then nothing mattered. There was no Alex; there was no Henry; there had been no terrible death for her father which must be avenged.

There was only this moment of dancing with him, round and round, beneath the soft iridescent chandeliers. The music surged; the other dancers seemed perilously close around them; but Ramses' steps were perfect for all their great breadth and strength.

Wasn't it enough that he should be a mystery? she thought desperately. Wasn't it enough that he'd torn the veil away completely? Did he have to be irresistible? Did she have to fall so hopelessly in love?

Far away, from the deep shadows of the darkly panelled bar, Elliott watched them dancing. They were going into the third waltz now, and Julie was laughing as Ramsey led her recklessly and madly, driving the other dancers out of his path.

No one seemed to take offense at it. Everyone respects those who are in love.

Elliott finished his whisky, then rose to go.

When he reached Henry's door, he knocked once and then opened it. Henry sat hunched over on the small couch, a thin green robe wrapped around him, his legs naked and hairy beneath it, his feet bare. He appeared to be trembling, as if he were terribly cold.

Elliott was appalled suddenly at the heat of his own anger. His voice came out hoarse and unfamiliar.

"What did our Egyptian King see?" he demanded. "What happened in that tomb when Lawrence died!"

Henry tried to turn away from him, in a pathetic moment of hysteria, as if he could claw his way through the wall. Elliott turned him around.

"Look at me, you miserable little coward. Answer my question. What happened in that tomb!"

"I was trying to get what you wanted!" Henry whispered. His eyes were sunken. There was a great bruise on his neck. "I was . . . trying to persuade him to advise Julie to marry Alex."

"Don't lie to me!" Elliott said. His left hand clutched at the silver walking stick, ready to lift it, to wield it like a club.

"I don't know what happened," Henry pleaded. "Or what it saw! It was wrapped up in the damned mummy case. What the hell could it have seen! Uncle Lawrence was arguing with me. He was upset. The heat . . . I don't know what happened. Suddenly he was lying on the floor."

He slumped forward, elbows on his knees, head in his hands. "I didn't mean to hurt him," he sobbed. "Oh, God, I didn't mean to hurt him! I did what I had to do." He bowed his head, fingers meshed in his dark hair.

Elliott stared down at him. If this had been his son, life would have no meaning. And if this miserable creature was lying . . . But he didn't know. He simply could not tell.

"All right," he murmured. "You have told me everything?"

"Yes!" Henry said. "God, I have to get off this ship! I have to get away from it!"

"But why does it despise you? Why did it try to kill you, and why does it seek to humiliate you?"

There was a moment of silence. All he heard were Henry's desperate broken gasps. Then the thin white face was turned up again, the sunken dark eyes imploring him.

"I saw it come alive," Henry said. "I'm the only one other than Julie who really knows what it is. You know, but I'm the one who saw it. It wants to kill me!" He stopped, as if he feared losing control altogether. His eyes were dancing as he looked at the carpet. "I'll tell you something too," he said, as he slumped back again on the couch. "It's unnaturally strong, that thing. It could kill a man with its bare hands. Why it didn't kill me the first time it tried, I don't know. But it could succeed if it tried again."

The Earl didn't respond.

He turned and left the stateroom. He went out onto the deck. The sky was black over the sea, and the stars were, as always on a cloudless night over the ocean, wonderfully clear.

He leaned on the railing for a long time, and then drew out a cheroot and lighted it. He tried to reason things out.

Samir Ibrahaim knew this thing was immortal. He was travelling with it. Julie knew. Julie had been swept off her feet. And now in his sheer obsession with this mystery, he had let Ramsey know that he knew as well.

Now, Ramsey clearly felt affection for Samir Ibrahaim. He felt something for Julie Stratford, though what that something was, still wasn't clear. But what did Ramsey feel for him? Maybe he would turn on him as he had on Henry, "the only witness."

But somehow that didn't make sense. Or at least if it did, it didn't frighten Elliott. It only fascinated him. And the whole question of Henry continued to puzzle him and repel him. Henry was a convincing liar. But Henry wasn't telling the whole truth.

Nothing to do but wait, he figured. And do what he could to protect Alex, his poor vulnerable Alex, who had failed so miserably at dinner to conceal his growing hurt. He had to help Alex through this, make it clear to his son that he was going to lose his childhood sweetheart, for there was no longer the slightest doubt of that.

But oh, how he himself was loving this. How secretly and completely it thrilled him. The truth was, no matter what the outcome, he was experiencing a rejuvenation because of this mystery. He was having the best time he'd had in years and years.

If he leafed back through the happy memories of his life, there had been one time only, when simply being alive had been this wondrous and strange. He'd been at Oxford then; he'd been only twenty; and he'd been in love with Lawrence Stratford, and Lawrence Stratford had been in love with him.

The thought of Lawrence now destroyed everything. It was as if the icy wind off the sea had frozen his heart. Something had happened in that tomb, something Henry did not dare to confess to him. And Ramsey knew it. And no matter what else happened in this dangerous little venture, Elliott was going to discover the truth of the matter.

12

BY THE fourth day out, Elliott realized that Julie would not dine again in the public rooms; that she would take all her meals in her stateroom from now on, and that Ramsey was probably dining with her.

Henry had also disappeared from view altogether. Sullen, drunk, he remained in his room round the clock, seldom wearing anything other than trousers, a shirt and a smoking jacket. However, this did not prevent him from running a fairly steady card game with members of the crew, who were not anxious to be discovered gambling with a first-class passenger. The gossip was that Henry was winning quite a lot. But that had always been the gossip about Henry. He would lose sooner or later, and probably everything that he had made; that had been the rhythm of his descent since the beginning.

Elliott could also see that Julie was going out of her way to be gentle with Alex. She and Alex took their afternoon walk on the deck, rain or shine. She and Alex danced now and then in the ballroom after supper. Ramsey was always there, watching with surprising equanimity, and ready at any moment to step in and become Julie's partner. But clearly it had been agreed that Alex should not be neglected by Julie.

On brief shore excursions, which Elliott could not physically endure, Julie, Samir, Ramsey and Alex always traveled together. Alex invariably came back faintly repelled. He didn't like foreigners very much; Julie and Samir had been thoroughly entertained; and Ramsey was overwhelmed with enthusiasm for the things he'd seen, especially if he'd been able to find a cinema or an English-language bookshop.

Elliott appreciated Julie's kindness to Alex. After all, this ship was no place for Alex to understand the full truth, and clearly Julie realized it. On the other hand, perhaps Alex already sensed that he'd lost the first major battle of his life; the truth was Alex was too pleasant and agreeable a person to reveal what he was feeling. Probably he did not know himself, Elliott figured.

The real adventure of the voyage for Elliott was getting to know Ramsey, and watching Ramsey from afar, and realizing things about Ramsey which others didn't appear to notice. It helped immensely that Ramsey was a ferociously social being.

By the hour Ramsey, Elliott, Samir and Alex played billiards together, during which time Ramsey discoursed on all manner of subjects and asked all kinds of questions.

Modern science in particular interested him, and Elliott found himself rambling on by the hour about theories of the cell, the circulatory system, germs and other causes of disease. The whole concept of inoculation fascinated Ramsey.

Almost every night Ramsey was in the library, poring over Darwin and Malthus or popular compendiums on electricity, the telegraph, the automobile and astronomy.

Modern art was also of more than passing interest. He was powerfully intrigued by the Pointillists and the Impressionists, and the novels of the Russians—Tolstoy and Dostoevsky, only newly translated into English—swept him up utterly. Clearly the speed of his reading and absorption was magical.

About the sixth day out, Ramsey acquired a typewriter. With the captain's permission he borrowed it from the ship's offices and thereafter he typed by the hour lists of what he meant to do, some of which Elliott managed to glimpse on trips to Ramsey's cabin. Common enough were entries such as "Visit the Prado in Madrid; ride in an aeroplane as soon as possible."

Elliott finally realized something. This man never slept. He didn't have to. At any hour of the night Elliott could find Ramsey doing something somewhere. If he was not in the cinema or in the library—or typing away in his room—then he was with the crew in the map room or the radio room. They had not been on board two days before Ramsey knew all the crew by name; and most of the staff as well. His capacity to seduce people into almost anything could not be overestimated.

On one very eerie morning, Elliott entered the ballroom to see a handful of musicians playing steadily for Ramsey, who danced alone, a curious slow and primitive dance much like that of Greek men today in their seaside tavernas. The figure of the lone dancing man, his white long-sleeve shirt open to the waist, had torn at Elliott's heart. It seemed a crime to spy on such a thing which came so totally from the soul. Elliott had turned away, going out on the deck to smoke in his own solitude.

That Ramsey was so accessible, that was a great surprise. But the oddest part of the whole exhilarating affair was how much Elliott was coming to like this mysterious creature.

In fact, if he dwelt on that aspect of it, he would feel real pain. He thought back many times on his hasty words before they'd left—"I want to know you." How true that had been. How tantalizing all this; how wondrously satisfying.

And then the agony; the fear: *something beyond all imagining is here!* Elliott did not wish to be closed off from it.

And how remarkable that his son, Alex, found Ramsey only peculiar and "funny" and not at all genuinely intriguing. But then what did Alex find intriguing? He'd made fast friends of the type of fast friends he always made with dozens of other passengers. He was having a good time, it seemed, as he always did, no matter what else was happening. And that will be his salvation, Elliott thought. That he feels nothing too deeply.

As for Samir, he was silent by nature; and he never said much no matter how the conversation raged between Elliott and Ramsey. But there was an almost religious quality about his attitude towards Ramsey. And he had become a complete servant to the man, that was obvious. He became agitated only when Elliott pressed Ramsey for opinions on the subject of history. And so did Julie.

"Explain what you mean," Elliott asked when Ramsey said that Latin made possible a whole new kind of thinking. "Surely the ideas came first and then the language to express them."

"No, that's not true. Even in Italy itself where the tongue was born, the language made possible the evolution of ideas which would have been impossible otherwise. Same partnership of languages and ideas in Greece as well, undoubtedly.

"But I shall tell you the strange thing about Italy. It is that culture developed there at all, for the climate is so pleasant. One must usually have a radical change of weather during the year for civilization to progress. Look at the people of the jungles and the far north, utterly limited, because the climate is the same all year round. . . ."

Julie would almost invariably interrupt these lectures. Elliott could hardly bear it.

Julie and Samir also became uneasy when Ramsey burst out with statements from the heart, such as "Julie, we must be done with the past as quickly as we can. There is so much to be discovered. X-rays, Julie, do you know what they are! And we must go to the North Pole in an aeroplane."

These remarks amused other people mightily. In fact, other passengers, charmed and seduced to a one, seemed to regard Ramsey as not a superintelligent being so much as one who was slightly retarded. Overly sophisticated themselves, never guessing the reason behind his odd exclamations, they treated him tenderly and indulgently, never availing themselves of the information he would give out at a moment's provocation.

Not so with Elliott, who pumped him mercilessly. "Ancient battle. What was it really like! I mean, we've seen the great reliefs on the temple of Ramses the Third. . . ."

"Ah, now that was a brilliant man, a worthy namesake. . . ."

"What did you say?"

"A worthy namesake of Ramses the Second, that's all, go on."

"But did a Pharaoh himself truly fight!"

"Oh, yes, of course. Why, he rode at the head of his troops; he was symbol in action. Why, in one battle, the Pharaoh himself might crush two hundred skulls with his bludgeon; he might make his way across the battlefield, executing the wounded and dying in the same manner. When he retired to his tent, his arms would be drenched in blood to the elbows. But remember, it was expected, you see. If the Pharaoh fell . . . well, the battle would be over."

Silence.

Ramsey: "You don't want to know these things, do you? And yet modern warfare is ghastly. That recent war in Africa; men were blown apart by gunpowder. And the Civil War in the United States, what a horror. Things change, but they do not change. . . ."

"Exactly. Could you yourself do such a thing? Crush skulls one after another?"

Ramsey smiled. "You are a brave man, aren't you, Lord Elliott, Earl of Rutherford. Yes, I could do it. So could you, if you were there, and you were Pharaoh; you could do it.''

The ship plowed on through the grey sea. The coast of Africa loomed. The party was almost over.

It had been another perfect night. Alex had retired early, and Julie had been left alone to dance with Ramses for hours. She'd drunk a little too much wine.

And now as they stood in the tiny low-ceilinged passage outside her stateroom, she felt as always the wrenching, the temptation and the desperation that she mustn't give in to it.

It caught her utterly off guard when Ramses spun her around, crushed her to his chest and kissed her more roughly than usual. There was a painful urgency to it. She found herself fighting, then drawing back on the edge of tears, her hand raised to hit him. She didn't.

"Why do you try to force me?" she said.

The look in his eyes frightened her.

"I'm hungry," he said, all semblance of courtesy lost, "hungry for you, for everything. For food and drink and sunshine and life itself. But above all, for you. It is a pain in me! I grow weary of it."

"God!" she whispered. She put her hands up delicately to cover her face. Why was she resisting? For the moment, she didn't know.

"It's what it does to me, the potion in my veins," he said. "I need nothing, yet nothing fills me. Only love, perhaps. And so I wait." His voice grew quieter. "I wait for you to love me. If that is what is required."

She laughed suddenly. How clear it all was.

"Ah, but with all your wisdom, you have it backwards," she said. "What is required is that you love *me*."

His face went blank. Then slowly he nodded. He seemed utterly at a loss for words. She could not guess what he was really thinking.

Quickly she opened the door and went inside and sat down alone on the sofa. She put her face in her hands. How childish it had sounded. And yet it was true, it was heartbreakingly true. And she began to cry softly, hoping Rita would not hear her.

Twenty-four hours, the navigator had told him, and we shall dock in Alexandria.

He leaned on the railing of the deck. And peered into the thick mist which covered the water completely.

It was four o'clock. Not even the Earl of Rutherford was about. Samir had been fast asleep when last Ramses visited their rooms. And so he had the deck to himself.

He loved it. He loved the deep rumble of the engines through the great steel hull. He loved the ship's pure power. Ah, the paradox of twentieth-century man amid his great machines and inventions, for he was the same two-legged creature he had ever been, and yet his inventions were begetting inventions.

He drew out a cheroot—one of the sweet, mild smokes which the Earl of Rutherford had given him, and cupping his hand around the match carefully lighted it. He could not see the smoke as it disappeared, yet the thing tasted divine. He closed his eyes and savored the wind, and let himself think of Julie Stratford again now that she was safely barricaded in her little bedchamber.

But Julie Stratford faded. It was Cleopatra he saw. *Twenty-four hours and we shall be in Alexandria.*

He saw the conference room in the palace of long ago, the long marble table, and she the young Queen—young as Julie Stratford was now—conversing with her ambassadors and advisers.

He watched from an antechamber. He had been gone for a long time, wandering far to the north and to the east, into kingdoms that had not been known to him at all in earlier centuries. And returning the night before, had gone directly to her bedchamber.

All night long they'd made love; the windows had been open to the sea; she had been as hungry for him as he had been for her; for though he had had a hundred women in the preceding months, he loved only Cleopatra. So feverish his lovemaking had been that finally he had almost hurt her; yet she had invited him to go on, her arms holding him tight, her body again and again receiving him.

The audience was over. He watched her dismiss her courtiers. He watched her rise from her chair and come towards him—a tall woman with magnificent bones, and a long slender neck beautifully exposed, her rippling black hair swept back from her face into a circle on the back of her head in the Roman manner.

There was a vaguely defiant expression on her face, and a lift to her chin which accentuated it. It gave an immediate impression of strength, badly needed to temper innate seductiveness.

Only when she had drawn the curtain did she turn to him and smile, her dark eyes firing beautifully.

There had been a time in his life when dark-eyed beings were all he knew; he alone was the blue-eyed one because he had drunk the elixir. Then he traveled to distant lands, lands of which Egyptians knew nothing; and he met pale-eyed mortal men and women. And dazzling though these things were, brown eyes for him remained the true eyes, the eyes he could fathom instantly.

Julie Stratford's eyes were deep brown, and large, and full of easy affection and response, as Cleopatra's eyes had been that day when she embraced him.

"Now, what are my lessons for this afternoon?" she'd asked in Greek, the only language they spoke to each other, something in her gaze acknowledging the long night of intimacy.

"Simple," he said. "Disguise yourself and come with me and walk among your people. To see what no Queen can ever see. That is what I want of you."

Alexandria. What would it be tomorrow? It had been a Greek city then of stone streets and whitewashed walls, and merchants who sold to all the world—a port full of weavers, jewelers, glass blowers, makers of papyri. In a thousand marketplace shops they worked above the crowded harbour.

Through the bazaar they had walked together, both of them in the shapeless cloaks all men and women wore who did not wish to be recognized. Two travellers through time. And he had spoken to her of so many things—of his wanderings north into Gaul, of his long trek to India. He had ridden elephants and seen the great tiger with his own eyes. He had come back to Athens to listen to the philosophers.

And what had he learned? That Julius Caesar, the Roman general, would conquer the world; that he would take Egypt if Cleopatra did not stop him.

What had her thoughts been that day? Had she let him ramble on without absorbing all the desperate advice he gave her? What had she seen of the common men about her? The women and children hard at work at the laundry tubs and the looms? Of the sailors of all nations searching for the brothels?

To the great university they had wandered, to listen to the teachers under the porticoes.

Finally in a dirt square they'd stopped. From the common well Cleopatra had drunk, from the common cup on its rope.

"It tastes the same," she had said with a playful smile.

He remembered so clearly the cup dropped down into the deep cool water. The sound echoing up the stone walls; the hammering that came from the docks, and the vision through the narrow street to his right of the masts of the ships, a leafless forest there.

"What is it you really want of me, Ramses?" she had asked.

"That you be a good and wise Queen of Egypt. I've told you."

She'd taken his arm, forced him to look at her.

"You want more than that. You're preparing me for something much more important."

"No," he said, but that had been a lie, the first lie he had ever told her. The pain in him had been sharp, almost unbearable. *I am lonely, my beloved. I am lonely beyond mortal endurance.* But he didn't say that to her. He only stood there, knowing that he, an immortal man, could not live without her.

What had happened after that? Another evening of lovemaking, with the sea beyond turning slowly from azure to silver, and finally black beneath a heavy full moon. And all around her the gilded furnishings, the hanging lamps and the fragrance of scented oil, and somewhere in an alcove just far enough away, a young boy playing a harp and singing a mournful song of ancient Egyptian words that the boy himself did not understand, but which Ramses understood perfectly.

Memory within the memory. His palace at Thebes when he had been a mortal man, and afraid of death, and afraid of humiliation. When he had had a harem of one hundred wives to pleasure, and it had seemed a burden.

"Have you had many lovers since I left?" he had asked Cleopatra.

"Oh, many men," she'd answered in a low voice that was almost as hard as a man's voice for all its feminine resonance. "But none of them were lovers."

The lovers would come. Julius Caesar would come; and then the one who swept her away from all the things he'd taught her. "For Egypt," she'd cry. But it wasn't for Egypt. Egypt was Cleopatra then. And Cleopatra was for Antony.

It was getting light. The mist above the sea had paled, and he could see now the sparkling surface of the dark blue water.

High above, the pale sun burnt through. And at once he felt it working on him. He felt a sudden breath of energy pass through him.

His cheroot had long ago gone out. He pitched it into the void, and drawing out his gold cigarette case, took another.

A foot sounded on the steel deck behind him.

"Only a few hours, sire."

The match came up to light the cheroot for him.

"Yes, my loyal one," he said, drawing in the smoke. "We wake from this ship as if from a dream. And what are we to do in the light of day with these two who know my secret, the young scoundrel, and the aged philosopher who may pose the worst threat of all with his knowledge?"

"Are philosophers so dangerous, sire?"

"Lord Rutherford has great faith in the invisible, Samir. And he is no coward. He wants the secret of eternal life. He realizes what it really is, Samir."

No answer. Only the same distant and melancholy expression.

"And I'll tell you another little secret, my friend," he went on. "I've grown to like the man mightily."

"I've seen it, sire."

"He is an interesting man," Ramses said. And to his surprise he heard his voice break. It was hard for him to finish, but he did, saying: "I like to talk to him."

Hancock sat at his desk in the museum office, looking up at Inspector Trent from Scotland Yard.

"Well, as I see it, we have no choice. We seek a court order to enter the house and examine the collection. Of course if everything is as it should be, and there are no coins missing. . ."

"Sir, with the two we have now, that's almost too much to hope for."

PART · 2

1

THE GRAND Colonial Hotel was a rambling pink confection of moorish arches, mosaic floors, lacquered screens and peacock wicker chairs, its broad verandas overlooking the shining sand and the endless blue of the Mediterranean beyond it.

Rich Americans and Europeans in perennial summer white thronged its immense lobby and other public rooms. An orchestra played Viennese music in one of its open bars. A young American pianist played ragtime in another. The ornate brass lifts, riding directly upwards beside the curving grand stair, seemed eternally in operation.

Surely if this resort had existed in any other place, Ramsey would have loved it. But Elliott could see in the very first hour of their arrival that Alexandria was a profound shock to him.

His vitality seemed immediately sapped. He fell quiet at tea, and excused himself to go wandering.

And that night at dinner, when the subject of Henry's abrupt departure for Cairo was raised, he was almost snappish.

"Julie Stratford's a grown woman," he said, glancing at her. "It's preposterous to think she requires the companionship of a drunken, dissolute being. Are we not, all of us, as you say, gentlemen?"

"I suppose so," Alex responded with predictable brightness. "Nevertheless he is her cousin and it was her uncle's wish—"

"Her uncle doesn't know her cousin!" Ramsey declared.

Julie cut the conversation short. "I'm glad Henry's gone. We'll join him in Cairo soon enough. And Henry in Cairo will be a cross as it is. Henry in the Valley of the Kings would be intolerable."

"Quite right." Elliott sighed. "Julie, I am your guardian now. Officially."

"Elliott, the trip is far too difficult for you. You ought to go on to Cairo and wait for us there, also."

Alex was about to protest when Elliott motioned for silence. "That's out of the question now, dearest, and you know it. Besides, I want to see Luxor again, and Abu Simbel, perhaps for the last time."

She looked at him thoughtfully. She knew that he was speaking the truth on both counts. He couldn't let her travel alone with Ramsey, no matter how much she wanted to. And he did want to see those monuments again. But she also sensed he had his own distinct priorities.

Regardless, her acceptance was quite enough for Elliott.

"And when do we go on to the Nile steamer?" Alex asked. "How much time do you need in this city, old boy?" he asked Ramsey.

"Not very much," Ramsey said dismally. "There is precious little left of the old Roman times which I hoped to see."

Ramsey, after devouring three courses without ever touching a knife or a fork, excused himself before the others had finished.

By the following afternoon, it was clear he was in a dismal state. He said almost nothing at luncheon; declined to play billiards and again went out walking. It was soon obvious that he was walking at all times of the night and day, and had left Julie entirely to Alex for the time being. Even Samir did not apparently have his confidence.

He was a man alone in the midst of a struggle.

Elliott watched all this; and then came to a decision. Through his man Walter he hired a young Egyptian boy, a hanger-on at the hotel who did nothing but continuously sweep off the red carpeted steps, to follow Ramsey. It was quite a risk. And Elliott felt ashamed. But this obsession was consuming him.

By the hour he sat in a comfortable peacock chair in the lobby reading the English papers, and watching all comings and goings. And then at odd moments, he would take reports from the Egyptian boy, who spoke tolerable English.

Ramsey walked. Ramsey stared for hours at the sea. Ramsey

explored great fields beyond the city. Ramsey sat in European cafes, staring at nothing, drinking huge quantities of sweet Egyptian coffee. Ramsey had also gone to a brothel, and there he had astonished the greasy old proprietor by taking every woman in the place between sunset and sunrise. That meant twelve couplings. The old pimp had never seen anything like it.

Elliott smiled. So he beds them in the same manner that he satisfies every other appetite, he thought. And this meant surely that Julie had not admitted him to her inner sanctum. Or did it?

Narrow alleyways, the old section of town, they called it. But it was no more than a few hundred years old, and no one knew that the great library had once stood here. That below on the hill had been the university where the teachers lectured to countless hundreds.

Academy of the ancient world, this city; and now it was a seaside resort. And that hotel stood on the very spot where her palace had been; where he had taken her in his arms and begged her to stop her mad passion for Mark Antony.

"The man will fail, don't you see?" he had pleaded. "If Julius Caesar had not been struck down, you would have been Empress of Rome. But this man will never give you that. He is weak, corrupt; he lacks the mettle."

But then, for the first time he'd seen the savage self-defeating passion in her eyes. She loved Mark Antony. She didn't care! Egypt, Rome, what did it matter? When had she ceased to be the Queen and become the mere mortal? He didn't know. He knew only that all his great dreams and plans were dissolving.

"What do you care about Egypt!" she had demanded. "That I be Empress of Rome? That's not what you want of me. You want that I should drink your magic potion, which you claim will make me immortal as you are. And to hell with my mortal life! You would kill my mortal life and my mortal love, admit it! Well, I cannot die for you!"

"You don't know what you're saying!"

Ah, stop the voices of the past. Listen only to the sea crashing on the beach below. Walk where the old Roman cemetery stood, where they laid her to rest beside Mark Antony.

He saw the procession in his mind's eye. He heard the weeping. And worst of all, he saw her again in those last hours. "Take away your promises. Antony calls me from the grave. I want to be with him now."

And now all trace of her was gone, save what remained inside him. And what remained in legend. He heard again the crowds who blocked the narrow streets, and flooded down the grassy slope to see her coffin placed within the marble tomb.

"Our Queen died free."

"She cheated Octavian."

"She was no slave of Rome."

Ah, but she could have been immortal!

The catacombs. The one place he had not ventured. And why had he asked Julie to come with him? How weak he'd become, that he needed her there. And to think, he'd told her nothing.

He could see the concern in her face. So lovely she looked in her long, lace-trimmed dress of pale yellow. These modern women had all seemed preposterously overdressed to him at first, but he understood the seductiveness of their clothing—the full sleeves tapering to tight cuffs at the wrists, the tiny waists and flowing skirts. They had begun to look normal to him.

And he wished suddenly that they were not here. That they were back in England again, or far away in America.

But the catacombs, he had to see the catacombs before they went on. And so with the other tourists they walked, listening to the droning voice of the guide, who spoke of Christians hiding here, of ancient rituals performed long before that in these rock chambers.

"You've been here before," Julie whispered. "It's important to you."

"Yes," he answered under his breath, holding her hand tightly. Oh, if only they could leave Egypt now and forever. What was the point of this agony?

The unwieldy party of chattering, whispering tourists came to a halt. His eyes moved anxiously over the wall. He saw it, the small passageway. The others moved on, cautioned again to remain with the guide, but he held Julie back, and then as the other voices died away, he switched on the electric torch and entered the passage.

Was it the same? He could not tell. He could only remember what had happened.

Same smell of damp stone; Latin markings on the wall.

They came to a large room.

"Look," she said. "There's a window there cut high in the rock, how amazing! And hooks in the wall, do you see it!"

It seemed her voice was very far away. He meant to answer, but that was not possible.

He stared into the gloom at the great rectangular stone to which she pointed now. She said something about an altar.

No, not an altar. A bed. A bed where he had lain for three hundred years, until that portal high up there had been opened. The ancient chains had pulled the heavy wooden blind, and the sun had come down, falling warm on his eyelids.

He heard Cleopatra's girlish voice:

"Ye gods, it's true. He's alive!" Her gasp echoing off the walls. The sun flooding down upon him.

"Ramses, rise!" she cried. "A Queen of Egypt calls you."

He'd felt the tingling in his limbs; felt the suddenly zinging sensation in his hair and skin. Half in sleep still he'd sat up and seen the young woman standing there, rippling black hair loose over her shoulders. And the old priest, shivering, jabbering under his breath, hands clasped as if in prayer, bowing from the waist.

"Ramses the Great," she had said. "A Queen of Egypt needs your counsel."

Soft dusty rays falling down from the twentieth-century world outside. The roar of motor cars on the boulevards of the modern city of Alexandria.

"Ramses!"

He turned. Julie Stratford was looking up at him.

"My beautiful one," he whispered. He took her in his arms, tenderly. Not passion, but love. Yes, love. "My beautiful Julie," he whispered.

In the lobby they took high tea. The whole ritual made him laugh. To eat scones, eggs, cucumber sandwiches, and not call this a meal. But why should he complain? He could eat three times what everyone else was eating and still be hungry for dinner.

He cherished this time alone with her. That Alex and Samir and Elliott were not about.

He sat staring at the parade of plumed hats, frilly umbrellas. And the big shiny open motor cars, chugging up to the side entrance, right along with the open leather carriages.

These were no longer the people of his time. The racial mix was different. She'd said he would see it was the same with the

Greeks when they went there. Oh, so many places to go. Was he feeling relief?

"You've been so patient with me," he said, smiling. "You don't ask me to explain anything."

Ah, but she looked radiant; her dress was a pale flowered silk; lace at the wrists and those tiny pearl buttons he was growing to love. Thank God she had not worn an open gown since that first night at sea. The sight of all that flesh drove him mad completely.

"You'll tell me when you want to tell me," she said. "What I can't bear is to see you suffering."

"It's all as you said," he murmured. He drank down the tea, a beverage he didn't much like. It seemed to be half of something. "All gone without a trace. The mausoleum, the library, the lighthouse. All that Alexander built; and Cleopatra built. Tell me, why are the pyramids still standing at Giza? Why is my temple still standing at Luxor?"

"Do you want to see them?" She reached across the little table and took his hand. "Are you ready to leave here now?"

"Yes, it's time to go on, isn't it? And then when we've seen it all, we can leave this land. You and I. . . . That is, if you want to remain with me."

Such lovely brown eyes with their deep fringe of brown lashes; and the pure sweetness of her mouth as she smiled. And wouldn't you know? The Earl had just come out of the lift, along with his charming nincompoop of a son, and Samir.

"I'll go with you to the ends of the earth," she whispered.

He held her gaze for a long moment. Did she know what she was saying? No. The question was, did he know what she was saying? That she loved him, yes. But the other, the other great question had never been asked, had it?

They had been heading up the Nile for the better part of the afternoon, the sun beating down with full force upon the striped awnings of the small, elegant steamer. The combination of Julie's purse and Elliott's gift for command had provided them with every luxury. The staterooms of the small boat were as fine as those of the P&O liner which had brought them across the sea. The saloon and dining room were more than comfortable. The cook was a European; the servants, with the exception, of course, of Walter and Rita, were Egyptian.

But the greatest luxury of all was that it was their craft. They shared it with no one else. And they had become, much to Julie's surprise, an extremely congenial group of travelers. Now that Henry was gone, that is. And for that she couldn't have been more grateful.

He'd fled like a coward as soon as they landed in Alexandria. And what a preposterous story, that he would prepare things for them in Cairo. Shepheard's Hotel would prepare things for them in Cairo. They had cabled before they ever started the journey south towards Abu Simbel. They did not know how long their cruise would be; but Shepheard's, the old standby of the British abroad, would be waiting.

Opera season was about to begin, they'd been advised. Should the concierge arrange for box seats for all of them? Julie had said yes, though she could not imagine how this trip would end.

She knew only that Ramses was in fine spirits; that he loved being on the Nile. That he had stared for hours from the deck at the palm trees and the golden desert on either side of the broad, gleaming strip of brown water.

No one had to tell Julie that these were the same airy, fanlike palms painted upon the walls of ancient Egyptian tombs. Or that the dark-faced farmers were drawing water from the river by the very same crude means they had used four thousand years ago. No one had to tell her that the many native boats which passed them were little changed since the time of Ramses the Great.

And the wind and the sun changed for no one.

But there was something she had to do, and it could wait no longer. She sat contentedly in the saloon, idly watching Samir and Elliott play chess. And then when Alex rose from his game of solitaire and went out on the deck alone, she followed him.

It was almost evening; the breeze was cool for the first time, and the sky was slowly turning a deep shade of blue which was almost violet.

"You're a darling," she said. "And I don't want to hurt you. But I don't want to marry you, either."

"I know," he said. "I've known for a long time. But I'm going to continue to pretend it isn't so. Just as I've always done."

"Alex, don't—"

"No, darling, don't give advice. Let me do things my own way. After all, it's a woman's privilege to change her mind, isn't it? And you may change yours, and when you do, I'll be waiting. No, don't say anything more. You're free. You've always been free, really."

She drew in her breath. A deep pain radiated through her. She felt it in her chest; in the pit of her stomach. She wanted to cry, but this was not the place. She kissed him quickly on the cheek, and then she went down the deck, and into her cabin.

Thank God, Rita wasn't there. She lay down on the small bed and cried softly in the pillow. And then, exhausted, she drifted into a half sleep, her last thought being, May he never find out that I never loved him. May he always think it was another man, an adversary who swept me off my feet. That he can understand, not the other.

It was dark beyond the windows when she opened her eyes. Rita had lighted a small lamp from the deck. And she realized Ramses was standing in the room, looking down at her.

She felt no anger, and certainly no fear.

And then suddenly she realized that she was still dreaming. Only now did she fully wake and find the room lighted and empty. Oh, if only he had been there. Her body ached for him. She no longer cared about past or future. She cared only for him, and surely he knew this.

When she came into the dining room, he was in fast conversation with others. The table was littered with exotic dishes.

"Should we have awakened you, my dear, we weren't sure," Elliott said, rising at once to help her with her chair.

"Ah, Julie," Ramses said, "these native dishes are simply delicious." He was gaily helping himself to shish kebab and grape leaves and spiced dishes for which she didn't know the names, fingers moving as always with great delicacy and deliberation.

"Wait a minute," Alex said. "You mean, you've never had this food before?"

"Well, no, in that crazy pink hotel we ate meat and potatoes if memory serves me right," Ramses said. "And this is a very fine dish, this chicken and cinnamon."

"But wait a minute," Alex said. "Are you not a native Egyptian?"

"Alex, please, I think Mr. Ramsey likes to be mysterious about his origins," Julie said.

Ramses laughed. He drank down a tumbler full of wine. "That's true, I must confess. But if you must know, I am . . . Egyptian, yes."

"And where in the world . . . ?"

"Alex, please," Julie said.

Alex shrugged. "What a puzzle you are, Ramsey!"

"Ah, but I don't offend you, do I, Alexander?"

"Call me that again and I'll call you out," Alex said.

"What does this mean?"

"Nothing," Elliott said. He patted his son's hand.

But Alex wasn't cross. And certainly he wasn't offended. He gazed at Julie across the table. He gave her a little sad secret smile, for which she knew she would be forever grateful.

It was burning hot at midday in Luxor. They waited until late afternoon before going ashore and taking the long stroll through the immense temple complex. Ramses had no need to be alone, she could see that. He walked among the pillars, now and then looking up, but for the most part deep in his own thoughts.

Elliott had refused to miss this part of the journey, no matter how difficult it was for him. Alex hung back to give his father an arm to lean on. And Samir walked with the Earl as well. They appeared to be in deep discussion.

"The pain's leaving you, isn't it?" Julie said.

"When I look at you I don't feel it at all," Ramses answered. "Julie is as beautiful in Egypt as she was in London."

"Were these ruins already when you last saw them?"

"Yes, they were, and covered over with sand so deep that only the very tops of the columns were visible. The avenue of the sphinxes was buried entirely. A thousand years had passed since I walked in this place a mortal man, a fool who thought the kingdom of Egypt was the civilized world and that no truth lay outside its boundaries." He stopped, turning to her and kissing her quickly on the forehead. Then there was a guilty glance in the direction of the party coming behind him. No, not guilty, only resentful.

She took his hand. They moved on.

"Someday I'm going to tell you all of it," he said. "I shall tell you so much that you'll tire of listening. I shall tell you how we dressed and how we spoke to each other; and how we dined and how we danced; and what these temples and palaces were when the paint still gleamed on the walls; and I came forth at dawn and noon and sunset to greet the god and say the prayers the people expected. But come, there's time for us to cross the river and ride out to the temple of Ramses the Third. I want so much to see it."

He signaled one of the turbaned Egyptians near at hand. He

wanted a buggy to take them to the landing. She was glad to be free of the others for a little while.

But when they had made the river crossing and reached the immense roofless temple with its court of pillars within, he fell strangely silent. He looked up at the great reliefs of the warrior King in battle.

"This was my first pupil," he said. "The one to whom I had come after hundreds of years of wandering. I'd come home to Egypt to die, but nothing could kill me. And then I conceived of what I should do. Go to the royal house, become a guardian, a teacher. He believed me, this one, my namesake, my distant child. When I spoke to him of history, of distant lands, he listened."

"And the elixir, did he want it?" Julie asked.

They stood alone in the ruins of the great hall, entirely surrounded by the carved pillars. The desert wind was cold now. It tore at Julie's hair. Ramses slipped his arms around her.

"I never told him I had been a mortal man," he said. "You see, I never told that to any of them. I knew from the last years of my own mortal life what the secret could do. I had seen it turn my son, Meneptah, into a traitor. Of course he failed in his attempt to imprison me and extract from me the secret. I gave him the kingdom, and left Egypt then for centuries. But I knew what the knowledge could do. It was centuries later that I told Cleopatra."

He stopped. It was clear that he didn't want to go on. The pain he'd felt in Alexandria had returned. The light had gone out of his eyes. They walked back to the carriage in silence.

"Julie, let us make this journey fast," he said. "Tomorrow the Valley of the Kings and then we sail south again."

They went at dawn, before the full heat of the sun came down on them.

Julie took Elliott's arm. Ramses was talking again, with spirit, prompted by any question Elliott asked, and they took their time on the path, descending through desecrated tombs, where the tourists were already thick as well as the photographers and the turbaned peddlers in their filthy *gellebiyyas*, selling trinkets and fakes with fantastical claims.

Julie was already suffering from the heat. Her big drowsy straw hat did not help much; she had to stop, take a deep breath. The smell of camel dung and urine almost overcame her.

A peddler brushed against her and she looked down to see a blackened hand outstretched, fingers curling like the legs of a spider.

She screamed before she could stop herself.

"Get away!" Alex said roughly. "These native fellows are intolerable."

"Mummy's hand!" cried the peddler. "Mummy's hand, very ancient!"

"I'm sure," Elliott laughed. "Probably came from some mummy factory in Cairo."

But Ramses was staring at the peddler and at the hand, as if transfixed. The peddler suddenly froze; there was a look of terror in his face. Ramses reached out and grabbed the withered hand, and the peddler let it go, stumbling to his knees and then scrambling backwards off the path.

"What in the world?" Alex said. "Surely you don't want that thing."

Ramses stared at the hand, at the ragged bits of linen wrapping still clinging to it.

Julie couldn't tell what was wrong. Was he outraged by the sacrilege? Or did the thing have some other fascination? A memory swept over her; the mummy in the coffin in her father's library, and this living being whom she loved had been that thing. It seemed a century had passed since then.

Elliott was watching all this with keen concentration.

"What is it, sire?" Samir said under his breath. Did Elliott hear it?

Ramses drew out several coins and threw them in the sand for the peddler. The man gathered them up and then took off at a dead run. Then Ramses took out his handkerchief, neatly covered the hand and slipped it in his pocket.

"And what were you saying?" Elliott said politely, resuming their conversation as if nothing had happened. "I believe you were saying that the dominant theme of our time is change?"

"Yes," Ramses said with a sigh. He appeared to be seeing the valley in an entirely new perspective. He stared at the gaping doors of the tombs, at the dogs lying there in the morning sun. Elliott went on:

"And the dominant theme of these ancient times was that things would remain the same, always."

Julie could see the subtle changes in his face, the faint shadow of despair; yet as they moved on, he answered Elliott smoothly.

"Yes, no concept of progress whatsoever. But then the concept of time was not as well developed, either. A new count of years began with each King's birth. You know that, of course. No one counted time itself in terms of centuries. I'm not sure the simple Egyptian had any sense at all . . . of centuries."

Abu Simbel. They had come at last to the greatest of Ramses' temples. The shore excursion had been brief on account of the heat, but now the night wind blew cold over the desert.

Stealthily Julie and Ramses climbed down the rope ladder into the dinghy. She wrapped her shawl tightly over her shoulders. The moon hung perilously low over the shimmering water.

With the help of a lone native servant, they mounted the camels awaiting them, and rode towards the great temple where stood the largest statues of Ramses the Great in existence.

It was thrilling to ride this mad, terrifying beast. Julie laughed into the wind. She dared not look at the ground moving unevenly beneath her. But she was glad when they came to a halt, and Ramses jumped down and reached up to catch her.

The servant took the beasts away. Alone they stood, she and Ramses, under the star-filled sky, the desert wind faintly howling. Far off she saw the lighted tent of their little camp waiting for them. She saw the lantern shining through the translucent canvas; she saw the tiny campfire dancing in the wind, winking out and then reappearing in a dazzle of yellow brilliance.

Into the temple they walked, past the giant legs of the Pharaoh god. If there were tears in Ramses' eyes, the wind carried them away, but his sigh she heard. The faint tremor in his warm hand she felt as she cleaved to him.

They walked on, hand in hand, his eyes roving over the great statues still.

"Where did you go," she whispered, "when your reign had ended? You gave the throne to Meneptah and then you went away. . . ."

"All over the world. As far as I dared. As far as any mortal man had dared. I saw the great forests of Britannia then. The people wore skins and hid in the trees to shoot their wooden arrows. I went to the Far East; I discovered cities which have now completely vanished. I was just beginning to understand that the elixir worked on my brain as it did on my limbs. The languages I could learn in a matter of days; I could . . . how do you say . . . adapt. But inevitably there came . . . confusion."

"How do you mean?" she asked. They had stopped. They stood on the hard-packed sand. A great soft light from the starry sky illuminated his face as he looked down at her.

"I was no longer Ramses. I was no longer a King. I had no nation."

"I understand."

"I told myself that the world itself was everything. What did I need but to wander, to see? But that was not true. I had to come back to Egypt."

"And that is when you wanted to die."

"And I went to the Pharaoh, Ramses the Third, and told him that I had been sent to be his guardian. That is, after I learned that no poison could kill me. Not even fire could kill me. Hurt me, yes, beyond endurance, but kill me, no. I was immortal. One draught of the elixir had done this to me. Immortal!"

"Oh, the cruelty of it," she sighed. But there were things she still did not understand, and yet she dared not ask him. Patiently she waited for him to tell her.

"There were many others after my brave Ramses the Third. Great Queens as well as Kings. I came when it pleased me. And I was a legend by then—the human phantom who spoke only to the rulers of Egypt. It was seen as a great blessing when I appeared. And of course, I had my secret life. I roamed the streets of Thebes, an ordinary man, seeking companions, women, drinking in the taverns."

"But no one knew *you*, or your secret?" She shook her head. "I don't know how you could bear it."

"Well, I could bear it no more," he said dejectedly, "when I finally wrote it down in the scrolls your father found in my secret study. But in those early days, I was a braver man. And I was loved, Julie. You must realize this."

He paused, as if listening to the wind.

"I was worshipped," he went on. "It was as if I *had* died, and become the very thing I claimed to be. Guardian of the royal house. Protector of the ruler; punisher of the bad. Loyal not to the King, but the kingdom."

"Don't even gods get lonely?"

He laughed softly.

"You know the answer. But you don't understand the full power of the potion that made me what I am. I myself do not fully comprehend. Oh, the folly of those first years, when I experimented with it like a physician." A look of bitterness came over his face. "To understand this world, that's our task, is it not? And even the simple things elude us."

"Yes, I have no quarrel with that," she whispered.

"In the hardest moments, I put my faith in change. I understood it, though no one around me did. 'This too shall pass,' the old axiom. But finally I was so . . . weary. So tired."

He put his arm around her, closing her against him gently, as they turned and made their way out of the temple. The wind had died down. He kept her warm. She shaded her eyes only now and then from the tiny grains of sand in the air. His voice was quiet, slow, as he remembered:

"The Greeks had come into our land. Alexander, the builder of cities, the maker of new gods. I wanted only the deathlike sleep. Yet I was afraid, as any mortal man might be."

"I know," she whispered. A shiver went through her.

"I made a coward's bargain finally. I'd go into the tomb, into the darkness, which I knew by then would mean a gradual weakening and then a deep sleep from which I couldn't wake. But the priests who served the royal house would know where I lay, and that sunlight could resurrect me. They would give the secret to each new ruler of Egypt with the warning that if I were awakened, it must be to serve the good of Egypt. And woe to anyone rash enough to wake me for curiosity only, or with evil intentions, because then I might take my revenge."

They passed out of the temple doors, stopping as he looked back and up at the colossal figures seated there. High above, the King's face was bathed in moonlight.

"Were you conscious at all as you slept?"

"I don't know. I ask myself this question! Now and then I'd come close to waking, of that I'm sure. And I dreamed, oh, how I dreamed. But whatever I knew, I knew as if in a dream. There was no urgency, no panic. And I could not wake myself, you see. I had no strength to pull the chain that would make the great iron-bound wooden shutter above admit the sunlight. Maybe I knew what had happened in the world outside. Surely it did not surprise me to learn it later. I had become legend—Ramses, the Damned; Ramses the Immortal, who slept in the cave waiting for a brave King or Queen of Egypt to wake him. I don't think they believed it anymore, not really. Until . . ."

"She came."

"She was the last Queen to rule Egypt. And the only one to whom I ever told the full truth."

"But Ramses, did she really refuse the elixir?"

He paused. It was as if he didn't want to answer. Then:

"In her own way, she refused it. You see, she couldn't understand finally what it was, the elixir. Later, she begged me to give it to Mark Antony."

"I see. It's a wonder I didn't guess it."

"Mark Antony was a man who had destroyed his life and hers also. But she didn't know what she was asking. She didn't understand. She did not realize what such a thing would have meant—a selfish King and Queen with such power. And the formula, they would have wanted that too. Would Antony not have wanted immortal armies?"

"Good God!" she whispered.

Ramses stopped suddenly and moved away from her. They had come some distance from the temple and he turned back, looking at the giant seated figures again.

"But why did you write the story in the scrolls?" she asked. She couldn't stop herself.

"Cowardice, my love. Cowardice, and the dream that someone would come who would find me and my strange tale, and take the burden of secrecy from my shoulders! I had failed, my love. My strength was gone. And so I slipped into dreams and left the story there . . . like an offering to fate. I could be strong no longer."

She came to him and threw her arms around him. He didn't look at her. He was looking at the statues still. The tears were in his eyes.

"Maybe I dreamed that someday I'd be awakened again, to a new world. To new and wise beings. Maybe I dreamed of someone who . . . would take the challenge." His voice broke. "And I would be the lone wanderer no more. Ramses the Damned would become once again Ramses the Immortal."

He looked as if his own words had surprised him. Then he looked down at her and, closing his hands tightly on her shoulders, lifted her as he kissed her.

With her whole soul she yielded. She felt his arm gathering her up. She leaned against his chest as he carried her towards the tent, and the flickering firelight. The stars fell down over the distant shadowy hills. The desert was a great tranquil sea stretching out on all sides from this sanctuary of warmth which they now entered.

Incense here; the smell of wax candles. He set her down on

silken pillows, on a carpet of dark woven flowers. The dancing flames of the candles made her close her eyes. Perfume rising from the silk beneath her. A bower he had made, for her, for himself, for this moment.

"I love you, Julie Stratford," he whispered in her ear. "My English Queen. My timeless beauty."

His kisses were paralyzing her. She lay back, eyes closed, and let him open her tight lace blouse, let him loosen the hooks of her skirt. Luxuriating in this helplessness, she let him rip away the chemise and the corset, and pull down the long lace undergarments. She lay naked, looking up at him as he knelt over her, peeling off his own garments.

Regal he seemed, his chest gleaming in the light; his sex hard and ready for her. Then she felt his delicious weight come down upon her, crushing her. The tears had sprung to her eyes, tears of relief. A soft moan escaped her lips.

"Batter down the door," she whispered. "The virgin door. Open it, I am yours forever."

He went through the seal. Pain; a tiny sputtering pain that burnt itself out in her mounting passion immediately. She was kissing him ravenously; kissing the salt and heat from his neck, his face, his shoulders. He drove hard into her, over and over again, and she arched her back, lifting herself, pressing herself against him.

As the first tide crested she cried out as if she truly would die. She heard the deep growl rise from his throat as he came. But it was only the beginning.

Elliott had watched the dinghy pull away. Through his binoculars he saw the tiny light of the camp far out over the low, hard-packed dunes. He saw the tiny figure of the servant, and the camels.

Then hurrying down the deck, not daring to use his cane for fear of the sound it would make, he turned the knob of Ramses' door.

Unlocked. He stepped into the darkened stateroom.

Ah, this thing has made me a sneak and a thief, he thought. But he didn't stop. He did not know how long he would have. And now, with only the moon through the portal to light his way, he searched the wardrobe full of neatly hung clothes, the bureau drawers of shirts and other such things; the trunk which contained nothing. No secret formula in this room. Unless it was well hidden.

Finally he gave up. He stood over the desk, staring down at the biology books spread open there. And then something black and ugly, glimpsed from the corner of his eye, frightened him. But it was only the mummy's hand, curled there on the blotter.

How foolish he felt. How ashamed. Yet he stood there staring at the thing, his heart knocking dangerously in his chest, and then he felt the burning pain that always followed such shocks and the numbness in his arm. He stood quite still, breathing very slowly.

Finally he went out and closed the door behind him.

A sneak and a thief, he thought. And leaning on his silver cane, he walked slowly back to the saloon.

It was almost dawn. They had left the warmth of the tent hours ago and come here into the deserted temple, with only the loose silk sheets around them. They had made love in the sand, over and over. And then he had lain in the dark, looking up at the stars, the King who had built this house.

No words now. Only the warmth of his naked body against hers, as he cradled her in his left arm. Only the smooth sheet wound tightly around her.

Just before sunrise. Elliott dozed in the chair. He heard the little boat come alongside; the lapping; the sound of the ropes creaking as the two lovers came back on board. He heard their furtive quick steps on the deck. Silence again.

When he opened his eyes, his son was there in the shadows. Dishevelled, as if he had not undressed to go to bed, his face unshaven. He watched as his son took a cigarette from the ivory box on the table and lighted it.

Then Alex saw him. For a moment, neither said a word, and then Alex smiled the familiar congenial smile.

"Well, Father," he said slowly. "It will be good to get back to Cairo and a little civilization."

"You're a good man, my son," Elliott said softly.

They must have all known, she realized. She lay beside Ramses beneath the warm blankets of her bed, the little steamer moving north again, towards Cairo.

Yet they were being discreet. He came and went only when

no one was about. There were no displays of affection. Yet they revelled in the freedom they had stolen; until dawn they made love, tumbling, struggling, coupling in the dark as the engines of the ship carried them ever onward.

Too much to wish for anything more. Yet she did. She wished to be rid of those she loved, save for him; she wished to be his bride or to be among those who questioned nothing. She knew when they reached Cairo, she would make her decision. And she would not see England again, for a long time, unless Ramses wanted it.

Four o'clock. Ramses stood by the bed. She was lovely beyond all reckoning in her sleep, her brown hair a great shadow beneath her against the white pillow. Carefully he covered her, lest she get cold.

He picked up his moneybelt from the tangle of his coat and pants, and feeling the four vials safely taped against the fabric, he put it around his waist again, buckled it and then dressed quickly.

No one on the deck. The light burned in the saloon, however. And when he peered through the wooden blinds, he saw Elliott fast asleep in the leather wing chair, a book open on his knee, a half-filled glass of red wine beside him.

No one else about.

He went into his room, locked the door and closed the little wooden blinds on the window. Then he went to his desk, turned on the green shaded lamp, sat down in the wooden chair and stared at the mummy's hand which lay there, fingers curled almost to the palm, nails yellowed like bits of ivory.

Did he have the stomach for what he meant to do? In ages past, had he not done enough of these ghastly experiments? But he had to know. He had to know just how powerful it was. He told himself he should wait for laboratories, equipment, wait until he'd mastered the chemistry texts; had listened to the learned physicians.

But he wanted to know now. It had come into his mind like an evil light in the Valley of the Kings when he had seen the hand, the leathery, shrivelled hand. No fake. He knew that. He'd known it the minute he'd examined the bit of bone protruding from the severed wrist, the moment he'd seen the black flesh cleaving to it.

Ancient as he was.

He shoved the biology books aside. He placed the thing directly under the lamp, and slowly he unwrapped the linen. There, very faintly, he could see the stamp of the embalmer—the words in Egyptian which told him the thing was from a dynasty before his time. Ah, poor dead soul, who had believed in the gods, and the makers of linen wrappings.

Do not do this. Yet he reached into his shirt, and reached inside the money belt and pulled out the half-full vial and opened the cap with his thumb without even consciously deciding to do it.

He poured the elixir on the blackened thing. Poured it into the palm, and over the stiffened fingers.

Nothing.

Was he relieved? Or disappointed? For a moment he didn't know. He stared at the window, where the pale dawn pushed at the blinds, making tiny seams of brightness. Maybe the sun was needed for the first effect. Though that had not been so when he'd stood in the cave with the priestess. He had felt that powerful alchemy before the sun's rays touched him. Of course they had strengthened him immeasurably. And without them, he would have gone into the sleep within a few days. But he had not needed them initially.

Well, thank the gods it could not work on an ancient dead thing! Thank the gods the horrid potion had its limits.

He drew out a cheroot now and lighted it, and enjoyed the smoke. He poured a little brandy in the glass and drank it.

Slowly the room lightened around him. He wanted to creep back into Julie's arms, and lie there. But that could not be done by day, he knew it. And the truth was, he liked young Savarell enough not to deliberately hurt him. And Elliott, of course, he did not want to injure on any count. Very little stood between real friendship with Elliott.

When he heard the first sounds of the others on deck, he capped the vial and slipped it back into his moneybelt. He got up to change his clothes. Then suddenly a sound startled him.

The cabin was now entirely visible in a bluish morning light. For a moment he dared not turn around. Then again he heard that sound! *A scratching.*

He could feel the blood pounding in his temples. At last he wheeled around and stared down at the thing. The hand was alive! The hand was moving. On its back it lay, groping, flexing, rocking on the desk, and finally it fell over like a great scarab onto its five legs, and scratched at the blotter.

He found himself shrinking back from it in horror. It moved forward on the desk, groping its way, struggling, and then suddenly it moved over the edge and fell to the floor with a thud at his feet.

A prayer in the oldest Egyptian escaped his lips. Gods of the underworld, forgive my blasphemy! Trembling violently, he resolved to pick it up, but he could not bring himself to do it.

Like a madman he looked around the room. The food, the tray of food that was always there for him. There would be a knife. Quickly he found it, a sharp paring knife, and grabbing it he stabbed the hand and thrust it down on the desk, its fingers curling as if reaching for the very blade.

He flattened it with his left hand and then stabbed it again and again, and finally cut the tough leathery flesh and bones into pieces. It was spurting blood, living blood. Ye gods, and the pieces were still moving. They were turning pink, the color of healthy flesh, in the growing light.

He hurried into the little bathroom, gathered up a towel and came back, and scooped all the bloody fragments into it. Then closing the towel over them, he pounded them with the handle of the knife, and then with the heavy base of the lamp, the cord of which he'd ripped from the socket. He could still feel movement in the bloody mass.

He stood there weeping. Oh, Ramses, you fool! Is there no limit to your folly! Then he gathered up the bundle, ignoring the warmth he could feel through the cloth, and went out on the deck and emptied the towel over the dark river.

In an instant the bloody little pieces disappeared. He stood there, bathed in sweat, the bloody towel hanging from his left hand, and then that too he committed to the deep. And the knife as well. And then he settled back against the wall, peering at the far bank of golden sand and the distant hills, still a pale violet in the morning.

The years dissolved. He heard the weeping in the palace. He heard his steward screaming before he had reached the throne room doors and forced them open.

"It's killing them, my King. They are retching, vomiting it up; they are vomiting blood with it."

"Gather it all up, burn it!" he'd cried. "Every tree, every bushel of grain! Throw it into the river."

Folly! Disaster.

But he had been only a man of his time, after all. What had the magicians known of cells and microscopes and true medicine?

Yet he couldn't stop hearing those cries, cries of hundreds, as they stumbled out of the houses; as they came into the public square before the palace.

"They are dying, my King. It's the meat. It is poisoning them."

"Slay the remaining animals."

"But, my King . . ."

"Chop them into pieces, do you hear? Throw them into the river!"

He looked down now into the watery depths. Somewhere far upstream, the tiny bits and pieces of the hand still lived. Somewhere deep, deep in the muck and mire, the grain lived. The bits and pieces of those ancient animals lived!

I tell you it is a horrible secret, a secret that could spell the end of the world.

He went back into his cabin, and bolting the door, he sank down in the chair at the desk, and wept.

It was noon when he came out on deck. Julie was in her favourite chair, reading that ancient history which was so full of lies and gaps it made him laugh. She was scribbling a question in the margin, which of course she would put to him, and he would answer.

"Ah, you're awake at last," she said. And then seeing the expression on his face, she asked: "What is it?"

"I'm done with this place. I want to visit the pyramids, the museum, what one must visit. And then I want to be gone from here."

"Yes, I understand." She motioned for him to take the chair beside her. "I want to be gone, too," she said. She gave him a quick, soft kiss on the lips.

"Ah, do that again," he said. "That comforts me mightily!"

She kissed him twice, slipping her warm fingers around the back of his neck.

"We won't be in Cairo more than a few days, I promise."

"A few days! Can we not take a motor car and see these things, or better yet, simply take the train to the coast and be done with it!"

She looked down. She sighed. "Ramses," she said. "You have to forgive me. But Alex, he wants badly to see the opera in Cairo. And so does Elliott. I more or less promised we would. . . ."

He groaned.

"And you see, I want to tell them farewell there. That I'm not going home to England. And . . . well, I need the time." She studied his face. "Please?"

"Of course," he said. "This opera. This is a new thing? Something I should see, perhaps."

"Yes!" she said. "Well, it's an Egyptian story. But it was written by an Italian fifty years ago and especially for the British Opera House in Cairo. I think you'll like it."

"Many instruments."

"Yes." She laughed. "And many voices!"

"All right. I give in." He bent forward, kissing her cheek, and then her throat. "And then you are mine, my beauty—mine alone?"

"Yes, on my soul," she whispered.

That night when he declined to go ashore at Luxor again, the Earl asked him if his trip to Egypt had been a success, if he had found what he wanted.

"I think I did," he said, scarcely looking up from his book of maps and countries. "I think I found the future."

2

THIS HAD been a Mameluke house, a little palace of sorts, and Henry liked it well enough though he wasn't entirely sure what a Mameluke was except they had once been rulers of Egypt.

Well, they could have it, as far as he was concerned. But for the moment he was enjoying himself and had been for days, and in this little house crammed with Eastern exotica and big comfortable old pieces of Victorian furniture, he had just about everything he wanted.

Malenka kept him fed on delicious spiced dishes that for some reason he craved when he was sick from drink, and which enticed him even when he was very drunk and all other food tasted like gruel to him.

And she kept him in booze, taking his winnings into British Cairo and coming back with his favourite gin, Scotch, and brandy.

And his winnings had been good for a straight ten days, as he kept the card game going from noon until late into the evening. So easy to bluff these Americans who thought all British were sissies. The Frenchman he had to watch; that son of a bitch was mean. But he didn't cheat. And he paid his debts in full, though where such a disreputable man got the money Henry couldn't imagine.

At night, he and Malenka made love in the big Victorian bed, which she loved; she thought that was very high class, that bed, with its mahogany headboard and yards of mosquito netting. So

219

let her have her little dreams. For the moment, he loved her. He didn't care if he never laid eyes on Daisy Banker again. In fact, he had more or less made up his mind that he wasn't going back to England.

As soon as Julie and her escorts arrived, he was heading on to America. It had even occurred to him that his father might go for that idea, might settle an income on him with the understanding that he stay over there, in New York, or even in California.

San Francisco, now that was a city that had an allure for him. They'd almost completely rebuilt it since the earthquake. And he had a feeling he might do well out there, away from all that he had come to loathe in England. If he could take Malenka with him, that wouldn't be half-bad either. And out there in California, who would give a damn that her skin was darker than his?

Her skin. He loved Malenka's skin. Smoky, hot Malenka. A few times he'd ventured out of this cluttered little house and gone to see her dance at the European club. He liked it. Who knows? Maybe she might be a celebrity in California, with him managing her, of course. That might bring in a little money, and what woman wouldn't want to leave this filthy hellhole of a city for America? She was already learning English from the gramophone, playing records she had bought in the British sector on her own.

It made him laugh to hear her repeating the inane phrases: "May I offer you some sugar? May I offer you some cream?" She spoke well enough as it was. And she was clever about money, that was obvious. Or she wouldn't have managed to keep this house, after her half-breed brother left it to her.

Trouble was his father had to be handled carefully. That was why he hadn't left Cairo already. Because his father had to believe he was still with Julie, and looking after her, and all that utter rot. He'd cabled his father for more money days ago, with some silly message that Julie was quite all right. But surely he did not have to follow her back to London. That was preposterous. He had to work something out.

Of course there was no rush to leave here, really. The game was going splendidly for the eleventh day.

And it had been some time since he'd set foot out of doors, except of course to take his breakfast in the courtyard. He liked the courtyard. He liked the world being completely shut out. He liked the little pond, and the tile, and even that screeching parrot of Malenka's, that African grey—the ugliest bird he'd ever seen—wasn't entirely uninteresting.

The whole place had a lush, overblown quality that appealed to him. Late at night he'd wake up dying of thirst, find his bottle and sit in the front room, amid all the tapestried pillows, listening to the gramophone play the records of *Aïda*. He'd blur his eyes and all the colours around him would run together.

This was exactly what he wanted life to be. The game; the drink; the utter seclusion. And a warm, voluptuous woman who'd strip off her clothes when he snapped his fingers.

He made her dress in her costumes about the house. He liked to see her shining flat belly and her mounded breasts over the gaudy purple satin. He liked the big cheap earrings she wore, and her fine hair, oh, very fine, he liked to see that down her back so that he could grab a handful of it, and tug her gently towards him.

Ah, she was the perfect woman for him. She had his shirts done, and his clothes pressed, and saw to it his tobacco never ran out. She brought him magazines and papers when he asked for them.

But he didn't care much for that anymore. The outside world didn't exist. Except for dreams of San Francisco.

That's why he was so annoyed when they brought a telegram to the door. He never should have left this address at Shepheard's. But then he had no choice. How else could he have gotten the money his father telegraphed? Or the other telegrams his father had sent? Important not to make his father angry until some sort of deal had been struck.

With a cold, nasty expression the Frenchman waited as he tore open the yellow envelope and saw that this message wasn't from his father. Rather, it had come from Elliott.

"Damn," he whispered. "They're on their way here." He handed it to Malenka. "Get my suit pressed. I have to go back to the hotel."

"You can't quit now," said the Frenchman.

The German took a long drag on his smelly cigar. He was even more stupid than the Frenchman.

"Who said I was going to quit?" Henry said. He upped the ante; then bluffed them out one by one.

He'd go to Shepheard's later and see to their rooms. But he wasn't sleeping there. They shouldn't expect that of him.

"That's quite enough for me," said the German, flashing his yellowed teeth.

The Frenchman would stay there until ten or eleven easily.

Cairo. This had been desert in Ramses' time, though somewhere to the south lay Saqqara, where he had come on a pilgrimage once to worship at the pyramid of Egypt's first King. And of course he had gone on to visit the great pyramids of the great ancestors.

And so now it was a metropolis, bigger even than Alexandria. And this the British sector looked for all the world like a part of London, except that it was too warm. Paved streets; neatly clipped trees. Motor cars in profusion, their engines and horns scaring the camels, the donkeys, the natives. Shepheard's Hotel—another "tropical" palace with broad porches, replete with wicker, slatted blinds, and vague Egyptian artifacts thrown in among the English furnishings, the whole crowded with the same rich tourists he'd seen everywhere.

A great advertisement for the opera stood in front of the two ironwork lifts. *Aïda*. And such a lurid, vulgar picture of ancient Egyptians entwined in each other's arms amid palms and pyramids. And in the foreground in an oval yet another sketch of a modern man and woman dancing.

OPERA BALL—OPENING NIGHT— SHEPHEARD'S HOTEL

Well, if this was what Julie wanted. He had to confess he wanted to see a large theater, and hear an orchestra of great power. Oh, so many things to see! He had heard talk of motion pictures.

But he must endure these last few days on his native soil without complaint. There was a good library here, Elliott had said. He'd load up with science textbooks and study, and then slip out at night to stand before the Sphinx and speak to the spirits of his ancestors.

Not that he believed they were really there. No. He did not. Even in ancient times he had not really believed in the gods, perhaps because men called him a god; and so much of his stamina had been sapped by ritual. He had known he was no god.

Would a god have struck down the priestess with one great

blow of his bronze sword, after drinking the elixir? But he was not the man who had done that thing. Oh, no, if life had taught him nothing else, it had taught him the meaning of cruelty.

It was the spirit of modern science that he worshipped now. He dreamed of a laboratory in some safe and isolated place, where he could break down the chemical components of the elixir. The ingredients he knew, of course. And he knew as well that he could find them today as easily as he had found them centuries ago. He had seen the very fish in the markets at Luxor. He had seen the very frogs hopping in the marshes along the Nile. The plants grew wild still in those marshes.

Ah, to think that such a chemical action came from such simple things. But who would have combined them but some ancient magician throwing things in a pot like an old woman making a stew?

But the laboratory would have to wait. He and Julie must travel first. And before this could begin, she must say her painful farewells. And when he thought of her saying farewell to her rich and beautiful world, it sent a coldness through him. Yet whatever his fears, he wanted her too much to do anything about them.

And then there was Henry, Henry who had not dared to show his face since their return—Henry who had made a gambling den in old Cairo of a belly dancer's house.

The clerks had been most forthcoming with that information. Seems that young Mr. Stratford had paid them very little not to talk of his excesses.

But what was Ramses to do with the information, if Julie would not let him act? Surely they could not leave the man alive when they departed. But how was it to be accomplished so that Julie did not suffer any more pain?

Elliott sat on his bed, his back to the ornate wooden headboard, the veils of mosquito netting pinned back on either side of him. It felt good to be settled into a suite at Shepheard's.

The pain in his hip was almost unbearable. The long walks at Luxor and Abu Simbel had left him utterly exhausted. There was a slight congestion in his lungs, and for days his heart had been beating just a little too fast.

He watched Henry in his rumpled linen suit pace the little Tunisian carpet in the quaint "Colonial" bedroom with its old-fashioned chunky Victorian pieces and Egyptian wall hangings, and the inevitable wicker chairs.

Henry now had the look of a round-the-clock drinker, skin waxy as well as florid, hands steady because he was now thoroughly fueled with Scotch.

As a matter of fact, his glass was empty and Elliott had not the slightest inclination to ask Walter to refill it. Elliott's antipathy for Henry had reached its zenith. The man's mumbling, half-incoherent speech left Elliott utterly repelled.

". . . no reason in the world why I should make that voyage back with her, she's perfectly capable of taking care of herself. And I don't intend to stay here at Shepheard's, either. . . ."

"Why are you telling me all this?" Elliott asked finally. "Write to your father."

"Well, I have. It's only you'd be advised not to tell him that I stayed here in Cairo while you went on that inane voyage south. You'd be advised to back me up."

"And why is that?"

"Because I know what you're up to." Henry wheeled around suddenly, eyes glittering with drunken drama. "I know why you came here. It's got nothing to do with Julie! You know that thing's a monster. You realized it during the voyage. You know what I said was true about its climbing out of the coffin. . . ."

"Your stupidity is beyond belief."

"What are you saying?" Henry leaned over the footboard, as if he meant to frighten Elliott.

"You saw an immortal man rise from his grave, you worthless fool. Why do you run from it with your tail between your legs?"

"You're the fool, Elliott. It's unnatural. It's . . . monstrous. And if it tries to come near me, I shall tell what I know. About it and about you."

"You're losing your memory as well as your mind. You have already told. You were the laughingstock of London for twenty-four hours, probably the only real recognition you will ever enjoy."

"You think you're so clever, you filthy aristocratic beggar. You dare to put on airs with me. Have you forgotten our little weekend in Paris?" He gave a twisted smile as he lifted the empty glass, then saw there was nothing in it. "You peddled your title for an American fortune. You've peddled your son's title for the Stratford money. And now you're chasing after that filthy thing! You believe in this mad, stupid idea of the elixir."

"And you don't?"

"Of course I don't."

"Then how do you explain what you saw?"

Henry paused, eyes working again in that feverish manner which had become shifty. "There's some trick to it, some twist. But there's no damned chemical that makes people live forever. That's insane."

Elliott laughed under his breath. "Maybe it was done with mirrors."

"What?"

"The thing coming out of the coffin and trying to strangle you," Elliott said.

The contempt in Henry's eyes hardened to hate.

"Maybe I should tell my cousin that you're spying on her, that you want the elixir. Maybe I should tell that thing."

"She knows. So does he."

Utterly stymied, Henry looked down into the empty glass.

"Get out of here," Elliott said. "Go where you please."

"If my father should contact you, leave a message for me at the desk."

"Oh? Am I not supposed to know that you're living with that dancer, Malenka? Everyone else knows it. It's the scandal of the moment, Henry in old Cairo with his card game and his dancing girl."

Henry sneered.

Elliott looked towards the windows. Soft bright sunshine. He did not look back until he'd heard the door close. He waited a few moments, then picked up the telephone and asked for the front desk.

"You have an address for Henry Stratford?"

"He asked that we not give it out, sir."

"Well, this is the Earl of Rutherford, and I am a friend of the family. Please do give it to me."

He memorized it quickly, thanked the clerk and put down the receiver. He knew the street in old Cairo. It was only steps from the Babylon, the French night club where the dancing girl, Malenka, worked. He and Lawrence used to sit and argue in that club by the hour, when there had been dancing boys.

He reaffirmed his vow: whatever else happened, he would find out what he could from Ramsey before they parted as to what had really happened to Lawrence in that tomb.

Nothing would deter him from that, not cowardice, nor

dreams of the elixir. He had to know what, if anything, Henry had done.

The door opened quietly. It had to be his man, Walter, the only one who would enter without a knock.

"Nice rooms, my lord?" Too solicitous. He had overheard the argument. He puttered about, wiping the bedside table, adjusting the shade of the lamp.

"Oh, yes, they're fine, Walter. They'll do. And my son, where is he?"

"Downstairs, my lord, and may I tell you a little secret?"

Walter leaned over the bed, hand up to his mouth as if they were in the midst of a crowd rather than in a large empty bedroom with nothing but an empty sitting room opening onto it.

"He's met a pretty girl, downstairs, an American. Name's Barrington, my lord. Rich family from New York. Father in the railroads."

Elliott smiled. "Now, how do you know all that already?"

Walter laughed. He emptied Elliott's ashtray of the cheroot, which had gone out because it burned Elliott's lungs so badly he couldn't smoke it.

"Rita told me, my lord. Saw him not an hour after we checked in. And he's with Miss Barrington now, taking a little walk about in the hotel gardens."

"Well, wouldn't that be interesting, Walter," Elliott said, shaking his head, "if our dear Alex married an American heiress."

"Yes, my lord, it certainly would be interesting," Walter said. "As for the other, do you want the same arrangements as before?" Again Walter assumed a highly confidential air. "Someone to follow *him*?"

He meant Ramses, of course. He referred to the shameful matter of the boy whom Elliott had hired in Alexandria.

"If you can do it quietly," Elliott said. "They're to watch him night and day, to report to me where he goes and what he does."

He gave Walter a wad of bills, which Walter tucked in his pocket immediately and then went out, closing the door behind him.

Elliott tried to take a deep breath, but the pain in his chest wouldn't allow it; very quietly he took one shallow breath after another. He stared at the white curtains ballooning over the open windows. He could hear the bustle and noise of British Cairo outside. He thought about the futility of all of this—following Ramses in the hope of discovering something, anything, about the elixir.

Absurd, really. A little bit of cloak-and-dagger that did no more than fuel Elliott's obsession. There was no doubt now as to what Ramses was; and if he had the elixir with him, undoubtedly he carried it on his person.

Elliott felt ashamed. But that was a small matter. The larger matter was the mystery from which he was utterly shut out. Might as well go to the man and beg for the gift. He had a good mind to call Walter back, to tell him it was all foolishness. But in his heart of hearts he knew he would try one more time to search Ramses' room; and the boy following Ramses might give him some clue as to the man's habits.

It was something to do, wasn't it, other than think about the pain in his chest and in his hip. He closed his eyes; he saw the colossal statues of Abu Simbel again. It seemed to him suddenly that this was the last great adventure of his life, and he realized that he had no regrets, that this excitement had been in itself a priceless gift to him.

And who knows, he laughed softly to himself. Perhaps Alex will find an American heiress.

Ah, she was lovely, and he so liked her voice and the divine sparkle in her eye, for that's just what it was; and how she'd push him lightly with her finger when she laughed. And what a pretty name she had, Miss Charlotte Whitney Barrington.

"And then we thought we'd go to London, but they say it's frightfully cold this time of year, and so gloomy, with the Tower of London and all, where they chopped off Anne Boleyn's head."

"Oh, it wouldn't be if I showed it to you!" he said.

"Well, when are you going home? You're staying for the opera, aren't you? Seems everybody in this place talks of nothing else. It's very funny, you know, to come all the way to Egypt to see an opera."

"But it's *Aïda*, my dear."

"I know, I know. . . ."

"And yes, we are going, as a matter of fact, it's all been arranged. And you'll be there, of course. Ah, what about the ball afterwards?"

What an adorable smile. "Well, I didn't know about the ball,

you see. I didn't really want to go with Mummy and Daddy
and—''

"Well, perhaps you'd go with me.''

Oh, what lovely white teeth.

"Why, Lord Rutherford, I'd simply love it.''

"Please call me Alex, Miss Barrington. Lord Rutherford's
my father.''

"But you're a Viscount yourself,'' she said with stunning
American frankness and the same ingratiating smile. ''That's
what they told me.''

"Yes, I guess that's true. Viscount Summerfield, actually . . .''

"What *is* a Viscount?'' she asked.

Such lovely eyes, and the way she laughed as she looked at
him. Suddenly he was no longer angry with Henry for being
holed up with that dancer, Malenka. Better that Henry should
be altogether out of sight with his drinking and gambling, rather
than hanging about the public rooms of the hotel.

Oh, what would Julie think of Miss Barrington? Well, he
knew what he thought!

High noon. The dining room. Ramses sat back laughing.

"Now, I insist you do it. Pick up the fork and the knife,''
Julie said. "Just try.''

"Julie, it's not that I can't do it! It's that it seems absolutely
barbaric to thrust food in one's mouth with pieces of silver!''

"Your trouble is, you know how perfectly handsome you are,
and how you charm everyone.''

"I learned a little tact over the centuries.'' He picked up the
fork, deliberately gripping the handle in his fist.

"Stop that,'' she said under her breath.

He laughed. He laid down the fork, and took a morsel of
chicken with his fingers again. She grabbed his hand.

"Ramses, eat properly.''

"Darling dear,'' he said, "I'm eating in the manner of Adam
and Eve, Osiris and Isis, Moses, Aristotle and Alexander.''

She dissolved with laughter. He stole a kiss from her quickly.
Then his face darkened.

"What about your cousin?'' he whispered.

It caught her completely off guard. "Must we speak of him?''

"Are we to leave him here in Cairo? Are we to leave the
murder of your father unavenged?''

Tears sprang to her eyes. Angrily, she searched in her bag for her handkerchief. She had not seen Henry since their return, and she didn't want to see him. In her letter to Randolph she had not mentioned him. And it was the thought of her uncle as much as anything else that made her cry now.

"Pass the burden to me," Ramses whispered. "I shall bear it easily. Let justice be done."

She put her hand up suddenly to his lips.

"No more," she said. "Not now."

He looked up, over her shoulder. He gave a little sigh, and squeezed her hand. "The museum party is here, it seems," he said. "And we mustn't keep Elliott standing about."

Alex swooped down suddenly to give her a little peck on the cheek. How chaste. She wiped at her nose quickly, and turned so that he wouldn't see the colour in her face.

"Well, are we all set?" Alex said. "We have our private guide meeting us at the museum in fifteen minutes. Oh, and before I forget, the opera has been completely arranged. Box seats and of course tickets to the ball afterwards. And Ramsey, old man, if you'll allow me to say so, I shan't compete with you that night for Julie's attentions."

Julie nodded. "Fallen in love already," she said with a mock whisper. She allowed Alex to help her to her feet. "A Miss Barrington."

"Please, darling, do give me your opinion. She's coming to the museum with us."

"Let's hurry," Ramses said. "Your father is not well. I'm surprised he doesn't remain behind."

"Good Lord, do you know what the Cairo Museum means to people?" said Alex. "And it's the dirtiest, dustiest place I've ever—"

"Alex, please, we are about to see the greatest collection of Egyptian treasures in existence."

"The last ordeal," Ramses said, taking Julie's arm. "And all the Kings are in one room? This is what you have been telling me?"

"My word, I should think you'd been there before," Alex said. "You are such a puzzle, old man. . . ."

"Give up on it," Ramses whispered.

But Alex scarcely heard. He was whispering to Julie that she must give him a candid opinion of Miss Barrington. And Miss Barrington was the rosy-cheeked blond woman standing in the lobby with Elliott and Samir. A pretty thing, obviously.

"To think," said Julie, "you need my approval!"

"Shhhh, there she is. With Father. They're getting along famously."

"Alex, she's perfectly lovely."

Through the broad dusty rooms of the first floor they trekked, listening to the guide, who spoke rapidly despite his thick Egyptian accent. Ah, treasures galore, there was no doubt of it. All the loot of the tombs; things he had never even dreamed of in his time. And here it was for all the world to see, under soiled glass and weak lights, yet nevertheless preserved from time and ruin.

He stared at the statue of the happy scribe—the little cross-legged figure with his papyrus on his lap, looking up eagerly. It should have moved him to tears. But all he felt was a vague joy that he had come, he had visited it all as he should, and now he would be leaving.

At last they proceeded up the grand stairway. The room of the Kings, the ordeal he was dreading. He felt Samir at his side.

"Why not forgo this gruesome pleasure, sire? For they are all horrors."

"No, Samir, let me see it through to the finish."

He almost laughed when he understood what it was—a great chamber of glass cases like the cases in the department stores where goods were displayed safe from prying fingers.

Nevertheless the blackened grinning bodies gave him a dull shock. It seemed he could scarcely hear the guide, and yet the words were coming clear:

"The Ramses the Damned mummy in England is still a controversial discovery. Very controversial. This is the true Ramses the Second, right before you, known as Ramses the Great."

Edging closer, he stared down at the gaunt horrid thing that bore his name.

". . . Ramses the Second, greatest of all Egypt's Pharaohs."

He almost smiled as he studied the dried limbs, and then the obvious truth hit him, like something physical pressing on his chest, that if he had not gone into that cave with the wicked old priestess, he would indeed be lying in this case. Or what was left of him. And all the world since faded; it was no more suddenly than those years. And to think he would have died without knowing so much; without ever realizing. . . .

Noise. Julie had said something, but he couldn't hear her.

There was a dull roaring in his head. Suddenly he saw them all, these ghastly corpses, like burnt things out of the oven. He saw the filthy glass; he saw the tourists pushing this way and that.

He heard Cleopatra's voice. *When you let him die, you let me die! I want to be with him now. Take it away, I won't drink it.*

Were they moving again? Had Samir said it was time to go? He looked up slowly from the awful sunken face and saw Elliott gazing at him, with the strangest expression. What was it? Understanding.

Oh, but how can you understand? I myself can scarcely understand.

"Let's go, sire."

He let Samir take his arm and lead him towards the doorway. It seemed Miss Barrington laughed at something Alex had whispered in her ear. And the din of the French tourists nearby was positively frightful. Such a harsh tongue.

He turned, staring back at the glass cases. Yes, leave this place. Why are we going down the corridor to the very back of the building? Surely we have seen it all; the dreams and fervor of a nation come to this; a great and dusty mausoleum where young girls laugh and rightly so.

The guide had stopped at the end of the hall. What was it now? Another body in a case, and how could anyone see it in the shadows? Only weak shafts of dusty light cut through the dirty window above.

"This unknown woman . . . a curious example of natural preservation."

"We cannot smoke, can we?" he whispered to Samir.

"No, sire, but we can slip away, surely. We can wait for the others outside, if you wish. . . ."

". . . combined to naturally mummify the body of this anonymous woman."

"Let's go," he said. He placed his hand on Samir's shoulder. But then he must tell Julie lest she be alarmed. He stepped forward and gave her sleeve a little tug, and glanced down at the body in the case as he did so.

His heart stopped.

". . . though most of the wrappings were long ago torn away—in the search for valuables, no doubt—the woman's body was perfectly preserved by the delta mud, much as bodies found in northern bogs. . . ."

The rippling hair, the long slender neck, the gently sloping shoulders! And the face, the very face! For a moment he did not believe his eyes!

The voice pounded in his head: ". . . unknown woman . . . Ptolemaic period . . . Graeco-Roman. But see the Egyptian profile. The well-molded lips . . ."

Miss Barrington's high-pitched laugh went through his temples.

He blundered forward. He had brushed Miss Barrington's arm. Alex was saying something to him, calling him sharply by name. The guide was staring up.

He looked down through the glass. *Her face!* It was *she*—the soft cerements molded into her flesh, her naked hands gently curved, her feet bare, the wrappings loose around her ankles. All black, black as the delta mud which had surrounded her, preserved her, hardened her!

"Ramses, what is it!"

"Sir, are you ill!"

They were speaking to him from all sides; they were surrounding him. Suddenly someone pulled him away, and he turned back furiously. "No, let me go."

He heard the glass shatter beside him. An alarm had gone off, shrieking like a woman in terror.

Look at her closed eyes. It's she! It's she. He needed no rings, no ornaments, no names to tell him. It's she.

The armed men had come. Julie pleaded. Miss Barrington was afraid. Alex was trying to make him listen.

"I cannot hear you now. I can hear nothing. It is she. Anonymous woman." She, the last Queen of Egypt.

Again, he jerked free of the hand on his arm. He hovered over the filthy glass. He wanted to shatter it. Her legs no more than bones; the fingers of her right hand dried almost to a skeleton. But that face, that beautiful face. My Cleopatra.

Finally he had allowed himself to be led away. Julie had questioned him. He had not answered. She had paid for the damage to the case, a small display of jewelry upset. He wanted to say that he was sorry.

He could not remember anything else. Except her face, and the whole picture she made—a thing created from the black earth and lifted up and placed on the bare polished wood of the case, linen wrappings still wrinkled as if by lapping water. And her hair, her thick rippling hair; why, the whole form had almost glistened in the dim light.

Julie spoke words. The lights were soft in the room at Shepheard's Hotel. He wanted to answer, but he couldn't. And then there was that other memory; that strange moment when he had turned in the confusion and the blur, and seen Elliott with those sad grey eyes watching him.

Oscar hurried after Mr. Hancock and the two chaps from Scotland Yard as they marched right through the drawing rooms and into the Egyptian room. Oh, he never should have let them into the house. They had no right to come into this house. And now they were marching right up to the mummy case.

"But Miss Julie will be so angry, sir. This is her house, sir. And you mustn't touch that, sir, why, it's Mr. Lawrence's discovery."

Hancock stared at the five gold Cleopatra coins in their case.

"But the coins could have been stolen in Cairo, sir. Before the collection was cataloged."

"Yes, of course, you're absolutely right," Hancock said. He turned and glared at the mummy case.

Julie poured the wine in his glass. He merely looked at it.

"Won't you try to explain?" she whispered. "You recognized it. You knew it. That has to be it."

For hours he'd sat there in silence. The late afternoon sun burned through the sheer curtains. The overhead fan churned slowly, monotonously, giving off a dull groan.

She didn't want to cry again.

"But it couldn't be . . ." No. She couldn't bring herself even to suggest it. Yet she thought of the woman again; of the gold tiara in her hair, now black and glossy as all the rest of her. "It's not possible that it's she. . . ."

Slowly Ramses turned and looked at her. Hard and brilliant his blue eyes were.

"Not possible!" His voice was low, hoarse, no more than an agonized whisper. "Not possible! You've dug up thousands of the Egyptian dead. You've raided their pyramids, their desert tombs, their catacombs. What is not possible!"

"Oh, my God." The tears flowed down her cheeks.

"Mummies stolen, traded, sold," he said. "Was there any man, woman or child ever buried in this land whose body has not been defiled, if not displayed, or dismembered? What is not possible!"

For a moment it seemed he'd lose control altogether; but then he was quiet, merely staring at her again. And then his eyes went dim as if he had not seen her. He sat back in the little chair.

"We don't have to stay in Cairo any longer if you don't want. . . ."

Again he turned slowly and looked at her. It was as if he were waking from a daze, that he had not just spoken to her.

"No!" he said. "We cannot leave. Not now. I don't want to leave. . . ."

And then his voice trailed off as if he'd just realized what he was saying. He rose and walked slowly out of the room, not even glancing back at her.

She saw the door close; she heard his tread in the hall; and then her tears flowed again.

What was she to do? What would comfort him? If she used all her influence, could she possibly have the body in the museum removed from public view and given proper burial? Not likely. The request would seem whimsical and foolish. Why, countless royal mummies were on display!

But even if she could accomplish such a thing, she feared it would not help now. It was the mere sight of the thing, not its desecration, which had crushed him.

The two officers from Scotland Yard watched the man from the British Museum uneasily.

"We should go now, sir. We don't have a court order to be disturbing the mummy's coffin. We came to check the coins, and we've done it."

"Nonsense," Hancock said. "We should check everything now while we have the court order. We came to see that the collection is intact. I want to see that the mummy's unharmed before I leave here."

"But, sir," Oscar intervened.

"Don't say another word, my good man. Your mistress ran off to Cairo and left a priceless treasure here. She did not have our permission." He turned to the two officers of the law. "Open the thing," he said sharply.

"Well, I don't like this, sir, I really don't," Trent said.

Hancock pushed past him and hefted the lid himself before the two men could stop him. Galton tried to catch it before the bottom struck the floor. Oscar gave a little gasp.

Inside stood the mummy, shrunken, blackened.

"What the hell is going on here!" Hancock raged.

"And what exactly do you mean, sir?" Trent asked.

"Everything goes back to the museum now."

"But, sir."

"That's not the same mummy, you fool. That's from a peddler's shop in London! I saw it myself. It was offered to me for sale. Damn that woman! She's stolen the find of the century!"

It was long past midnight. No more music came from the public rooms. Cairo slept.

Elliott walked alone in the dark courtyard between the two wings of Shepheard's Hotel. His left leg was going numb; but he paid no heed to it. Now and then he glanced up at the figure pacing in the suite above; a shadow moving back and forth across the slatted blinds. Ramsey.

Samir's room was dark. Julie's light had gone out an hour ago. Alex was long gone to bed, worried about Ramsey, and thoroughly confused as to whether Julie had fallen in love with a madman.

The figure stopped. It moved to the blinds. Elliott stood stockstill in the chilly darkness. He watched Ramsey peer out at the sky, and perhaps at the great web of stars flung out over the rooftops.

Then the figure disappeared altogether.

Elliott turned and hobbled awkwardly towards the doors to the lobby. He had just reached the shadowy foyer beyond the front desk when he saw Ramsey come down the grand staircase and make for the doors, his loose mane of brown hair in unkempt tangles.

I am mad, Elliott thought. I am madder than he has ever been.

Firmly gripping his cane, he made to follow. When he emerged from the front doors, he saw the dark figure ahead of him, walking fast across the square. The pain in his leg was now so bad he had to grit his teeth, but he pressed on.

Within a few minutes, Ramsey had reached the museum. Elliott watched him turn from the main entrance, and walk slowly to the far right side of the building, towards a light burning behind a barred window.

The yellow light spilled out of the small rear alcove. The guard was slumped in the chair, snoring blissfully. The rear door was open.

Elliott slowly entered the museum. He passed quickly through the empty chambers of the ground floor, past towering gods and goddesses. At last he reached the grand stairs and, clutching the railing, moved up step by step, hoisting his weight off his painful leg, trying not to make a sound in the thinning darkness.

A gray murky light filled the corridor. The window at the far end was paling visibly. And there stood Ramsey beside the low shallow display case, in which the mass of the dead woman in her petrified rags gleamed like black coal. Ramsey bowed his head in the gray light, like a man praying.

It seemed he whispered something in the dark. Or was he weeping? His profile was sharply clear, and so was the movement of his hand as he reached into his coat and drew out something that sparkled in the shadows.

A glass vial full of luminescent liquid.

Dear God, he cannot mean to do this. What is this potion that he would even attempt it? Elliott almost cried out. He almost went to Ramsey and tried to stay his hand. But when Ramsey opened the vial, when Elliott heard the faint grinding of the metal cap, he shrank to the far side of the corridor, and concealed himself from view behind a tall glass cabinet.

How eloquent of suffering the distant figure was, poised there over the case, the open vial in his hand, the other hand rising to wipe his hair out of his forehead.

Then Ramsey turned as if to go and came down the corridor towards Elliott without seeing him.

Something changed in the light. It was the first palpable glow of the sun, a dull steel-grey radiance; a soft grey shimmer firing all the glass cases and cabinets of the long corridor.

Ramsey turned. Elliott could hear him sigh. He could feel his torment. Ah, but this is madness; this is unspeakable.

Helplessly, he watched as Ramsey approached the case again and broke loose the light wood-framed glass lid, and folded it silently backwards and away like the cover of a book, so that he might touch the dead thing inside.

With sudden speed, he produced the vial again. The gleaming white liquid flowed in droplets down on the corpse as Ramsey passed the vial back and forth above it.

"It's vain, it cannot possibly work," Elliott whispered half-aloud. He found himself shrinking even closer to the wall, peering now through the glass sides of the cabinet.

In horror and fascination, he watched Ramsey smooth the fluid over the dead woman's limbs. He saw him bend tenderly, as if placing the glittering vial to her mouth.

A hiss echoed through the darkness. Elliott let out a silent gasp. Ramsey stumbled back, pressing himself to the wall. The vial fell from his hand and rolled on the stone floor, a tiny bit of fluid still shimmering inside it. Ramsey stared down at the thing in front of him.

Movement of the dark mass in the low shallow bed of the case. Elliott saw it. He heard a low raw sound like breath.

Dear God, man, what have you done! What have you awakened!

The wood of the case gave a violent creak; the thin wooden legs appeared to shudder. The thing inside the case was stirring, rising.

Ramsey backed away into the corridor. A muffled cry escaped his lips. Beyond him, Elliott saw the figure sit up. The wooden case shattered and then collapsed, the noise echoing loudly throughout the museum. The thing stood square on its feet! Its great head of shaggy black hair poured down like thick smoke over its shoulders. The blackened skin was lightening, changing. A ghastly moan came out of the being. It raised its skeletal hands.

Ramsey moved backward away from it. A desperate prayer escaped him, full of the old Egyptian names of the gods. Elliott clamped a hand over his mouth.

Moving forward, its bare feet scratching the stones with the rough, dry sound of rats in the walls, the figure lowered its arms and reached out towards Ramsey.

The light shone in its huge staring eyes, the eyelids eaten away, the hair thickening and writhing as it grew sleeker and blacker and tumbled down longer over the bony shoulders.

But dear God, what were the patches of white all over it? They were the bones of the thing, the bare bones where the flesh had been torn away, perhaps centuries ago! Bare bone showing in the left leg, bare bone in the right foot, bare bones in the fingers struggling to reach Ramsey.

It's not whole. You've raised a thing which is not whole.

The light brightened in the window above. The first distinct rays pierced the ashen gloom. As Ramsey backed away again, passing Elliott, half stumbling towards the far railing of the stair, the thing came on, gaining speed until it reached the sunlight.

And there it reached up as if trying to catch the rays, its moaning breaths coming rapid and desperate and full of panic.

The shriveled flesh of the hands was now bronze. The face was bronze, and growing lighter and paler and more truly human as the sun struck it.

It turned and rocked on its feet, as if drinking up the light, and the blood began to ooze from the torn wounds that everywhere exposed the skeleton.

Elliott closed his eyes. For one moment he almost lost consciousness. He was aware of noise below. A door slamming far to the back of the huge building.

He opened his eyes to see the thing drawing nearer. Glancing over his shoulder, he saw Ramses plastered to the rail of the stairs, staring in undisguised horror.

God in heaven, drive it back. Elliott felt the burning in his chest, the familiar tightening. The pain shot down his left arm, and with all his strength he clutched the silver cane. He willed himself to breathe, to remain standing.

The skeletal thing was filling out. Its flesh was now the color of Elliott's own flesh; and the hair a great wavy mop veiling its shoulders completely. And its clothing—even its clothing had changed. Its clothing was once again white linen where the elixir had splashed. The creature bared its white teeth to the roots as it moaned. Its breasts heaved and the ragged linen fell loose from the womanly shape, tangling in the legs that trudged doggedly forward.

Its eyes were fixed on the man at the end of the hall. Its breath came in heaves. Its mouth became a grimace.

Noises from below. The shrill sound of a whistle. A man shouting in Arabic.

Ramses reeled. They were coming up the staircase. Their shouts could only mean that they had seen him.

In panic, he turned back to the female figure drawing ever closer.

A rasping cry escaped her lips.

"Ramses!"

The Earl closed his eyes. Then he opened them again and stared at the skeletal hands outstretched as the woman passed him.

There was a cry of "Halt!" and then a shot. The creature screamed and clamped her fingers over her ears. She staggered backwards. Ramses had been struck by the bullet, and pivoted to face the men coming up the stairs. Desperately he turned back to the female. Another volley of shots! The deafening roar resounded through the corridor. Ramses fell back against the marble rail.

The female shuddered, hands still covering her ears. She appeared to lose her balance, staggering between the stone sarcophagi on the opposite side of the hall. When the whistle shrieked again, she roared in terror.

"Ramses!" It was the cry of a wounded animal.

3

AGAIN, ELLIOTT almost lost consciousness. Again he closed his eyes, and struggled to fill his lungs with air. His left hand, clutching the walking stick, was now entirely numb.

He could hear the sounds of the guards dragging Ramses down the stairs. Clearly Ramses was fighting. But there were too many of them.

And the woman! She'd disappeared. Then he heard her feet scraping the stone floor again. He peered through the glass beside him to see her retreating to the far end of the hall. Whimpering, her breath still coming in gasps, she vanished through a side door.

All sound had died away below. Apparently Ramses had been removed from the museum. But undoubtedly men would come to search within minutes.

Ruthlessly ignoring the pain in his chest, Elliott hurried down the corridor. He reached the side door in time to see the female just disappearing from view at the foot of a service stair. Quickly he turned back, glancing under the display cases. There lay the vial, still gleaming in the grey light. Going down on one knee, he managed to get hold of it; and closing its cap, he put it in his coat.

Then, fighting a wave of dizziness, he crept down the stairs after the female, his numbed left leg almost tripping him. Halfway down he saw her—bewildered, staggering, one clawlike hand raised as if groping in the dimness.

A door opened suddenly, leaking yellow light into the passage; and a servant woman emerged, her hair and body draped in the Moslem manner by a garment of black wool. She carried a mop in her right hand.

At once she saw the skeletal figure approaching, and she let out a shrill scream, the mop falling from her hands. She fled back into the lighted room.

A low hiss came out of the wounded one and then that awful roar again as she went after the serving maid, skeletal hands out as if to stop the piercing scream.

Elliott moved as fast as he could. The screams stopped before he reached the door of the lighted room. As he entered, he saw the body of the servant woman slumping, dead, to the floor. Her neck had apparently been broken and the flesh torn from her cheek. Her glassy black eyes stared at nothing. And the ragged wounded one stepped over her and moved towards a small mirror over the washbasin on the wall.

A wretched agonized sobbing broke from her when she saw her reflection. Gasping, shuddering, she reached out and touched the glass.

Again, Elliott almost collapsed. The sight of the dead body, and the ghastly creature before the glass, were more than he could bear. But a ruthless fascination sustained him, as it had all along. He must use his wits now. Damn the pain in his chest and the panic rising like nausea in his throat.

Quickly he closed the door of the room behind him. The noise startled her. She wheeled about, hands poised again for the attack. For a moment, he was paralyzed by the full horror of what he now beheld. The light from the ceiling bulb was merciless. Her eyes bulged from their half-eaten sockets. White rib bones gleamed through a huge wound in her side. Half of her mouth was gone, and a bare stretch of clavicle was drenched in oozing blood.

Dear God, what must her suffering be! Poor, tragic being!

Giving a low growl, she advanced on him. But Elliott spoke quickly in Greek:

"Friend," he said. "I am a friend and offer you shelter." And as his mind went blank on the ancient tongue, he switched to the Latin: "Trust in me. I shall not let you come to harm."

Not taking his eyes off her for a second, he groped for one of

several black cloaks hanging on the wall. Yes, what he wanted—
one of those shapeless robes worn by Moslem women in public.
It was easily large enough to drape her from head to toe.

Fearlessly, he approached her, throwing the cloak over her
head and winding it over her shoulders, and at once her hands
went up to assist, closing it over her face save for her frightened
eyes.

He ushered her out into the corridor, closing the door behind
him to conceal the dead body. Noises and shouts were coming
from the floor above. He could hear voices coming from a room
at the far end of the hall. Spotting the service door to his right,
he opened it, and led her out into the alleyway, where the bright
sun came down upon them both.

Within moments, he was clear of the building. And they had
entered the great endless crowd of Moslems, Arabs and West-
erners one saw everywhere in Cairo, thousands of pedestrians
moving in all directions, despite the blast of motor-car horns
and the progress of donkey-drawn carts.

The woman stiffened when she heard the motor horns. At the
sight of a motor car rocking past her, she drew back, crying
through clenched teeth. Again, Elliott spoke to her in Latin,
reassuring her that he would take care of her, he would find her
shelter.

What she understood he could not possibly guess. Then the
Latin word for food came from her in a low, tortured voice.
"Food and drink," she whispered. She murmured something
else, but he did not understand. It sounded like a prayer or a
curse.

"Yes," he said in her ear, the Latin words coming easily now
that he knew she understood them. "I shall provide all you
require. I shall take care of you. Trust in me."

But where could he take her? Only one place came to mind.
He had to reach old Cairo. But did he dare put the creature into
a motor taxi? Seeing a horse-drawn cab passing, he hailed it.
She climbed willingly up to the leather seat. Now, how was he
to do it, when he could scarce breathe and his left leg was almost
useless? He planted his right foot firmly on the step and swung
himself up with his right arm. And then, near to collapse as ever
he'd been in his life, he slumped down beside the hunched figure
and told the driver where he must go with his last breath.

The cab shot forward, the driver shouting at the pedestrians and cracking his whip. The poor creature beside him cried brokenheartedly, drawing the veil completely over her face.

He embraced her; he ignored the cold hard bone he could feel through the thin black cloth. He held tight to her and, gradually catching his breath, told her again in Latin that he would care for her, that he was her friend.

As the cab sped out of the British district, he tried to think. But shocked and in pain, he could achieve no rational explanation for himself for what he'd witnessed or what he'd done. He only knew on some inchoate level that he'd seen a miracle and a murder; and that the former meant infinitely more to him than the latter; and he was set now upon an irrevocable course.

Julie was only half-awake. Surely she was misunderstanding the British official who stood in the door.

"Arrested? For breaking into the museum? I don't believe it."

"Miss Stratford, he's been wounded, badly. There seems to be some confusion."

"What confusion?"

The doctor was furious. If the man was badly wounded, he should be in hospital, not in the back of the jail.

"Make way," he shouted to the uniformed men in front of him. "What in God's name is this, a firing squad?"

No less than twenty rifles were pointed at the tall blue-eyed man standing against the wall. Dried blood covered the man's shirt. The shoulder had been blown away from his coat. There was dried blood there as well. Panic-stricken, he stared at the doctor.

"Come no closer!" he cried. "You will not examine me. You will not touch me with your medical instruments. I am unharmed and I want to leave this place."

"Five bullets," whispered the officer in the doctor's ear. "I saw the wounds, I tell you. He can't possibly have withstood such a—"

"Let me have a look at you!" The doctor attempted to move in.

Instantly the man's fist shot towards him, knocking the black bag to the ceiling. One of the rifles went off as the man charged the policemen, slamming several of them backwards, against the wall. The doctor fell to his knees. His glasses fell on the ground before him. He felt the heel of a boot come down on his hand as the soldiers stampeded into the hall.

Again the rifle cracked. Shouts and curses in Egyptian. Where were his glasses! He must find his glasses.

Suddenly someone was helping him to his feet. The glasses were in his hand and quickly he put them on.

A civilized English face came into focus.

"Are you all right?"

"What the devil's happened? Where is he? Did they shoot him again?"

"The man's as strong as a bull. He broke the back door out, bars and all. He's escaped."

Thank God, Alex was with her. No one could find Elliott. Samir had gone on to the police station to find out what he could. As she and Alex were ushered into the office, she saw with relief that it was the governor's assistant, Miles Winthrop, and not the governor himself. Miles had gone to school with Alex. Julie had known him since he was a little boy.

"Miles, this is a misunderstanding," Alex said. "It has to be."

"Miles," she said. "Do you think you can get him released?"

"Julie, the situation is more complicated than we realized. First off, the Egyptians aren't too fond of those who break into their world-famous museum. But now there's a theft and a murder to be considered as well."

"What are you talking about!" Julie whispered.

"Miles, Ramsey couldn't murder anybody," Alex said. "That's patently absurd."

"I hope you're right, Alex. But there's a maid dead in the museum with her neck broken. And a mummy's been stolen from a display case on the second floor. And your friend has escaped the jail. Now, tell me, both of you. How well do you really know this man?"

Running at full sprint across the roof, he took the alleyway before him in one leap. Within seconds, he covered another roof, and dropped down to another, and then cut across another narrow street.

Only then did he look back. His pursuers had lost him. He

could hear the faint, very distant crack of the rifle. Perhaps they were shooting at each other. He did not care.

He dropped down into the street and ran. Within a short distance, the street became an alley. The houses hemming him in had high windows covered over with wooden screens. He saw no more British shops or English signs. Only Egyptians passed him, and for the most part they were old women in pairs, with veils over their faces and their hair. They averted their eyes at once from his bloodstained shirt and torn clothes.

Finally he stepped into a doorway and rested, and then slowly slipped his hand into his coat. The wound was healed on the outside, though he could still feel the throbbing inside. He felt the broad strip of the moneybelt. The vials were intact.

The cursed vials! Would that he had never taken the elixir from its hiding place in London! Or that he had sealed the powder into a clay vessel and sunk the vessel into the sea!

What would the soldiers have done with the liquid if they had got their hands on it? He could not bear to dwell on how close he had come to that possibility.

But the thing now was to return to the museum! He must find her! And to dwell on what had befallen her in the interim was more than he could bear.

Never in all his existence had he experienced the regret which he was feeling now. But it was done! He had succumbed to the temptation. He had awakened the half-rotted body lying in that case.

And he must find the results of his folly. He must learn whether a spark of intellect existed inside it!

Ah, but whom was he deceiving! *She had called his name!*

He turned and hurried down the alley. A disguise, that's what he needed. And he had no time to purchase it. He must take it where he could. Laundry, he had seen ropes of laundry. He rushed on, until he saw another such rope sagging across a narrow passageway to his left.

Bedouin garments—the long-sleeved robe and the headdress. He tore these down at once. Discarding his jacket, he put them on, and then cut a bit of the rope itself to tie around his head.

Now he looked like an Arab except for the blue eyes. But then he knew where he might get a pair of dark glasses. He'd seen them in the bazaar. And that was on the way back to the museum. He headed out at a dead run.

* * *

Henry had been almost dead drunk since he'd come from Shepheard's the day before. The brief talk with Elliott had had a peculiar effect on him somehow; it had sapped his nerve.

He tried to remind himself that he loathed Elliott Savarell and that he himself was pressing on to America, where he'd never see Elliott or anyone like him again.

Yet the meeting haunted him. Every time he sobered up just a little he saw Elliott again, staring at him with absolute contempt. He heard the cold hatred in Elliott's voice.

A lot of nerve Elliott had, turning on him like this. Years ago, after a brief and stupid affair, Henry had had it in his power to destroy Elliott, but he had not done so for no other reason than it would have been a cruel thing to do. He had always presumed that Elliott was grateful for that; that Elliott's patience and politeness signaled that gratitude. For Elliott had been unfailingly courteous to him over the years.

Not so yesterday. And the awful thing about it was that the hatred Elliott evinced had been a mirror image of the hatred Henry felt for everyone he knew. It had soured Henry and embittered him.

And it had also frightened him.

Have to get away from them, all of them, he reasoned. They do nothing but criticize me and misjudge me when they are not worth a tinker's damn themselves.

When they had left Cairo, he would clean himself up, stop drinking, go back to Shepheard's and sleep in peace for a few days. Then he'd strike the bargain with his father and head out to America with the considerable little fortune he'd saved.

But for the moment, he had no intention of curtailing the party. There would be no card game today; he would take it easy, and enjoy the Scotch without distraction; merely dozing in his rattan chair, and eating the food Malenka prepared for him if and when he chose.

Malenka herself had become a bit of a nag. She had just cooked an English breakfast for him and wanted him to come to the table. He had slapped her with the back of his hand, and told her to leave him alone.

Nevertheless she went on with her preparations. He could hear the kettle whistling. She had set china out on the small rattan table in the courtyard.

Well, to hell with her. He had three bottles of Scotch, which was plenty. Maybe he would lock her out later if there was a chance. He loved the idea of being all alone here. Of drinking and smoking and dreaming. And maybe listening to the gramophone. He was even getting used to that damned parrot.

As he dozed off now, the parrot was screeching and clucking and walking back and forth, upside down, on the ceiling of its cage. African greys liked to do things like that. In truth the thing looked like a giant bug to him. Maybe he should kill it when Malenka wasn't here.

He felt himself drifting, dozing, on the edge of dream. He took one more sip of Scotch, so smooth, and let his head roll to the side. Julie's house; the library; that thing at his shoulder; the scream curled at the back of his throat.

"God!" He shot forward out of the chair, and the glass fell out of his hands. If only that dream would stop. . . .

Elliott had to stop to catch his breath. The two bulbous eyes stared at him over the black serge. It seemed they tried to squint in the sunlight, but the half-eaten lids would not fully close. The woman's hand pulled the veil tighter as if she wanted to hide herself from his gaze.

Whispering softly in Latin, he begged for patience. The carriage had been unable to get very close to the house to which they were going. It was only a few paces more.

He mopped his forehead with his handkerchief. But wait a moment. The hand. The hand which was holding the black serge over her mouth. He looked at it again. It was changing in the burning sun. The wound exposing the knucklebone had almost closed.

He stared at it for a moment; then he looked at her eyes again. Yes, the eyelids had filled in somewhat and long beautiful black lashes were now curving upwards, hiding the leprouslike ruin of the flesh.

He put his arm about her again: at once she cleaved to him, a soft and trembling thing. A soft sigh escaped her.

He was aware suddenly of a perfume rising from her, a rich, sweet and altogether lovely perfume. There was the smell of dust, of mud, actually, of the deep river silt—but that was very faint. The perfume was strong and musky. He could feel her warmth coming through the black serge.

Dear God, what is this potion! What is it capable of!

"There, there, my dear," he said in English. "We're very close. That door at the end."

He felt her arm slip around him. With a powerful grip she lifted him slightly, taking the pressure off his numb left foot. The pain in his left hip slackened. He gave a little laugh of relief. In fact, he almost broke into outright laughter. But he didn't. He simply moved on, allowing her to assist him, until he reached the door.

There he rested for a moment, and then he pounded with his right fist.

He could not have gone another step.

There was a long moment in which he heard nothing. He pounded again, and again.

Then came the sound of the bolt sliding, and Henry appeared, squinting, his face unshaven, dressed only in a green silk robe.

"What the hell do you want?"

"Let me in." He pushed the door back and brought the woman with him into the room. Desperately she crowded against him, hiding her face.

Dimly, he saw that the place was luxurious—carpets, furniture, decanters gleaming on a marble sideboard. Through the archway, a dark-skinned beauty in a satin dancing costume—obviously Malenka—had just set down a tray of steaming food. Small orange trees crowded against the whitewashed garden wall.

"Who is this woman!" Henry demanded.

Holding tight to her still, Elliott struggled to the chair. But he could see that Henry was staring at the woman's feet. He'd seen the bare bones showing in the instep. A look of disgust passed over Henry; of puzzlement.

"Who is she! Why did you bring her here!"

Then convulsively, Henry moved back, slamming into the pillar that divided the archway to the courtyard, his head thudding dangerously against the stone.

"What's wrong with her!" he gasped.

"Patience, I'll tell you everything," Elliott whispered. The pain in his chest was so bad now that he could hardly form the words. Easing down in the rattan chair, he felt the woman's grip loosen. He heard her make a faint sound. He looked up, and realized she had seen the cupboard across the room, the glass bottles gleaming in the light from the courtyard.

She went towards the liquid, groaning. The black serge garment fell from her head and then from her shoulders, fully revealing the bones of her ribs gleaming through the gaping holes in her back, and the remnants of cloth that barely concealed her nakedness.

"For the love of God, don't panic!" Elliott shouted.

But it was too late. Henry's face went white, his mouth twisted and shuddering. Behind him, in the courtyard, Malenka let out a full-throated scream.

The wounded creature dropped the bottle with a great piteous moan.

Henry's hand rose from his pocket, sun glinting on the barrel of a small silver gun.

"No, Henry!" Elliott cried. He tried to rise, but he couldn't. The shot exploded with the same nerve-shattering volume of the guns in the museum. A parrot screeched in its cage.

The wounded woman cried out as she took the bullet in her chest, staggering backwards, and then let out a great bellow as she ran at Henry.

The sounds coming from Henry were scarcely human. All reason had left him. He backed into the courtyard, firing the gun again and again. Crying in agony, the woman closed on him, knocking the gun out of his hand and taking him by the throat. In an ugly waltz they struggled, Henry clawing at her desperately, her own bony fingers holding fast to his neck. The wicker table went over, china shattering on the tiles. Into the orange trees they stumbled, tiny leaves pouring down in a shower.

In terror Malenka crouched against the wall.

"Elliott, help me!" Henry screamed. He was being bent over backwards, knees buckling and hands flailing, catching stupidly in the creature's hair.

Elliott managed somehow to reach the edge of the archway. But only in time to hear the bones snap. He winced as he saw Henry's body go limp and tumble softly, in a heap of green silk, on the ground.

The creature staggered backwards, whimpering, and then sobbing, her mouth making a grimace again, as it had in the museum, teeth bared. The ragged cloth covering her had been torn from one shoulder; her dark pink nipples showed through the sheer linen. Great gouts of blood hung in the wrappings still clinging to her torso, strips of fabric falling from her thighs with each step. Her eyes, bloodshot and running with tears, stared at the dead body and then at the spilt food, the hot tea steaming in the sun.

Slowly she went down on her knees. She grabbed up the muffins and stuffed them into her mouth. On all fours she lapped the spilt tea. She scraped up the jam with her fingers and sucked them frantically. She gnawed on the bacon and then swallowed the rasher whole.

In utter silence, Elliott watched her. He was vaguely conscious of Malenka running silently towards him, and then hovering behind him. Deliberately, he took one short breath after another, listening at the same time to the hammer trip of his heart.

The creature devoured the butter; the eggs she crushed and scraped with her teeth from the shells.

Finally there was no more food. Yet she remained there, on her knees. She was staring at her outstretched hands.

The sun beat down on the little courtyard. It gleamed on her dark hair.

In a daze, Elliott continued to watch. He could not absorb what he was seeing or judge it. The continuing shock of all he'd witnessed was too great.

Suddenly the creature turned and lay down on the paved ground. She stretched out full length, crying as if into a soft pillow, her hand scratching at the hard-baked tiles. Then she rolled over on her back into the full sunlight, free of the soft dancing green shadows from the small trees.

For a moment she stared up into the burning sky, and then her eyes appeared to roll up in her head. Only a half-moon of pale iris showed.

"Ramses," she whispered. Her bosom moved faintly with her breathing. But otherwise she lay still.

The Earl turned and reached for Malenka. Leaning heavily on her, he struggled back towards the chair. He could feel the dark-skinned woman trembling. He settled down silently on the tapestried cushions, and rested his head against the high rounded chair back of prickly rattan. This is all a nightmare, he thought. But it was not a nightmare. He had seen this creature raised from the dead. He had seen her kill Henry. What in God's name was he to do?

Malenka remained at his elbow, then went down slowly on her knees. Her eyes were wide and empty, her mouth agape. She stared towards the garden.

Flies circled over Henry's face. They swooped down on the remnants of the overturned meal.

"There, there, nothing will harm you," Elliott whispered. The burning in his chest subsided very slowly. He felt a dull warmth in his left hand. "She won't hurt you. I promise you." He moistened his dry lips with his tongue, then somehow managed to go on. "She is ill; and I must take care of her. She will not harm you, you understand."

The Egyptian woman clutched at his wrist, her forehead against the arm of the chair. After a long moment, she spoke.

"No police," she pleaded in a barely audible voice. "No English take my house."

"No," Elliott murmured. "No police. We don't want the police."

He wanted to pat her head, but he could not bring himself to move. He stared dully out into the sunlight, at the prone creature, her glossy black hair spread out in the sunlight; and at the dead man.

"I take care of . . ." the woman whispered. "I take my English away. No police come."

Elliott didn't understand her. What was she saying? Then slowly it dawned on him.

"You can do this?" he said under his breath.

"Yes, I do this. Friends come. Take English away."

"Yes, all right then." He sighed and the pain in his chest intensified. Tentatively he pushed his right hand into his pocket and brought out his money clip. Barely able to move his left fingers, he took out two ten-pound notes.

"For you," he said. He closed his eyes again, exhausted by the effort. He felt the money taken from his hand. "But you must be careful. You must tell no one what you saw."

"I tell no one. I take care of . . . This is *my* house. My brother give."

"Yes, I understand. I shall be here only a little while. That I promise you. I shall take the woman with me. But for now, you will be patient, and there'll be more money, much more." Once again he looked at the money clip. He peeled the notes off without counting and forced them into her hand.

Then he lay back again, and closed his eyes. He heard her pad softly across the carpet. Then her hand touched him again.

When he looked up he saw her draped in black, and she held another folded black robe in her hand.

"You cover," she whispered. And with her eyes, she gestured to the courtyard.

"I cover," he whispered. And closed his eyes again.

"You cover!" he heard her say desperately. And again he said that he would.

With great relief he heard her go out, and shut the door to the street.

In the long flowing Bedouin robes, Ramses walked through the museum, among the milling tourists, peering ahead through the dark glasses at the empty space at the end of the corridor where the display case had stood. No sign that it had ever been there! No broken glass, no splintered wood. And the vial he had dropped. Gone.

But where could she be! What happened to her! In anguish, he thought of the soldiers who'd surrounded him. Had she fallen into their hands?

He walked on, turning the corner, eyes moving over the statues and the sarcophagi. If he had known misery like this ever in all these centuries, he could not remember it now. He had no right to be walking here with men and women, to be breathing the same air.

He could not think where to go or what to do. If he did not discover something soon, he would go completely mad.

Perhaps a quarter of an hour passed, maybe less. Cover her, yes. No, get her out of the garden before the men come. She lay in the sun, stuporous, now and then murmuring in her sleep.

Gripping his walking stick, he rose to his feet. There was feeling in his left leg again, and that meant there was pain.

He went into the bedroom. A high old-fashioned Victorian bed stood against the far right wall, its white mosquito netting catching the flood of sunlight from the open blinds of the window.

A dressing table stood just to the left of the window. And an armoire stood farther away in the left corner, its mirrored doors open, revealing a row of wool jackets and coats.

A small portable gramophone with a horn stood on the dressing table. Beside it were a set of gramophone records in a cardboard case. "Learn English," said the bold lettering. There was another dance hall record. An ashtray. Several magazines and a half-full bottle of Scotch.

He could see a proper bathroom through a far door on the right side of the bed. Copper tub there; towels.

He went the other direction, through a door into another chamber which formed the north wall of the courtyard, with all its blinds shut. Here the dark beauty kept her tawdry dancing costumes and junk jewelry. But one cabinet was bursting with frilly Western dresses as well. There were Western shoes, and frilly umbrellas and a couple of impossible wide-brimmed hats.

But what good were these clothes when the wounded thing needed to be hidden from prying eyes? He found the usual Moslem robes folded neatly on a bottom shelf. So he could give her fresh covering—that is, if Malenka would allow him to buy these clothes.

He paused in the doorway to catch his breath. He stared at the regal bed in the sunlight, the netting flowing down from a circular tester, much like a crown above. The moment seemed trancelike, elastic. Images of Henry's death flashed before his eyes. Yet he felt nothing. Nothing—except perhaps for a cold horror that took away the very will to live.

Will to live. He had the vial in his pocket. He had a few drops of the precious fluid!

That, too, did not affect him; did not dispel his languor. The maid dead in the museum; Henry dead in the courtyard. The thing lying out there in the sun!

He could not reason. Why bother to try? He had to reach Ramses, of that much he was certain. But where was Ramses? What had the bullets done to him? Was he being held by the men who had dragged him away?

But first, the woman, he had to bring her in and hide her so that Henry's body could be taken away.

She might well attack the men who came to get Henry. And one glimpse of her might do them even more harm.

Limping out to the courtyard, he tried to clear his head. He and Ramses were not enemies. They were confederates now. And perhaps . . . But then he had no spirit for such dreams and ambitions anymore—only what must be done now.

He took a few cautious steps towards the woman asleep on the tiled patio floor.

The midday sun was burning hot, and suddenly he feared for her because of it. He shaded his eyes as he looked at her: for surely he could not be seeing what he thought he saw.

She moaned uneasily; she was suffering—but a woman of great and exceptional beauty lay there!

A large patch of white bone gleamed through her raven hair,

true, and a small bit of bare cartilage showed in her jaw. Indeed, her right hand still had two fingers which were bones only, blood trickling from the gristle in the joints. And the wound in her chest was still there, gaping, revealing a stretch of white rib, overlaid with a thin membrane full of tiny red veins.

But the face had assumed its full human contour! High colour bloomed in the beautifully moulded cheeks. The mouth was exquisitely shaped and ruddy. And the flesh had over all a lovely even olive tone.

Her nipples were a dark rose colour, her breasts plump and firm.

What was happening? Did the elixir take time to work?

Timidly he drew closer. The heat pounded upon him. His head began to swim. Struggling once again not to lose consciousness, he groped for the pillar behind him and steadied himself, eyes still fixed on the woman who now opened her pale hazel eyes.

She stirred, lifting her right hand and staring at it again. Surely she felt what was happening to her. In fact, it seemed the wounds hurt her. Gasping, she touched the bleeding edge of open flesh on her hand.

But if she understood that she was actually healing, she gave no sign. She let her arm drop limply and once again she closed her eyes. She cried again, softly.

"Ramses," she said as if in half sleep.

"Come with me," Elliott spoke to her softly in Latin. "Come inside, to a proper bed."

Dully she looked at him.

"The warm sun is there too," he said. And no sooner had he said these words than he realized. It was the sun that was healing her! He had seen it working on her hand as they came through the streets. It was the only part exposed save for her eyes, and they too had been healing.

And it had been the sun that waked Ramses. That was the meaning of all the strange language on the coffin, that the sun must not be allowed into the tomb.

But there was no time to ponder it or question it. She had sat up; the rags had fallen away from her naked breasts completely, and her face, looking up at him, was beautifully angular, cheeks softly shadowed, eyes full of cold light.

She gave him her hand, then saw the bony fingers and drew it back with a hiss.

"No, trust in me," he said in Latin. He helped her to her feet.

He led her through the little house and into the bedroom. She studied objects around her. With her foot, she examined the soft Persian carpet. She stared at the little gramophone. What did the black disk look like to her?

He tried to steer her towards the bed, but she would not move. She had seen the newspaper lying on the dressing table; and now she snatched it up and stared at the advertisement for the opera—at the quaintly Egyptian woman and her warrior lover, and the sketch of the three pyramids behind them and the fanlike Egyptian palms.

She gave a little agitated moan as she studied this. Then her finger moved over the columns of English, and she looked up at Elliott, her eyes large and glossy and slightly mad.

"My language," he said to her in Latin. "English. This advertises a drama with music. It is called an opera."

"Speak in English," she said to him in Latin. Her voice was sharp yet lovely. "I tell you, speak."

There was a sound at the door. He took her arm and moved her to one side, out of sight. "Strangers," he said in English and then immediately in Latin. He went on in this vein, alternating languages, translating for her. "Lie down and rest, and I shall bring you food."

She cocked her head, listening to the noises from the other room. Then her body moved with a violent spasm and she put her hand to the wound in her chest. Yes, they hurt her, these awful oozing ulcers, for that's what they looked like. But there was something else wrong with her, accounting for her sudden jerky movements, and the way every sound startled her.

Quickly he led her to the bed, and, shoving back the netting, he urged her to lie back on the lace pillows. A great look of relief came over her as she did so. She shivered violently again, fingers dancing now over her eyes, as she turned instinctively towards the sun. Surely he should cover her; only a few rags now clung to her, thin as paper, but then she needed the sun.

He opened the blinds opposite, letting the full heat come in.

Then he hurried to close the door to the sitting room, and he peered out the window that opened onto the yard.

Malenka was just opening the garden gate. Two men had come in with a rolled-up carpet. They unrolled it on the pavement, lifted the body of Henry, dumped it down on the carpet and rolled it up again.

The sight of the heavy flopping limbs sickened Elliott. He swallowed, and waited out the sudden increased pressure in his chest.

Then he heard a soft weeping coming from the bed. He went back to the woman and looked down at her. He could not tell if the healing was continuing. And then he thought of the vial in his coat.

For a moment he hesitated. Who would not? But there were only a few droplets. And he could not bear the sight of her pain.

The deaths she'd caused; they had been almost blunders. And how impossible to measure her confusion and torments.

She looked up at him, squinting as though the brightness hurt her. And softly in Latin, she asked his name.

For a moment he couldn't respond. Her simple tone had evinced a natural intelligence. And it was intelligence now that he beheld in her eyes.

That is, she seemed no longer mad or disoriented. Only a woman suffering.

"Forgive me," he said in Latin. "Elliott, Lord Rutherford. In my land, I am a lord."

Shrewdly she studied him. She sat up, and reaching for the folded comforter at the foot of the bed, she brought it up to cover her to the waist. The sunlight sparkled on her black hair, and once again he saw the tendrils dancing about her face.

Her black eyebrows were beautifully drawn, high and just wide enough apart. Her hazel eyes were magnificent.

"May I ask your name?" he said in Latin.

A bitter smile came over her. "Cleopatra," she said. "In my land, I am a Queen."

The silence shimmered. A soft heat washed through him, utterly unlike the pain of other shocks. He stared into her eyes, unable to answer. And then a great exhilaration seized him, obliterating every fear and regret of his soul.

"Cleopatra," he whispered, awestruck, respectful.

In Latin she said, "Speak to me in English, Lord Rutherford. Speak the tongue you spoke to the slave girl. Speak the tongue written there in the book. Bring me food and drink, for I am ravenous."

"Yes," he said in English, nodding to her. He repeated the assent in Latin. "Food and drink."

"And you must tell me—" she started, but then stopped. The pain in her side hurt her, and then frantically she touched the wound on her head. "Tell me—" she tried again, then looked at him in pure confusion. She was obviously struggling to remember; then panic seized her, and clamping her hands to her head, she closed her eyes and started to weep.

"Here, wait, I have the medicine," he whispered. He eased himself down slowly on the side of the bed. He drew the vial out of his coat. A half inch of fluid remained in it, sparkling unnaturally in the sun.

She studied the vial suspiciously. She watched him open it. He raised it, gently touching her hair with his left hand; but she stopped him. She pointed to her eyelids and he saw that there were still small places there where the skin appeared eaten away. She took the vial from him, poured a drop or two onto her fingers and smoothed this on her lids.

Elliott narrowed his eyes as he watched the action of the chemical. He could almost hear it, a faint rustling, crackling sound.

Now, desperately, she took the whole vial and poured the fluid over the gaping hole in her chest. She smeared it with her left fingers, whimpering softly, and then lay back, gasping faintly, head tossing on the pillows, then still.

Several minutes passed. He was fascinated by what he saw. But the healing went only so far, then stopped. Her lids, they were now entirely normal, and indeed her lashes were a dark unbroken fringe. But the wound in her side was as evil as ever.

It was only just penetrating to him that she *was* Cleopatra, that Ramses had stumbled upon the body of his lost love. It was only just coming clear to him why Ramses had done what he had done. Dully he wondered what it meant to have such power. He had dreamed of immortality, but not the power to convey it. And this was the power not only to grant immortality, but to triumph over death.

But the implications . . . they staggered him. This creature, what was going on in her mind? Indeed, where had her mind as such come from? God, he had to reach Ramsey!

"I'll get more of the medicine," he said in English, translating it immediately into Latin. "I'll bring it here to you, but you must rest now. You must lie here in the sun." He pointed to the window. Using both languages, he explained that the sun was making the medicine work.

Drowsily she looked at him. She repeated his English phrases, mimicking his accent perfectly. But her eyes had a glazed and utterly mad look now. She murmured something in Latin about not being able to remember and then she began to weep again.

He could not bear the sight of it. But what more could he do? As quickly as he could, he went into the other room and brought back a bottle of liqueur for her, a thick spicy brandy, and at once she took it from him and drank it down.

Her eyes went dim for a moment. And then she moaned aloud in pure distress again.

The gramophone. Ramsey loved music. Ramsey was spellbound by it. Elliott went to the little machine, and examined the few records beside it in a pile. Lots of the English-language foolishness. Ah, here was what he wanted: *Aïda*. Caruso singing Radames.

He wound the box, and set the needle on the record. At the first thin sound of the orchestra, she sat up in the bed; she stared in horror. But he went to her and touched her shoulder gently.

"Opera, *Aïda*," he said. He groped for words in Latin to explain it was a music box; it worked by parts fitted together. "The song was from a man to his Egyptian love."

She climbed out of the bed and stumbled past him. She was now almost entirely naked, and her form was quite beautiful, her hips narrow and her legs beautifully proportioned. He tried not to stare at her; not to stare at her breasts. Approaching slowly, he lifted the gramophone needle. She screamed at him. A volley of curses broke from her in Latin. "Make the music go on."

"Yes, but I want to show you how," he told her. He cranked the handle of the machine again. He set the needle on the record again. Only then did the utter savagery go out of her expression. She began to moan in time with the music, and then she put her hands on her head, and shut her eyes very tight.

She began to dance, rocking frantically from side to side. It terrified him to watch her, but he knew he'd seen this very kind of dancing before. He had seen it among severely damaged children—an atavistic response to the rhythm and sound.

She didn't notice as he slipped away to bring her food.

Ramses bought the newspaper from the British newsstand and walked on, slowly, through the crowded bazaar.

MURDER IN THE MUSEUM
MUMMY STOLEN; MAID KILLED

Beneath the headline was the column heading:

MYSTERIOUS EGYPTIAN
SOUGHT IN GRISLY DEATH

He scanned the details, then crumpled up the newspaper and threw it away. He walked on with his head bowed, arms folded under the Arab robe. Had she slain this serving woman? And why had she done it? And how had she managed to escape?

Of course the officials might be lying, but that seemed unlikely. Not enough time had elapsed for such cleverness. And she had had the opportunity, for the guards had been busy taking him away.

He tried to see again what he had seen in that shadowy hallway—the horrid monstrosity which he had resurrected from the case. He saw the thing trudging towards him; he heard the hoarse, almost gurgling voice. He saw the attitude of suffering stamped on the half-eaten-away face!

What was he to do? This morning for the first time since he had been a mortal man, he had thought of his gods. In the museum as he had stood over her remains, ancient chants had come back to him; ancient words he'd spoken before the populace and in the darkened temple surrounded by priests.

And now in the hot teeming street, he found himself whispering under his breath old prayers again.

Julie sat on the small white chintz sofa in the sitting room of her cluttered hotel suite. She was glad that Alex was holding her hand. Samir stood quietly beside the only empty chair. Two British officials sat opposite. Miles Winthrop, standing near the door, hands clasped behind his back, looked miserable. The elder of the two officials, a man named Peterson, held a telegram in his hand.

"But you see, Miss Stratford," he said with a condescending smile, "with a death in London and now a death here in Cairo . . ."

"How do you know they are connected?" Samir asked. "This man in London. You say he was a maker of illegal loans!"

"Ah, Tommy Sharples, yes, that was his profession."

"Well, what would Mr. Ramsey have to do with him?" Julie asked. How remarkable that I sound so calm, she thought, when I am going mad inside.

"Miss Stratford, the Cleopatra coin found in the dead man's pocket connects these murders. Surely it came from your collection. It is identical with the five coins cataloged."

"But it is not one of the five coins. You've told me that."

"Yes, but you see, we found several others, here at Shepheard's."

"I don't follow you."

"In Mr. Ramsey's room."

Silence. Samir cleared his throat. "You searched his room?"

It was Miles who answered:

"Julie, I know this is a very dear friend of yours, and the whole situation is painful. But you see, these killings—they're extraordinarily vicious. And you must tell us anything that can help us to apprehend this man."

"He did not kill anyone in London!"

Miles went on as if he hadn't heard this outburst, with maddening civility.

"Now, the Earl, we must talk to the Earl also, and at the moment we can't find him." He looked to Alex.

"I don't know where my father is," Alex said helplessly.

"And Henry Stratford, where can we find him?"

The two Egyptians hurried through the narrow streets of old Cairo, with the blanket over their shoulders, the bulging body quite a weight in the noon heat.

But it was well worth the sweat and time taken, for the body would bring them plenty. As the winter months approached, tourists would descend in droves upon Egypt. They had found a good and handsome corpse just in time.

Finally they reached Zaki's house, or "the factory," as it was known to them in their own tongue. Through the courtyard gate they entered, hurrying with their trophy into the first of a series of dimly lighted rooms. They had taken no notice of the mummies propped against the stone wall as they passed, or of the numerous dark, leathery bodies on tables in the room.

Only the stench of the chemicals bothered them. And they waited impatiently for Zaki to come.

"Good body," said one of the men to the workman who stirred a giant pot of bitumen in the centre of the room. A great bed of coals beneath it kept it bubbling, and it was from this pot that the foul smell came.

"Good bones?" asked the man.

"Ah, yes, beautiful English bones."

The disguise was a good one. Thousands of such Bedouins roamed Cairo. He might as well have been invisible, that is, when he took off the sunglasses which did occasionally bring stares.

He pocketed them now beneath the striped robe as he entered the rear yard of Shepheard's Hotel. The brown-skinned Egyptian boys, lathering a motor car, did not even look up from their labor as he passed.

Moving along the wall, behind the fruit trees, he approached a small nondescript door. An uncarpeted rear stairs lay within. Mops, brooms, a wash pail in the alcove.

He took the broom and made his way slowly up the stairs. He dreaded the inevitable moment when Julie would ask what he had done.

She sat on the side of the bed, eating from the tray he'd put before her on the small wicker table from the yard. She wore a thin chemise now, the only undergarment he'd found in Malenka's closet. He had helped her put it on.

Malenka had prepared the food for him—fruit, bread, cheese and wine—but she would not come near the room.

The creature's appetite was fierce and she ate almost savagely. The bottles of wine she'd drunk as if they were water. And though she had remained in the sun steadily, no more healing had taken place, of that he was fairly sure.

As for Malenka, she remained shivering in the front room. How long he could control her, Elliott was unsure.

He slipped away now and went in search of her. He found her crouched, her arms folded, against the far wall.

"Don't be frightened, dear," he said to her.

"My poor English," she said in a whisper.

"I know, my dear, I know." But that's just it, he didn't know. He sat down in the peacock chair again, and took out a few more bills. He gestured to her to come and take them. But she merely stared at him, dull-eyed, shivering, and then turned her head to the wall.

"My poor English," she said, "is in the boiling vat by now."

Had he heard her properly?

"What vat?" he asked her. "What are you saying?"

"They make a great Pharaoh of my English. My beautiful English. They put him in the bitumen; they make a mummy of him for tourists to buy."

He was too shocked to answer her. He looked away, unable to form the simplest words.

"My beautiful English, they wrap him in linen; they make him a King."

He wanted to say, Stop, he could hear no more. But he only sat there in silence until suddenly the sound of the gramophone startled him—the sound of a pinched voice speaking English grinding out from the other room. The English records. She had found them. He trusted that they would content her, that they would give him this little time to rest.

But there came a great shattering crash. The mirror. She had broken it.

He rose and hurried towards her; she stood rocking back and forth on the carpet, the broken glass all over the dressing table, all over the floor around her, the gramophone droning on.

"Regina," he said. *"Bella Regina Cleopatra."*

"Lord Rutherford," she cried. "What has happened to me! What is this place?" A long string of words in a strange tongue she spoke rapidly, and then the words gave out altogether into hoarse hysterical cries breaking one after another, and finally forming one great roaring sob.

Zaki inspected the operation. He watched them sink the naked body of the Englishman deep into the thick, viscous green fluid. On occasion, he would embalm these bodies; he would carry the replication of the original process to the extreme. But that was no longer necessary. The English weren't so keen anymore to unwrapping them at their parties in London. It was only necessary to have them thoroughly soaked in bitumen, and then the wrappings could be applied.

He approached the vat; he studied the face of the Englishman floating below the surface. Good bones, that was true. That's what the tourists like—to see a real face beneath the linen. And this one would look very good indeed.

A soft knock on her door.

"I don't want to see anyone," Julie said. She sat on the couch in the sitting room of her suite, beside Samir, who had been holding her as she cried.

She could not understand what had happened. There was no doubt Ramses had been in the museum, that he had been badly wounded, and that he had escaped. But the murder of the maid, she could not believe he would do such a thing.

"The theft of the mummy, this I understand," she had told Samir only moments before. "He knew that woman; he knew who she was. He could not bear to see the body desecrated any longer, and so he sought to remove her."

"But none of the pieces fit together," Samir said. "If he was taken prisoner, who then removed the mummy?" He paused as Rita answered the door.

Julie turned, caught a glimpse of a tall Arab standing there, in full flowing robes. She was about to turn away when she saw a flash of blue eyes.

It was Ramses. He pushed his way past Rita and shut the door. At once she rushed into his arms.

She did not know what her doubts had been, or her fears. She held him, burying her face in his neck. She felt his lips graze her forehead, and then his embrace tightened. He kissed her hard, yet tenderly, on the mouth.

She heard Samir's urgent whisper. "Sire, you are in danger. They are searching for you everywhere."

But she couldn't release him. In the graceful robes, he looked more than ever otherworldly. The pure precious love she felt for him was sharpened to the point of pain.

"Do you know what's happened?" she whispered. "A woman in the museum was murdered and they are accusing you of the crime."

"I know, my dearest," he said softly. "The death is on my head. And worse horrors than that."

She stared at him, trying to accept his words. Then the tears rose once again, and she covered her face with her hands.

She sat on the bed, staring stupidly at him. Did she understand when he told her the dress was a very fine dress? She mimicked the words of the gramophone in perfect English. "I should like a little sugar in my coffee. I should like a bit of lemon in my tea." Then she fell silent again.

She let him button the pearl buttons; she stared down in

amazement as he tied the sash of the pink skirt. She gave an evil little laugh and lifted her leg against the heavy gores of the skirt.

"Pretty, pretty," she said. He had taught her that much in English. "Pretty dress."

She brushed past him suddenly and picked up a magazine from the dressing table and looked at the pictures of the women. Then in Latin, she asked again, What is this place?

"Egypt," he told her. He had told her over and over. Then would come the blank look, then the look of pain.

Timidly he lifted the brush, and brought it down through her hair. Lovely, fine hair. Hair so black there were faint glints of blue in it. She sighed, lifted her shoulders; she loved him brushing it. A low laugh came from her lips.

"Very good, Lord Rutherford," she said in English. She arched her back and moved her limbs languidly, a cat stretching, her hands exquisitely graceful as she held them poised in the air.

"Bella Regina Cleopatra," he sighed. Was it safe now to leave her? Could he make her understand? Perhaps if Malenka stood outside in the street before the bolted door until he came back.

"I must go now, Your Majesty. I must get more of the medicine if I can."

She turned, stared at him blankly. She didn't know what he was talking about! Was it possible she could not even remember what had happened moments before? She was trying to remember.

"From Ramses," he said.

There was a spark in her eye, then a deep shadow over her face. She whispered something, but he didn't hear it. "Kind Lord Rutherford," she said.

He pulled firmly on the hairbrush. Her hair was now a great soft drift of rippling waves.

The strangest light had come into her expression; her mouth was slack; her cheeks flushed.

She turned and stroked his face. She said something quickly in Latin that meant he possessed an older man's knowledge and a young man's mouth.

He puzzled over it, trying to think as she looked into his eyes. It seemed his own awareness of things drifted in and out; one moment she was this deeply afflicted creature he must care for;

the next the great Cleopatra, and the full shock of it struck him again.

Luscious, this woman; the seducer of Caesar. She drew closer to him. It seemed the shrewdness had returned. Then her arm went up around his neck. Her fingers stroked his hair.

Warm her flesh. Dear God, the same flesh that had lain rotted and black beneath that dirty glass, thick and impenetrable as tar, that mass.

But these eyes, these deep hazel eyes with the tiny flecks of yellow in the pupils, impossible that they had sprung alive again from the dark filth. The filth of death. . . . Her lips touched his suddenly. Her mouth opened against his and he felt her tongue sliding between his teeth.

Instantly, his sex stirred. But this was madness. He was incapable. His heart, the pain in his bones, he could not possibly . . . She pushed her breasts against him. Through the cloth he felt their throbbing heat. The lace, the pearl buttons; they only made her seem all the more deliciously savage.

His vision blurred, he saw the naked bones of her fingers as she reached to force his hair back off his forehead, as her kiss became more insistent and her tongue plunged deep into his mouth.

Cleopatra, the lover of Caesar, of Antony, and of Ramses the Damned. He closed his arms around her waist. She went back on the lace pillows, pulling him down on top of her.

He groaned aloud, his mouth gnawing at her. God, to take her. His hand gathered up the silk skirts and plunged between her legs. Moist, hot hair there, moist lips.

"Good, Lord Rutherford," she said in Latin. Her hips knocked against him, against his sex bulging and ready to be free.

He opened the few buttons quickly. How many years had it been since the thing was done in such haste? But there was no question now of what was meant to happen.

"Ah, take me, Lord Rutherford!" came her hissing whisper. "Plunge your dagger into my soul!"

And this is how I die. Not from the horrors I've beheld. But from this, this which is beyond my strength yet irresistible. He kissed her almost cruelly, his sex pumping between her damp thighs. The sweet evil laughter was bubbling out of her.

He shut his eyes as he thrust against the tight little fount.

* * *

"You cannot stay here, sire," Samir said. "The risk is too great. They're watching the entrance. Surely we are being followed wherever we go. And sire, they searched your room, they found the ancient coins. They may have found . . . more than that."

"No. There was nothing else for them to find. But I must speak with you, both of you."

"Some sort of hiding place," Julie said. "Where we can meet."

"I can arrange this," Samir said. "But I need a couple of hours. Can you come to me outside the Great Mosque at three o'clock? I shall dress as you are dressed."

"I'm coming with you!" Julie insisted. "Nothing is going to keep me away."

"Julie, you don't know what I've done," Ramses whispered.

"Ah, then you must tell me," she said. "These robes, Samir can get them for me as well as for himself."

"Oh, how I love you," Ramses whispered very low under his breath. "And I need you. But for your own sake, Julie, do not—"

"Whatever it is, I stand with you."

"Sire, leave now. There are policemen everywhere in this hotel. They will come back to question us. At the mosque. Three o'clock."

The pain in his chest was bad, but he wasn't dying. He sat slumped in a small wooden chair near the bed. He needed a drink from the bottle in the other room, but he had no stamina to get it. It was all he could manage to slowly button his shirt.

He turned to look at her again, her smooth waxen face in sleep. But now her eyes were open. She sat up and held out the glass vial to him.

"Medicine," she said.

"Yes, I shall get it. But you must stay here. You understand?" In Latin first he explained it. "You are safe here. You must remain in this house."

It seemed she did not want to do this.

"Where will you go?" she asked. She looked around her; she looked at the window beside the bed, open onto the slanting afternoon sun and a barren whitewashed wall. "Egypt. I do not believe this is Egypt."

"Yes, yes, my dear. And I must try to find Ramses."

That spark again, and then the confusion, and suddenly the panic.

But he rose; he could delay this no longer. He could only hope and pray that Ramses had somehow gotten free of his captors. Surely Julie and Alex had marshalled the appropriate lawyers. Whatever the case, he must try to reach the hotel.

"Not very long, Your Majesty," he said to her. "I shall return with the medicine as soon as I can."

She did not appear to trust him. She watched suspiciously as he went out of the room.

Malenka sat crouched still in the corner of the sitting room. She was shivering and she stared at him with empty, stupid eyes.

"My dear, listen to me," he said. He found his cane by the drinks cupboard and took it in hand. "I want you to go out with me, lock the door and stand guard."

Did the girl understand? She was staring past him; he turned around and saw Cleopatra in the door—barefoot, her hair streaming, so that again she looked utterly savage in the proper pink silk English dress. She stared at Malenka.

The girl recoiled, whimpering. Her loathing and fear were plain.

"No, no, dearest. Come with me," Elliott said. "Don't be afraid, she won't hurt you."

Malenka was too terrified to listen or obey. Her piteous cries grew louder. Cleopatra's blank face had changed to a mask of rage.

She came towards the helpless woman, who stared at the naked bones in her hand and in her foot.

"She's only a servant girl," said the Earl, reaching out for Cleopatra's arm. She pivoted and slapped him, knocking him backwards so that he fell against the parrot's cage. As Malenka screamed in pure hysteria, the bird began to screech frantically, beating his wings against the bars.

Elliott tried to steady himself. The girl must stop screaming. This was a disaster. Cleopatra, looking from the screeching bird to the screaming woman, appeared on the verge of hysteria herself. Then she lunged at the woman, grabbing her by the throat and forcing her down on her knees as she had done to Henry only hours before.

"No, stop it." Elliott hurled himself at her. This time he could not let it happen, and once again he felt her powerful blow knocking him yards across the room. He fell against the wall, his hand up on the plaster. Then came that sound, that unspeakable sound. The girl was dead. Cleopatra had broken her neck.

The bird had ceased its screeching. It stared with one round senseless eye into the room. Malenka lay on her back on the carpet, her head wrenched to one side at an impossible angle, her brown eyes half-closed.

Cleopatra stood staring down at her. Thoughtfully she looked at the girl. Then she said in Latin:

"She is dead."

Elliott didn't answer. He gripped the edge of the marble-top cupboard and pulled himself to his feet. The throbbing in his chest meant nothing to him. Nothing could equal the pain in his soul.

"Why did you do it!" he whispered. Oh, but was he mad to ask such a question of this being? This thing whose brain was damaged, without doubt, as her body was damaged, beautiful though she was.

Almost innocently she stared at Elliott. Then she looked back at the dead woman.

"Tell me, Lord Rutherford, how did I come to be here!" Her eyes narrowed. She approached him. In fact, she reached out and effortlessly helped him to stand upright. She picked up the walking stick and put it in his left hand. "Where did I come from?" she asked. "Lord Rutherford!" She bent forward, her eyes growing wide and full of terror. "Lord Rutherford, was I dead?"

She didn't wait for him to answer; her scream came in pulses. He embraced her, and put his hand over her mouth.

"Ramses brought you here. Ramses! You called out to him. You saw him."

"Yes!" She stood still, not struggling, merely clutching his wrist. "Ramses was there. And when I . . . when I called out to him, he ran from me. Like the woman, he ran from me! That same look in his eyes."

"He wanted to come back to you. Others stopped him. Now I must go to get him. Do you understand? You must stay here. You must wait for me." She stared past him. "Ramses has the medicine," he said. "I shall bring it back here."

"How long?"

"A few hours," he said. "It's midafternoon. I'll be back before dark."

She moaned again, and pressed her curved thumb to her teeth, staring at the floor. She looked like a child suddenly, a child wrestling with an enormous puzzle. "Ramses," she whispered. Clearly she was not certain who he was.

He patted her shoulder gently; then with the aid of his cane, he approached the body of the girl. What in the name of heaven was he to do with it? Let it lie here and rot as the hours passed? How could he bury it in the garden, when he could barely walk as it was? He closed his eyes and laughed to himself bitterly. It seemed a thousand years since he had seen his son, or Julie, or the civilized rooms of a common place like Shepheard's Hotel. It seemed a thousand years ago that he had done anything normal or loved anything normal; or believed in it; or made the sacrifices that normality required.

"Go, get the medicine," she said to him. She stepped between him and the dead woman. She reached down and lifted Malenka by her right arm. Effortlessly she dragged the woman across the carpet, past the clucking bird, which had the good fortune to be silent, and threw the corpse of the woman out into the yard as if it were a stuffed doll. The body landed on its face against the far wall.

Do not think now. Go to Ramses. Go!

"Three hours," he said to her, again using the two languages. "Bolt the door after me. You see the bolt?"

She turned and looked at the door. She nodded.

"Very well, Lord Rutherford," she said in Latin. "Before dark."

She did not bolt the door. She stood there, her hands on the bare wood, listening as he walked away. It would take him a long time to move out of sight.

And she must get out of this place! She must see where she was! This could not be Egypt. And she could not understand why she was here, or why she hungered so, and could not be satisfied, or why she felt this sharp, enervating desire to be in a man's arms. She would have forced Lord Rutherford again if she had not wanted him to go on his errand.

But the errand; it was not clear to her suddenly. He meant to get the medicine, but what was the medicine! How could she live with the great gaping wounds she had?

Yet only a moment ago she'd realized something about this, something to do with that dead woman, that shrieking slave girl whose neck she'd snapped.

Ah, but the thing to do was leave here, while Lord Rutherford was not here to scold her like a teacher and tell her to remain.

In a haze, she remembered the streets she had glimpsed earlier, full of great rumbling monstrous things made from metal; full of foul smoke and deafening noise. Who were the people she had seen around her? Women in dresses such as she wore.

She'd been terrified then; but her body had been full of aches and misery. Now her body was full of cravings. She must not be terrified. She must go.

She went back into the bedchamber. She opened the "magazine" called *Harper's Weekly* and looked at the drawings of pretty women in these strange dresses that pinched them in the middle like insects. Then she looked at herself in the mirror on the cabinet door.

She needed a covering for her head, and sandals. Yes, sandals. Quickly she searched the bedchamber, and found them in a wooden closet—sandals with gold worked into the leather, and small enough for her feet; and a great strange thing with silk flowers all over it, a thing such as one would wear to keep off rain.

She laughed as she looked at it. Then she put it on her head, and tied the ribbons under her chin. Now she looked very much like the women in the pictures. Except for her hands. What was she to do about her hands!

She stared at the naked bones of the first right finger. A thin covering of skin overlaid them, but it was like silk, more sheer than the dress. She could see blood in it; but it was transparent. And the mere sight of the bones caused her to become dizzy, confused again.

A memory—someone standing above her. No, don't let it begin again. She must wrap her hand in something, a bandage. The left hand would do well enough. She turned and began to search through the cabinet of female clothes.

And then she made the loveliest discovery! Here were two little silk garments made for hands. They were white; they had pearls sewn on them! Each had five fingers and had been cut to fit closely over the hand. This was perfect. She slipped them on; they hid the naked bone completely.

Ah, the wonder of what Lord Rutherford had called these "modern times." These times of music boxes and "motor cars," as he called them, the things she had seen this morning, all around her, like great roaring hippopotami from the river.

What would Lord Rutherford call these things, these clothes for hands?

She was wasting time. She went to the dressing table, gathered up a few small coins that lay there and put these in the deep hidden side pocket of the heavy skirt.

As she opened the front door of the house, she glanced over at the dead body, out in the courtyard, heaped against the wall. Something, what was it, she had to understand it, but it simply would not come clear to her. Something . . .

She saw again that hazy figure standing over her. She heard again those sacred words. A tongue she knew speaking to her. *This was the tongue of your forefathers, you must learn it.* No, but that had been another time. They had been in a bright room full of Italian marble, and he had been teaching her. This time, it had been dark and hot and she'd been struggling upwards as if from deep water, her limbs weak, the water crushing her, her mouth full of water so that she couldn't scream.

"Your heart beats again; you come to life! You are young and strong once more; you *are* now and forever."

No, do not weep again! Do not struggle to grasp it, to see it. The figure moving away; blue eyes. She had known those blue eyes. *As soon as I drank it, it happened. The priestess showed me in the mirror . . . blue eyes.* Ah, but whose voice was this! This voice that had said the prayer in the darkness, the ancient sacred prayer for the opening of the mummy's mouth.

She had called out his name! And here, in this strange little house, Lord Rutherford had spoken the name also. Lord Rutherford was going . . .

Be back before dark.

It was no use. She stared through the archway at the dead body. She must get out into this strange land. And she must remember that it was extremely easy to kill them, to snap their necks like brittle stems.

She hurried out, without closing the door. The whitewashed houses on either side of her looked familiar and good to her. She had known such cities. Maybe this was Egypt, but no, that could not be.

She rushed along, holding the ribbons tight so that the strange headdress would not fly from her hair. So easy to walk fast. And the sun felt so good to her. The sun. In a flash she saw it flooding down from a high portal in a cave. A wooden shutter had opened. She heard the creak of the chain.

Then it was gone, the memory, if it had even been a memory. *Wake, Ramses*.

That was his name. But she didn't care now. She was free to roam this strange city; free to discover, to see!

4

SAMIR PURCHASED several Bedouin garments in the first shop in old Cairo that sold such clothes. He ducked into a small restaurant, a filthy alleyway of a place full of down-on-their-luck Frenchmen, and there put on the loose, concealing garb and tucked the other garments— those he'd bought for Julie—under his arm, inside his robes.

He liked this loose peasant costume, which was infinitely older than the tailored robes and hats which most Egyptians wore. In fact, it was probably the oldest mode of dress still in active existence—the long, loose drapery of the desert wanderers. He felt free in it, and safe from all eyes.

He hurried along through the winding honeycomb streets of Arab Cairo, towards the house of his cousin Zaki, a man he disliked dealing with but one who would give him exactly what he wanted more easily and efficiently than anyone else. And who knew how long Ramses must hide in Cairo? Who knew how these murders would be solved?

When he reached the mummy factory of his cousin—surely one of the most distasteful places in the entire known world— he entered by the side gate. A load of freshly wrapped bodies baked in the harsh afternoon sunshine. Inside, no doubt, others were being stewed in the pot.

A lone worker dug a trench now into which these fresh mum-

273

mies would be laid for a few days, "browning" as it were in damp earth.

It disgusted Samir completely, though he had come to this little factory as a boy long before he had known there were real mummies, the bodies of the ancient ancestors to be studied, to be saved from theft and mutilation, and preserved.

"Look at it this way," his cousin Zaki once argued. "We are better than the thieves who sell our ancient rulers bit by bit to the foreigners. What we sell isn't sacred. It's fake."

Good old Zaki. Samir was about to signal to one of the men inside the place, a man who was in fact engaged in wrapping a body. But then Zaki himself emerged from the reeking little house.

"Eh, Samir! So good to see you always, cousin. Come have a coffee with me, cousin."

"Not now, Zaki, I need your assistance."

"Of course, you would not be here if you did not."

Samir accepted the rebuke with a humble little smile.

"Zaki, I need a safe place, a little house with a heavy door and a back entrance. Secret. For a few days, maybe longer. I don't know."

Zaki laughed good-naturedly, but a little smugly.

"Ah, so, the educated one, the one whom all respect, and he comes to me for a hiding place?"

"Don't question me, Zaki." Samir produced a roll of bills from under his robe. He held this out to his cousin. "A safe house. I can pay."

"All right, I know just the thing," said Zaki. "Come into the house and take coffee with me. One whiff, and you get used to the smell."

For decades Zaki had been saying that. Samir never got used to the smell. But he felt compelled now to do what his cousin wanted, and he followed him into the "embalming room," a miserable place where a vat of bitumen and other chemicals was always simmering, waiting for a new body to be thrown in.

As he passed, Samir saw that the pot had a new victim. It sickened him. He looked away, but not before he had glimpsed the poor devil's black hair billowing free on the surface as his face floated just beneath it.

"How about a nice fresh mummy?" Zaki teased him. "Straight from the Valley of the Kings. Name a dynasty, I give it to you! Male, female, whatever you wish!"

"The hiding place, cousin."

"Yes, yes. I have several such houses vacant. Coffee first and I send you off with a key. Tell me what you know of this robbery in the museum! The mummy which was stolen! Was it genuine, do you think?"

In a daze, Elliott walked into the lobby of Shepheard's. He knew that he was dishevelled, that dirt and sand clung to his trousers and even his coat. His left leg ached, but he no longer truly felt it. He did not care that beneath his rumpled shirt and suit coat he was drenched in sweat. He knew that he should be relieved to be here—safe and away from all the horrors he'd witnessed, the horrors in which he had shared. But it seemed unreal to him; he had not escaped the atmosphere of the little house.

All the way back from old Cairo, as the cab jolted him through the insufferable traffic, he had thought, Malenka is dead because I brought the woman there. Henry he could not grieve for. But Malenka would be forever on his soul. And the murderer, his monstrous resurrected Queen. What would he do with her if he could not find Ramsey? When would she turn on him?

The thing to do now was to find Samir, for he would know where Ramsey was.

He was quite unprepared for Alex rushing to him, and embracing him and trying to stop his progress to the desk.

"Father, thank God you're here."

"Where's Ramsey? I have to talk to him at once."

"Father, don't you know what's happened? They're searching for him all over Cairo. He's wanted for murder, Father, both here and in London. Julie's beside herself. We've been going out of our minds. And Henry, we cannot find Henry! Father, where have you been!"

"You stay with Julie, you take care of her," he said. "Let your American Miss Barrington wait." He tried to move on to the desk.

"Miss Barrington's gone," Alex said with a dismissive gesture. "Whole family changed their plans this morning, after the police came to question them about Ramsey and about us."

"I'm sorry, son," he murmured. "But you must leave me now, I have to find Samir."

"Then you're in luck. He's just come in."

Alex gestured to the cashier. Samir had apparently just written a bank draft for some money. He was counting it and putting it away. He had a bundle under his arm. He seemed to be in a hurry.

"Let me alone now, my boy," Elliott said as he hurried towards him. Samir looked up just as Elliott reached the marble desk. He drew Samir aside.

"I have to see him," Elliott whispered. "If you know where he is, I must see him."

"My Lord, please." Samir glanced around, slowly and casually taking in the entire lobby. "The authorities are searching for him. People are watching us now."

"But you know where he is. Or how to get a message to him. You know all about him, you have from the beginning."

Samir's eyes became unreadable. It was as if a door closed firmly in his soul.

"You give him this message for me."

Samir started to walk away.

"Tell him I have *her*."

Samir hesitated. "But who?" he whispered. "What do you mean?"

Elliott took his arm roughly again.

"He knows. And *she* knows who she is as well! Tell him I took her from the museum. And I have her in a safe place. I've been with her all day."

"I don't understand you."

"Ah, but he will. Now listen carefully. Tell him that the sun helped her. It healed her, and so did the . . . the medicine in the vial."

The Earl drew out the empty vial now and put it in Samir's hand. Samir stared down at it as if he were afraid of it; as if he did not want it to touch him and did not know what in the world he would do now that it had.

"She needs more of it!" Elliott said. "She's damaged, inside and outside. She's mad." Out of the corner of his eye, he saw Alex moving towards him, but he gestured for patience, drawing even closer to Samir. "Tell him he's to contact me at seven this evening. At the French cafe called the Babylon in the Arab quarter. I shall talk to no one but him."

"But wait, you must explain—"

"I told you. He will understand. And under no circumstances is he to contact me here. It's too dangerous. I won't have my son mixed up in this. The Babylon at seven. And tell him this also. She has killed three times. And she will kill again."

He left Samir abruptly, turning to his son and reaching out for Alex's helping hand.

"Come, take me upstairs," he said. "I have to rest. I'm near fainting."

"Good Lord, Father, what is going on!"

"Ah, that you have to tell me now. What's happened since I left? Oh, and the desk. Tell the desk I will speak to no one. They are not to ring the room. No one is to be allowed up."

Only a few steps more, he thought as the elevator doors opened. If he could only make it to a clean bed. He was dizzy now; and close to nausea. He was grateful for his son, who held him firmly around the shoulders, and would not let him fall.

As soon as he reached his room, he lost his balance altogether. But Walter was there, and Walter and Alex together helped him onto the bed.

"I want to sit up," he said crankily like an old invalid.

"I'll run you a bath, my lord, a good hot restful bath."

"Do that, Walter, but you'll bring me a drink first. Scotch, and set the bottle beside the glass."

"Father, I've never seen you like this. I'm going to ring the house doctor."

"You are not!" Elliott said. His tone startled Alex, which was all well and good. "Would Lady Macbeth have benefited from a doctor? I don't think a doctor would have helped her."

"Father, what is all this about?" Alex's voice had dropped to a whisper, as it always did when he was truly upset. He watched as Walter put the glass in Elliott's hand.

Elliott drank a swallow of the whisky. "Ah, that's good," he sighed. In that horrid little house, that house of death and madness, there had been a dozen bottles of Henry's liquor, yet he could not bring himself to touch them; could not bring himself to drink from a glass that had been Henry's, or to eat a morsel of Henry's food. He had given it to her, but he could not himself touch it. And now he luxuriated in the sweet warmth of the Scotch, so utterly different from the burning in his chest.

"Now, Alex, you must listen," he said, taking another swallow. "You are to leave Cairo immediately. You're to pack your bags now and be on the five o'clock train to Port Said. I'm taking you to the train myself."

How utterly defenseless his son looked suddenly. Just a boy, a sweet young boy. And this is my dream of immortality, he thought; and it has always been there. My Alex, who must go home now to England where he will be safe.

"That's out of the question, Father," Alex said with the same gentleness. "I can't leave Julie here."

"I don't want you to leave Julie. You're taking Julie with you. You're to go to her now. Tell her to get ready! Do as I say."

"Father, you don't understand. She won't leave until Ramsey's been cleared. And no one can find Ramsey. And no one can find Henry, either. Father, until this matter's settled, I don't think the authorities would let any of us leave."

"Dear God."

Alex took out his handkerchief; he folded it carefully and blotted Elliott's forehead. He folded it again and offered it to Elliott. Elliott took it and wiped his mouth.

"Father, you don't think Ramsey really did these dreadful things, do you? I mean, I was rather fond of Ramsey!"

Walter came to the door. "Your bath's ready, my lord."

"Poor Alex," Elliott whispered. "Poor decent and honorable Alex."

"Father, tell me what's the matter. I've never seen you like this. You're not yourself."

"Oh, yes, I am myself. My true self. Desperate and cunning and full of mad dreams as always. Too much myself. You know, my son, when you inherit the title, you will probably be the only decent and honorable Earl of Rutherford in our whole history."

"You're being the philosopher again. And I'm not all that decent and honorable. I'm merely well bred, which I hope is a tolerable substitute. Now, get into the bath. You'll feel much better. And don't drink any more Scotch, please." He called out to Walter to come and give him a hand.

Miles Winthrop stared at the telegram placed in his hand by the man standing before him.

"Arrest her? Julie Stratford! For the theft of a priceless mummy in London? But this is madness, all of it. Alex Savarell and I went to school together! I'm contacting the British Museum myself."

"Very well, but do it promptly," said the other. "The governor's furious. The Department of Antiquities is up in arms. And find Henry Stratford. Track down that mistress of his, that dancing girl, Malenka. Stratford's somewhere in Cairo, and pretty well besotted, you can be sure of it. In the meantime arrest somebody or the old man will blow his top.''

''The hell I will,'' Miles whispered as he picked up the phone.

Ah, such a bazaar. Everything was for sale here—rich fabrics, perfumes, spices, and strange ticking devices with Roman numbers on them; jewelry and pottery; and food! But she had no money to buy the food! The first peddler had told her in English and with age-old indisputable gestures that the money she had was no good.

She walked on. She was listening to the voices on all sides of her, picking out the English, trying to understand.

''I won't pay that much. That's too dear, the man's trying to rob us. . . .''

''Just a little drink, come on now. It's burning hot.''

''Oh, and these necklaces, how pretty.''

Laughter, horrid noises; loud grating noises! She had heard these before. She put her hands over her ears under the broad floppy headdress. She walked on, trying to shut out what hurt her and still hear what she needed in order to learn.

Suddenly a monstrous sound—an inconceivable sound—shook her and she looked up, on the verge of screaming. Her hands would not shut it out. She stumbled forward, realizing in her panic that those around her were not frightened! Those around her were scarcely paying any attention at all.

She had to fathom this mystery! And though the tears were welling in her eyes, she moved on.

What she beheld suddenly filled her with a nameless dread. She had no words in any tongue to describe it. Immense, black, it moved forward, on wheels made of metal, a chimney atop it belching smoke. The sound was so loud all other sounds vanished. Great wooden wagons following, coupled to it by huge hooks of black iron. The whole monstrous caravan thundering along a thin strip of metal that ran along the ground. And the noise grew even louder as the thing rolled past her and entered a great yawning tunnel in which hundreds crowded as if trying to get near to it.

She sobbed aloud, staring at it. Oh, why had she left her hideaway? Why had she left Lord Rutherford, who would have protected her? But just when it seemed she could see nothing worse than this awful chain of wagons rattling past her, the last one entered the tunnel and she beheld, beyond the metal pathway, a great granite statue of the Pharaoh Ramses, standing with arms folded, his scepters in his crossed hands.

In dizzying shock she looked at this colossus. Ripped from the land she had known, the land she had ruled, this thing stood here, grotesque, abandoned, ludicrous.

She backed away. Another one of the demonic chariots was coming. She heard a great searing screech from it, and then it roared by, obliterating the statue.

She felt herself turning, inward, away from all of it, back into the darkness, into the dark water whence she'd come.

When she opened her eyes a young Englishman stood over her. He had his arm around her and was lifting her and telling others to get away. She understood that he was asking after her and what he might do.

"Coffee," she whispered. "I should like some sugar in my coffee." Words from the talking machine Lord Rutherford had revealed to her. "I should like a bit of lemon in my tea."

His face brightened. "Well, yes, of course. I shall get you some coffee. I shall take you there, into the British cafe!"

He lifted her to her feet. What a fine muscular youth he was. And blue eyes he had, so rich in color, almost like the other. . . .

She glanced back over her shoulder. It had not been a dream. The statue stood there towering over the iron pathways; she could hear the roar of the chariots, though none was in sight.

She was weak again for a moment, stumbling; he caught her. He helped her right along.

She listened keenly to the words he spoke.

"It's a nice place; you can sit, rest. You know, you gave me quite a scare there a moment ago. Why, you fell just as if you'd been struck over the head."

The cafe. The voice on the gramophone had said, "I shall meet you in the cafe." A place for drinking coffee, obviously, for meeting, talking. And full of women in these dresses, and young men clothed like Lord Rutherford and this fine creature, with the powerfully built arms and legs.

She sat down at the small marble-top table. Voices everywhere. "Why, I frankly think everything here is super, but you know Mother, the way she carries on." And "Gruesome, isn't it? They say her neck was broken." And "Oh, this tea is cold. Call that waiter."

She watched the man at the next table peel off slips of printed paper for the servant. Was this money? The servant was giving him coins in return.

A tray of hot coffee had been set down before her. She was so hungry now she could have drunk the pot entirely, but she knew it was proper to let him pour it in the cups. Lord Rutherford had showed her that much. And yes, the young man did it. Pretty smile he had. How to tell him that she wanted to bed him immediately? They should find a small inn. Surely these people had inns.

Across from her a young woman spoke rapidly:

"Well, I don't even like opera. I wouldn't go if I were in New York at all. But since we're in Cairo, we're all supposed to go to the opera and love it. It's ridiculous."

"But darling, it's *Aïda*."

Aïda. "Celeste Aïda." She began to hum it, then sing it softly, too low for these people to hear. But her companion heard her. He smiled at her, positively beamed. Getting him into bed would be nothing. Finding the bed, that might be hard. Of course she could take him back to the little house, but that was too far away. She stopped singing.

"Oh, no, you mustn't stop," he said. "Go on singing."

Go on singing, go on singing. Waiting just a moment was the secret, then the meaning came surprisingly clear.

Ramses had taught her that. In the beginning, each tongue sounds impenetrable. You speak it; you listen; and gradually it comes clear.

Ramses; Ramses, whose statue stood among the iron chariots! She turned, craning her neck to see through the window—why, the window was covered over with a giant piece of very clear glass. She could see the dirt on it. However did they make such a thing? "Modern times," as Lord Rutherford said. Well, if they could make those monstrous chariots, they could make such glass.

"You've a lovely voice, positively lovely. Are you by any chance going to the opera? Everyone in Cairo is going, or so it seems."

"The ball will last till dawn," said the woman opposite to her female companion.

"Well, I think it's super. We're just too far from civilization to complain."

He laughed. He had overheard the women too.

"The ball's supposed to be the event of the season here. They hold it at Shepheard's.'' He drank a swallow of his coffee. That was the signal she'd been waiting for. She downed her entire cup.

He smiled. He poured her another from the little pot.

"Thank you," she said, carefully mimicking the record.

"Oh, but didn't you want sugar?"

"I think I prefer cream, if you don't mind."

"Of course not." He poured a dollop of milk in her cup. Was that cream? Yes, Lord Rutherford had given her the last of it that the slave woman had in the house.

"Are you going to the ball at Shepheard's? We're staying at Shepheard's, my uncle and I. My uncle's in trade here."

He stopped again. What was he staring at? Her eyes? Her hair? He was very pretty; she loved the fresh new skin of his face and throat. Lord Rutherford was a fine-looking man, for certain; but this one had the beauty of youth.

She reached across the table and felt his chest through the linen of his clothing, through the silk that covered her fingers. Don't let him feel the bone. How surprised he looked. Her fingertips touched his nipple and she pinched it ever so slightly with her fourth finger and thumb. Why, he blushed like a vestal virgin. The blood was roaring in his face. She smiled.

He glanced around, at the two women opposite. But they went right on talking. "Simply super!"

"I bought this gown, you know, spent a fortune on it. I said, well, if I'm going to be here, and everyone's going . . ."

"The opera." She laughed. "Going to the opera."

"Yes," he said, but he was still amazed at what she'd done. She emptied the pot into her cup and drank it. Then she picked up the little pitcher of milk and drank that too. She picked up the sugar and poured it into her mouth. Ah, she did not like that. She set it down, and then slipped her hand under the small table and squeezed his leg. He was ready for her! Ah, poor young boy, poor wide-eyed young boy.

She remembered that time when she and Antony had brought those young soldiers in the tent, and stripped them, before making a choice. That had been a lovely game. Until Ramses found out about it. Was there anything he hadn't accused her of in the end? But this one was powerfully amorous! He wanted her.

She rose from the table. She beckoned and went towards the doors.

Noise outside. The chariots. She did not care. If they didn't frighten all these people, surely they were something explainable. What she had to do now was find a place. He was right behind her, talking to her.

"Come," she said in English. "Come with me."

An alleyway; she led him back, stepping over the puddles. Shadowy here, and quieter. She turned around and slipped her arms under his. He bent to kiss her.

"Well, not here, right here!" he asked nervously. "Miss, I don't think . . ."

"I say here," she whispered, kissing him and thrusting her hand into his clothes. Hot his skin, what she wanted. Hot and sweet smelling. And so ready he was, the young fawn. She lifted the skirts of the pink dress.

It was over too quickly; she shuddered as she held on to him, her body clamped to him, her arms wrapped around his neck. She heard him moan as he spilled into her. He was still for a moment, too still. The shudders were still passing through her; but she could not coax him anymore. He released her and leaned back against the wall, staring, as if he was ill.

"Wait, please, give me a moment," he said when she started to kiss him again.

She studied him for a few seconds. Very easy. Snap. Then she reached up, took a firm hold of his head with both her hands, and twisted it until his neck broke.

He stared off, the way the woman had stared off, and the way the man had also. Nothing in his eyes. Nothing. Then he slipped down the wall, his legs wide apart.

She studied him. There was that nagging sense of a mystery again, something to do with her. Something to do with what she'd just done.

She remembered that dim figure standing over her. Had it been a dream? "Rise, Cleopatra. I, Ramses, call you!"

Ah, no! Merely trying to remember caused a searing pain in her head. But the pain was not physical. Pain of the soul it was. She could hear women crying, women she had known. Women weeping. Saying her name to her. Cleopatra. Then someone covered her face with a sheer black cloth. Was the snake still alive? Strange it seemed to her that the snake should outlive her. She felt again the sting of the fangs in her breast.

She gave a dull little groan as she stood there, leaning against the wall, looking down at the dead boy. When had all that happened? Where? Who had she been?

Don't remember. "Modern times" await.

She bent over, and slipped the money out of the boy's coat. Lots and lots of money in a little leather book. She slipped it deep into her pocket. Other things here as well. A card with English writing and a tiny portrait of the boy, how remarkable. Very beautiful work. And then two small bits of stiff paper with AIDA written on them. And OPERA. They bore the same tiny drawing she had seen in the "magazine" of an Egyptian woman's head.

Surely these were worth taking as well. She threw away the dead man's picture. Slipping the little opera papers into her pocket also, she sang "Celeste Aïda" again softly to herself as she stepped over the dead boy and walked out again into the noisy street.

Be not afraid. Do as they do. If they walk near the metal pathways, you must do this too.

But no sooner had she started off again than there came one of those shrill blasts from the iron chariots. She covered her ears, crying in spite of herself, and when she looked up another fine man was standing in her path.

"Can I help you, little lady? You're not lost down here, are you? You mustn't go about down here by the railway station with that money showing in your pocket like that."

"Railway station . . ."

"Don't you have a handbag?"

"No," she said innocently. She allowed him to take her arm. "You help me?" she said, remembering the phrase Lord Rutherford had used a hundred times to her. "I can trust you?"

"Oh, of course!" he said. And he meant it. Another young one. With smooth, lovely skin!

Two Arabs left the rear of Shepheard's, one slightly taller than the other, both striding very fast.

"Remember," Samir said under his breath, "take very big steps. You are a man. Men do not take small steps, and swing your arms naturally."

"I should have learned this trick a long time ago," Julie answered.

The Great Mosque swarmed with the faithful as well as tourists who had come to see this wonder, and come to see the sight of devout Moslems in worship on their knees. Julie and Samir moved lazily through the crush of tourists. Within minutes they had spotted the tall Arab with the dark glasses, in his flowing white robes.

Samir placed a key in Ramses' hand. He whispered the address and the directions. Ramses should follow him. It would not be a long walk.

He and Julie moved on, with Ramses a few paces behind.

Ah, she liked this one, who called himself an American and spoke in such a strange voice. They rode along together in the horse-drawn "taxi" carriage, among the "motor cars." And she was no longer afraid.

Before they'd left the "railway station" she'd realized that the big iron chariots pulled people about. Just a common means of transportation. How strange.

This one was not as elegant as Lord Rutherford, by any means, but he spoke more slowly and it was becoming quite simple for her to understand, especially as he pointed to things as he spoke. She knew now what was a Ford automobile, and a Stutz Bearcat, and also a little roadster. This man sold such things in America. He was a merchant of Ford automobiles in America. Even poor people could buy these driving machines.

She clutched the canvas bag he'd brought her, which held the money and the bits of paper with OPERA written on them.

"And this here is where the tourists live," he said to her, "more or less. I mean, this is the British sector. . . ."

"English," she said.

"Yes, but all the Europeans and Americans pretty much come here, too. And that building there—that's where all the best people stay, the British and the Americans, that's Shepheard's, *the* hotel, if you know what I mean."

"Shepheard's—*the* hotel?" She gave a little laugh.

"That's where the opera ball's going to be tomorrow night. That's where I'm staying. I don't much like opera"—he made a little face—"never did much care for it. But here in Cairo, well, this is an important thing, you see."

"Important thing, you see."

"Real important. So I figured pretty much I'd go, you see, and to the ball afterwards, though I had to rent a tailcoat and all that." He had a lovely light in his eyes as he looked down at her. He was enjoying himself immensely.

And she was enjoying herself as well.

"And *Aïda* being all about ancient Egypt."

"Yes, Radames singing."

"Yes! So you know it. Bet you like opera, bet you appreciate it." Suddenly he made a little frown. "Are you okay, little lady? Maybe you'd find the old city more romantic. You want something to drink? How about a little ride in my car. It's parked right behind Shepheard's."

"Motor car?"

"Oh, you're quite safe with me, little lady, I'm a real safe driver. Tell you what. Have you been out to the pyramids?"

Pee-ra-mids.

"No," she said. "Drive in your car, super!"

He laughed. He shouted a command to the taxi and the driver pulled the horse to the left. They rode around *the* hotel, Shepheard's, a handsome building with pretty gardens.

When he reached up to help her down from the carriage, he almost touched the tender opening in her side. She shivered. But it had not happened. Yet it had reminded her that the wound was there. How could one live with such awful sores? That was the mystery. Whatever happened now, she must return at dusk to see Lord Rutherford again. Lord Rutherford had gone to speak with the man who could explain these things—the man with the blue eyes.

They arrived together at the hideout. Julie agreed to wait as Samir and Ramses entered, inspected the three little rooms and their neglected garden; then they motioned for her to come in, and Ramses bolted the door.

There was a small wooden table with a candle in the middle, stuck in an old wine bottle. Samir lighted the candle. Ramses drew up two of the straight-backed chairs. Julie brought the other.

This was comfortable enough. The afternoon sun came through the old garden and through the back door, and the place was hot, but not unbearable, as it had been locked up for a long time. A damp musky odor of spices and hemp hung in the air.

Julie took off the Arab headdress, and shook out her hair. She had not pinned it up because of the headdress, and now she loosened the ribbon that kept it tied at the back of her neck.

"I don't believe you killed that woman," she said immediately, looking up at Ramses as he sat across from her.

Like a sheikh he looked in the desert robes, his face partially in shadow, the candle glinting in his eyes.

Samir sat down quietly to her left.

"I didn't kill the woman," Ramses said to her. "But I am responsible for the woman's death. And I need your help, both of you. I need someone's help. And I need your forgiveness. The time has come for me to tell you everything."

"Sire, I have a message for you," Samir said, "which I must give you at once."

"What message?" Julie asked. Why hadn't Samir told her of this?

"Is it from the gods, Samir? Are they calling me to account? I have no time for less important messages. I must tell you what has happened, what I've done."

"It's from the Earl of Rutherford, sire. He accosted me at the hotel. He looked like a madman; he said that I must tell you that he has *her*."

Ramses was obviously stunned. He glared at Samir almost murderously.

Julie could not bear this.

Samir removed something from under his robe and gave it to Ramses. It was a glass vial, such as those she'd seen among the alabaster jars in the collection.

Ramses looked at this, but he didn't move to touch it. Samir went to speak again, but Ramses gestured for quiet. His face was so heavily disfigured with emotion that he scarce looked like himself.

"Tell me what this means!" Julie said, unable to stop herself.

"He followed me to the museum," Ramses whispered. He stared at the empty vial.

"But what are you talking about? What happened at the museum?"

"Sire, he says that the sun has helped her. That the medicine in the vial helped her, but that she needs more of it. She is damaged, inside and out. She has killed three times. She is mad. He keeps her safe in hiding, he wants a meeting with you. He has given me the time and place."

For a moment, Ramses said nothing. Then he rose from the table and headed towards the door.

"No, stop!" Julie cried out, rushing towards him.

Samir was also on his feet.

"Sire, if you try to find him sooner, you may be apprehended. The hotel is surrounded. Wait till he leaves and goes to this place for the meeting. It is the only safe thing to do!"

Ramses was clearly stymied. Reluctantly, he turned, looking past Julie with dull, crazed eyes. He moved back sluggishly to the chair and sat down.

Julie wiped her tears with her handkerchief and took her chair again.

"Where and when?" Ramses asked.

"Seven tonight. The Babylon, it's a French night club. I know it. I can take you there."

"I cannot wait until then!"

"Ramses, tell us what all this means. How can we help you if we don't know?"

"Sire, Julie is right. Take us into your trust now. Allow us to assist in this. If you are captured again by the police . . ."

Ramses waved it away in disgust. His face was working silently with emotion.

"I need you, and when I tell you, I may lose you. But so be it. For I have wreaked havoc with your lives."

"You will never lose me," Julie said, but her fear was mounting. A great dread of what was to come was building in her soul.

Until these last few moments she thought she understood what had happened. He had taken the body of his love from the museum. He had wanted to see it properly put in a tomb. But now, faced with the vial and these strange words from Elliott, she considered other more ghastly possibilities, denying them in the same instant, but returning to them again.

"Put your trust in us, sire. Let us share this burden."

Ramses looked at Samir, then at her.

"Ah, the guilt you can never share," he said. "The body in the museum. The unknown woman . . ."

"Yes," Samir whispered.

"She was not unknown to me, my dear ones. The ghost of Julius Caesar would have known her. The shade of Mark Antony would have kissed her. Millions once mourned for her. . . ."

Julie nodded, tears rising again.

"And I have done the unspeakable. I took the elixir to the museum. I did not realize how much her body had been ravaged, that whole hunks of flesh were no longer there. I poured the elixir over her! After two thousand years life stirred in her ruined body. She rose! Bleeding, wounded, she stood upright. She walked. She reached out for me. She called my name!"

* * *

Ah, it was better than the finest wine, better even than making love, racing over the road in the open American motor car, the wind whistling past her, the American shouting convivially as he jerked the "stick shift" this way and that.

To see the houses flying past. To see the Egyptians trudging with their donkeys and camels and to leave them in a spray of gravel.

She adored it. She looked up at the open sky above, letting the wind lift her hair completely as she kept one hand firmly on her hat.

Now and then she studied what he did to make this chariot move. Pump the "pedals," as he called them, over and over again; pull the stick; turn the wheel.

Ah, it was too thrilling; too marvellous. But suddenly that horrid shrill sound caught her off guard. That roaring she had heard in the "railway station." Her hands flew to her ears.

"Don't be frightened, little lady, it's just a train. See there, the train's coming!" The motor coach came to a jerking halt.

Metal pathways side by side in the desert sand before them. And that thing, that great black monster bearing down from the right. A bell was clanging. She was dimly aware of a red light flashing, like a lantern beam. Would she never get away from these hideous things?

He put his arm around her.

"It's all right, little lady. We just have to wait for it to pass."

He was still speaking, but now the great rattle and clatter of the monster drowned out his words. Horrid, the wheels rumbling by in front of her, and even the long procession of wooden wagons, filled with human beings who sat inside against the wooden slats as if this were the most simple thing in the world.

She tried to regain her composure. She liked the feel of his warm hands on her; the smell of the perfume rising from his skin. She watched dully as the last of the cars rolled by. Again the bell clanged. The light atop the pillar flashed.

The American pumped the pedals again, pulled the stick; the car began to rumble, and they drove over the metal pathways and on into the desert.

"Well, most people in Hannibal, Missouri, you tell them about Egypt, they don't even know what you're talking about. I said to my father, I'm going over there, that's what I'm going to do. I'm taking the money I've made and going over there, and then I'll settle down back here. . . .''

She caught her breath. She was settling into the pleasure of it again. Then far away to the left, on the horizon, she saw the pyramids of Giza! She saw the figure of the Sphinx coming into view.

She gave a little cry. This was Egypt. She was in Egypt in "modern times," but she was still at home.

A lovely sadness softened her all over. The tombs of her ancestors, and there the sphinx to whom she had gone as a young girl, to pray in the temple between its great paws.

"Ah, yes, that's a pretty sight, isn't it? I tell you, if people in Hannibal, Missouri, don't appreciate it, it's their tough luck.''

She laughed. "Their tough luck," she said.

As they drew closer, she saw the crowds. A great field of motor cars and carriages. And women in frilly dresses with tiny waists, like her own. Men in straw hats like the American. And many Arabs with their camels, and armfuls of cheap necklaces. She smiled.

In her time they had sold cheap jewelry here to the visiting Romans. They had peddled rides on their camels. They were doing the very same thing now!

But it took her breath away, the great tomb of King Kufu looming above her. When had it been that she had come here, a small girl, and seen this huge structure made up of square blocks? And then with Ramses, later, alone in the cool of the night, when she'd been wrapped in a dark robe, a common woman, riding with him along this very same road.

Ramses! No, something horrid that she did not want to remember. The dark waters rushing over her. She had been walking towards him, and he had been backing away!

The American motor car jerked to a halt again.

"Come on, little lady, let's get out and see it. Seventh wonder of the world.''

She smiled at the chubby-faced American; so gentle with her he was.

"Okaaaay! Super!'' she said. She jumped down from the high open seat before he could give her a helping hand.

Her body was very close to his. His chubby nose crinkled as he smiled at her. Sweet young mouth. She kissed him suddenly. She stood on tiptoe and embraced him. Hmmmm. Sweet and young like the other. And so surprised!

"Well, you sure are an affectionate little thing," he said in her ear. He didn't seem to know what to do now. Well, she would show him. She took his hand and they walked over the beaten sand towards the pyramids.

"Ah, look!" she said, pointing to the palace that had been built to the right.

"Ah, that's the Mena House," he said. "Not a bad hotel, either. It's not Shepheard's, but it's okay. We can have a bite to eat there later, if you like."

"I tried to fight them," Ramses said. "It was impossible. There were simply too many. They took me away to the jail. I needed time to heal. It must have been a half hour before I managed to escape."

Silence.

Julie had buried her face in her handkerchief.

"Sire," Samir said gently. "You knew this elixir could do such a thing?"

"Yes, Samir. I knew, though I had never put it to such a test."

"Then it was human nature, sire. No more and no less."

"Ah, but Samir, I have made so many blunders over the centuries. I knew the dangers of the chemical. And you must know those dangers now too. You must know if you are to help me. This creature—this mad thing which I've brought back to life cannot be destroyed."

"Surely there is some way," Samir said.

"No. I've learned this through trial and error. And your modern biology books, they've sharpened my understanding. Once the cells of the body are saturated with the elixir, they renew themselves constantly. Plant, animal, human—it is all the same."

"No age, no deterioration," Julie murmured. She was calmer now, she could trust her voice.

"Precisely. One full cup made me immortal. No more than the contents of that vial. I am eternally in the prime of life. I don't need food, yet I am always hungry. I don't need sleep, yet I can enjoy it. I have perpetually the desire to . . . make love."

"And this woman—she did not receive the full measure."

"No, and she was damaged to begin with! That was my folly, don't you see! The body was not all there! But damaged or no, she is now virtually unstoppable. I understood that when she came towards me through the corridor! Don't you see?"

"You're not thinking in terms of modern science," Julie said. She wiped both her eyes slowly. "There must be a way to halt the process."

"On the other hand, if you were to give her the full measure— more of the medicine, as the Earl put it . . ."

"That's madness," Julie interjected. "You can't even consider it. You'll make the thing stronger."

"Listen, both of you," Ramses said, "to what I have to say. Cleopatra is only part of this tragedy. The Earl knows the secret now with certainty. It is the elixir itself that is dangerous, more dangerous than you know."

"People will want it, yes," Julie said, "and they will do anything to get it. But Elliott can be reasoned with, and Henry is a fool."

"There's more to it than that. We are speaking of a chemical which changes any living substance by which it is absorbed." Ramses waited a moment, glancing at both of them. Then he went on: "Centuries ago, when I was still Ramses, ruler of this land, I dreamed I would use this elixir to make food and drink aplenty for my people. We would have famine no more. Wheat that would grow back instantly after every harvest. Fruit trees that would bear forever. Do you know what came to pass?"

Fascinated, they stared at him in silence.

"My people could not digest this immortal food. It stayed whole in their insides. They died in agony as if they had eaten sand."

"Ye gods," Julie whispered. "Yet it's perfectly logical. Of course!"

"And when I sought to burn the fields and slaughter the immortal hens and milk cows, I saw the burnt wheat spring to life as soon as the sun shone on it. I saw burnt and headless carcasses struggle to rise. Finally it was all cast into the sea, weighted and sent to the very bottom, where surely it remains, whole and intact, to this day."

Samir shuddered; he folded his arms over his chest as if he were cold.

Julie looked steadily at Ramses. "So what you're saying is . . . if the secret fell into the wrong hands, whole regions of the earth could be rendered immortal."

"Whole peoples," Ramses answered soberly. "And we who are immortal hunger as much as the living. We would crowd out the living to consume what has always been theirs!"

"The very rhythm of life and death would be endangered," Samir said.

"This secret must be destroyed utterly!" Julie said. "If you have the elixir in your possession, destroy it. Now."

"And how do I do that, dearest? If I hurl the dry powder into the wind, the tiny particles cleave as they fall to the earth, waiting for the first rain to liquefy them and carry them down to the roots of the trees, which they will make immortal. If I pour the liquid into the sand, it pools there until the camel comes to drink. Pour it into the sea and I give birth to immortal fishes, serpents, crocodiles."

"Stop," she whispered.

"Can you consume it yourself, sire, without harm coming to you?"

"I don't know. I would imagine that I could. But who knows?"

"Don't do it!" Julie whispered.

He gave her a faint, sad smile.

"You care still what becomes of me, Julie Stratford?"

"Yes, I care," she whispered. "You're only a man; with a god's secret in your possession. I care."

"That's just it, Julie," he said. "I have the secret in here." He tapped the side of his forehead. "I know how to make the elixir. What happens to the few vials I possess does not ultimately matter, for I can always brew more."

They looked at each other. The full horror of it was impossible to encompass steadily. One had to view it, draw away from it and then reexamine it again.

"Now you understand why for a thousand years I shared the elixir with no one. I knew the danger. And then, with the weakness of a mortal man—to use your modern phrase—I fell in love."

Julie's eyes again filled with tears. Samir waited patiently.

"Yes, I know." Ramses sighed. "I've been a fool. Two thousand years ago, I watched my love die rather than give the elixir to her lover—Mark Antony, a dissolute man, who would have hounded me to the ends of the earth for the formula itself. Can you imagine those two, immortal rulers? 'Why can we not make an immortal army?' she said to me when his influence had thoroughly corrupted her. When she had become his pawn. And now, in this day and age of astonishing wonders, I overruled her last words to me and brought her back to life.''

Julie swallowed. The tears poured down silently. She no longer even wiped at them with the little handkerchief. She reached across the table and touched the back of his hand.

"No. Ramses, it isn't Cleopatra. Don't you see? You've made a terrible mistake, yes, and we must find a way to undo it. But it isn't Cleopatra. It cannot possibly be.''

"Julie, I made no mistake on that account! And she knew me! Don't you understand? She called my name!''

Soft music drifted from the Mena House. There were twinkling yellow lights in its windows. Tiny figures moved back and forth on its broad terrace.

Cleopatra and the American stood in a dark tunnel, high up on the pyramid; the burial shaft.

Feverishly she embraced him, slipping her silk-covered fingers into his shirt. Ah, the nipples of men, so tender; such a key to torment and ecstasy; how he writhed as she twisted them ever so gently, her tongue darting in and out of his mouth.

All the bravado and high spirits were gone now. He was her slave. She ripped the linen fabric back off his chest, and plunged her hand down under his leather belt to the root of his sex.

He moaned against her. She felt him gathering up her skirts. Then suddenly his hand stopped. His whole body stiffened. Awkwardly she turned her head; he was staring down at her naked leg, her foot.

He was staring at the great strip of bloody bone exposed in her leg, at the fan of bones in her foot.

"Jesus Christ!'' he whispered. He drew back from her against the wall. "Jesus Christ!''

A low growl of rage and hurt broke from her. "Take your eyes off me!'' she screamed in Latin. "Turn your eyes away from me! You will not look at me in disgust.''

She sobbed as she grabbed his head with both hands and banged it against the stone wall. "You will die for this!'' she spit at him. And then the twist, the simple little twist. And he was dead, too.

That was all that was required, and now there was blessed

silence and his body lying there, like the body of the other, with the money showing under his sagging coat.

Her wounds could not kill her. The blast of heat from the one called Henry had not killed her; the blast which made the horrible, unbearable noise. But all it took to kill them was this.

She looked out of the opening of the shaft, down over the dark ocher sands towards the soft lights of the Mena House. Again, she heard the music, so sweet, drifting on the cool air.

Always cool at night, the desert. And almost dark, wasn't it? Tiny stars above in the azure sky. She felt a strange moment of peace. Nice to walk alone, away from them in the desert.

But Lord Rutherford. The medicine. Almost dark.

She bent down now, took the American's money. She thought of the beautiful yellow motor car. Ah, that would take her back to where she'd come from very swiftly. And now it was hers all alone.

Suddenly she was laughing, thrilled by the prospect. She rushed down the side of the pyramid, dropping easily from one stone block to the one below it; so much strength now, and then she ran towards the car.

Simple. Press the electric starter button. Then push the "gas pedal." At once it began to roar. Then forward on the stick, as she had seen him do it, as she depressed the other pedal, and miracle of miracles, she was racing forward, giving a mad turn to the wheel

She drove in a great circle before the Mena House. A few terrified Arabs scurried out of her path. She hit the throbbing "horn," as he had called it. It frightened their camels.

Then she made for the road, pulling the stick back again to make it go faster, then shoving it forwards, just as she had seen him do.

When she came to the metal pathway, she stopped. She clutched the wheel, trembling. But no sound came from the great empty reaches of the desert to right and left. And ahead lay the lights of Cairo, such a sweet spectacle under the paling, star-filled sky.

" 'Celeste Aïda!' " she sang as she started up and raced forward once more.

* * *

"You asked for our help," Julie said. "You asked for our forgiveness. Now I want you to listen to me."

"Yes, I want to," Ramses said in a heartfelt voice, but he was puzzled. "Julie, it is she . . . beyond question."

"The body, yes," Julie responded. "It was hers, without doubt. But the being who lives now? No. It is not the same woman you once loved. That woman, wherever she is, has no consciousness now of what is happening to this body."

"Julie, she knew me! She recognized me!"

"Ramses, the brain in that body knew you. But think about what you are saying. Think about the implications. The implications are everything, Ramses. Our intellects—our souls, if you will—they don't reside in the flesh, slumbering for centuries as our bodies rot. Either they go on to higher realms or they cease to exist altogether. The Cleopatra you loved ceased to exist in that body the day it died."

He stared at her, trying to grasp this.

"Sire, I think there is wisdom here," Samir said. But he too was confused. "The Earl says that she knows who she is."

"She knows who she is supposed to be," Julie said. "The cells! They are there, revitalized, and possibly some memory is encoded within them. But this thing is a monstrous twin of your lost love. How *can* it be more than that?"

"This could be true," Samir murmured. "If you do what the Earl suggests—if you give her more of the drug, you may only be revitalizing a . . . a demon."

"This is beyond my understanding!" Ramses confessed. "It is Cleopatra!"

Julie shook her head. "Ramses, my father has been dead no more than two months. There was no autopsy performed on his remains. The only embalming done upon him was the age-old miracle of the Egyptian heat and desert dryness. He lies, intact, in a crypt here in Egypt. But do you think I'd take this elixir, if I had it in my hands, and raise him from the dead?"

"God in heaven," Samir whispered.

"No!" Julie said. "Because it wouldn't be my father. The connection has been fatally broken! A duplicate of my father would rise. A duplicate who knew perhaps all that my father had known. But my father wouldn't be there. He wouldn't know the duplicate was walking about. And what you have brought back to life is a duplicate of Cleopatra! Your lost love is not there.''

Ramses was silent. This seemed to shake him as profoundly as everything else. He looked at Samir.

"What religion, sire, holds that the soul remains in the rotted flesh? It was not so with our forefathers. It is not so in any land in the world.''

"You are truly immortal, my beloved," Julie said. "But Cleopatra has been dead for twenty centuries. She is still dead. The thing you resurrected must be destroyed.''

5

NO, I'M sorry, Miles. My father's not here. Yes, I will. Immediately." Alex hung up the telephone. Elliott watched him from the desk in the corner of the room.

"Thank you, Alex. Lying is actually an underrated social skill. Some clever person should write a polite guide to lying. And all the charitable principles which justify lying so well."

"Father, I am not letting you go out alone."

Elliott turned back to the work at hand. His bath and brief rest had done much to restore his strength, even though it had been impossible to really sleep. He had had a quiet hour to think out what he meant to do now; and he had made his decision, though he had little hope that his scheme would work. Nevertheless the elixir was worth it. If only Samir had reached Ramses. And everything in the man's manner had indicated to him that Samir knew where Ramses was.

He sealed the last of the three envelopes, which he had just addressed, and turned again to his son.

"You will do exactly as I've told you," he said firmly. "If I do not return by tomorrow noon, post these letters. To your mother and to Randolph. And leave Cairo as soon as you possibly can. Now give me my walking stick. And I need my cloak, also. It's damned cold in this city after dark."

Walter fetched the stick immediately. He had the cloak over his arm. He put it over Elliott's shoulders, adjusting it snugly.

298

"Father," Alex pleaded, "for the love of—"

"Good-bye, Alex. Remember. Julie needs you. She needs you here."

"Sire, it's past six now," Samir said. "I must show you how to find this tavern."

"I can find it on my own, Samir," Ramses answered. "Go back to the hotel, both of you. I must see for myself . . . the state of things. And then I shall get word to you as soon as I can."

"No," Julie said, "let me go with you."

"Unthinkable," Ramses said. "It's much too dangerous. And this is something I must face alone."

"Ramses, I'm not leaving you," she insisted.

"Julie, we must return now," Samir said. "We must be seen before they start searching for us."

Ramses rose to his feet slowly. He turned away from the flickering light of the candle, which was now the only illumination in the dark room. He lifted his hands as if in prayer. He looked for all the world like one of the Moslems in the mosque as he stood there, a tiny speck of light shining in his eyes.

"Julie," he said, turning back to her with a deep sigh. "If you go home to England now, you can still recover your old life."

"Oh, you hurt me, Ramses!" she said. "You wound me to the quick. Do you love her, Ramses? Do you love this thing you've raised from the grave?"

She had not meant to say this. She stopped, defeated, and now it was she who turned away.

"I know I love you, Julie Stratford," he whispered. "I've loved you from the first moment I saw you. I braved discovery to save you. And I want your love now."

"Then don't speak of my leaving you," she said, her voice breaking. "Ramses, if I never see you again after this night, my life is destroyed."

"On my honour, you shall see me."

He took her in his arms.

"My love, my brave love," he whispered, caressing her. "I need you—both of you—more than I can say."

"May the old gods be with you, sire," Samir whispered. "We will count the minutes until we receive some word."

* * *

Only a dim light burned in Winthrop's office. He was staggered by the report on his desk. The young official standing before him waited for orders.

"And his head was crushed, you said?"

"Neck broken also. Like the maid in the museum. And all his money had been taken, though his passport had been left in the mud."

"Double the watch on Shepheard's," said Winthrop. "And get the Earl of Rutherford over here immediately. We know he's there, I don't care what his son says. We saw him go in."

Out of the back door of the wing, Elliott walked swiftly, stiffening his left leg to take the weight off the knee. He crossed the dark parking lot and headed towards old Cairo. Only when he was two streets away from Shepheard's did he hail a passing cab.

Julie slipped into her suite, and locked the door. The Arab robe was folded tightly under her arm. She had removed it in the cab, and she stuffed it now in the bottom of the wardrobe behind her trunk.

Going into the bedroom, she drew the small suitcase down from the wardrobe shelf. What few things did she need? So much she possessed did not matter to her. Only freedom mattered now, freedom with Ramses, to somehow escape this hideous tangle of events.

But what if she never again laid eyes upon this man who had thrown her entire past life into shadow? What was the point of packing this suitcase until she knew what had happened?

Suddenly the entire thing overwhelmed her. She lay down on the bed, weak, sick at heart.

She was crying softly when Rita came in.

The Babylon. He could hear the drums and cymbals as he hurried down the crooked little stone street. How odd that at this moment, he would remember Lawrence so keenly, his beloved Lawrence.

Suddenly a soft collection of sounds behind him forced him to stop. Someone had dropped down off the roof! He turned around.

"Keep walking," said the tall Arab. It was Ramsey! "There

is a bar around the corner which I prefer for this meeting. It is quiet. Go in ahead of me and sit down.''

Elliott was weak with relief. He obeyed immediately. Whatever happened, he was no longer alone in this nightmare. Ramsey would know what to do. He pushed on to the little bar, and went inside.

Beaded curtains; low flickering oil lamps; wooden tables; the usual collection of disreputable Europeans. An indifferent serving boy swabbing a table with a filthy rag.

A tall blue-eyed Arab in handsome robes sat at the last table, his back to the right wall. Ramsey. He must have entered from the rear.

Several patrons eyed Elliott arrogantly as he made his way to the back. He was conspicuous in his proper clothes. The least of his worries.

He took the chair to the right of Ramsey, with its back to the rear door.

The sputtering little lamp on the table reeked of scented oil. Ramses already had a drink in his hand. There was a bottle without a label and a clean glass.

''Where is she?'' Ramsey said.

''I have no intention of telling you,'' Elliott said.

''Oh? What are the rules of this game? Or am I to remain at a major disadvantage?''

Elliott was quiet for a moment. He reflected upon his decision again. Worth it. Worth the shame of the moment. He cleared his throat.

''You know what I want,'' he said to Ramsey. ''You've known since the beginning. I didn't make this journey to Egypt to protect my future daughter-in-law's chastity. That's absurd.''

''I believed you were an honorable man.''

''I am, though today I've witnessed things that would sicken a monster.''

''You should never have followed me to the museum.''

Elliott nodded. He picked up the bottle, uncorked it and filled the glass. Whisky. Ah, yes. He took a stiff drink.

''I know I shouldn't have followed you,'' he said. ''It was a young man's folly. And maybe I would be young again . . . forever.''

He looked at Ramsey. There was more than a touch of majesty to the man in these white robes. He looked biblical, larger than life. His blue eyes were rimmed with red, however. And he was weary, and suffering. That was quite clear.

"I want the elixir," Elliott said politely. "Once you've given it to me, once I've drunk it, then I'll tell you where she is. And she shall become your responsibility. And believe you me, I don't envy you. Though I have done all that I could."

"What state is she in? I want to know precisely."

"Healed, but not enough. She is beautiful and she is deadly. She killed Henry, and his Egyptian mistress, Malenka."

Ramsey said nothing for a moment, then:

"Well, young Stratford got what he deserved, to use your modern expression. He murdered his uncle. He tried to murder his cousin. I rose from the grave to stop him. The story he told you of my trying to strangle him was true."

Elliott sighed. Another great wash of relief passing through him, but not without bitterness, deep bitterness. "I knew it . . . the part about Lawrence. About Julie I never guessed."

"With my poisons," Ramses sighed.

"I loved Lawrence Stratford," Elliott whispered. "He was my . . . my lover, once, and always my friend."

Ramses gave a small nod of respect.

"This killing, was it easy for her? How did it come about?"

"She is incalculably strong. I'm not sure she fully understands what death is. She killed Henry because he was firing a gun at her. Malenka she killed because the girl was frightened and had begun to scream. She broke the necks of these two people. The maid in the museum, the same."

"She speaks?"

"Clearly. She picks up English from me as if imbibing it. She told me who she was. But something's wrong with her, something profound. She does not really know where she is, or what's happening to her. And she suffers. She suffers unspeakably because of the great gaping sores on her body, through which the bones are visible. She suffers anguish and physical pain." Elliott took another drink of the whisky. "The damage to her body—surely there is similar damage to her brain."

"You must take me to her immediately!"

"I gave her what was left in the vial, the one you so carelessly dropped in the museum. I applied it to her face and her hands. But much more is needed."

"You saw it work? It shrank these wounds?"

"Yes. But the sunlight had already healed her enormously."

Elliott paused; he studied Ramsey's seemingly impassive face, the blue eyes staring forward. "But surely this is no mystery to you!"

"You're wrong."

Mechanically Ramses lifted the glass and drank.

"A quarter of the vial, that's all that was left," Elliott said. "Would it have been enough for me, if I had drunk it instead of giving it to her?"

"I don't know."

Elliott smiled bitterly.

"I am not a scientist. Only a King."

"Well, you have my proposition, Your Royal Highness. You give me the elixir. And in a quantity sufficient to resolve all doubts. And I shall give you Cleopatra, Queen of Egypt, to do with as you like."

Ramses looked at him directly. "And suppose I told you I would kill you if you did not tell me where she was?"

"Kill me. Without the elixir I'll die anyway. Those are the only two things I think of now: death and the elixir. I'm not sure I can distinguish between the two any longer." One more glass of whisky, that was all he could handle. He drank it down and made a faint bitter face. "Look, I'll be frank with you. I have no stomach for what I've seen today. But I want that potion. And all else collapses in the face of that desire."

"Yes, how well I remember. Yet it didn't for her. She chose death. To be with her beloved Mark Antony, though I held it out to her. That was her choice."

"Then she didn't really know what death was."

Ramses smiled.

"In any case, that, I am certain, she doesn't remember. And if she does, I doubt she cares. She's alive now, suffering, struggling with her wounds, her hungers . . ." He stopped.

Ramses leaned forward. "Where is she!"

"Give it to me. And I will help you with her. I will do anything that I can. We won't be enemies, you and I. We aren't enemies now, are we?"

"No, not enemies!" Ramses whispered. His voice was soft, but his eyes were full of anger. "But I can't give it to you. It's far too dangerous. You simply do not understand."

"Yet you raised her from the dead like a bloody alchemist!" Elliott said heatedly. "And you will give it to Julie Stratford, will you not? And your devoted friend, Samir?"

Ramses didn't answer. He rested back against the wall, eyes forward again.

Elliott stood up.

"I'll be at Shepheard's. When you've brewed the elixir, call me there. I'll know your voice when you call. But be careful. Then we shall arrange another meeting."

Gathering up his walking stick, he started for the door. He did not look back, hard as that was for him. His face was burning with shame. But this was the only feeble chance that remained to him, and he played it out, miserable though he was.

There was a moment of fear as he walked in the dark alleyway alone. He was keenly aware not only of all the familiar aches and pains that plagued him, but also of the general weakness from which he was suffering, the premature curse of old age. Then it occurred to him that Ramses would follow!

He stopped, listened. Not a sound in the darkness. He went on.

She stood in the front room; she had not made up her mind whether or not she should kill this noisy bird. It was being quiet at this moment, clucking, dancing on its perch. And it was beautiful. If it did not scream, she would not kill it. That seemed fair enough.

The body of the dancing girl had begun to rot. She had dragged it into the farthest corner of the garden and there thrown a great cloth over it; but still she could smell it.

Even in the back kitchen she could smell it. But that had not stopped her from consuming all the food she could find. A few lemons, very sweet: a loaf of stale bread.

After that she had changed into one of the other "frocks," to use the American's word for frilly dress. This one was white; she liked it because it made her skin look very fine and faintly golden; and it had even bigger skirts with great ruffles to hide her feet.

The pain in her feet was bad. So was the pain in her side. If Lord Rutherford did not come soon, she would go out again. Though how to find him, she had no idea. It had been hard enough finding this house again. She had driven the American motor car to the outskirts of this curious part of the city where the houses were old and without colour or decoration, and then she had wandered through the narrow streets until she saw the open door. Now she was growing impatient.

Suddenly she heard a knock.

"Your name?" she said in English.

"Elliott, Lord Rutherford. Open for me."

She opened the door at once.

"I have waited a long while for you, Lord Rutherford. You have brought the elixir to me? You know where is the man with the blue eyes?"

Lord Rutherford was startled by her English. She gave a little shrug of her shoulders as she closed the door. "Oh, yes, your language is no puzzle to me," she said. "In the streets of this city today I heard much of it and other such tongues. I learned many things. It's the past that's the puzzle, the world I can't remember!" Suddenly she felt angry. Why was he staring at her like that! "Where is Ramses!" she demanded. She was certain that that was the name of the man with the blue eyes.

"I spoke with him. I told him what was needed."

"Yes, Lord Rutherford." She approached him. He backed away from her. "Do you fear me?"

"I don't know. I want to protect you," he whispered.

"Ah, true. And Ramses, the blue-eyed one. Why does he not come?" Something unpleasant, something very unpleasant. A dim image of Ramses backing away from her. Of Ramses standing many feet away from her as she cried out. Something about the venom of the snake and . . . she was screaming, but no one could hear her! And then they pulled the black cover over her face. She turned away from Lord Rutherford. "If I remembered nothing, it would be easier," she whispered. "But I see it, and then I see it no more." She turned back to him.

"You have to be patient," Lord Rutherford said. "He will come."

"Patient! I don't want to be patient. I want to find him. Tell me where he is. I shall go to him."

"I can't. That's impossible!"

"Is it!" Her voice had risen to a shriek. She saw the fear in him, she saw the . . . what was it? He was not repelled as the others had been. No, it was something else as he stared at her. "Tell me where to find him!" she screamed. She took another step towards him, driving him towards the wall. "I will tell you a secret, Lord Rutherford. You are weak, all of you. Strange beings! And I like killing you. It soothes my pain to watch you die."

She rushed at him, grabbing him by the throat. She would

shake the truth from him, and then kill him if he did not tell her. But suddenly strong hands laid hold of her, wrenching her backwards. For a moment she could not get her bearings; she screamed, blundering, and then saw the blue-eyed man standing before her. Who was this! She knew, ah, but it was just beyond her grasp. Yet the word broke from her: "Ramses!" Yes, this was Ramses, the blue-eyed one. . . . She ran at him with her hands out.

"Get out," he shouted to the other. "Get away from here. Go."

His throat felt like marble. She could not snap the bones! But he could not throw her off, either, no matter how hard he tried. Vaguely, she knew that Elliott, Lord Rutherford, had left the house, slamming the door behind him. And she was alone now, battling her nemesis, Ramses, who at another time had turned away from her; Ramses, who had hurt her. It didn't matter that she couldn't remember. It was like the name. She knew!

Through the room they struggled and into the other. She freed her right hand only long enough to scratch at him with her bone-bare fingers, before he caught her wrist again. With all her strength she fought him, seething with rage. Then she saw his hand go up. She tried to duck, but the blow caught her, and she fell back on the bed. Sobbing, she turned and pushed her face into the pillows. She could not kill him! She could not snap his neck.

"Damn you," she roared, not in the new tongue but in the old one. "Evil Ramses!" She spat at him as she lay there, hands drawn under her breast, gazing up at him, wishing she had the strength of a cat to spring at him and slice open his eyes.

Why did he look at her like that? Why did he weep?

"Cleopatra!" he whispered.

Her vision blurred for an instant; a load of memories so vast and heavy hovered just near her, ready to wipe out the moment utterly, should she give in. Dark, awful memories, memories of suffering she never wanted to revisit again.

She sat up on the bed, looking at him, puzzling over the tender, wounded expression of his face.

Handsome man he was; beautiful. Skin like the young ones; firm, sweet mouth. And the eyes, the large, translucent blue eyes. She saw him in another place, a dark place, as she rose up out of the abyss. He'd been bending over her saying the ancient prayer in Egyptian. *You are, now and for always.*

"You did this to me," she whispered. She heard the glass breaking, the boards shattering, felt those stones under her feet. Her arms had been blackened, withered! "You brought me here, to these 'modern times,' and when I reached out to you, you ran from me!"

Like a boy, he bit his lip; trembling, tears washing down his cheeks. Should she pity him in his suffering!

"No, I swear it," he said in the old familiar Latin. "Others came between us. I would never have left you."

This was a lie. An awful lie. She had tried to rise off the couch. The poison of the snake was paralyzing her. Ramses! In panic, she'd called out; she could hear her own call. But he hadn't turned from the window. And the women around her, they pleaded with him. Ramses!

"Liar!" she hissed. "You could have given it to me! You let me die!"

"No." He shook his head. "Never."

But wait. She was confusing two different crucial events. Those women. They hadn't been there when he said the prayers. She'd been alone . . . forever and ever. "I'd been sleeping, in a dark place. And then you came. And I felt pain again. Pain and hunger, and I knew you. I knew who you were! And I hated you!"

"Cleopatra!" He came towards her.

"No, stay back. I know what you've done! I knew it before. You've brought me back from the dead!" she whispered. "That's what you've done. From the grave, you raised me. And this is the evidence of it, these wounds!" Her voice had almost dried in her throat from pure bitterness. Then she felt the scream coming; she gasped, unable to hold it off.

He grabbed her by the arms, shook her.

"Let me go!" she cried. Calm now. No scream.

For a moment, he held on to her and she allowed it; after all, fighting him was useless. But then she smiled slowly. The thing was to use her wits. To understand all this once and for all.

"Oh, but you are very handsome, aren't you?" she said. "Were you always so beautiful? When I knew you before, we made love, didn't we?" She lifted her fingers and touched his lip. "I like your mouth. I like the mouths of men. Women's mouths are too soft. I like the silkiness of your skin."

Slowly she kissed him. Before it had happened; before it had been so heated that all other men had meant nothing to her. If only he had given her the freedom, the patience, she would have always returned to him; why hadn't he understood? She had to live and breathe as the Queen of Egypt. Hmmmmm, kissing him, hot as it had been then.

"Don't stop," she moaned.

"Is it you?" he said. Such pain in his voice. "Is it really you?"

She smiled again. That was the horror, wasn't it? She didn't know the answer herself! She laughed. Ah, it was very funny. She threw back her head laughing, and she felt his lips on her throat.

"Yes, kiss me, take me," she said. His mouth moved down her throat, his fingers opening her dress, his mouth closing on her nipple. "Aaaaah!" She could scarcely stand it, the searing pleasure of it. He held her captive suddenly, his mouth clamped to her, tongue stroking the nipple, pulling on her with the ferocity of a suckling child.

Love you? I've always loved you. But how can I leave my world? How can I leave behind everything that I cherish? You speak of immortality. I can't grasp such a thing. I know only that here I am Queen, and you're moving away from me, threatening to leave me forever. . . .

She pulled away from him. "Please," she begged him. Where and when had she spoken those words?

"What is it?" he said.

"I don't know . . . I can't . . . I see things and then they vanish!"

"There's so much I must tell you, so much to be revealed. If only you'll try to understand."

She struggled to her feet and walked away from him. Then looking down, she ripped off the dress, tore the fabric of the skirt to its hem. Pulling it back, she pivoted and faced him.

"Yes! Cast your blue eyes on what you've done! This is what I understand!" She touched the wound in her side. "I was a Queen. And now I am this horror. What is this that you brought back to life with your mysterious elixir! Your medicine!"

She lowered her head slowly, hands up once more to her temples. A thousand times she did it, but it didn't stop the pain inside her mind. Moaning, she rocked back and forth. Her moaning was like a singing. Did that soothe the pain? She hummed with her lips sealed, that strange soft song, "Celeste Aïda."

Then she felt his hand on her shoulder. He was turning her around. Like waking it was to look up at him. Handsome Ramses.

Only slowly did she lower her eyes and see the shining vial in his hand.

"Ah!" She seized it and went to pour its contents into her cupped palm.

"No, drink it!"

She hesitated. But he had poured it into her mouth, she remembered. Yes, down her throat in the blackness.

With his left hand, he grabbed the back of her head, and with his right he lifted the vial to her lips.

"Drink it down."

She did. Gulp after gulp and it was gone into her. The light brightened in the room around her. A great lovely vibration shook her from the roots of her hair to her toes. The tingling in her eyes was almost unbearable. She closed her eyes, and then opened them and saw him staring at her in astonishment. He whispered the word "Blue."

But the wounds, were they healing! She held up her fingers. The itching tingling sensation was tantalizing. The flesh was covering the bone. And her side, yes, closing.

"Oh, ye gods, thank you. Thank the gods!" she sobbed. "I am whole, Ramses, I am whole."

Once again his hands stroked her, sending the chills through her. She let him kiss her, let him pull off the torn clothes. "Suckle me, hold me," she whispered. On the tingling flesh where the wound had been he kissed her, his mouth open, his tongue licking her. As he kissed the moist hair between her legs, she pulled him upwards. "No, into me. Fill me!" she cried. "I am whole."

His sex jutted against her. He lifted her and thrust her down on it; ah, yes, nothing remembered now, nothing but the flesh; she went limp in ecstasy, her head thrown back, her eyes closed.

Defeated, he dragged his left foot like a cripple, drawing ever closer to the hotel. Had he been a coward to leave? Should he have stayed, struggling to be of assistance in that war between Titans? With malice in his eyes, Ramsey had said, Go. And Ramsey had saved his life by intervening; by following him, by making a joke of his last feeble attempt to get the elixir of life.

Ah, what did it matter now? He must somehow get Alex out of Egypt; get himself out of Egypt. Wake from this nightmare once and for all and completely. That was the only thing left for him to do.

He approached the front steps of Shepheard's, eyes down.

And he did not see the two men who stopped him until they were blocking his path.

"Lord Rutherford?"

"Let me alone."

"Sorry, my lord, I wish I could. We're from the governor's office. There are some questions we must ask you."

Ah, the last humiliation. He did not fight.

"Help me up the steps, then, young man," he said.

She stepped out of the copper bathtub, the long coarse white towel around her, her hair still damp and curling in the steam. It was a bath for a palace, this room of painted tiles, and hot water running through a tiny pipe. And the perfumes she had found; how sweet the scent, like crushed lilies.

She walked back into the bedroom and saw herself again in the mirrored cabinet door. Whole. Perfect. Her legs had their proper contour. Even the pain inside her, where the evil one called Henry had wounded her, that was no more.

Blue eyes! How the sight shocked her.

Had she been this beautiful when she was alive? Did he know? Men had always said she was beautiful. She did a little dance, loving her own nakedness, enjoying the softness of her own hair against the backs of her arms.

Ramses watched her sullenly from the corner. Well, that was nothing out of the ordinary, was it? Ramses, the secret watcher. Ramses, the judge.

She reached out for the wine bottle on the dressing table. Empty. She smashed it on the marble top. Bits and pieces of glass fell to the floor.

No response from him; only that hard unyielding gaze.

So what did it matter? Why not go on dancing? She knew that she was beautiful, that men would love her. The two men she'd killed this afternoon had been charmed by her, and now there was no dreadful secret evidence of death to hide.

Pivoting, letting her hair fly about her, she cried out: "Whole! Alive and whole."

From the other room came the sudden frantic cry of that parrot, that evil bird. Now was the time to kill it, a sacrifice to her happiness, like buying a white dove in the marketplace and letting it go in thanks to the gods.

She went to the cage, opened the little door and thrust her hand inside, catching the fluttering, screeching thing at once.

She killed it by pressing her fingers together. Then shook out her hand and watched it drop to the floor of the cage.

Turning, she looked at Ramses. Ah, such a sad face, so full of disapproval! Poor dearest!

"I can't die now. Isn't that true?"

No answer. Ah, but she knew. She'd been pondering ever since . . . ever since all of this began. When she looked at the others, it had been the realization hovering in the back of her mind. He'd raised her from the dead. Now she couldn't die.

"Oh, how disconsolate you look. Aren't you pleased with your magic?" She came towards him, laughing under her breath. "Am I not beautiful? And now you weep. What a fool you are! It was all your design, wasn't it? You came into my tomb; you brought me back; and now you weep as if I were dead. Well, you turned away from me when I was dying! You let them pull the shroud over my face!"

He sighed. "No. I never did that. You don't remember what happened."

"Why did you do it? Why did you bring me back? What were we to each other, you and I?" How did all these little shimmering bits and pieces of memory fit together? When would they make one cloth?

She drew closer, peering at his skin, touching it again. Such resilient skin.

"Don't you know the answer?" he asked. "Isn't it deep inside you?"

"I know only that you were there when I died. You were someone I loved. I remember. You were there and I was frightened. The poison from the snake had paralyzed me, and I wanted to cry out to you, but I couldn't. I struggled. I said your name. You turned your back."

"No! No, that could not have happened! I stood there watching you."

The women weeping, she heard it again. Move away from that room full of death, the room where Antony had died, beloved Antony. She wouldn't let them take the couch away, though the blood from his wounds had soaked into the silk.

"You let me die."

He took her by the arms again, roughly. Was that always his way?

"I wanted you to be with me, the way you are now."

"As I am now. And how is that? What is this world? Is it the Hades of myth? Will we come upon the others . . . upon . . . ." But it had been right there a moment ago. "Upon Antony!" she said. "Where is Antony!" Oh . . . but she knew.

She turned away. Antony was dead and gone; laid in the tomb. And he would not give the magic to Antony; it was all there again.

He came up behind her, and embraced her.

"When you called out to me," he said, "what was it you wanted? Tell me now."

"To make you suffer!" She laughed. She could see him in the mirrored door of the cabinet, and she laughed at the pain in his face. "I don't know why I called out to you! I don't even know who you are!" She slapped him suddenly. No effect. Like slapping marble.

She wandered away from him into the dressing room. She wanted something beautiful. What was the finest dress that miserable woman had possessed? Ah, this one of rose-colored silk with fragile cutwork trimming. She took it up, slipped her arms into it and quickly snapped the little hooks up the front. It flattered her breasts beautifully; and the skirt was full and beautiful, though she no longer had to hide her feet.

Once again she put on the sandals.

"Where are you going?"

"Out in the city. This is the city of Cairo. Why should I not go out into it?"

"I must talk to you. . . ."

"Must you?" She gathered up her canvas bag. In the corner of her eye she could see a great sliver of broken glass on the marble dressing table top. A shard from the bottle she'd smashed.

She moved lazily towards it. Her hand played with the pearls there. She should take these too. Of course he followed her.

"Cleopatra, look at me," he said.

She turned abruptly and kissed him. Could he be so easily fooled? Yes, his lips told her that, oh, so delicious. How splendidly he suffered! Groping blindly at her side, she found that shard and, lifting it, gashed his throat.

She stepped backwards. He stood staring at her. The blood poured down his white robe. But he wasn't afraid. He did not move to stop the bleeding. His face showed only sadness, not fear.

"I cannot die either," he whispered softly.

"Ah!" She smiled. "Did someone wake you from the grave?"

Again she rushed at him, kicking at him, clawing at his eyes.

"Stop, I beg you."

She raised her knee, jamming him hard between his legs. That pain he felt, oh, yes. He doubled over with it, and she kicked him hard in the side of the head.

Through the courtyard she raced, gripping the canvas bag with her left hand, as with her right she reached for the top of the wall. In a second she was over it and racing through the narrow unlighted street.

Within minutes she reached the motor car. Instantly she turned on the engine, gave it fuel with a stab of the pedal and roared out of the small alleyway and onto the main road.

Ah, the wind in her face again; the freedom; and the power of this great iron beast at her command.

"Take me to the bright lights of British Cairo," she said, "dear sweet little beast. Yes!"

6

THE FRONT lounge at Shepheard's. Good gin from the bar, with plenty of ice and just a little lemon. He was grateful that they had allowed him that. What a drunkard he had become. A lovely realization came over him. When he got back to England, he was going to drink himself to death.

But would they never stop? Surely they had realized he would tell them nothing. They looked like mannequins to him, their mouths jerking as if worked by wires. Every gesture seemed artificial. Even the handsome little boy who came in and out with the ice and the gin appeared to be acting. All of it false. Grotesque the figures moving past in the lobby; and the music drifting from the bars and the ballroom, why, it sounded like what they might be playing tonight in hell.

Sometimes the words they said made no sense. He knew the definition of each word, but what was the meaning? Dead men with their necks broken. Had she done it in the short time that he had absented himself?

"I'm tired, gentlemen," he said finally. "The heat here does not agree with me. I took a bad fall today. I need my rest now. You must allow me to go to my room."

The two men looked at each other. Mock frustration. Nothing was real here. What was real? Cleopatra's hands closing on his throat; the white-draped figure behind her, catching hold of her?

"Lord Rutherford, we are now dealing with several murders!

314

Clearly, the stabbing in London was only the beginning. Now we must ask for your full cooperation. These two young men murdered this afternoon. . . ."

"I have told you. I know nothing about it! What is it you want from me, young man, that I spin fancies for you? This is absurd."

"Henry Stratford. Do you know where we can find him? He was here at Shepheard's to see you two days ago."

"Henry Stratford frequents the worst parts of Cairo. He walks dark streets alone at night. I don't know where he is, God help him. Now, I really must go."

He rose from his chair. Where was that damned walking stick now?

"Do not attempt to leave Cairo, sir," said the young one, the arrogant one, the one with the pinched nose. "We have your passport."

"You what! That's outrageous," Elliott whispered.

"I'm afraid the same applies to your son. And to Miss Stratford. I've already collected their passports from the desk as well. Lord Rutherford, we must get to the bottom of this."

"You idiot," Elliott said. "I'm a British citizen! You dare do this to me!"

The other man stepped in.

"My lord, let me speak to you candidly! I know of your close relationship with the Stratford family, but do you think Henry Stratford could be connected to these killings? He knew this man in London, the one who was stabbed. As for the American found out at the pyramids, the fellow had been robbed of quite a good deal of money. Now we know Stratford had his ups and downs with regard to money."

Elliott held his gaze without speaking. Pinning it on Henry. That had not occurred to him. Oh, but it was obvious! Pinning it all on Henry, of course. And Henry knew the fellow in London. What luck. What supremely marvellous luck. He eyed the two gentlemen who stood now before him, awkwardly. What if this could work!

"My lord, there's even more to it than that. We have two mysterious thefts as well. Not only the mummy stolen from the Cairo museum; but it seems the mummy's been stolen from Miss Stratford's house in Mayfair too."

"Really."

"And a bit of priceless Egyptian jewelry was found in the

possession of Henry Stratford's mistress, a Daisy Banker, a music hall singer. . . ."

"Yes. . . ." Elliott eased back down into his chair.

"Well, what I'm driving at, my lord, is perhaps Stratford was involved in something, you know, some sort of smuggling arrangement . . . the jewelry and the coins and the mummies. . . ."

"Mummies . . . Henry and mummies . . ." Oh, it was too beautiful, and Henry, poor Henry, who had murdered Lawrence, was floating in the bitumen right now. He would begin to laugh, thinly, hysterically, if he weighed it all too deeply.

"You see, Lord Rutherford, we might be looking for the wrong man."

"But then what was Ramsey doing at the museum?" said the younger official a bit impatiently.

"Trying to stop Henry," Elliott murmured. "He must have followed him. He was desperate to talk to Henry, for Julie's sake. Of course."

"But how do we explain the coins!" asked the young man, getting a little steamed now. "We found seven gold Cleopatra coins in Ramsey's room."

"But that's obvious," said Elliott, looking up, the light just dawning. "He must have taken them away from Henry when they quarreled. He knew what Henry was up to. He must have been trying to stop it. Of course."

"But none of this makes sense!" said the younger man.

"Well, it makes a hell of a lot more sense now than it did before," Elliott said. "Poor Henry, poor mad, doomed Henry."

"Yes, I'm beginning to see a pattern," said the old man.

"You are?" Elliott said. "But of course you are. Now, if you'll allow me, I want to consult a lawyer. I want my passport back! I presume I may still consult a lawyer? That privilege of British citizenship has not been revoked?"

"By all means, Lord Rutherford," said the older man. "What could make young Stratford run amok like that?"

"Gambling, old man. Gambling. It's an addiction. It destroyed his life."

Whole, alive, and a madwoman! Madder than she'd been before he gave it to her. That is what his elixir had accomplished. Ah, the fruits of his genius. And how could this nightmare conceivably end?

Back and forth through the honeycombed streets of old Cairo he searched. She had vanished. How could he hope to find her until she gave him some sign?

Had he never gone into the dark shadowy corridors of the Cairo Museum, he would never have gazed on her neglected remains; a different path would have been taken into the future. With Julie Stratford at his side, all the world might have been his.

But he was linked now forever to the monster he'd created, dragging through time with her the suffering he'd sought to put to rest; the mad creature who could remember only the hatred she'd once known for him, and none of the love. Ah, but what then had he expected? That in this new and shining age, a great spiritual transformation would be worked upon her ancient soul?

What if Julie was right, and that soul was not even the soul of Cleopatra! What if the thing was a horrid twin!

The fact was, he didn't know. When he'd held her in his arms, he'd known only that this was the flesh he had once cherished; this was the voice that had spoken to him both in anger and in love; this was the woman who had broken him finally; and taken her own life rather than the elixir—who now taunted him with a fragment of memory, that she'd cried out to him in her dying moments centuries ago; or tried to; and he had not heard her last plea. He loved her, just as he loved Julie Stratford. He loved them both!

On he walked, faster and faster, out of the strange eerie quiet of old Cairo and back towards the bustle of the new city. All he could do was continue to search. And what clue would she give him finally? Another senseless killing; and that murder too would be blamed on the man known as Reginald Ramsey and it would drive another sword through Julie's heart.

But there was little chance that Julie would ever forgive him now. He had hopelessly compounded his folly, and she had expected greater wisdom from him, greater courage. And he had been a man standing in that little house, a man staring at the suffering image of his lost love.

And so he had sacrificed a finer, stronger love for a passion that had enslaved him centuries ago. He no longer deserved that finer lover, and he knew it. Yet he wanted it, lusted for it; just as he lusted for the doomed one whom he must somehow control or somehow destroy.

All consolation was now quite beyond his reach.

* * *

Now there were gorgeous garments, dresses she could love, for they had the old softness to them and the old simplicity, and they were threaded through and through with silver and gold.

She came up to the brightly lighted window, and placed her hand on it. She read the sign in English:

ONLY THE FINEST FOR THE OPERA BALL

Yes, she required the finest. And there was plenty of money in this bag. She needed shoes like that, high shoes with daggers for heels. And jewels as well.

She went to the door and tapped. A tall woman with silver hair came to answer.

"We're about to close, my dear. I'm sorry, if you come back . . ."

"Please, that dress!" she said. She opened the bag and withdrew a great handful of the money. A few pieces of it fluttered out and down to the ground.

"My dear, you mustn't display that much money at this time of night," the woman said to her. She bent down and gathered up the loose pieces. "Come inside. Are you all alone?"

Oh, but it was quite lovely in here; she touched the rich fabric of the small gilded chair. And behold, more of the statues she'd seen in the window, and these were decked not only with rich flowing silks, but furs as well. The long strip of white fur in particular attracted her.

"I want this," she said.

"Of course, my dear, of course," said the proprietress.

She flashed her sweetest smile at the baffled woman. "Is this . . . is this . . . for the opera ball?" she asked.

"Oh, it would be perfectly lovely! I shall wrap it for you."

"Ah, but I need a gown, you see, and those slippers, and I need pearls and rubies, if you have them, for you see, I have lost all my finery, I have lost my jewels."

"We shall take care of you! Please be seated. Now, what would you like to see in your size?"

It was going to work. It was an absurd story: Henry breaking into the Museum of Antiquities to steal a mummy in order to pay his debts. But the simple fact was—and he must remember this—the truth was even more absurd! No one would believe the truth at all.

He rang his old friend Pitfield as soon as he reached the suite.

"Tell him it's Elliott Rutherford, I'll hold on for him. Ah, Gerald. I'm sorry to interrupt your dinner. It seems I'm in a bit of legal trouble here. I think Henry Stratford's mixed up in it. Yes. Yes, this evening if you could. I'm at Shepheard's, of course. Ah, wonderful, Gerald. I knew I could count on you. Twenty minutes from now. In the bar."

He looked up to see Alex coming through the door as he put down the phone.

"Father, thank God you're back. They've confiscated our passports! Julie is frantic. And Miles has just been at her with another wild story. Some poor American murdered at the pyramids, and an English fellow killed outside the International Cafe."

"Alex, pack your trunk," he said. "I've already heard that whole story. Gerald Pitfield's on his way over. He'll have your passports back for you before morning, I promise, and then you and Julie are to be on the train."

"You'll have to tell her that, Father."

"I will, but right now I have to see Pitfield. Give me your arm, and help me to the lift."

"But, Father, who is responsible . . . ?"

"Son, I don't want to be the one to tell you. And certainly not the one to tell Julie. But it looks as if Henry may be deeply involved."

Quiet up here. One could scarcely hear the music from the lighted windows below. She had crept up the stairs all alone, wanting only to see the stars, and be away from the unwelcome knocks and the unwelcome jangling of the phone.

And there was Samir, standing there at the edge of the roof, looking out over the minarets and the domes, and the myriad little rooftops of Cairo. Samir, looking up at the heavens as if he were in prayer.

He slipped his arm around her as she approached.

"Samir, where is he?" she whispered.

"He will send word to us, Julie. He will not break his promise."

* * *

This had been an exquisite choice: pale green "satin" with rows of pearl "buttons" and layers of "Brussels lace." And the loose fur wrap looked quite becoming, said the woman, and the woman should know, should she not?

"Your hair, so beautiful, it seems quite a sin to tie it up, but my dear, you really should, you know. It looks rather . . . Perhaps tomorrow I can make an appointment for you with a hairdresser."

Of course she was right. The other women all had hair upswept, off the neck, not unlike the manner in which she'd worn hers always before this, except their coifs were shaped in a different way, more like a great heart with fancy curls. Yes, she would like this hairdresser.

"Especially for the opera ball!" Indeed. And the gown for the opera ball was a lovely creation, too, now hidden safely in a bundle of stiff and shining paper. And so were all the other things—the pretty lace "knickers" and the flimsy "underskirts" and the countless dresses, and shoes and hats, and various trifles she could no longer now remember. Lace handkerchiefs, scarves, and a white parasol for carrying in the sun! What delightful nonsense. It had been like walking into a great dressing closet. What were modern times that such things were everywhere ready made for the body?

The proprietress had almost finished her sums, as she called them. She had counted out many "bills" from the money. And now she opened the drawer of a big bronze machine, the "cash register," and there was much more money, more money by far than Cleopatra possessed.

"I must say you look stunning in that colour!" said the woman. "It makes your eyes change from blue to green."

Cleopatra laughed. Heaps of money.

She rose from the chair, and walked delicately towards the woman, rather liking the clicking sound of these high heels on the marble floor.

She took hold of the woman's throat before the poor creature so much as looked up. She tightened her grip, pressing her thumb right on the tender bone in the middle. The woman appeared astonished. She gave a little hiccuping noise. Then Cleopatra lifted her right hand and carefully twisted the woman's head hard to the left. Snap. Dead.

No need now to reflect upon it, to ponder the great gulf that existed between her and this poor sad being who lay now on the floor behind her little table, staring up at the gilded ceiling. All of these beings were for killing when it was wanted, and what could they possibly do to her?

She scooped the money into the new satin evening bag she had found here. What would not fit she put into the old canvas bag. She took also all the jewels left in the case beneath the "cash register." Then she piled the boxes one atop another until she had a mountainous stack of them; and she carried them out and heaved them into the rear seat of the car.

Off now, to the next adventure. Throwing the long thick tails of the white fur over her shoulders, she fired up the beast again.

And headed fast for the place where "all the best people stay, the British and the Americans, that's Shepheard's, *the* hotel, if you know what I mean."

She gave a deep laugh when she thought of the American and his strange way of talking to her, as if she were an idiot; and the merchant woman had been the same. Maybe at Shepheard's she would meet someone of charm and graceful manners, someone infinitely more interesting than all these miserable souls whom she had sent into the dark waters whence she'd come.

"What in God's name has happened here!" whispered the older of the two officials. He stood in the doorway of Malenka's house, reluctant to enter without a warrant or permission. No answer to his knock; no answer when he had called Henry Stratford's name.

He could see broken glass over the dressing table in the lighted bedroom. And that looked like blood on the floor.

The younger man, as ever impatient and strong-willed, had ventured into the courtyard with his electric torch. Chairs overturned. Broken china.

"Good Lord, Davis. There's a woman dead out here!"

The older man didn't move for a moment. He was staring at the dead parrot on the floor of its cage. And at all the empty bottles ranged from one end of the bar to the other. And the suit coat hanging on the corner rack.

Then he forced himself to go out into the dark little garden and see this corpse for himself.

"That's the woman," he said. "That's Malenka from the Babylon."

"Well, I don't think we need a warrant under these circumstances."

The older man came back into the sitting room. He moved cautiously into the bedroom.

He stared at the torn dress lying on the floor, and at the curious rags pushed in a pile against the wall. He paid little heed to the young man passing him; the young man who moved about, vaguely exhilarated by these obvious signs of disaster, searching and scribbling in his little book.

Those rags—why, they looked like mummy wrappings, yet some of the linen appeared to be new. He looked up as the young man held a passport before him.

"Stratford's," said the young man. "All of his identification is in there, in his coat."

Elliott leaned on Alex's arm as they stepped out of the glass lift.

"But what if Pitfield can't straighten all this out?" Alex asked.

"We will continue to conduct ourselves like civilized people as long as we must remain here," Elliott said. "You'll take Julie to the opera as planned tomorrow night. You will accompany her to the ball afterwards. And you will be ready to leave as soon as your passport is released."

"She's in no mood for it, Father. And she'd rather have Samir accompany her, if you want the truth. Since all this started, it's Samir she confides in. He's always at her side."

"Nevertheless, you are to stay close to her. We are going to be seen together tomorrow. Everything right and proper. Now why don't you go out on the veranda and have a nightcap and leave the legal business to me?"

Yes, she liked Shepheard's, she knew it already. She had liked it this afternoon when she had seen the long chain of motor cars before it, with exquisitely dressed men and women climbing out of them and walking up the steps.

Now there were very few cars. She managed to stop right before the entrance; and a charming young male servant came to open her door. Carrying her canvas bag and satin purse, she walked serenely up the carpeted stairs as other servants scrambled to retrieve her many packages.

The lobby delighted her at once. Oh, she had no idea the rooms of this palatial building would be so grand. And the crowds moving to and fro—shapely women and handsomely clad men—excited her. This was an elegant world—"modern times." One had to see such a place as this to grasp the possibilities.

"May I help you, miss?" Another servile male approached; how strange was his clothing, especially his hat. If there was one thing about "modern times" she did not like, it was these hats!

"Oh, would you be so kind!" she said carefully. "I would like to have lodgings here. This is Shepheard's Hotel? *The* hotel?"

"Yes, indeed, miss. Let me take you to the desk."

"Wait," she whispered. Some feet away from her, she spied Lord Rutherford! No mistake. It was he. And an exquisite young man was with him, a tall, slender creature of fine porcelain features who made her earlier companions seem quite crude.

She narrowed her eyes, concentrating, trying to hear what this young man was saying. But there was too great a distance. And the two were moving in and out of sight, beyond a row of high potted palms. Then the young one clasped Lord Rutherford's hand and left him, moving towards the front doors. And Lord Rutherford moved into a large shadowy room.

"That's Lord Rutherford, miss," said the helpful young man beside her.

"Yes, I know," she said. "But the beautiful one. Who is he?"

"Ah, that's his son, Alex, miss, the young Viscount Summerfield. They're frequent guests of Shepheard's. Friends of the Stratfords, miss."

She looked at him quizzically.

"Lawrence Stratford, miss," he explained as he took her arm and gently guided her forward. "The great archaeologist, the one who just made the discovery of the Ramses tomb."

"What did you say!" she whispered. "Speak slowly."

"The one that dug up the mummy, miss, of Ramses the Damned."

"Ramses the Damned!"

"Yes, miss, quite a story, miss." He pointed now to a long ornate table in front of her, which in fact looked like an altar. "There's the desk, miss. Anything else I can do for you?"

She gave a little laugh of pure amazement. "No," she said. "You have been simply super. Very okay!"

He gave her a sweet indulgent look, the look all these men gave her. And then he gestured for her to step up to the "desk."

* * *

Elliott went right to it as Pitfield sat down across from him. He was aware that he was talking too fast, and likely to say strange things, but he could not break his momentum. Get Alex out of here. Get Julie out if at all possible. Those were the only thoughts in his mind, and worry about Randolph later.

"None of us has the slightest connection to any of it," he said. "They must all be allowed to go home. I can stay here, if it's absolutely necessary, but my son must be allowed to leave."

Gerald, ten years his senior, white-haired and heavy about the middle, listened keenly. He was a man not given to strong drink, who tended to work round the clock so that his family might enjoy every pleasurable aspect of colonial existence.

"Of course not," he said now, with complete sympathy. "But wait, there's Winthrop in the doors. He has two men with him."

"I can't talk to him!" Elliott said. "Not now, for the love of heaven."

"You leave it to me completely."

How astonished they were when she paid them in advance with piles and piles of the strange money they called "pound notes," though they weighed nothing. The young servants would take her many bundles to her suite, they said. And indeed, there were kitchens working now to produce whatever food she desired; there lay the dining room to the right; and she could banquet in her room if that was her wish. As for the hairdresser which she dearly required to tie up her hair, that lady would not be available until tomorrow. Very well. Thank you!

She dropped the key into her satin bag. She would find suite number 201 later. She hurried to the door of the dark room into which Lord Rutherford had gone, and spied him drinking there alone. He did not see her.

Out on the broad front terrace, she could see his son, Alex, leaning against the white pillar—such a comely youth—in fast conversation with a dark-skinned Egyptian. The Egyptian came back into the hotel. The young one seemed at a loss.

She went to him immediately. She crept up and stood beside him and studied his delicate face—yes, a beauty. Of course Lord Rutherford was a man of considerable charm; but this one was so young that his skin was still petal soft, and yet he was tall and his shoulders were strong and straight, and he had a clear, confident look in his brown eyes when he turned to her.

"The young Viscount Summerfield," she said. "Son of Lord Rutherford, I am told?"

A great flash of a smile. "I'm Alex Savarell, yes. Forgive me, I don't believe I've had the pleasure."

"I'm hungry, Viscount Summerfield. Won't you show me to the banquet room of *the* hotel? I should like to eat something."

"I'd be delighted! What an unexpected pleasure."

He hooked his arm for her to take it. Oh, she liked him very much; there was no reticence in him at all. He escorted her back into the crowded main room, past the dark tavern where his father drank, and on towards a great open place under a high gilded ceiling.

Tables draped in linen filled the sides of the immense room. In the centre men and women danced, the women's skirts like great softly ruffled flowers. And the music, oh, so lovely, though it almost hurt her ears. It was far more shrill than that of the music box. And it was sweetly sad!

At once he asked an imperious old man to show them to a "table." What an ugly person was this imperious man who appeared as finely dressed as anyone present. But he said, "Yes, Lord Summerfield" with great respect. And the table was fine indeed, set with gorgeous plate, and sweet-scented flowers.

"What is this music?" she asked.

"From America," he said. "From Sigmund Romberg."

She began rocking back and forth a little.

"Would you like to dance?" he asked.

"That would be super!"

Oh, such a warm hand he had as he clasped hers and led her out on the floor. How peculiar that each couple should be dancing as if entirely alone and engaged in a private ritual. At once the melancholy rhythm swept her up. And this adorable young man, how lovingly he looked at her. This really was a lovely young man, this Alex, Lord Summerfield.

"How enchanting it is here," she said. "A true palace. And the music, so piercing, but beautiful. It hurts my ears, but then I do not like loud noises—screeching birds, guns!"

"Of course you don't," he said with surprise. "You're such a fragile creature. And your hair, may I tell that your hair is lovely? It's a rare thing to see a woman who wears her hair free, and natural. It makes you look like a goddess."

"Yes, that is very okay. Thank you."

He had a sweet laugh. So honest. No fear in his eyes, no

shrinking. He was like a prince who had been reared with kind nurses in a palace. Altogether too gentle for the real world.

"Would you mind terribly telling me your name?" he asked. "I know we've not been properly introduced, so we must introduce ourselves, it seems."

"My name is Cleopatra, Queen of Egypt." How she loved this dancing, being carried along, turned about; the floor shimmered like water beneath her.

"Oh, I could almost believe you," he said. "You look like a Queen. May I call you Your Highness?"

She laughed. "Your High-ness. Is that the proper address for a Queen! Yes, you may call me Your High-ness. And I shall call you Lord Summerfield. These men here, are they all . . . lords?"

Through the dark mirror on the panelled wall, Elliott saw Winthrop and his cohorts withdraw. Pitfield came directly back and took his chair opposite. He signaled for another drink.

"More mayhem," he said. "What in God's name has happened to young Stratford!"

"Tell me."

"Astonishing! Some belly dancer, Henry Stratford's mistress. They found her dead, neck broken, in the garden of the house she was sharing with Henry. All Henry's things were there. Passport, money, everything."

Elliott swallowed. He needed another drink badly. It occurred to him that he ought to take some supper just so that he could go on drinking without passing out.

"Same thing that happened to the Oxford student this afternoon, neck broken, and the American kid out at the pyramids, and the maid at the museum. Wonder why he bothered to use a knife on Sharples! You'd better tell me everything you know about this."

The waiter set down the fresh glasses of Scotch and gin. Elliott took his drink and sipped it thoughtfully.

"Just what I was afraid of, the whole thing. He was going out of his mind with guilt."

"Over the gambling."

"No. Over Lawrence. It was Henry, you see, and the poisons in the tomb."

"Good Lord, man, are you serious?"

"Gerald, that's how it all started. He had papers for Lawrence to sign. He probably forged them. But that's not the point. He admitted the killing.''

"To you."

"No, to someone else." He broke off, had to think this through, but there was no time. "To Ramsey."

"Ramsey, the one they're searching for."

"Yes, Ramsey tried to talk to him, early this morning, before Henry went on the rampage and broke into the museum. By the way . . . you said they'd been to the belly dancer's house. Did they find any evidence of a mummy there, any wrappings? That would certainly tie it up and then they'd stop persecuting poor Ramsey. Ramsey is entirely innocent, you see. He went to the museum to reason with Henry.''

"You know this for a fact?"

"It was all my fault. I can't sleep of late, pain in my joints is too severe. Five o'clock this morning I was just coming in from my walk. I'd seen Henry, roaring drunk, near the museum, as I told you. I thought he was pub crawling. And I made the mistake of telling Ramsey, who had just come down for his morning coffee. Ramsey had tried to reason with Henry earlier. And off he went to find him again, for Julie's sake.''

"Julie and this Ramsey, they're . . ."

"Yes. The engagement's off with Alex. It's all quite amicable; Alex and Ramsey are friends. And the whole thing must be straightened out.''

"Of course, of course."

"Ramsey was trying to stop the robbery when the police apprehended him. He's a strange man. He panicked. But surely you can get this cleared up.''

"Well, I can do my damnedest. But why in the world would Stratford break into the museum to steal a mummy?''

"That part I can't quite figure." Understatement of the year, he thought. "All I know is that the mummy of Ramses the Damned in London is missing too and apparently he stole some coins and jewelry as well. I believe somebody may have put him up to it. Steal a pair of valuable relics, get some ready cash, that sort of thing.''

"So he goes blundering into the most famous museum in the entire world?''

"Egyptian security isn't very good, old boy. And you haven't seen Henry in the last few months, have you? He's quite deteriorated, my friend. This may be a case of pure insanity. The thing is, I can't have Alex and Julie detained in Cairo. And they won't leave until Ramsey's cleared, and Ramsey has not done anything.''

He finished off the gin.

"Gerald, get us off the hook, all of us. I'll make a statement, if you advise it. I'll try to reach Ramsey. If he's granted immunity, then surely he'll back me up. You can handle it, Gerald, you know these colonial idiots! You've put up with them for years.''

"Yes, I certainly have. This has to be handled delicately, but immediately. And the fact is, they're on to Stratford. It's merely a question of exonerating Ramsey.''

"Yes, and protocol and propriety and paperwork and all the other colonial rot. Go to it, Gerald. I don't care what you do, I have to get my son home. I've used my son badly in all this. . . .''

"What?''

"Nothing. Can you work it out?''

"Yes, but Henry himself . . . Have you any idea where he could be?''

In the vat of bitumen. Elliott shuddered. "No," he said. "No idea at all. But he has many enemies out there, people whom he owes money. I need another drink. Get the attention of the pretty little nitwit, will you?''

"Young Lord Summerfield," she said, gazing at his beautiful mouth, "let us banquet in my rooms. And leave this place to be alone there.''

"If you wish." The inevitable flame in the cheeks. Oh, what would the rest of the young body look like? Pray there was a priapic organ there worthy of all the other charms!

"Indeed, but do *you* wish?'' she asked him. She ran the backs of her fingers along his cheek. Then slid her fingers under the stiff cloth of his garment.

"Yes, I do,'' he whispered.

She led him off the dance floor, collecting her handbags as they went out of the swimming music and lights, back into the crowded grand room.

"Suite two-oh-one," she said, producing the key. "How do we find it?''

"Well, we'll just take the lift to the second floor,'' he said, beaming at her. "And walk to the very front of the building.''

The lift? He led her towards a pair of brass gates. He pressed a small button in the wall.

A huge drawing stood between these gates: *Aïda*, the opera. And there were the same Egyptian figures she'd seen before. "Ah, the opera," she said.

"Yes, quite an event," he said. The brass gate had opened, and a man inside the small chamber appeared to be waiting for them. She stepped inside. It was like a cage. And it frightened her suddenly. The doors clanged shut. Some sort of trap, and the room began to rise.

"Lord Summerfield," she cried.

"It's quite all right, Your Highness," he said. He threw his arms around her, and turning, she bowed her head against his chest. Oh, he was so much sweeter than all the others, and when a strong man is sweet, even goddesses look down from Mount Olympus.

At last the doors opened. He led her out and into a silent passageway. They walked towards a distant window.

"What frightened you so?" he asked. But his intonation had no mockery or disapproval. It was almost soothing. He took the key from her, and put it in the lock.

"The room moved," she sighed. "Are those not the right English words?"

"Yes, they are," he said. He paused as they entered the long sitting room, with rich hangings and chairs that looked for all the world like giant cushions. "Why, you are the strangest creature. So out of this world."

She reached out and caressed his face, and slowly kissed him. His brown eyes were troubled, suddenly. But then he kissed her back, and the sudden fire surprised her and thrilled her.

"For this night, Lord Summerfield," she said, "this is my palace; and now we must go and seek the royal bedchamber."

Elliott walked to the door of the bar with Pitfield. "I can't thank you enough for coming immediately."

"Have every confidence, old boy, and do see if you can get some word to your friend. Of course, I can't advise you to—"

"I know, I know. Let me handle that." Elliott went back into the bar, settled down into the leather chair and picked up the gin. Yes, definitely he would slowly drink himself to death when this was over.

He would go out to the country, stock the finest sherry and

port and Scotch and gin, and just drink day in and day out until he was dead. It would be very simply wonderful. He saw himself there, by the great log fire, one foot on the leather ottoman. The image shimmered; then faded. The sickness rose in his throat, and he was near to breaking down completely.

"Get Alex home; get him home and safe," he whispered, and then he began to tremble almost uncontrollably. He saw her again, moving through the museum with her arms out. And then in the bed looking up at him: he felt her caress, and the bare bones in her side as she'd pressed against him. He remembered the crazed look in Ramsey's eyes when he'd fought her.

The trembling got worse. Much worse.

No one noticed in the dark bar; a pianist had come in—a young man, who began to play a slow ragtime.

He had helped her with her fine dress of green satin. He laid it over the chair; and when the lights went out, she saw the city through the pale curtains. She saw the river.

"The Nile," she whispered. She wanted to say how beautiful, this gleaming strip of water winding through the built-up city; but a shadow fell over her soul. An image came to her like all the rest; descending complete and entire and then vanishing; only this one had been so quick. A catacomb, a priest walking before her.

"What is it, Your Highness?"

She lifted her head slowly. She'd moaned; that's what had frightened him.

"You're so tender with me, young Lord Summerfield," she said. Where was the inevitable unkindness in this boy? The inevitable need to hurt which all men evinced sooner or later?

She looked up and saw that he was now naked as well, and the sight of his strong, youthful body pleased her intensely. She placed her hand on his flat belly, and then gently on his chest. It was always the hardness of men all over that excited her; even the hardness of their mouths, that they tensed their mouths when they kissed; she liked even to feel their teeth behind their lips.

She kissed him roughly and pressed her breasts against him. He could hardly control himself; he wanted to carry her to the bed; he tried to be gentle.

"Such an unearthly thing," he whispered. "Wherever did you come from?"

"From darkness and coldness. Kiss me. I am only warm

again when I'm kissed. Make a fire, Lord Summerfield, to burn both of us.''

She went back against the pillows, tugging him down on top of her. Her hand plunged, grasped his sex and stroked it, pinching the tip. When he moaned, she opened his lips with her own, licking at his tongue and his teeth.

''Now,'' she said. ''Into me. The second time is for the slow song.''

Julie's suite. Samir set the newspapers down on the table. Julie drank a second cup of the sweet Egyptian coffee.

''You mustn't leave me tonight, Samir. Not till we hear from him,'' she said. She stood up. ''I'm going to change into my robe. Promise me you won't leave me.''

''I'll be here, Julie,'' he said, ''but perhaps you should sleep. I'll wake you as soon as I hear anything.''

''No, I can't do that. I want only to get out of these tired clothes. I won't be but a minute.''

She went into the bedroom. She had sent Rita off an hour ago to her own room, and thank God for that; she wanted only to be with Samir. Her nerves were worn thin. She knew Elliott was in the hotel, but she could not bring herself to ring him. She did not want to see him or talk to him. Not until she knew what Ramses had done, and she could not break the feeling of foreboding.

Slowly she took the pins out of her hair, gazing absently in the mirror. For a moment, she noticed nothing amiss, and then suddenly she realized that a tall Arab in white robes was standing in the corner of the room, still as the shadows, merely watching her. Her Arab, Ramses.

She spun around, her hair tumbling down all at once over her shoulders. Her heart was about to burst.

She might have fainted again for the second time in her life, if he hadn't caught her. Then she saw the deep bloodstain on his robe and again she felt weak; blackness rising all around her.

Silently he embraced her, pressing her to himself.

''My Julie,'' he said, his voice heartbroken.

''How long have you been here?''

''Only a little while,'' he said. ''Let me be silent now; let me hold you.''

''Where is she?''

He let her go, backing off. "I don't know," he said in a defeated voice. "I have lost her."

Julie watched him as he paced, turned and looked at her from a distance. She was keenly aware that she loved him, and would go on loving him no matter what had happened. But she could not say such a thing to him, not until she knew. . . .

"Let me call Samir," she said. "He's there, in the sitting room."

"I want to be alone with you for a moment," he said. And for the first time, he appeared just slightly afraid of her. It was a subtle thing, but she felt it.

"You must tell me what's happened."

He remained impassive, looking at her, the sheikh robes doing their damnedest to make him irresistible. And then suddenly his expression broke her heart; no use denying it.

In a tremulous voice, she said, "You gave her more of it."

"You haven't seen her," he said quietly, his voice unhurried, his eyes full of undisguised sorrow. "You have not heard the sound of her voice! You have not heard her weeping. Don't judge me. She is as alive as I am! I brought her back. Let me judge myself."

She clasped her hands tightly, hurting the fingers of her right hand with the fingers of the other.

"What do you mean, you don't know where she is?"

"I mean she escaped from me. She attacked me; she tried to kill me. And she is mad. Lord Rutherford was right. Absolutely mad. She would have killed him if I hadn't stopped her. The elixir hasn't changed that. It merely healed her body."

He took a step towards her, and before she could stop herself she turned her back. She was going to cry again; oh, so many tears. And she didn't want to.

"Pray to your gods," she said, looking at him through the mirror. "Ask them what to do. My God would only condemn you. But whatever happens with this creature, one thing is certain." She turned and looked him in the eye. "You must never, never brew the elixir again. Whatever remains, consume it. Do it now in my presence. And then erase the formula from your mind."

No response. Slowly he removed the headdress, and ran his hand back through his hair. For some reason this only made him look all the more gallant and seductive. A biblical figure now with flowing hair and flowing robes. It maddened her slightly, and made the threat of tears all the more sharp.

"Do you realize what you're saying?"

"If it's too dangerous to consume it, then find someplace far out in the desert sands, and make a deep shaft into which to pour it! But get rid of it."

"Let me put a question to you."

"No." She turned her back again. She covered her ears. When she looked up she saw in the mirror that he was right at her shoulder. There was that awareness again of her own world destroyed, of a brilliant light having thrown all else into hopeless shadow.

Gently, he took her hands, and lowered them from her ears. He looked into her eyes through the mirror, his body warm and close to her.

"Julie, last night. If instead of taking the elixir with me to the museum, if instead of pouring it over Cleopatra's remains— if instead, I'd offered it to you, wouldn't you have taken it?"

She refused to answer. Roughly he grabbed her wrist and turned her around.

"Answer me! If I had never seen her lying there in that glass case . . ."

"But you did."

She meant to hold firm, but he surprised her with his kiss, with the roughness and the desperation of his embrace, with his hands moving over her face and her cheek almost cruelly. He was saying her name like a prayer. He murmured something in the ancient Egyptian tongue, she didn't know what it was. And then he said softly in Latin that he loved her. He loved her. It seemed both explanation and apology, somehow, the reason for all this suffering. He loved her. He said it as if he were just realizing it, and now her tears were coming again, stupidly. It infuriated her.

She pulled back; then kissed him and let him kiss her again, and sank against his chest, merely letting him hold her.

Then softly she said:

"What does she look like?"

He sighed.

"Is she beautiful?"

"She always was. She is now. She is the woman who seduced Caesar, and Mark Antony, and the whole world."

She stiffened, drawing away from him.

"She is as beautiful as you are," he said. "But you are right. She is not Cleopatra. She is a stranger in Cleopatra's body. A monster looking through Cleopatra's eyes. And struggling to use Cleopatra's wits to her own purposeless advantage."

What more was there to say? What could she do? It was in his hands, it had been since the beginning. She forced him to release her and then she sat down and leaned her elbow on the arm of the chair and rested her forehead in her hand.

"I'll find her," he said. "And I will undo this awful error. I will put her back into the darkness from which I took her. And she will suffer only a little while. And then she will sleep."

"Oh, but it's too awful! There must be some other way. . . ." She broke into sobs.

"What have I done to you, Julie Stratford?" he said. "What have I done to your life, all your tender dreams and ambitions?"

She took her handkerchief out of her pocket and pressed it to her mouth. She forced herself to stop this foolish crying. She wiped her nose, then looked up at him, the great handsome dreamy figure he was standing there with that tragic expression. A man, only a man. Immortal, yes, a ruler once, a teacher always, perhaps, but human as we all are. Fallible as we all are. Lovable as we all are.

"I cannot live without you, Ramses," she said. "Well, I could. But I don't want to." Ah, tears from him now. If she didn't look away, she'd be weeping again. "Reason has nothing to do with it anymore," she went on. "But it's this creature you've wronged. It's this thing you've resurrected that will be hurt. You speak of burying her alive. I cannot . . . I cannot . . ."

"Trust in me that I shall find a painless way," he whispered.

She couldn't speak. She couldn't look at him.

"And know this, for what it's worth. Know it now because later it may bring confusion. Your cousin Henry is dead. Cleopatra killed him."

"What!"

"It was to Henry's abode in the old Cairo that Elliott took her. He did follow me to the museum. And when the soldiers took me away, Elliott gave shelter to the creature I'd resurrected. He took her there, and there she killed both Henry and the woman, Malenka."

She shook her head, and once again her hands went up to her ears. All the things she knew of Henry, of her father's death, of his attempt on her life, somehow could not help her now; they could not touch her. She heard only the horror.

"Trust in me when I say that I shall find a painless way. For that I must do before more innocent blood is shed. I cannot turn my back until it's finished."

"My son left no message?" Elliott had not forsaken the leather chair, or the gin, and had no intention of doing so. But he knew he had to call Alex before he got any drunker. And so he'd sent for the telephone. "But he wouldn't go out without telling me. All right. Samir Ibrahaim, where is he? Can you ring his room for me?"

"He's in Miss Stratford's suite, sir. Two-oh-three. He requests that any messages be sent there. Shall I ring? It is eleven of the clock, sir."

"No, I'll go up, thank you."

She leaned over the marble lavatory. She slapped the cold water on her face. She didn't want to look into the mirror. Then slowly she wiped her eyes with the towel. When she turned around, she saw him standing in the sitting room. She could hear Samir's low, comforting voice.

"Of course I will help you, sire, but where do we begin?"

There was a sharp rap on the hall door.

Ramses stepped back into the bedroom. Samir went to answer. It was Elliott. Their eyes met for only a moment, and then she looked away, unable to judge him and unable to face him. She thought only, He has had a hand in this. He knows it all; he knows more than I know. And suddenly her revulsion for the whole nightmare was insupportable.

She went into the sitting room, and took the chair in the far corner.

"I shall come right to the point," Elliott said, looking directly at Ramses. "I have a plan and I need your cooperation. But before I begin, let me remind you that it isn't safe here for you."

"They find me, I escape again," Ramses said with a shrug. "What is this plan?"

"A plan to get Julie and my son out of here," Elliott said. "But what happened after I left? You want to tell me?"

"She is as you described her. Mad, incalculably strong, and

dangerous. Only she is whole now. No longer disfigured. And her eyes are the colour of the blue sky, just as mine are.''

''Ah.''

Elliott fell silent, as if he'd felt a sharp pain inside and had to hold his breath to let it pass. Julie realized suddenly he was drunk, really drunk. It was perhaps the first time she'd seen him this way. He was dignified, restrained, but drunk. He reached out for Samir's glass, still half-full of brandy, and drank it almost absently.

Quietly Samir went to the small rattan drinks cupboard in the corner and got a bottle for him.

''You saved my life,'' Elliott said to Ramses. ''I thank you for that.''

Ramses shrugged. But the tone of all this struck Julie as curious. It was intimate, as though these two men knew each other quite well. There was no animosity.

''What is this plan?'' Ramses said.

''You must cooperate. You must tell lies. You must do that effectively. And the end result will be that you are cleared of the crimes of which you're suspected, and Julie and Alex will be free to leave here. Samir also will no longer be under suspicion. Then other matters can be attended to. . . .''

''I'm not going anywhere, Elliott,'' Julie said wearily. ''But Alex must be allowed to go home as soon as possible.''

Samir poured another drink of brandy for Elliott, and Elliott took it mechanically and drank it. ''Any gin, Samir? I prefer gin for getting drunk,'' he said.

''Come to the point, my lord,'' said Ramses. ''I must be taking my leave. The last Queen of Egypt roams this city alone, with a penchant for killing; I must find her.''

''This will take a strong stomach,'' Elliott said, ''but there's a way that all of this can be pinned on Henry. He laid the ground himself. But Ramsey, you have to lie as I told you. . . .''

The quiet of the night. Alex Savarell lay naked and asleep on the snow-white sheets of the soft feather bed, the thin wool blanket covering him only to the waist, his face smooth and waxen in the moonlight.

In the sweet stillness, she had undone her many parcels quietly, examining the fine robes, gowns, slippers. She had laid out the little rectangular stolen opera papers which said ''Admit One'' on the dressing table.

The moon shone on the rich silks. It sparkled in the rope of pearls, coiled like a snake on the table. And beyond the sheer finespun curtains on the window, it shone upon the Nile flowing into the soft tangle of rounded roofs and towers that was Cairo.

Cleopatra stood at the window, her back to the soft bed and the godlike young man who lay there. Divinely he had pleasured her; divinely she had pleasured him. His innocence and simple male power were treasures to her; her mystery and skill had overwhelmed him. Never had he placed himself in the hands of a woman thus, he had said. Never had he given vent to all his whims with such abandon.

And now he slept the sleep that children sleep, safe in the bed, as she stood at the window. . . .

. . . As dreams came to her, pretending to be memories. It occurred to her that she had not known the night since she'd been awakened. She had not known the cool mystery of the night, when thoughts tend naturally to deepen. And what came to her now were images of other nights, of real palaces, resplendent with marble floors and pillars, and tables laden with fruit and roasted meat and wine in silver pitchers. Of Ramses speaking to her, as they lay together in the dark.

"I love you, as I've loved no other woman. To live without you . . . it would not be life."

"My King, my only King," she had said. "What are the others, but toys on a child's battlefield? Little wooden emperors moved by chance from place to place."

It dimmed; it moved away from her. She lost it as she had lost the other memories. And what was real was the voice of Alex stirring in his sleep.

"Your Highness, where are you?"

Misery like a spell had descended upon her, and he could not pierce the veil. It was too heavy; too dark. She sang to herself, that song, that sweet song from the music box, "Celeste Aïda." And then when she turned and saw his face in the moonlight, his eyes closed, his hand open on the sheet, she felt a deep and soulful longing. She hummed the song, her lips closed as she approached the bed and looked down at him.

Tenderly she stroked his hair. Tenderly her fingertips touched his eyelids. Ah, sleeping god, my sweet Endymion. Her hand moved down, lazily, and touched his throat, touched the tender bones she had broken in the others.

Frail and mortal thing for all your strength, your finely muscled arms, your smooth flat chest, powerful hands that pleasure me.

She didn't want him to know death! She didn't want him to suffer. A great protectiveness rose in her. She lifted the white blanket and snuggled down into the warm bed beside him. She would never harm this one, never, that she knew. And suddenly death itself seemed a frightful and unjust thing.

But why am I immortal when he is not? Ye gods. For one second it seemed a great portal opened on a vast place of light and all answers were revealed; her past, who she was, what had happened, all those things were clear. But it was dark and quiet in this room. There was no such illumination.

"My love, my pretty young love," she said, kissing him again. At once he stirred; responded. He opened his arms to her.

"Your Highness."

She felt the hardness again between his legs; she wanted it to fill her again, to bruise her. She smiled to herself. If one cannot be immortal, one should at least be young, she thought ruefully.

Ramses had listened silently for a long time before he spoke.

"So what you are saying is that we must tell this elaborate tale to the authorities, that I argued with him, followed him inside, saw him take the mummy from the case, and then the soldiers apprehended me."

"You lied for Egypt when you were King, did you not? You lied to your people when you told them you were the living god."

"But, Elliott," Julie broke in. "What if these crimes continue?"

"And they very well might," said Ramses impatiently, "if I don't get out of here and find her."

"There is no proof that Henry's dead," Elliott said, "and no one is going to find any. It's perfectly plausible that Henry's roaming around Cairo. And what is plausible is what they'll accept. Pitfield leapt at this nonsense. So will they. And they can hunt for Henry as you hunt for her. But Alex and Julie will be safely out of it by then."

"No, I told you," Julie said, "I'll persuade Alex to go. . . ."

"Julie, I can come to you later in London," Ramses said. "Lord Rutherford's a clever man. He would have made a good King, or a King's wily adviser."

Elliott gave a bitter smile and drank down his third glass of straight gin.

"I shall make this poetry of lies as convincing as I can. What else must we discuss?" Ramses said.

"It's settled. Ten A.M. you must call me. By then I'll have a guarantee of immunity for you from the governor himself. Then you must come to the governor's palace and make your statement. And we do not leave without the passports."

"Very well," Ramses said. "I leave you now. Wish me good fortune."

"But where will you begin to search?" Julie asked. "And when will you sleep?"

"You forget, my beauty. I don't need to sleep. I'll search for her until we meet here again before ten o'clock. Lord Rutherford, if this fails to work . . ."

"It will work. And we shall go to the opera tomorrow night precisely as planned and to the ball afterwards."

"That's absurd!" Julie said.

"No, my child. Do it for me. It's the last demand I shall ever make on you. I want the social fabric restored. I want my son to be seen with his father, and his friends; with Ramsey, whose name shall be cleared. I want us all to be seen together. I want no shadows over Alex's future. And whatever the future holds for you, don't shut the gate on the life you once lived. It's worth the price of one night's pomp and ceremony to keep that gate open."

"Ah, Lord Rutherford, how you always amuse me and satisfy me," Ramses said. "In another world and another life, I used to say such inane things myself to those around me. It's palaces and titles which do such things to us. But I've remained here long enough. Samir, come with me if you will. Otherwise I'm going alone now."

"I'm with you, sire," Samir said. He rose and made a ceremonial little bow to Elliott. "Until tomorrow, my lord."

Ramses went out first; then Samir. For a moment Julie couldn't move; then she rose out of the chair and went running out of the door after Ramses. She caught him in the dark stairwell at the rear of the wing, and once again, they held each other.

"Please love me, Julie Stratford," he whispered. "I am not always such a fool, I swear it." He held her face in his hands.

"You'll go to London where you are safe, and you shall see me when this horror is finished."

She went to protest.

"I do not lie to you. I love you too much for that. I have told you everything."

She watched him slip down the stairs. He put the headdress on again and became the sheikh before he went out into the darkness, one hand raised in a graceful farewell.

She didn't want to return to her rooms. She didn't want to see Elliott.

She knew now why he had made this journey; she had sensed it all along, but now she knew for certain. Following Ramses to the museum, that he had ever gone to such an extreme, astonished her.

On second thought, why should it astonish her? After all, he had believed; he had been the only one, other than Samir, perhaps, who believed. And so the mystery and the promise had lured him.

As she walked back to her rooms, she prayed he understood the full evil that had unfolded. And when she thought of any creature—no matter how evil or dangerous or cruel—being shut up in the dark, unable to wake, she shuddered and began to cry again.

He was there still, drinking the last of the gin as he sat in the overstuffed chair, so self-contained and elegant even in his drunkenness, hands curved around the cane.

He did not look up when she came in. He did not gather his strength to leave. She shut the door and faced him.

Her words came swiftly, without thought. But she made no accusations. She told him only all that Ramses had said. She told the tale of the food that could not be eaten, and the cattle that could not be slaughtered, the tale of the insatiable hunger and craving of the flesh; she told the tale of loneliness, of isolation; it all came in a rush, as she paced back and forth, not looking at him, not meeting his eyes.

And finally it was done and the room was still.

"When we were young," he said, "your father and I, we spent many months in Egypt. We pored over our books; we studied the ancient tombs; we translated the texts; we roamed the sands by day and by night. Ancient Egypt; it became our muse, our religion. We dreamed of some secret knowledge here that would transport us from all the things that seemed to lead to boredom and finally hopelessness.

"Did the pyramids really contain some secret yet undiscovered? Did the Egyptians know a magic language to which the gods themselves listen? What undiscovered tombs lay within these hills? What philosophy remained to be revealed? What alchemy?

"Or did this culture produce a mere semblance of high learning; a semblance of true mystery? We wondered now and then if they had been not wise, and mystical, but a simple, literal, brutal people.

"We never knew. I don't know now. I see now it was the quest that was the passion! The quest, you understand?"

She didn't answer. When she looked at him, he looked very old. His eyes were leaden. He climbed out of the chair, and came towards her, and kissed her cheek. He did this as gracefully as he did all things. That strange thought came to her again which had come so often in the past. She could have loved him and married him, had there been no Alex and no Edith.

And no Ramses.

"I fear for you, my dear," he said. And then he left her.

The night, the silent empty night, with only the thinnest echo of the music below, lay before her. And all her past countless nights of good and dreamless sleep seemed like the lost comforts and delusions of childhood.

7

DAWN. THE great endless rosy sky spread out beyond the dim shadows of the pyramids and the roughened, disfigured Sphinx, with his paws sprawled on the yellow sand before him.

The dim shape of the Mena House lay still and quiet with only a few tiny lights in its rear rooms.

Only a solitary man, draped in black, rode his ugly camel across the horizon. Somewhere a steam train gave its deep, throbbing whistle.

Ramses walked through the sand, his garments blown back by the cold wind, until he came to the giant Sphinx and stood between its feet looking up at the ruined face, which in his time had been beautiful still, covered over in a fine casing of shining limestone.

"But you stand here still," he whispered in the ancient tongue, surveying this ruin.

In the cool still morning, he let himself remember a time when all answers had seemed to him to be so simple; when he the brave King had taken life with a swift blow of his sword or his cudgel. When he'd struck down the priestess in her cave so no one else would possess the great secret.

A thousand times he'd wondered if that had not been his first and most terrible sin—to kill the innocent crone whose laughter still echoed in his ears.

I am not fool enough to drink it.

Was he truly damned for that? A wanderer on the face of the earth like the biblical Cain, marked by this great eternal vigour which separated him from all humankind forever?

He did not know. He knew only that he could not bear to be the only one any longer. He had blundered, he would blunder again. It was a certainty now.

Yet what if his isolation was meant? And every attempt would end in such disaster?

He laid his hand on the hard rough stone of the Sphinx's paw. The sand was deep and soft here, and the wind stirred it as it ruffled his robes, and tore at his eyes cruelly.

Again he looked up at the disfigured face. He thought back to the age when he had come here in pilgrimage and in procession. He heard the flutes, the drums. He smelled the incense again and heard the soft, rhythmic incantations.

He made his own prayer now, but it was in the language and the manner of those times which gave him some sweet childish comfort.

"God of my fathers; of my land. Look down on me with forgiveness. Teach me the way; teach me what I must do to give back to nature what I have taken. Or do I walk away in all humility, crying that I have blundered enough? I am no god. I know nothing of creation. And little of justice.

"But one thing is certain. Those who made us all know little of justice, either. Or what they do know, great Sphinx, is like your wisdom. A very great secret."

The great grey shadow of Shepheard's Hotel grew darker and ever more solid in the rising light as Samir and Ramses approached it—two robed figures moving swiftly and silently together.

A cumbersome black truck, rocking on its four wheels, pulled into the front drive before they reached it. Newspapers in tightly bound bundles were thrown down upon the pavement.

Samir removed one quickly from the first bundle as the bellboys came out to collect the others. He felt in his pocket for a coin and gave it to one of the boys, who took little heed of it.

ROBBERY AND MURDER IN DRESS SHOP

Ramses read the headline over his shoulder.
The two men looked at each other.

Then they walked away from the sleeping hotel, in search of some early morning cafe where they might sit and think and read this evil news, and ponder what to do about it.

Her eyes were open when the first rays of the sun pierced the thin curtains. How beautiful it looked to her, the great arms of the god, reaching out to touch her.

How stupid the Greeks had been to think the mighty disk the chariot of a deity, driven wildly over the horizon.

Her ancestors had known: the sun was the god Ra. The giver of life. The one and only god before all gods, without whom all gods were nothing.

The sun struck the mirror; and a great golden glare filled the room, blinding her for an instant. She sat up in the bed, her hand resting lightly on the shoulder of her lover. A dizziness overcame her. It seemed her head was teeming suddenly.

"Ramses!" she whispered.

The warm sun fell silently over her face, her knotted brows and her closed eyelids. She felt it on her breasts and on her outstretched arm.

Tingling; warmth; a sudden great breath of well-being.

She rose from the bed, and moved on swift feet across the deep green carpet. Softer than grass, it ate the sound of her steps completely.

She stood in the window looking out over the square, looking out again to the great silver glare of the river. With the back of her hand, she touched her own warm cheek.

A deep ripple of sensation passed through her. It was as if a wind had caught her hair and lifted it lightly off her neck; a hot desert wind, stealing over the sands, slipping into the palace halls, and creeping over her, and somehow into her, and through her.

Her hair made a soft zinging sound as if being stroked by a hairbrush.

In the catacombs it had begun! The old priest had told the tale, and they all laughed at supper. An immortal slumbering in a deep rock tomb, Ramses the Damned, counsel to dynasties past, who had gone to sleep in the dark in the time of her great-great-grandfathers.

And when she'd awakened, she'd called for him.

"It is an old legend. My father's father told it to him, though he did not believe it. But I have seen him with my own eyes, the sleeping King. Yet you must be aware of the danger.''

Thirteen years old. She did not believe in such a thing as danger; not in the ordinary sense; there had always been danger.

They walked together through the rough-cut stone passage. Dust fell from the loose ceiling above. The priest carried the torch before them.

''What danger? These catacombs are the danger. They may cave in on us!''

Several rocks had fallen at her feet.

''I tell you I don't like this, old man.''

The priest had pushed on. A thin baldheaded man with stooped shoulders.

''The legend says that once awakened, he cannot easily be dispatched. He is no mindless thing, but an immortal man with a will of his own. He will counsel the King or Queen of Egypt, as he has done in the past, but he will do as he pleases as well.''

''My father knew of this?''

''He was told. He did not believe. Neither did your father's father, or his father. Ah, but King Ptolemy, in the time of Alexander, he knew, and he called Ramses forth saying the words: 'Rise, Ramses the Great, a King of Egypt needs your counsel.' ''

''And he returned, this Ramses, to his darkened chamber? Leaving only the priests with the secret?''

''So I have been told, as my father was told, and that I should come to the sovereign of my time and tell the story.''

It was hot, suffocating, in this place. No coolness of the deep earth here. She did not like to go any further. She did not like the flickering of the torch; the evil light on the rounded ceiling. Here and there were marks on the walls, scribbles in the ancient picture language. She could not read them; who could? It made her afraid, and she loathed being afraid.

And they had taken so many twists and turns that she could never find her own way out now.

''Yes, tell the Queen of your time the tale,'' she said, ''while she is young enough and fool enough to listen.''

''Young enough to have faith. That is what you have; faith and dreams. Wisdom is not always the gift of old age, Majesty. Rather, it is sometimes the curse.''

''And so we go to this ancient one?'' She had laughed.

''Courage, Majesty. He lies there, beyond those doors.''

She'd peered ahead. There *were* a pair of doors—enormous doors! Layered over with dust, and covered beneath the dust with inscriptions. Her heart had quickened.

"Take me into this chamber."

"Yes, Majesty. But remember the caution. Once waked he cannot be sent away. He is a powerful immortal."

"I don't care! I want to see this!"

She'd gone ahead of the old man. In the dancing glow from his torch she'd read the Greek aloud:

"Here lies Ramses the Immortal. Called by himself Ramses the Damned, for he can not die. And sleeps eternally, waiting the call of the Kings and Queens of Egypt."

She'd stepped back.

"Open the doors! Hurry!"

Behind her, he had touched some secret place in the wall. With a great grinding the doors had slid back slowly, revealing a vast unadorned chamber.

The priest had raised the torch high as he entered beside her. Dust, the clean pale yellow dust of a cave unknown to the wild beasts or the poor wanderers and haunters of hills and caves and tombs.

And there on the altar, a gaunt shriveled being, withered limbs crossed on his breasts; brown hair wisps about his skull.

"You poor fool. He's dead. The dry air here preserves him."

"No, Majesty. See the shutter high above, and the chains hanging from it. It must be opened now."

He had given her the torch, and with both hands tugged upon the chains. Again, the grinding, the creaking; dust filling the air, stinging her eyes, but then high above a great iron-bound shutter had opened. Like an eye into the blue heavens.

The hot summer sun poured down upon the sleeping man. Her eyes had grown wide; what words were there to describe what she had seen, the body filling out; reviving. The brown hair flowing from the scalp, and then the eyelids, shuddering, eyelashes curling.

"He lives. It's true."

She'd thrown aside the torch and run to the altar. She'd bent over him, as far as she dared not to shade him from the sun.

And the brilliant blue eyes had opened!

"Ramses the Great, rise! A Queen of Egypt needs your counsel."

Motionless, silent, staring up at her.

"So beautiful," he had whispered.

She stared out at the square before Shepheard's Hotel. She saw the city of Cairo coming to life. The carts, the motor cars, moved noisily through the clean paved streets; birds sang in the neatly trimmed trees. Barges moved on the smooth river water.

The words of Elliott Rutherford came back to her. "Many centuries have passed . . . modern times . . . Egypt has had many conquerors . . . wonders such as you cannot imagine."

Ramses stood before her in the Bedouin robes, weeping, begging her to listen.

In the dark place of glinting glass and statues and coffins on end, she'd risen up, in pain, her arms out, crying his name!

The blood had poured down his shirt where they'd wounded him. Yet he'd staggered towards her. Then the second shot had struck his arm. Same evil pain that the one called Henry had given to her, same blood and pain, and in the murky morning light, she'd seen them drag him away.

I can't die now. Isn't that right?

Ramses had stood at the door of her bedchamber. She'd been crying, a young queen in torment. "But for how many years?"

"I don't know. I only know you cannot give up all this now. You don't know the meaning of what I offer you. So let me go. Use the knowledge I've given you, I'll return. Be sure of it. I'll return when you most have need of me, and then perhaps you will have had your lovers and had your warm and had your grief, and you will welcome me."

"But I love you."

The bedroom of Shepheard's Hotel was awash in blinding light; the furnishings vanished in the pulsing glow. The soft curtains touched her face as they blew out past her. She leaned forward over the windowsill, drowsing; her head swimming.

"Ramses, I remember!"

In the dress shop, the look on the woman's face! The serving girl screaming. And the young man, the poor young man who had looked down and seen the bone!

Ye gods, what have you done to me!

She turned, staggering away from the light, but it was all around her. The mirror was ablaze. She went down on her knees, her hands on the warm green rug. She lay down, tossing, turning, trying to push away the fierce power that penetrated her brain; that penetrated her heart. A great pulsing vibration had caught her entire form. She floated in space. And finally lay still in the great vibrating drift, the hot light blanketing her skin, an orange fire against her eyelids.

Elliott sat alone on the deep veranda. The empty bottle sparkled in the light of the morning sun. He dozed as he lay against the cushioned back of the chair, mind now and then wandering. Fasting, drinking, the long sleepless night, all had sharpened him and left him slightly mad; it seemed the light itself was a miracle streaking the sky; it seemed the great glossy silver car rumbling up the drive was a joke of sorts; and so was the funny grey-haired man who climbed down off the high seat and came towards him.

"I've been with Winthrop all night."

"You have my sympathies."

"Old man, we have an appointment at ten-thirty to clear everything up. Can you manage it?"

"Yes. I shall manage it. You may depend upon me. And Ramsey can be there if . . . if . . . you've obtained full immunity."

"Full and complete as long as he'll sign a sworn statement against Stratford. You know of course he struck again last night, robbed a shop—woman was in there with a full drawer of cash. He took everything."

"Hmmmmm. Bastard," Elliott whispered.

"Old man, it's very important you get up out of this chair, have a good bath and a good shave and be there. . . ."

"Gerald, on my word. I shall. Ten-thirty, the governor's palace."

Blessed quiet. The ugly car had gone away. The boy came again. "Breakfast, my lord?"

"Bring a little something, and some orange juice with it. And ring my son's room again. And check the desk. Surely he's left a message!"

It was late morning before her young lord finally awoke.

Rome had fallen. And two thousand years had passed.

For hours she'd sat at the window, dressed in a "fine blue frock," watching the modern city. All the bits and pieces of what she'd seen and heard were now a complete tapestry. Yet there was so much to know, to understand.

She'd feasted, and had the servants take away the evidence;

she did not want anyone to see the bestial manner in which she'd consumed so much food.

Now his small banquet waited for him. And when he came towards her out of the bedroom, "So beautiful," she said under her breath.

"What is it, Your Highness?" He bent to kiss her. She wrapped her arms around his waist and kissed his naked chest.

"Take your breakfast, young lord," she said. "There are so many things I must discover. So many things I must see."

He seated himself at the small draped table. He lighted the candles with the "matches."

"Aren't you joining me?"

"I've already feasted, my love. Can you show me the modern city? Can you show me the palaces of the British who rule this land?"

"I'll show you everything, Your Highness," he said, with the same unguarded gentleness.

She sat across from him.

"You're very simply the strangest person I've ever met," he said, and again there was no mockery or meanness in it. "In fact, you remind me of someone I know, a very enigmatic man . . . but that doesn't matter. Why are you smiling at me like that? What are you thinking?"

"So beautiful," she whispered again. "You and all of life, my young lord. It is everything and nothing. So beautiful."

He blushed like a girl and then laid down the silver tools and leaned across the table and once again kissed her.

"You're crying," he said.

"Yes. But I am happy. Stay with me, young lord. Do not leave me just now."

He appeared startled, then transfixed. She combed the past slowly; had she ever known anyone so gentle? Perhaps in childhood, when she'd been too stupid to know what it meant.

"I don't want to leave you for the world, Your Highness," he said. He appeared sad again for a second, half disbelieving. And then at a loss.

"And the opera tonight, my lord, shall we go together? Shall we dance at the opera ball?"

Lovely the light that came to his eyes. "That would be heaven," he whispered.

She gestured to the plates before him. "Your food, my lord."

He picked at it in mortal fashion. Then lifted a bundle from beside his plate, which she had taken no notice of before. He tore off the wrapping and opened what appeared to be a thick manuscript covered over with tiny writing.

"Tell me what this is."

"Why, a newspaper," he said, half laughing. He glanced at it. "And awful news, too."

"Read aloud."

"You wouldn't really want to hear it. Some poor woman in a dress shop, with her neck broken like all the rest. And they've got a picture of Ramsey with Julie. What a disaster!"

Ramses?

"It's the talk of Cairo, Your Highness. You may as well know now. My friends have been involved in a fair bit of trouble, but that's just it, they've nothing to do with it. They've only been associated with it. There . . . you see this man?"

Ramses. *They are friends of Lawrence Stratford, the archaeologist, the one who dug up the mummy of Ramses the Damned.*

"He's a dear friend of my father and of me. They're searching for him. Some foolishness about stealing a mummy from the Cairo Museum. It's all hogwash. It will soon blow over." He broke off. "Your Highness? Don't let this story frighten you. There's nothing to it, really."

She stared at this "picture," not a drawing like the rest but a dense image, rather like a painting, yet it was all done in ink, undoubtedly. The ink even rubbed off on her fingers. And there he stood. Ramses, beside a camel and a camel driver, dressed in the curious heavy clothes of this age. The print beneath said "Valley of the Kings."

She almost laughed aloud; yet she did not move or say a word. It seemed the moment stretched into eternity. The young lord was talking, but she couldn't hear him. Was he saying that he must call his father, that his father must need him now?

In a trance, she watched him move away from her. He had laid the paper down. The picture. She looked at him. He was picking up a strange instrument from the table. He was talking into it. Asking for Lord Rutherford.

At once she was on her feet. Gently she took the thing away from him. She set it down.

"Don't leave me now, young lord," she said. "Your father can wait for you. I need you now."

Baffled, he looked at her; he made no move to stop her as she embraced him.

"Don't bring the world to us just yet," she whispered in his ear, kissing him. "Let us have this time together."

So completely he gave in. So quickly came the fire.

"Don't be timid," she whispered. "Caress me; let your hands do what they will as they did last night."

Once again he belonged to her, enslaving her with his kisses, stroking her breasts through the blue frock.

"Have you come to me by magic?" he whispered. "Just when I thought . . . when I thought . . ." And then he was kissing her again, and she led him towards the bed.

She picked up the newspaper as they went into the bedroom. As they sank down on the sheets together, she showed it to him, just as he removed the robe.

"Tell me," she said, pointing to the little group of figures standing by the camel in the sun. "Who is that woman beside him?"

"Julie, Julie Stratford," he said.

Then there were no words, only their frantic, hurried and delicious embraces; his hips grinding against her; his sex pumping into her again.

When it was all over, and he lay still, she ran her fingers through his hair.

"This woman; does he care for her?"

"Yes," he said sleepily. "And she loves him. But that doesn't matter now."

"Why do you say this?"

"Because I have you," he said.

Ramsey was at his best, evincing that easy charm that had subdued everyone on the voyage out; he sat back, spotless and carelessly fashionable in the white linen suit, his hair tousled, blue eyes sparkling with a near boyish vigour.

"I tried to reason with him. When he broke the case and removed the mummy, I realized it was hopeless. I tried to get out on my own, but the guards, well, you know the story."

"But they said they shot you, they—"

"Sir, these men are not the soldiers of ancient Egypt. They're hirelings who barely know how to fire their guns. They would not have beaten the Hittites."

Winthrop laughed in spite of himself. Even Gerald was charmed. Elliott glanced at Samir, who dared not crack the smallest smile.

"Well, if only we could find Henry," Miles said.

"No doubt his creditors are looking for him, too," Ramsey said quickly.

"Well, let's get back to this question of the jail. It seems there was a doctor there when you—"

Gerald finally intervened:

"Winthrop," he said, "you know very well that this man's innocent. It's Henry. It's been Henry all along. Everything points to it. He broke into the Cairo Museum, stole the mummy, sold it for profit, went on a drunken rampage with the money. You found the wrappings in the belly dancer's house. Henry's name was found in the loan shark's book in London."

"But the whole story is so . . ."

Elliott motioned for silence.

"Ramsey has been subjected to enough, and so have we. He's already made the crucial statement that Henry confessed to the murder of his uncle."

"He made this very plain to me," Ramsey said dryly.

"I want our passports returned immediately," Elliott said.

"But the British Museum . . ."

"Young man," Gerald began.

"Lawrence Stratford gave a fortune to the British Museum," Elliott declared. Finally he could take no more. He had reached his limit with this farce. "Listen, Miles," he said, leaning forward. "You clear this up, and now, unless you intend to become a social recluse. For I assure you that if my party, including Reginald Ramsey, is not on the noon train tomorrow for Port Said, you will never be received again by any family in Cairo or London which hopes to receive the seventeenth Earl of Rutherford. Do I make myself clear?"

Silence in the office. The young man blanched. This was excruciating.

"Yes, my lord," he answered under his breath. At once he opened the desk drawer and produced the passports one by one, laying them down on the blotter before him.

Elliott managed to scoop them up with a neat quick gesture before Gerald could do it.

"I find this as disagreeable as you do," he said. "I've never said such words before to any human being in my life, but I want my son released so he can go back to England. Then I'll stay in this bloody place as long as you want me here. I'll answer any question you like."

"Yes, my lord, if I can tell the governor that you will stay . . ."

"I just told you that, didn't I? Do you want a blood oath?"

Enough said. He felt Gerald's hand on his arm. He had what he wanted.

Samir helped him to his feet. They led the party out of the anteroom, through the hallway and onto the front veranda.

"Well done, Gerald," he said. "I'll call you if I need you. I'd appreciate your notifying Randolph about this. It's a little more than I can bear at the moment. But I'll write a long letter soon. . . ."

"I'll soften everything. No need at all for him to know the details. When Henry's arrested, it's going to be dreadful enough."

"Let's worry about that when it happens."

Ramsey was clearly impatient. He started down the steps towards the waiting car. Elliott shook Gerald's hand and then followed.

"Are we quite finished with this little performance?" Ramsey said. "I am wasting valuable time here!"

"Well, you have a lot of time, don't you?" Elliott said with a polite smile. He was a little light-headed suddenly. They had won. The children could get out. "It's imperative that you come back to the hotel now," he said, "that you be seen there."

"Foolishness! And the idea of the opera tonight is positively ludicrous."

"Expediency!" said Elliott, climbing into the backseat of the car first. "Get in," he said.

Ramsey stood there, angry, dejected.

"Sire, what can we do until we have some further evidence of where she might be?" Samir asked. "On our own, we cannot find her."

This time the little room that moved did not scare her. She knew what it was, and that it was to serve the people of these times, as the railroad served them and the motor cars, and all the strange devices that had seemed to her earlier as instruments of horror, things exquisitely capable of bringing suffering and death.

They didn't torture people by packing them into the little room and making them travel up and down. They didn't drive the big locomotives into advancing armies. How strange that she had interpreted things in terms of their most malicious uses.

And he was explaining things to her now, freely and easily—in fact, he had been talking for hours. It wasn't important to ask him specific questions, except occasionally; he liked telling her all about the mummy of Ramses the Damned, and how Julie Stratford was a modern woman; and how Britain ran its great empire, and so forth and so on. That he had loved Julie Stratford was obvious; Ramsey had "stolen" her, but again, it didn't matter. Not at all. What he'd thought was love wasn't love but something paler, more convenient, and altogether too easy. But did she really want to hear about his family? No, talk of history, then, and Cairo, and Egypt, and the world. . . .

It had been a great chore to keep him from calling his father. He felt guilty. But she had used all her persuasion and all her wiles. He did not require fresh garments; his shirt and jacket looked every bit as fine as they had last night.

And so off they were going now through the crowded lobby of Shepheard's, to drive in his Rolls-Royce, to see the Mamluke tombs and all the "history" that she had asked about; and the tapestry was becoming fuller and fuller.

But he'd remarked more than once on how changed she seemed from last night, when she had been almost playful. And that made her faintly afraid. How strong her affection was for him.

"And do you like this?" she asked as they moved towards the front doors.

He paused. It was as if he were seeing her for the first time. It was so simple to smile at him; he deserved one's tenderest smile. "You're the loveliest, most wonderful thing that's ever come into my life," he said. "I wish I could put into words the effect you have upon me. You are . . ."

They stood amid the crowds of the lobby, lost in each other's gaze.

"Like a ghost?" she suggested. "A visitant from another realm?"

"No, you're much too . . . too real for that!" He laughed softly. "You're altogether vivid and warm!"

They crossed the veranda together. His car was waiting, just as he'd said it would be. A long black saloon, he'd called it, with deep velvet seats and a roof. They would still feel the wind through the windows.

"Wait, let me just leave word at the desk for my father, that we'll see him tonight."

"I can do that for you, my lord," said the servant who held the door for them.

"Oh, thank you, I do appreciate it," Alex said politely, that same generosity evinced for the lowest underling. As he gave the man a small gratuity, he looked him directly in the eye. "Tonight, I shall see him at the opera—if you please."

She admired the subtle grace with which he did the smallest things. She took his arm as they went down the steps.

"And tell me," she said as he helped her into the front seat, "about this Julie Stratford. What is a modern woman?"

Ramsey was still arguing as the car pulled into the drive before Shepheard's.

"We will do everything society expects of us," Elliott said. "You have the rest of eternity to search for your lost Queen."

"But what puzzles me is this," Ramsey insisted. He opened the door carelessly, almost wrenching one of the hinges. "If her cousin is wanted for high crimes, how can Julie dance at a ball as if this thing is not happening?"

"Under English law, my friend, a man is innocent until proved guilty," Elliott explained, accepting Ramsey's helping hand. "And publicly we presume Henry is innocent; and we know nothing of these atrocities, so in private we have done our duty as citizens of the Crown."

"Yes, you definitely should have been an adviser to a King," Ramsey said.

"Good Lord, look at that."

"What?"

"Just my son driving off with a woman. At a time like this!"

"Ah, but perhaps he is doing what society expects of him!" Ramsey said contemptuously, leading the way up the steps.

"Lord Rutherford, excuse me—your son said to tell you that he would see you tonight, at the opera."

"Thank you," Elliott said, with a short ironic laugh.

Elliott wanted only to sleep as he entered the sitting room of his suite. Some drunk he was going to be; he was already thoroughly bored with being inebriated. He wanted a clear head, though he understood the dangers.

Ramsey helped him to a chair.

He suddenly realized that they were alone. Samir had gone

on to his own room; and Walter for the moment was nowhere about.

Elliott sat there, trying to collect his strength.

"And what do you do now, my lord?" Ramsey asked. He stood in the center of the room, studying Elliott. "You go back home to England after your precious opera ball, as if none of this ever happened?"

"Your secret's safe. It always was. No one would believe what I've seen. And I wish only to forget it, though I never will."

"And the lust for immortality has burnt itself out?"

Elliott thought for a moment. Then he answered in unhurried fashion, rather relieved himself at the resignation in his voice.

"Perhaps in death, I'll find what I seek, rather than what I deserve. There's always the chance of that." He smiled up at Ramsey, who appeared completely surprised by the response. "Now and then," Elliott continued, "I picture heaven as a vast library, with unlimited volumes to read. And paintings and statues to examine galore. I picture it as a great doorway to learning. Do you think the hereafter could be like that? Rather than one great dull answer to all our questions?"

Ramsey gave him a sad wondering smile.

"A heaven of man-made things. Like our ancient Egyptian heaven."

"Yes, I suppose so. A great museum. And a failure of the imagination."

"I think not."

"Oh, there are so many things I wanted to discuss with you, so much I wanted to know."

Ramsey didn't answer him. The man just stood there, looking at him; and Elliott had the weirdest sense of being listened to, studied. It made him aware of how inattentive most human beings were in general.

"But it's too late for all that." Elliott sighed. "My son Alex is the only immortality that matters to me now."

"You're a wise man. I knew that when I first looked into your eyes. And by the way, you are bad at treachery. You told me where you were keeping Cleopatra when you told me she'd slain Henry and his mistress. It had to have been the belly dancer's house. I played out your game with you. I wanted to see how far you'd go with it. But you gave yourself away. You are not so good at such things."

"Well, my brief career at them is over. Unless you want me

to remain here when the children go home. But I don't see how a crippled, prematurely old man can help you. Do you?''

Ramsey seemed perplexed. ''Why weren't you afraid of her when you saw her in the museum?'' he asked.

''I was afraid of her. I was horrified.''

''But you sheltered her. It couldn't have been merely for your own ends.''

''Ends? No. I don't think so. I found her irresistible, as I found you irresistible. It was the mystery. I wanted to seize it. Move into it. Besides . . .''

''Yes.''

''She was . . . a living thing. A being in pain.''

Ramsey thought about this for a moment.

''You *will* persuade Julie to go back to London—until this is over,'' Elliott asked.

''Yes, I'll do that,'' Ramsey said.

He went out quietly, closing the door behind him.

They walked through the City of the Dead, ''the place of the exalted ones,'' as they said in Arabic. Where the Mamluke Sultans had built their mausoleums; they had seen the fortress of Babylon; they had wandered the bazaars; now the heat of the afternoon wore on Alex, and her soul was chastened and shocked by the things she'd discovered, the long thread of history having connected the centuries for her from this radiant afternoon to the time she'd been alive.

She wanted to see no more of the ancient ruins. She wanted only to be with him.

''I like you, young lord,'' she said to him. ''You comfort me. You make me forget my pain. And the scores I must settle.''

''But what do you mean, my darling?''

She was overcome again by that sense of his fragility, this mortal man. She laid her fingers on his neck. The memories rose, threatening inundation; all too similar to the black waves from which she'd risen, as if death were water.

Was it different for each being? Had Antony gone down in black waves? Nothing separated her from that moment if she wanted to seize it, to see Ramses turn his back again and refuse to give Antony the elixir; to see herself on her knees, begging. ''Don't let him die.''

''So fragile, all of you . . .'' she whispered.

''I don't understand, dearest.''

And so I'm to be alone, am I? In this wilderness of those who can die! Oh, Ramses, I curse you! Yet when she saw the ancient bedchamber again, when she saw the man dying on the couch, and the other, immortal, turning his back on her, she saw something she had not seen in those tragic moments. She saw that both were human; she saw the grief in Ramses' eyes.

Later, when she'd lain as if dead herself, refusing to move or speak, after they'd buried Antony, Ramses had said to her: "You were the finest of them all. You were the one. You had the courage of a man and the heart of a woman. You had the wits of a King and a Queen's cunning. You were the finest. I thought your lovers would be a school for you; not your ruin."

What would she say now if she could revisit that chamber? I know. I understand? Yet the bitterness welled in her, the dark uncontrollable hatred when she looked at young Lord Summerfield walking beside her, this fair and fragile mortal boy-man.

"Dearest, can you confide in me? I've only known you for a short while, but I . . ."

"What is it you want to say, Alex?"

"It sounds so foolish."

"Tell me."

"That I love you."

She lifted her hand to his cheek, touched it tenderly with her knuckles.

"But who are you? Where did you come from?" he whispered. He took her hand and kissed it, his thumbs rubbing her palm. A faint ripple of passion softened her all over; made the heat throb in her breasts.

"I'll never hurt you, Lord Alex."

"Your Highness, tell me your name."

"Make a name for me, Lord Alex. Call me what you will, if you do not believe the name I gave you."

Troubled, his dark brown eyes. If he bent to kiss her, she would pull him down here on the stones. Make love to him till he was spent again.

"*Regina,*" he whispered. "My Queen."

So Julie Stratford had left him, had she? The modern woman who went everywhere on her own and did as she pleased. But then it had been a great King who had seduced her. And now Alex had his Queen.

She saw Antony again, dead on the couch. *Your Majesty, we should take him away now.*

Ramses had turned to her and whispered, "Come with me!"

Lord Summerfield stoked the heat in her, his mouth on her mouth, oblivious to the tourists who passed them. Lord Summerfield, who would die as Antony had died.

Would Julie Stratford be allowed to die?

"Take me back to the bedchamber," she whispered. "I starve for you, Lord Alex. I shall strip the clothes off you here if we don't go."

"Your slave forever," he answered.

In the motor car, she clung to him.

"What is it, Your Highness, tell me?"

She looked out at the hordes of mortals passing her; the countless thousands of this ancient city, in their timeless peasant robes.

Why had he brought her to life? What had been his purpose? She saw his tearstained face again. She saw the picture in which he stood, smiling at the miracle of Camera, with his arm around Julie Stratford, whose eyes were dark.

"Hold me, Lord Alex. Keep me warm."

Through the streets of old Cairo, Ramses walked alone.

How could he persuade Julie to get on that train? How could he let her go back to London, but then was it not best for her, and mustn't he think of that for once? Had he not caused evil enough?

And what about his debt to the Earl of Rutherford; this much he owed the man who had sheltered Cleopatra; the man he liked and wanted so to be near, the man whose advice would always have been good for him, the man for whom he felt a deep and uncertain affection that just might be love.

Put Julie on the train. How could he? His thoughts gave out in confusion. Over and over he saw her face. *Destroy the elixir. Never brew the elixir again.*

He thought of the headlines in the paper. Woman on the floor of the dress shop. *I like to kill. It soothes my pain.*

In the old-fashioned Victorian bed in his suite, Elliott slept. He dreamed a dream of Lawrence. They were talking together in the Babylon and Malenka was dancing, and Lawrence said: It's almost time for you to come.

But I have to go home to Edith. I have to take care of Alex, he had said. And I want to drink myself to death in the country. I've already planned it.

I know, said Lawrence, that's what I mean. That won't take very long.

Miles Winthrop didn't know what to make of any of it finally. They had issued a warrant for Henry's arrest, but frankly at this moment everything pointed to the possibility that the bastard was dead. Clothes, money, identification, all left behind at the scene of Malenka's murder. And no telling when the shopkeeper had been killed.

He had a premonition that this whole grisly case might never be solved.

The only thing to be thankful for was that Lord Rutherford was not at the moment his sworn enemy. A stigma like that would never be overcome.

Well, at least the day so far had been peaceful. No more hideous corpses with their necks broken, staring off as they lay on the slab, saying in a silent whisper, Will you not find the one who did this to me?

He dreaded the opera tonight, the continuous questions he would get from the entire British community. And he knew that he could not take refuge in Lord Rutherford's shadow. On the contrary, he dreaded another run-in. He would keep to himself.

Seven o'clock.

Julie stood before the mirror in her sitting room. She had put on the low-cut gown that violently disturbed Ramses, but then she had no other appropriate clothing for this inane occasion. As she watched Elliott through the mirror, he fastened her pearls at the back of her neck.

Elliott always looked better than almost anyone around him. Trim, still handsome at fifty-five, he wore white tie and tails as if they were entirely natural to him.

And it struck her as faintly horrible that they could resume like this, as if nothing had happened. They might as well have been in London; Egypt was a nightmare suddenly; only Julie was not ready to wake up.

"And so here we are in our feathers," she said, "ready to do our ritual dance."

"Remember, until he's apprehended, which he won't be, we

have every right to presume he's innocent. And carry on as if he were.''

''It's monstrous and you know it.''

''It's necessary.''

''For Alex, yes. And Alex hasn't seen fit to call us all day. As for myself, it doesn't matter.''

''You have to go back to London,'' he said. ''I want you to go back to London.''

''I'll always love you,'' she said. ''You're flesh and blood to me, really, you always have been. But what you want doesn't matter anymore.'' She turned around.

Up close she could see the evidence of the strain in him; he'd aged, the way Randolph had suddenly aged when he'd heard of Lawrence's death. He was as handsome as ever, but now there was a tragic quality to it; a certain philosophical sadness had replaced the old twinkle in his eye.

''I can't go back to London,'' she said. ''But I will get Alex on that train.''

Destroy the elixir. He stood before the mirror. He had put on most of the required garments, taken from the trunk of Lawrence Stratford—the shining black trousers, shoes, belt. Naked from the waist up, he stared at his own reflection. The money-belt girded him as it had since he left London. And the vials gleamed in their canvas pockets.

Destroy the elixir. Never use it again.

He lifted the stiff white shirt and put it on carefully, working the impossible buttons. He saw Elliott Savarell's drawn and weary face. *You will persuade Julie to go back to London—until this is over.*

Beyond the windows, the city of Cairo seethed quietly with the great noise of modern cities, a sound he had never heard in ancient times.

Where was she, the dark-haired queen with the violent blue eyes? He saw her again, sighing under him, her head thrown back on the pillows, *same flesh*. ''Suckle me!'' she'd cried out as she had done so long ago; back arched like a cat. And then the smile on her face; a stranger's smile.

''Yes, Master Alex,'' Walter said into the telephone, ''to suite two-oh-one, I'll bring your clothes right away. But do call your father in Miss Stratford's suite. He's eager to get in touch with you. He's worried that he hasn't seen you all day. So much has happened, Master Alex—'' But the connection was already broken. Quickly he rang Miss Stratford. No answer. He had no time. He had to hurry with the clothes.

Cleopatra stood at the window. She had dressed in the gorgeous gown of pure silver which she had taken from the poor woman in the little shop. Ropes of pearls fell down over the swell of her breasts. She had never done her hair properly; in a dark black veil it hung down about her, moist still from the bath, and full of perfume, and she liked it. It made her smile bitterly to think it was like being a girl again.

Running through the palace gardens, her hair her cloak.

"I like your world, Lord Alex," she said as she watched the winking lights of Cairo under the paling evening sky. The stars seemed so lost above this dazzling splendour. Even the headlamps moving through the streets had a soothing beauty. "Yes, I like your world. I like everything about it. I want to have money and power in it; and for you to be at my side."

She turned. He was staring at her as if she'd hurt him. She ignored the knock at the door.

"Dearest, those things don't always go hand in hand in my world," he said. "Lands, a title, education—these I have, but money I do not."

"Don't worry," she said, so relieved it was only that. "I shall acquire the wealth, my lord, that's nothing. Not when one is invulnerable. But there are some scores I must settle first. I must hurt someone who has hurt me. I must take from him . . . what he took from me."

The knock sounded again. As if waking from a dream, he took his eyes off her and went to the door. A servant. His evening clothes had come.

"Your father's already left, sir. Your tickets will be at the box office under his name."

"Thank you, Walter."

There was barely time for him to dress. As he shut the door, he looked at her again, curiously, with that little touch of sadness.

"Not now," she said, quickly kissing him. "And we may use these tickets, may we not?" She picked up off the dressing table the pair she'd stolen from the poor dead boy in the alleyway, the little papers which said "Admit One."

"But I want you to meet my father, I want you to meet all of them. I want them to meet you."

"Of course you do, and I shall, soon enough. But let us be alone somewhere lost in the crowd so that we can be together. We shall see them when it suits us. Please?"

He wanted to protest, but she was kissing him, stroking his hair again. "Let me have a chance to see your lost love Julie Stratford from a distance."

"Oh, but none of that matters now," he said.

8

ANOTHER MODERN palace—the Opera House, swarming with bejeweled women in gowns the colours of the rainbow, and the men beside them, elegant in white and black. How curious it was, all colours belonging to the females. The males wore uniforms, it seemed, each perfectly identical with the other. She blurred her eyes, to see the reds and blues dancing independently of all detail.

She watched the great surge up the grand staircase. She felt admiring glances on her; the soft glaze of admiration like a light on her skin.

Lord Summerfield beamed at her with pride and affection. "You are the Queen here," he whispered, cheeks flushed again for an instant. He turned to one of the merchants peddling strange little instruments the purpose of which she couldn't guess.

"Opera glasses," he said as he handed them to her. "And the program, yes, please."

"But what are they?" she asked.

He gave a startled little laugh. "You did fall from heaven, didn't you?" His lips touched her neck and then her cheek. "Put them to your eyes, adjust them until they come into focus. Yes, that's it. You see?"

She was shocked. She jumped back as the people on the upper gallery appeared to loom over her.

"What a curious thing. What makes it happen?"

"Magnification," he said. "Pieces of glass." How delighted

he seemed that she'd never heard of it. She wondered how Ramses had mastered all these little secrets; Ramses, whose "mysterious tomb" had been discovered only a month ago by "poor Lawrence," who was now dead. Ramses, who told "in the scrolls" of his love for Cleopatra. Was it really possible that Alex didn't know that the mummy and his nemesis Ramsey were the same?

But how could he grasp it? With only the inane story of the disreputable cousin to link the two? Had she believed when the old priest had led her into the cave?

Chimes sounded. "The opera's going to begin."

They moved up the stairs together. It seemed to her a brilliant light surrounded both of them, separated them from others, and others could see this light, and cast their glances carefully, perceiving that it was love. Love. She did love him; it was not a full-blooded love such as she'd known for Antony; that hurtling through darkness and destruction because one cannot resist another, one cannot live with him or without him, and one goes on, knowing full well that one is being destroyed.

No, this was a newborn love, fresh and gentle as Alex was, but it was love. Julie Stratford had been a fool not to love him; but then Ramses could seduce the goddess Isis. Had there not been Antony, she would never have loved anyone but Ramses. That he had always understood.

Ramses the father, the judge, the teacher; Antony the bad boy with whom she'd run away. Playing in the royal bedchamber like children; drunk; mad; answerable to no one; until Ramses had appeared after all those years.

This is what you've done with your freedom? Your life?

The question was, what would she do with her freedom now? Why did the pain not cripple her? Because this newborn world was too magnificent. Because she had what she had dreamed of in those last few months, when the Roman armies swarmed over Egypt, when Antony was desperate and full of delusions: *another chance.* Another chance, without the weight of a love that was dragging her down into those dark waves forever; another chance without a hatred for Ramses, who wouldn't save her doomed lover; who wouldn't forgive her for being doomed herself.

"Your Highness, I'm losing you again," he said intimately.

"No, you're not," she said. The lights swam around her. "I'm with you, Lord Alex." The high crystal light fixture above was full of tiny sparkling rainbows; she could hear the faint tinkle of glass as it moved in the breeze from the open doors.

"Oh, but look, there they are!" Alex said suddenly, pointing up to where the banister curved and ran away from the top of the stairs.

The noise died around her; the lights; the crowds, the soft communal excitement. Ramses stood there!

Ramses in modern raiment, and beside him the woman, of considerable beauty, young and fragile as Alex was fragile, her auburn hair brushed exquisitely back from her face. A flash of dark eye as she looked at them and did not see them. And Lord Rutherford, dear Lord Rutherford, struggling on his silver cane. Did Ramses really fool the mortals around him? This giant of a man, his face glistening with immortal vigour, hair a tousled mane. And the woman—she had not been given it. She was mortal still. Desperately, fearfully, she clung to Ramses' arm.

"Darling, not now," she begged.

Onward the party moved, the crowd swallowing them.

"But dearest, just to tell them that we're here. Why, this is splendid, it means Ramsey's been cleared. Everything's back to normal. Pitfield worked the miracle."

"Give me this time, Alex, I beg you!" Had her tone become imperious?

"All right, Your Highness," he said with a forgiving smile.

Away from them! She felt desperate, as if she were suffocating. Reaching the top of the stairs, she glanced back. They had gone into a far doorway draped with velvet. And Alex was taking her in another direction. Thank the gods for this.

"Well, it seems we're at the opposite end of the dress circle," he said to her, smiling. "But how can you be so shy when you're so lovely? When you're more beautiful than any woman I've ever beheld?"

"I'm jealous of you, of the hours we've spent together. Believe me, the world will ruin it, Lord Alex."

"Ah, that's not possible," he said with utter innocence.

Elliott stood at the curtained doorway. "Where on earth can Alex be? What could possess him to wander off at a time like this? Oh, this is past all patience."

"Elliott, Alex is the least of our worries!" Julie said. "He's probably found another American heiress. The third consecutive love of his life in one week."

Elliott gave a faintly bitter smile as they went on into the box. The woman he'd glimpsed in the car had been all hat, ribbons and hair flying. Maybe it was just the bit of good fortune his son required.

A curved tier; a giant amphitheatre save it was covered over; and only one-half of the oval. At the far end lay the stage, obviously, hidden by a wall of soft shimmering curtains; and sunk beneath and before it, a gathering of men and women making horrid sounds with their stringed instruments and horns. She put her hand to her ears.

Alex led her down the little step to the front row of this small section. The soft red chairs at the railing were theirs. She turned to her left. Across the dimly lighted gulf she saw Ramses! She saw the pale-faced woman, with large sad eyes. Lord Rutherford had settled directly behind them; and at his arm was a dark-skinned Egyptian, beautifully clad as the other men.

She tried to take her eyes off them; she did not fully understand the tumult inside her, as she continued to stare. Then Ramses put his arm around the woman. He embraced her tightly as if to comfort her, and the woman lowered her eyes, and there was a sudden glisten of tears on her cheeks! Ramses kissed this woman, and the woman, inclining towards him, returned his kiss!

How the pain passed through her as she saw this! It was like a knife travelling down her face suddenly, slicing her open. She turned her head, shaken; staring before her in the dark.

It seemed she would have cried out if she could. But why, what did she feel? A hatred for the woman swelled inside her; burning her. *Give Antony the elixir.*

Suddenly the great theatre went dark. A man appeared before the audience; applause broke out all around her, then rose in a deafening noise. Like so much in modern times, it was overwhelming yet strangely contained.

The man bowed, lifted his hands, then turned and faced the musicians, who had become quiet and still. At his signal, they played in concert; the sound rose, huge and searing and beautiful.

It seemed to touch her, this sound. She felt Alex's hand cover her hand. The sound surrounded her, swept her away from her pain suddenly.

"Modern times," she whispered. Was she too weeping? She

did not want to hate! She did not want this pain! In memory
again, she saw Ramses above her in the darkness; had it been a
tomb? She felt the elixir filling her mouth. And then he backed
away from her in terror. *Ramses*. But was she sorry that he had
done it? Could she really curse him?

She was alive!

Elliott ducked outside the curtain into the lighted foyer behind
the box, to read the note in the electric light.

"It was at the desk at Shepheard's, sir," said the boy, waiting
for the coin which Elliott fished from his pocket and held out.

Father, will see you at the opera or at the ball afterwards. Sorry to be so mysterious, but have met the most
entrancing female companion. Alex.

Infuriating. But so be it! He went back into the darkened hall.

Ramses hadn't thought it possible to enjoy this spectacle. He
was furious still with Elliott that he had been dragged here
against his will. And indeed, the opera would have been ludicrous had it not been so beautiful—the fat "Egyptian" figures
down there singing in Italian against a backdrop of painted temples and statues which appeared to be utterly grotesque. But the
melodies overcame him, even as they worsened Julie's pain.
Julie leaned against his shoulder in the privacy of the darkness.
The lovely voices rising in the gloom touched his heart. These
hours wouldn't be the agony he had imagined; it even occurred
to his cowardly soul that perhaps Cleopatra had fled Cairo, that
she was lost now in the modern world, beyond all hope of his
finding her. And this both released him and terrified him. What
would her loneliness be as the weeks and months passed; what
would her rage demand?

She lifted the magical opera glasses. She peered at Ramses and
Julie, astonished at the intimate focus. The woman was crying,
no doubt of it. Her dark eyes were fixed on the stage, where the
ugly little man sang the beautiful song, "Celeste Aïda," his
voice enormous, the melody enough to break the heart.

She was about to put down the glasses when suddenly Julie
Stratford whispered something to her partner. They rose to-

gether, Julie Stratford hurrying through the curtain, and Ramses following.

Quickly, Cleopatra touched Alex's hand.

"You stay here," she whispered in his ear.

He seemed to think it quite the normal thing. He didn't try to stop her. She hurried through the alcove behind their little section of the theater, and moved slowly and cautiously out into the grand room of the second floor.

It was almost empty. Servants behind a marble-top counter poured drinks for a few old men who looked quite miserable in their black-and-white uniforms, one of them pulling at his collar in obvious annoyance.

At a far table, against a great arched window hung with tapestried drapery, Julie Stratford and Ramses talked in whispers that she could not possibly hear. She moved closer, behind a stand of potted trees, and lifted the opera glasses, bringing their faces close again; but not the words.

Julie Stratford shook her head, recoiling. Ramses held her hand, he would not let her go. What was she saying with such passion? And how he pleaded with her; she knew that authority, that insistence, but Julie Stratford was strong just as she herself had been strong.

Suddenly Julie Stratford rose, clutching a small bag in her hand, and walked swiftly away with her head bowed. Ramses was in despair. He rested his forehead on his hand.

Swiftly, she followed after Julie Stratford, cleaving to the wall, praying that Ramses did not look up.

Julie Stratford passed through a wooden door.

POWDER ROOM

She was confused, uncertain. Suddenly a voice spoke to her; it was a young servant.

"Looking for the ladies' room, miss? It's right there."

"Thank you," she said, and she went towards it. It was obviously a public room.

Thank God, the powder room was empty. Julie sat down at the last velvet stool before the long dressing table, and merely rested for a moment, her hand covering her eyes.

The thing was out there, the monster, the creation, whatever one could call such a being; and they were locked in this stupid auditorium listening to music, as if horrors had not been committed, as if they would not be committed again.

But the worst of it was Ramses pushing it to this conclusion between them, holding her hand and telling her that he couldn't bear to lose her.

And she, she had burst out with it: "I wish I'd never laid eyes on you. I wish you had let Henry do his work."

Had she meant it? He'd hurt her wrist as he held her; it was hurting her now as she cried softly in this quiet room, her softest murmurs echoing off the cold mirrored walls.

"Julie," he'd said, "it was a horrible thing I did, yes, I know. But I'm speaking now of you and me. You're alive, you're whole and beautiful, soul and body united—"

"No, don't say it," she'd pleaded.

"Take the elixir, and come with me, forever."

She had been unable to remain there. She'd broken away and run. And now alone in this room she wept. She tried to quiet her soul; she tried to think, but she could not. She told herself that she must envision her life, years from now, when this seemed a dark adventure that she would confide only to those she dearly loved. She would tell of the mysterious man who had come into her life. . . . But this was unbearable.

As the door of the powder room opened, she covered her face with her handkerchief, keeping her head down, trying only to be calm; to breathe.

How dreadful to be noticed now, when she wanted to withdraw and go back alone to the hotel. And this other woman who had come in, why in the world was she sitting so close to her, right on the next stool? She turned her head away to the right. She had to get a grip on herself. Get through this night somehow for Elliott, though she was losing faith in the meaning of any sustained direction. She folded the handkerchief, the miserable little ruin of lace and linen now soaked with tears, and blotted her eyes.

Almost by accident she looked up into the mirror. Was she losing her mind! The woman directly on her left was staring at her with great ferocious blue eyes. Why, the woman was scarcely inches from her, and what a creature she was, with all her long rippling black hair pouring down over her naked shoulders and her back.

She turned and faced the woman, drawing back as far as she could on the stool, her hand out to the mirror to brace herself.

"Good Lord!" A shock went through her; she was trembling so violently, she couldn't hold her hand steady!

"Oh, you are lovely, yes," said the woman in a low, perfect British accent. "But he has not given you his precious elixir. You're mortal. There's no doubt."

"Who are you!" she gasped. *But she knew.*

"Do you call it by another name?" the woman said, pressing in on her, the strong, beautifully modeled face looming over her, the rippling black hair seeming to eat the very light. "Why has he waked me from my sleep and not given the magic potion to you?"

"Leave me alone!" Julie whispered; violent tremors coursed through her. She tried to rise, but the woman had forced her securely into the corner. In panic, she almost screamed.

"So alive you are nevertheless," the woman whispered. "Young, delicate, like a flower; so easy to pick."

Julie sank back against the mirrored wall. If she shoved the woman, could she knock her off balance? It seemed a virtual impossibility; and once again, as she had when Ramses rose from the coffin, she felt she was going to faint.

"It seems monstrous, does it not?" the woman went on in the same clipped British accent. "That I should pluck this flower because what I loved was allowed to die. What have you to do with the loss suffered so long ago? Julie Stratford for Antony. It seems unfair."

"God help me!" Julie gasped. "God help us both, you and me. Oh, please let me go."

The woman's hand flew towards her, grabbing her about the throat; she couldn't bear it, the fingers closing out her life's breath; her head struck the mirror behind her, once, twice. She was losing consciousness.

"Why should I not kill you! *You* tell me!" came the seething voice in her ear.

The hand suddenly let her go. Gasping, she fell forward over the dressing table.

"Ramses!" she screamed, the breath rushing out of her. "Ramses!"

The door of the powder room opened; two women stopped dead in their confusion. Beside her, Cleopatra rose from the table and plunged past them, knocking one of them to the side. In a flurry of streaming black hair and shimmering silver cloth she vanished.

Julie fell sobbing to the floor.

People shouting; hurried footsteps. An old woman with soft wrinkled hands was helping her to her feet.

"Have to get to Ramses," she said. She struggled towards the door. The other women tried to stop her. She should sit down. "Someone get a glass of water!" "No, let me go!"

Finally she reached the door, and forced her way through it, through the small knot of ushers gathered. Ramses came rushing towards her; she collapsed in his arms.

"She was there," she gasped in his ear. "She spoke to me. She touched me." She moved her hand to her aching throat. "She ran away when the others came in."

"What is it, miss?"

"Miss Stratford, what happened?"

"No, I'm all right now." He almost lifted her off her feet, and carried her away from them.

"Well, all I saw was another woman with her; yes, a tall woman, black hair."

Into the foyer of the box, he led her, a quiet private space. She tried to clear her vision; Elliott and Samir stood over her suddenly, and the music, the music was a ghastly din pouring through the curtains. Samir filled a glass with champagne for her. How absurd! Champagne.

"Here in the auditorium somewhere. Dear God, she was like a terrible angel! A goddess! Ramses, she knew me, my name. She knew me. She spoke of vengeance for Antony. Ramses, she knew who I was!"

His face was a mask of rage. He started for the door. She grabbed hold of him, knocking the champagne glass over. "No, don't go! Don't leave my side!" she whispered. "She could have killed me. She wanted to. But then she couldn't. Ramses! She's a living, feeling creature! Oh, God, what have you done, what have *I* done!"

A bell had sounded within the auditorium. People were streaming out into the open spaces. And Alex would be searching for her; and perhaps he would find them.

She could not clear her head; she could not bring herself to move.

She stood on the high iron balcony, above the iron steps that descended to a dark, neglected alleyway, the door open to the lights and the noise to her right. The city was a haze of soft lamps and rooftops, of shining domes, and towers piercing the deep azure sky. She could not see the Nile from here, but it didn't matter. The air was cool and sweet; full of the scent of the green trees below.

Suddenly, she heard his voice:

"Your Highness, I've been searching for you everywhere."

"Hold me, Alex," she whispered. "Hold me in your arms." She took a deep breath as she felt him close to her, his warm hands on her. Gently he moved her back to sit on the iron steps that went upward to yet another balcony above.

"You're ill," he said. "I must get something for you to drink."

"No, stay close to me," she said. She knew her voice was barely audible. She stared out at the lights of the city almost desperately. She wanted somehow to cling to this vision of the modern city; to move towards it mentally out of her anguish. It was her only escape. That and the boy beside her, the clean innocent male thing that held her and kissed her.

"What do I do?" she murmured in the old Latin. "Is it grief I feel, or rage? I only know it's suffering."

She was torturing him, but she didn't mean to. Had he understood her words?

"Open your heart to me," he said earnestly. "I love you, Your Highness. Tell me what's troubling you. I won't let anything hurt you. If it's in my power to stop it, I shall."

"I believe you, young lord," she said. "I feel love for you too."

But what was it she wanted? Would revenge cure the rage that was tearing her apart? Or should she retreat now, taking young Lord Alex with her, and move as far away from her mentor, her creator, as she could? It seemed for one moment the ache in her would consume everything—thought, hope, will. But then she realized something and it was like the sun again, the warm sun.

To love and to hate so fiercely, it was the essence of life itself. And life she had again with all its blessings and all its pain.

The last act was nearing the end. Elliott sat staring dully at the beautiful stage, the doomed lovers suffocating in the tomb, Amneris the princess praying above.

Thank God it was almost finished! Verdi at his finest seemed absolutely ludicrous under these circumstances. As for the ball, they would pass through it for no more than a moment or two before taking Julie to her room.

Julie was on the verge of collapse. She sat still in the foyer of the box behind him, shivering, clinging to Ramses.

She'd refused to let Ramses leave her; so Elliott and Samir had searched the crowds at the intermissions. They had moved up and down the staircase, looking for the woman whom only Elliott would surely recognize, but whom Samir could spot for her flowing hair and silver gown.

She was nowhere to be found. And it wasn't surprising. She may well have left the hall altogether after the brief attack. The mystery was: how did she know about Julie! How had she found Julie here!

Another maddening aspect of all this was that they had not found Alex either! But perhaps that was a blessing in disguise. Alex remained somehow miraculously untouched by what had happened. Maybe he could be taken home with no further explanations, yet that seemed too much to expect.

There was no doubt in Elliott's mind now that Julie would be on that noon train tomorrow with Alex. He himself would remain in Cairo until this thing was seen to the finish. Samir would go back to London with Julie, it had already been decided; for Alex surely couldn't protect her or comfort her, since he did not know and must not know what was going on.

Samir would stay with Julie in Mayfair until Ramses returned. What good Elliott would be was uncertain. But he would remain. He had to. And Julie had to be taken far, far away.

The last heartrending duet of the opera was at its most poignant. He could not bear it for much longer. He lifted his opera glasses and began scanning the hall. Alex, where the hell are you! He scanned the left side of the dress circle slowly, and then gradually turned to the right.

Grey heads, sparkling diamonds; men half-asleep, mouths agape under white mustaches. And a gorgeous woman with black rippling hair over her shoulders walking quickly down to the front row of a far box, her hand in Alex's hand.

He froze.

He turned the little dial on the glasses, bringing the image even closer. The woman had settled down on Alex's left, but the curve of the dress circle placed them both clearly in view! Don't have a heart attack now, Elliott, not after all you've been through. Alex turned and kissed the woman's cheek as she stared at the stage—the tomb, the doomed lovers—and then in a little silent frenzy she turned to Alex with heartbroken eyes and nestled into the crook of his arm.

"Ramsey," he whispered. He had disturbed those around him, even woken up somebody in the next box. But Ramsey had heard him and had come through the curtain, kneeling down beside his seat.

"There, look! With Alex; it's she." The whisper was a gasp. Shoving the opera glasses at Ramsey, he stared at the two distant figures. He didn't need the glasses to see that Cleopatra had lifted her own and was staring at them!

He heard Ramsey's low moan of distress.

Alex had turned. Alex was making a little cheerful gesture to them, a discreet little wave with his left hand.

The last dying notes of the duet ended. Applause broke out all around them. The inevitable "Bravos!" came from all directions. The house lights were rising. People were climbing to their feet.

Julie and Samir stood in the open doorway.

"What is it!" Julie demanded.

"They're leaving. I'm going after them!" Ramses said.

"No!" Julie cried.

"Julie, she's with Alex Savarell," Ramsey said. "She has ensnared the Earl's son! Both of you, stay with Julie. Take Julie back to the hotel."

He knew it was no good as soon as he had reached the box. They were gone. At least three exits opened on iron stairways down the side of the building. And people were using all of them. He rushed along the mezzanine, scanning those who descended the grand stairway. Not a chance of finding them now.

He was at the front doors when Elliott, Samir and Julie came down the stairs. Julie looked like the ghost of herself, clinging to Samir. Elliott was clearly drawing upon the very last of his stamina, and his face had turned a deathly white.

"It's no use," Ramses explained. "They are lost again."

"Our only chance then is the ball," Elliott said. "It's a game, don't you see! Alex doesn't understand what's happening. He said he would meet us here, or at the ball."

9

THEY HAD followed the flow of the guests, streaming out of the Opera House, and walking across the broad square towards the hotel.

There was no doubt in her mind that Ramses was following them. Undoubtedly Lord Rutherford would come in the hope of rescuing his son.

She made no decision as to what she should do. The meeting was inevitable. Words must be spoken; and beyond that? She saw only freedom, but she did know where she must go or what she must do to be free.

Killing the other, that was not the answer. A great revulsion rose in her against all the lives she'd thoughtlessly taken—even the life of the man who had fired the gun at her, whoever he had been.

Solving the riddle of why Ramses had resurrected her; of how precisely he'd done it—that must be part of what she had to do. But maybe she should run from that and run from him.

She glanced at the motor cars nosing their way up the circular drive before the entrance of Shepheard's. Why couldn't they run away, she and Alex, right now? There was time enough, wasn't there, for her to seek her old teacher, this man who had dominated all of her mortal life, and had now recreated her for reasons she couldn't understand?

And for one second a dreadful foreboding shook her. She clasped Alex's hand all the more tightly. There came his reassuring smile again. She said nothing. Her mind was confusion as they entered the bright hotel lobby and followed the crowds up another grand stairway.

The ballroom opened before them on the second floor, a vast space far larger than the ballroom she had seen last night below. Linen-draped tables lined the walls on either side; and the room itself seemed to go on forever, music surging from an orchestra now hidden by the milling crowd.

Gold draperies hung from the high-panelled ceiling. How these people loved plaster ornament; doors and windows were covered with it, as if with carefully sculpted whipped cream. Couples had already begun to dance to the music. Light appeared to drip from the great tinkling glass fixtures. Young servants moved about offering white wine in exquisite glasses from silver trays.

"How are we going to find them?" Alex said. "Oh, I'm so eager for them to meet you."

"Are you?" she whispered. "And if they fail to approve your choice, Lord Alex, what will you do?"

"What a strange thing to say," he said with characteristic innocence. "They can't fail. And it doesn't matter finally whether or not they do."

"I love you, Lord Alex. I didn't think that I would when I first saw you. I thought you were pretty and young and that it would be lovely to have you in my arms. But I love you."

"I know perfectly what you are saying," he whispered, with a strange look in his eyes. "Does that surprise you?" It seemed he wanted desperately to say something else to her but could not find the words. That sadness came; the little shadow of sadness she'd seen in him from the beginning, and for the first time she realized it was something in her which aroused it; it was a response to something he saw in her face.

Someone called his name. His father calling. She knew the voice before she turned to see for herself. "Remember, I love you, Alex," she said again. She had the strangest feeling that she was saying farewell. Too innocent, those were the only words that came clear to her.

Turning, she saw them all moving towards her from the open doors.

"Father, and Ramsey! Ramsey, old man," Alex said, "I'm so glad to see you."

In a dream she watched them, Alex pumping Ramses' hand and Ramses staring at her.

"My darling." Alex's voice sought to reach her. "Let me present my father, and my dearest friends. Why, Your Highness—" He broke off suddenly. And in a low whisper he confided, "I don't even know your real name."

"Yes, you do, my beloved," she said. "I told you when first we met. It's Cleopatra. Your father knows me and so does your good friend Ramsey, as you call him. And I have met your friend Julie Stratford as well."

She fixed her gaze on Lord Rutherford; the music and the noise of the crowd was a roar in her ears.

"Allow me to thank you, Lord Rutherford, for your recent kindness to me. What would I have done without you? And I was so unkind in return."

The feeling of foreboding grew stronger. She was doomed if she remained in this room. Yet she stood there, her hand trembling as she held on to Alex, who looked from her to his father in complete confusion. "Why, I don't understand; you mean you've met?"

Ramses stepped forward suddenly. He took her arm roughly, and pulled her away from Alex.

"I must speak to you," he said, glaring down at her, "now, alone."

"Ramsey, what in the world are you doing?"

Others had turned to stare at them.

"Alex, stay here!" said his father.

Ramses pulled her farther away. She turned her ankle in the high shoes. "Let me go!" she whispered.

In a blur, she saw pale Julie Stratford turning desperately to the dark-faced Egyptian, and old Lord Rutherford physically restraining his son.

In a rage, she drew back from Ramses, startling him, freeing herself at once. Gasps from all these strange modern people, who looked as they pretended not to look. A hush had fallen around them, though the music roared over it.

"We will speak when I say, my beloved teacher! You interfere just now with my pleasures, just as you always did in the past."

Alex rushed to her side. She slipped her arm around him as once again Ramses advanced on her.

"What in God's name is the matter with you, Ramsey!" Alex protested.

"I tell you now, we are to speak, you and I, alone," Ramses said to her, ignoring her lover.

Her anger went before her words and her words went before her thoughts.

"You think you can force me to do your will! I'll pay you out for what you've done to me! I'll pay you in kind!"

He grabbed her, swinging her away from Alex, whose father moved in again to take his arm. She glanced back to see Alex vanishing as the crowds closed in front of him, Ramses forcing her deeper into the dancers, refusing to let her go, though she struggled, his right hand clutching her left wrist, his left hand locked on her waist.

All about them couples whirled to the deafening music and its deep throbbing rhythmic beat. He forced her into the dance as he towered over her, lifting her off her feet as he turned her about.

"Let go of me!" she hissed. "You think I'm the same mad creature you left in that hovel in old Cairo. You think I am your slave!"

"No, no, I can see you are different," dropping into the old Latin. "But who are you, really?"

"Your magic has restored my mind, my memory. All that I suffered—it is there, and I hate you now more truly than I did before."

How stunned he was; how he suffered. Was she supposed to pity him?

"You have always been magnificent at suffering!" She spat the words at him. "And in your judgments! But I am not your slave or your property. What you have brought back to life would be free to live."

"It is you," he whispered. "The Queen who was wise as well as impulsive? Who loved recklessly but knew always how to conquer and rule?"

"Yes, precisely. The Queen who begged you to share your gift with one mortal man, but you refused her. Selfish, spiteful and petty in the end."

"Oh, no, you know it is not true." Same old charm, same old persuasiveness. And the same fierce and unyielding will. "It would have been a ghastly error!"

"And I? Am I not an error!"

She struggled to free herself. She couldn't. Again he turned her in a great circle to the rhythm of the music, skirts brushing her as others danced around them, oblivious, it seemed, to her struggle.

"Last night you told me that when you were dying, you tried to call out to me," he said. "The venom of the snake had paralyzed you. Were you telling me the truth?"

Again she tried to pull loose. "Do not say these things to me!" she said. She jerked her left arm away from him, but he caught it again. Now the others did see what was happening. Heads were turning. A pair of dancers had stopped in alarm.

"Answer me," he demanded. "Did you try to call out to me in those last moments? Is that true?"

"You think that justifies what you have done!" She forced him to a halt. She would not be dragged along by him. "I was afraid. I was at death's door!" she confessed. "It was fear, not love! You think I could ever forgive you for letting Antony die?"

"Oh, it's you," he said softly. They stood motionless together. "It is really you. My Cleopatra, with all your duplicity and passion. It is you."

"Yes, and I speak the truth when I say I hate you," she cried, the tears springing to her eyes. "Ramses the Damned! I curse the day I let the light of the sun into your tomb. When your sweet mortal Julie Stratford is lying dead at your feet as Antony lay dead at mine, you will know the meaning of wisdom, of love, the power of she who always conquers and rules. Your Julie Stratford is mortal. Her neck can be snapped like a river reed."

Did she mean these words? She didn't know. She knew the hatred and all the love that had heated it, made it possible. In a fury she drew back, at last free of him, and turned to flee.

"No, you will not hurt her. You will not hurt Alex, either," he cried out in Latin. "Or anyone else."

She shoved the dancers out of her path. A woman screamed; a man stumbled into his partner. Others struggled to make way for her. She turned and saw him bearing down on her, calling out to her.

"I will put you back into the grave before I will let you do it. Into the darkness."

In terror, she plowed through the crowd before her. The air was rife with screams everywhere. But the door lay ahead, and freedom, and she ran towards it with all her strength.

"Wait, stop, listen to me," Ramses shouted.

Glancing back as she reached the doors, she saw that Alex

had a hold of him. "Stop, Ramsey, let her go!" Other men were surrounding Ramses.

She ran on to the top of the stairs. Now it was Alex's voice calling her, begging her to wait, not to be afraid. But Ramses would get free of his captors. They could not hold him, and his threats rang in her ears.

Down the steps she ran, clutching to the railing, badly hampered by the high-heeled shoes.

"Your Highness," Alex shouted.

She rushed through the lobby and out the front doors. A car had just stopped at the foot of the steps. The man and woman were already out of it, the servant holding the door open.

She glanced back. Alex was running down the staircase, and Ramses was right behind him.

"Your Highness! Wait!"

She dashed around the car, and shoved the baffled servant out of her path. She slid behind the wheel and slammed her foot on the pedal. As it raced forward, Alex vaulted over the side door and fell down into the seat beside her. She struggled to control the wheel, barely missing the garden, turning back onto the street that led to the boulevard.

"God in heaven," Alex shouted over the wind. "He's taken the car behind us. He's following us."

She forced the pedal to the floor, turning dangerously to avoid the car directly in front of her, and then racing ahead into the open lane.

"Your Highness, you'll kill us!"

The cold air struck her face as she leaned forward, twisting and turning the wheel to pass the sluggish cars that would not get out of her way. Alex pleaded with her. But she heard only Ramses' voice in her ears: "I will put you back into the grave . . . into the darkness." To get away, she had to get away.

"I won't let him hurt you."

At last the boulevard had given way to the open country road. Nothing in her path now. Yet she kept the pedal jammed to the floor.

Somewhere far out there lay the pyramids, and then the desert, the open desert. But how could she hide there; where would she go?

"Is he still behind us?" she screamed.

"Yes, but I won't let them hurt you, I told you! Listen to me."

"No," she screamed. "Do not try to stop me!"

She shoved at him as he went to embrace her. The car twisted, went off the paving. Over the packed sand it plowed, plunging into the blackness, headlamps shining dimly on the open desert. She had lost the road!

Far off to the right she saw a twinkling light moving as if towards her. Then she heard that sound, that awful sound: the scream of the steam locomotive! Ye gods, where was it!

Panic seized her. She could hear the low rumble of the iron wheels!

"Where is it!" she screamed.

"Stop, you have to. Don't try to race it!"

A glare of lights struck the little mirror above her, blinding her. She threw up her hands for an instant, then grabbed the wheel again. Then she saw the horror of horrors, the great roaring monster that had terrified her more than anything else. The giant black iron locomotive looming down on her right.

"The brakes!" Alex cried.

The motor car bumped, rose up in the air and caught at a dead halt. The locomotive passed only a foot in front of her, the huge grinding wheels directly before her eyes.

"We're caught on the tracks, damn it, come on, get out!" Alex cried.

The whistle came again, screaming over the iron rumbling. Another one was coming towards her from the left! She saw its round yellow eye, the beam sweeping over her, its great flaring iron skirt as it thundered down the metal path.

They had her, these things; they had her. How could she escape them? And Ramses was behind her, Ramses was shouting her name. She felt Alex grab her arm and try to pull her out of the seat. The hideous locomotive was on top of her; as it struck the car she screamed.

Her body was thrown upwards. In one glaring moment she felt herself flying, high above the desert, tossed like a doll into the wind. Below the horrid iron monsters travelled past each other, over the endless sands. Then a searing flash of orange fire rose under her; unendurable heat enveloped her with a great deafening sound the like of which she had never before heard.

Ramses was thrown backwards by the explosion. He landed sprawling on the sand. One instant he had seen her body, thrown up and out of the car. The next the car had exploded, and she had been swallowed in midair by a great plume of orange flame. Again the explosion rocked the earth with its force, the fire spewing even higher. And for a moment he could see nothing at all.

As he scrambled to his feet, the great northbound locomotive was trying to stop. Wheezing, grinding still, it lumbered on the burning wreckage of the car shoved to the side, off the track. The southbound train roared on, oblivious, its rattling boxcars adding to the unbearable noise.

He ran towards the burning car. The mangled frame looked like blackened timbers in the rolling, greasy blaze.

He could see no life, no movement, no sign of her! He was about to run into the fire itself when Samir grabbed him. When he heard Julie scream.

In a daze he turned and looked at them. Alex Savarell was struggling to get up, his clothes blackened and smoking. His father stood beside him, a burnt garment hanging from his hand. He would live, the young man. That was clear.

But she! Where was she! Appalled, he stared at the giant trains, the one stopped now, the other fast disappearing; had ever the world known such power? And the explosion; it had been like a volcano.

"Cleopatra!" he cried out. Then he felt himself, for all his immortal strength, slowly crumpling. Julie Stratford held him in her arms.

The dawn came with a fiery glow on the horizon; the sun, caught in a mist, seemed not so much a disk but a great layer of simmering heat. The stars faded slowly.

Once again he walked back and forth over the same stretch of railroad track. Samir watched him patiently. Julie Stratford had gone to sleep in the backseat of the car.

Elliott and his son had returned to the hotel.

Faithful Samir alone stood with him, as once again he examined the burnt mangled car. Horrid the skeleton of the thing. Horrid the bits and pieces of charred leather clinging to the blackened springs.

"Sire," Samir said patiently, "nothing could survive such an explosion. In the olden times, sire, such heat was unknown."

It *was* known, he thought. It was known in the eye of an erupting mountain, the very image that had come to him last night.

"But there must be some trace, Samir. Something must remain."

But why punish this poor mortal who had never done anything but give him comfort? And Julie, his poor Julie. He must take her back to the safety and quiet of the hotel. She had not spoken since it happened. She had stood by him, holding on to him, but she had not spoken a word.

"Sire, give thanks for what has taken place," Samir said tentatively. "Death has reclaimed her. Surely she is at peace again."

"Is she?" he whispered. "Samir, why did I frighten her! Why did I drive her out into the night? Samir, we quarrelled as we had always quarrelled. We strove to hurt each other! There was no time suddenly; we stood outside it, warring with each other." He broke off, unable to go on.

"Come rest now, sire. Even immortals must rest."

10

THEY STOOD all together in the train station. For Ramses, a moment of the most pure and undiluted anguish. But he had no more words to use to persuade her; when he looked into her eyes, he saw not a coldness, but a deep and unhealing hurt.

And Alex, he was changed now into another human being with Alex's face and form. He had listened resentfully to the half-truths they'd given him. A woman Ramsey had known; mad; dangerous. Then he had closed himself off; he wanted to hear no more.

They were older now, this young man and this young woman. There was a faint greyness in Julie's expression; there was a numbness and sullen quiet to Alex as he stood at her side.

"They won't keep me here more than a few days," Elliott said to his son. "I'll be home perhaps a week after your arrival. Take care of Julie. If you take care of Julie . . ."

"I know, Father, it will be the best thing for me."

Icy the smile that had once been so warm.

The conductor made his call. The train was ready to roll out of the station. Ramses did not want to see it moving; did not want to hear that noise. He wanted to escape now, but he knew that he would stay till the end.

"You will not change your mind," he whispered.

She continued to look away.

"I'll always love you," she whispered. He had to bend down

385

to hear it, let her lips almost touch him. "To my dying day, I shall love you. But no, I cannot change my mind."

Alex took his hand suddenly. "Good-bye, Ramsey. Hope I see you in England."

The ritual was almost over; he turned to kiss Julie, but she'd already pulled away. She was on the metal stair into the passenger car, and then for one instant their eyes met.

It wasn't reproach; it wasn't condemnation; she couldn't do anything else. She had explained it a thousand times in those same few words.

Finally the noise again, the awful engulfing sound. With uneven chugs, the string of windowed cars began to move forward; he saw her face at the window. She pressed her hand to the glass and looked down at him again, and again he tried to interpret the look in her eyes. Was there a moment's regret?

Dully, miserably, he heard Cleopatra's voice. *I called out for you in those last moments.*

The train was sliding by; the window was suddenly bright silver as it moved into the sunlight; he couldn't see her anymore.

It seemed the Earl of Rutherford led him out of the station to where the motor cars waited, with the uniformed chauffeurs at their open doors.

"Where will you go?" the Earl asked him.

Ramses was watching the train disappear, the last car with its little iron gate growing smaller and smaller, the noise entirely manageable now.

"Does it matter?" he answered. Then as if waking from a spell, he looked at Elliott. Elliott's expression surprised him almost as much as Julie's. No reproach; only a thoughtful sadness. "What have you learned from all this, my lord?" he asked suddenly.

"It will take time to know that, Ramses. Time, perhaps, which I do not have."

Ramses shook his head. "After all you have seen," he asked, dropping his voice so that only Elliott could hear him, "would you still ask for the elixir? Or would you refuse as Julie has refused?"

The train was gone now. Silence reigned in the empty station. If one did not count the low hum of conversation here and there.

"Does it really matter now, Ramses?" Elliott asked, and for the first time Ramses saw a flash of bitterness and resentment in Elliott.

He took Elliott's hand. "We shall meet again," he said. "Now I must go, or I will be late."

"But where are you going?" Elliott asked him.

He didn't answer. He turned and waved as he crossed the train yard. Elliott acknowledged it with a polite little nod and a scant movement of his hand, then moved on to his waiting car.

Late afternoon. Elliott opened his eyes. The sun fell in slashes through the wooden blinds, the fan churning slowly overhead.

He lifted his gold pocket watch from the bedside table. Past three. Their ship had sailed. He enjoyed the relief for a long moment before thinking of anything else that he must do.

Then he heard Walter open the door.

"Have those damned people from the governor's office called yet?" Elliott asked.

"Yes, my lord. Twice. I told them you were sleeping and I had not the slightest intention of disturbing your rest."

"You're a good man, Walter. And may they burn in hell."

"My lord?"

"Never mind, Walter."

"Oh and Your Lordship, the Egyptian fellow's been by."

"Samir?"

"Brought the bottle of medicine from Ramsey. It's right there, my lord. Said you'd know what it was."

"What?" Elliott rose on his elbows. Then, slowly, he turned his gaze away from Walter to the table on his right.

It was a flask bottle, the kind used for vodka or whisky, but with no color to the glass. And it was filled entirely with a milk-white liquid, which gave off strange, almost luminescent glints in the light.

"I'd be careful of that, my lord," Walter said, opening the door, "if it's some kind of Egyptian thing, I'd watch my step."

Elliott almost laughed aloud. There was a note by the bottle with his name on it. He sat up and remained there motionless until Walter was gone. Then he reached for the note, and tore it open.

It was printed in block letters very like Roman printing, angular and clean.

Lord Rutherford, it is now your decision. May your philosophy and your wisdom sustain you. May you choose the right path.

He couldn't absorb it. No, he simply couldn't believe it. He stared at the note for a long moment; then he looked at the flask.

She lay in half sleep on the pillow. When she opened her eyes, she realized that it was her own voice that had awakened her. She'd been calling Ramses. She rose from bed slowly and pulled on her robe. Did it matter if anyone saw her out on the deck of the ship in her robe? But it was dinnertime, wasn't it? She had to dress. Alex needed her. Oh, if only she could think straight. She went to the wardrobe and began pulling things out. Where were they? How many hours had they been at sea?

When she reached the table, he was sitting there staring forward. He did not greet her, or rise to help her with her chair. As if any of that mattered. He started talking.

"I still don't understand any of it. Truly I don't. She didn't seem mad at all, really."

This was excruciating, but she forced herself to listen.

"I mean, there was something sombre and sad about her," he said. "I only know that I loved her. And that she loved me." He turned to Julie. "Do you believe what I'm saying?"

"Yes, I do," she said.

"You know, she said the strangest things. She said that she hadn't planned to love me! But it had happened, and you know, I told her I knew just what she meant. I'd never thought I . . . I mean, it was altogether different. As if all your life you've thought that pink roses were red roses!"

"Yes, I know."

"And that tepid water was hot."

"Yes."

"Did you get a good look at her? Did you see how beautiful she was?"

"It's not going to help to dwell on it. You can't make her come back."

"I knew I would lose her. I knew from the start. I don't know why. I simply knew it. She wasn't of this world, do you understand? And yet she was the world more truly than anything I'd ever . . ."

"I know."

He stared forward; he appeared to be looking at the other diners; the black-jacketed waiters moving about; maybe listening to the hushed civilized voices. Almost entirely a British ship. There seemed something utterly revolting about that.

"It's possible to forget!" she said suddenly. "It is possible, I know that it is."

"Yes, forget it," he said, and he smiled coldly, though not at her in particular. "Forget it," he repeated. "That's what we'll do. You'll forget Ramsey, as clearly something's happened to separate you. And I'll forget her. And we will go through the motions of living as if we had never loved like that, either of us. You and Ramsey and I with her."

Julie found herself looking at him in mild shock. She narrowed her eyes.

"The motions of living!" she whispered. "What a horrible thing to say."

He hadn't even heard her. He had picked up the fork and started eating, or rather picking at the food. Going through the motions of eating it.

She sat there trembling, looking down at the plate.

It was dark outside now. A blue light shone through the slatted blinds. Walter had come again to ask him if he wanted supper. He had said no. Only to be alone.

He sat in his robe and slippers, looking at the flask on the table. It shimmered in the darkness. The note lay where he had left it, beside the flask.

Finally he got up to dress. It took him several minutes, because each part of it made some special demand on his patience, but finally it was finished. He had on his grey wool, a bit too heavy for the days here, yet perfect for the night.

And then he went to the table, leaning on his cane with his left hand, and lifted the flask with his right. He put the flask in his inside pocket, where it just barely fit, making a weight against his chest.

Then he went out. The pain in his leg grew worse after he had walked a short distance from Shepheard's. But he continued, now and then shifting the cane to the other side to see if that made it any better. He stopped when he had to; then when he'd caught his breath he moved on.

In about an hour, he'd reached old Cairo. He made his way through the alleyways, aimlessly. He did not search for Malenka's house. He merely walked. And walked. By midnight, his left foot was numb again. But it didn't matter.

Everywhere that he walked, he looked at things. He looked at walls, and doors, and people's faces; he stopped in front of cabarets and listened to the dissonant music. Now and then he glimpsed a belly dancer going through her seductive little performance. Once he paused to listen to a man playing a flute.

He didn't linger very long anywhere, except when he was very tired; then he sat, and sometimes even dozed. The night was quiet; peaceful. It seemed to harbor none of the dangers of London.

As two o'clock came he was still walking. He had covered the medieval city, and he was moving back to the newer districts again.

Julie stood at the rail, clutching the ends of her shawl. She looked down at the dark water, vaguely conscious that she was bitterly cold, that her hands were freezing. But it didn't matter. And it seemed lovely suddenly that such things weren't hurting her. That she didn't care.

She wasn't here at all. She was at home in London. She was standing in the conservatory, and it was all full of flowers. Ramses stood there, the linen wrappings covering him; he raised his hand as she watched and tore them loose from his face. The blue eyes looked directly at her, at once full of love.

"No, it's wrong," she whispered. But to whom was she speaking? There was no one here to hear what she said. All the ship slept, all the civilized British travellers going home after their little sojourn in Egypt, so happy to have seen the pyramids, the temples. *Destroy the elixir. Every drop of it.*

She stared down into the turbulent sea. The wind suddenly ripped at her hair, at the edges of the shawl. She gripped the railing, and the shawl was lifted off her shoulders and blown away, rolling into a ball as it was carried up and out into the dark.

The mist swallowed it. She never saw it hit the water. And the sound of the wind and the sound of the engines merged suddenly, and seemed to be of the same fabric as the mist.

Her world, gone. Her world of faded colors and dim noises, gone. She heard his voice speaking to her, "I love you, Julie Stratford." She heard herself say, "I wish I'd never laid eyes on you. That you had let Henry do his work."

She smiled suddenly. Had she ever been this cold in her life? She looked down. She was wearing only a thin nightgown. No wonder. And the truth was, she ought to be dead now. Dead like her father. Henry had put the poison in her cup. She closed her eyes, turning her face this way and that in the wash of the wind.

"I love you, Julie Stratford," his voice came again in memory, and this time she heard herself answer with the old cliché, so beautiful. "I shall love you till my dying day."

It was no use going home. It was no use, any of it. The motions of living. The adventure had ended. The nightmare had ended. And now the normal world would be the nightmare, unless she was with her father, or alone sealed off from all reality, her last thoughts only of all the glorious moments that had been.

In the tent with him, making love to him, his at last. In the temple under the stars.

She would tell no children in old age why she had never married. She would tell no young man the story of the voyage to Cairo. She would not be that woman, harbouring all her life a terrible knowledge, a terrible regret.

But this was too harsh, all of this. No need for such literal thoughts. The dark waters waited. She'd be carried far, far away from the ship within moments; there would be no chance of salvation. And that seemed to her to be inexpressibly beautiful suddenly. She had only to climb up, which she did now, and let herself go into the cold wind.

Why, the wind would even carry her partway. It had caught her gown and was blowing it out behind her. She stretched out her arms and pitched herself forward. It seemed the wind grew louder and she was flying out towards the water. *It was done!*

In one split second she knew that nothing could save her, nothing could possibly intervene; she was already falling, and she wanted to say her father's name. But it was Ramses' name that came to her mind. Ah, the sweetness of it, the utter sweetness of all of it.

Then two strong arms caught her. She hung suspended above the sea, stunned, groping to see through the mist.

"No, Julie." It was Ramses pleading with her. Ramses who lifted her over the railing and held her tightly in his arms. Ramses standing on the deck with her in his arms. "Not death over life, Julie, no."

In a torrent the sobs broke from her; like ice she shattered, the warm tears spilling down her face as she hugged him and buried her face against his chest.

She said his name over and over. She felt his arms closing her off from the searing wind.

Cairo woke with the sun. The heat seemed to rise from the dirt streets themselves as the bazaar came to life, as the striped awnings fell down over doorways, as the sounds of camels and donkeys rose.

Elliott was thoroughly tired now. He couldn't resist sleep much longer, but still he walked. Sluggishly he moved past the brass merchants and the rug merchants, and the sellers of *gellebiyyas* and of fake antiquities—cheap Egyptian "treasures" for a few pence. The sellers of mummies, who claimed now to offer for a pittance the bodies of Kings.

Mummies. They stood along the whitewashed wall in the burning sunlight; mummies, soiled, worn, in their bedraggled wrappings, yet the features of their faces distinguishable beneath the layer of linen and grime.

He stopped. All the thoughts with which he'd wrestled the night long seemed to leave him. The images of those he loved which had been so close to him suddenly faded. He was in the bazaar; the sun was burning down on him; he was looking at a row of dead bodies against a wall.

Malenka's words came back to him.

"They make a great Pharaoh of my English. My beautiful English. They put him in the bitumen; they make a mummy of him for tourists to buy. . . . My beautiful English, they wrap him in linen; they make him a King."

He moved closer; irresistibly drawn by what he saw, though it repelled him completely. He felt the first wave of nausea strike him as his eyes locked on the first mummy, the tallest and leanest, propped at the near end of the wall. Then the second wave came as the merchant stepped forward, belly preceding him beneath his striped cotton robes, hands clasped behind his back.

"Allow me to offer you a great bargain!" said the merchant. "This one here is not like the others. See? If you look you can see the fine bones of this one, for he was a great King. Come! Come closer. Have a good look at him."

Slowly Elliott obeyed. The wrappings were thick, moldering, as ancient in appearance as any he had ever seen! And the smell rising from them, the rotting, stinking smell of earth and bitumen; but there, beneath that thick veneer, he could see the face; see the nose and the broad plain of the forehead, see clearly the sunken eyes, the thin mouth! He was staring at the face of Henry Stratford, and there was no doubt.

The morning sun broke in glorious rays through the round porthole, piercing the sheer white veils of the small brass bed.

They sat together against the barred bedstead; warm from their lovemaking; warm from the wine they'd drunk.

Now she watched as he filled the tumbler from the vial. Tiny lights danced in the strange liquid. He held it out to her.

She took it from him, then looked into his eyes. For one tiny moment she was afraid again. And it seemed suddenly she was not in this room. She was on the deck in the mist and it was cold. The sea was waiting. Then she shivered, and the warm sun melted over her skin, and she saw the touch of fear in his eyes too.

Only human, only a man, she thought. He does not know what will happen any more than I do! And she smiled.

She drank the tumbler down.

"The body of a King, I tell you," said the merchant, leaning forward in farcical confidentiality. "I give to you for nothing! Because I like you. I see you are a gentleman. You have good taste. This mummy, you can get it out of Egypt, it's nothing. I pay the bribe for you. . . ." On and on went the chant of lies, the song of commerce, the idiot imitation of truth.

Henry under that gauze! Henry locked in the filthy bandages forever! Henry whom he had caressed in that little room in Paris a lifetime ago.

"Come now, sir, don't turn your back upon the mysteries of Egypt, sir, deepest darkest Egypt, sir. Land of magic . . ."

The voice faded; echoed for a moment as he stumbled a few steps away and towards the full light of the sun.

A great burning disk, it hung over the rooftops. It flashed in his eyes as he looked up at it.

And never taking his eyes off it, he grasped the cane firmly as he reached into his coat and pulled out the flask. Then dropping the cane altogether, he opened the flask and drank the contents in great easy gulps to the very last drop.

Petrified as the chills passed through him, he let the flask fall into the dirt. He felt the heat in spasms. He felt his numb leg come to life. The great weight in his chest slowly melted; and stretching his limbs with the utter abandon of an animal, he stared wide-eyed at the glaring sky; at the golden disk.

Before him the world pulsed, shimmered, then became solid again as he had not seen it since his middle years when his vision had begun to slowly fail. He saw the grains of earth at his feet.

Stepping over the silver walking stick, ignoring the shouts of the merchant behind him that he had lost his cane and must wait, he walked out of the bazaar with long easy strides.

The sun was high above in the noon sky as he left Cairo, as he walked on along the thin road to the east. He did not really know where he was going and it didn't matter. There were monuments and wonders and cities enough to behold. His steps were quick, and the desert had never seemed so beautiful to him, this great monotonous ocean of sand.

He had done it! And there was no undoing of it now. Eyes fixed on the vast azure emptiness above him, he gave a soft cry intended for no one, merely the smallest, most spontaneous expression of his joy.

They stood on the deck, the warm sun blanketing them as they embraced one another. She could feel the magic moving through her skin and her hair. She felt his lips graze hers, and suddenly they were kissing as they had never really kissed before. It was the same fire, yes, but now her strength and her urgency came to the fore to meet his.

He lifted her and carried her back into the little bedroom and laid her down on the bed. The veiling fell silently around them, snaring the light and wrapping them up in it.

"You are mine, Julie Stratford," he whispered. "My Queen forever. And I am yours. Always yours."

"Lovely words," she whispered, smiling at him almost sadly. She wanted always to remember this moment; to remember the look in his blue eyes.

Then slowly, yet feverishly, they began to make love.

11

T HE YOUNG doctor grabbed his bag and ran towards the infirmary, the young foot soldier running beside him.

"Just dreadful, sir, burned to a crisp, sir, and wedged down there under the crates at the very bottom of the freight car. I don't know how she can be alive."

What in God's name was he going to be able to do for her, out here at this godforsaken outpost in the jungles of the Sudan?

He steadied himself against the doorjamb as he came to a halt inside the room.

The nurse shook her head as she came towards him. "I don't understand it," she said in a stage whisper, with a pointed glance at the bed.

"Let me see her." He pulled back the mosquito netting. "Why, this woman's not burned at all."

She lay asleep against the white pillow, her black wavy hair stirring in the sunlight, as if there actually were a ghost of a breeze coming from somewhere through this infernally hot room.

If he had ever seen a woman this beautiful, he couldn't remember it and frankly didn't want to be reminded of it just now. It was almost painful to look at her, she was so beautiful. And it wasn't a china doll prettiness she had; her features were strong though exquisitely proportioned. Her rippling hair, parted in the middle, made a great shining pyramid of darkness beneath her head.

As he came round the side of the bed, she opened her eyes. How remarkable that they should be so startlingly blue. Then the miracle of miracles. She smiled. He went weak looking down at her. Words like "fate" and "destiny" came to his mind, idly, yet persistently. Who in the world could she be?

"What a handsome man you are," she whispered. Perfect British accent. One of us, he thought, hating himself instantly for the snobbish thought. But her voice was purely aristocratic.

The nurse mumbled something. There were whispers behind his back. He drew up the camp chair and sat down beside her. As casually as he could he lifted the white sheet up over her half-naked breasts.

"Get this woman some clothing," he said without looking up at the nurse. "You gave us all quite a scare, you realize. They thought you were burned."

"Did they?" she whispered. "It was kind of them to help me. I was in some close place where I could scarcely breathe. I was in the dark."

She blinked up at the sunlight coming in the window. "You must help me up and out into the sunshine," she said.

"Oh, it's much too soon for that."

But she sat up, clearly undeterred, and started to wrap the sheet about her like a gown. The fine dark eyebrows gave her a distinct look of will and determination, which he found oddly exciting in a very direct physical way.

Like a goddess she looked, with the thing draped over one shoulder as she rose to her feet. Again that smile flashed at him, subduing him utterly.

"Listen, you must tell me who you are. Your family, your friends, we'll send word."

"Walk outside with me," she said.

He followed her almost stupidly, taking her hand. Let them whisper! They'd come running with stories that she was burnt like overdone beef! There was nothing at all wrong with this woman! Had the world gone mad?

She went across the dusty yard, leading him through the gate into the small garden, which was his actually, not for the patients, just adjacent to his bedroom and his office doors.

She sat down on the wooden bench, and he sat beside her. She threw back her hair as she looked up into the hot sky.

"But it's no use your being out in this terrible heat," he told her. "Especially if you have been burned." But this was stupid. Her skin was flawless and radiant all over; her cheeks were beautifully flushed. He'd never seen a healthier human being in his life.

"Is there someone I should contact?" he tried again. "We have a telephone and a telegraph out here now."

"Don't concern yourself about it," she said, lifting his left hand and playing idly with his fingers. He was ashamed suddenly of what this aroused in him. He couldn't stop staring at her, at her eyes and then at her mouth. He could see her nipples through the sheet.

"I have friends, yes," she said almost dreamily, "and appointments to keep. And accounts to settle. But tell me about yourself, Doctor. And tell me about this place."

Did she want him to kiss her? He could scarcely believe it and he had no intention of passing it up. He bent to touch her lips, hmmm. He didn't care who was watching. He ran his arms around her, and gathered her against him, stunned by the manner in which she yielded completely, breasts hot against his chest.

In another second he would drag her to the bed, if she wouldn't come of her own free will. But he knew she would.

"There's no great hurry to contact anyone," she whispered as she ran her hand inside his shirt. They were on their feet, moving together across the flags towards the bedroom door. She stopped as if she could not even wait for that. He picked her up and carried her.

Sinful, wicked, but he couldn't stop himself. She clamped her mouth on his and he almost dropped in his tracks. He set her down on the mattress, and shut the wooden blinds. To hell with everyone else.

"You're sure you . . ." he faltered. He was ripping off his shirt.

"I like men who blush," she whispered, gazing up, "And yes, I'm sure. I want to be prepared before I see my friends again." She unwound the sheet. "Very well prepared."

"What?" He lay down beside her, kissing her throat, running his hand down over her breast. Her hips rose against him as he climbed on top of her. She was undulating like a serpent in the bed, but she was no serpent. She was warm and fragrant and ready for him!

"My friends . . ." she whispered, staring at the ceiling as if faintly dazed, a tiny spark of distress in her blue eyes. But then she looked at him—all hunger suddenly, voice dropping to a monotone as she stroked him, her nails deliciously grazing his shoulders. "My friends can wait. We have time to see each other. All the time in the world!"

He hadn't the slightest idea what she meant. And he didn't care.

THE END

THE ADVENTURES

OF

RAMSES THE DAMNED

SHALL

CONTINUE

ABOUT THE AUTHOR

ANNE RICE is the author of many novels, including *Interview with the Vampire, The Feast of All Saints, Cry to Heaven, The Vampire Lestat*, and *The Queen of the Damned*. She also writes under the names Anne Rampling and A. N. Roquelaure. Anne Rice was born in New Orleans, where she now lives with her husband, the poet Stan Rice, and their son, Christopher.